*A small voice in the back of her
mind told her to resist,*

. . . but she could neither ignore nor overcome
the tremendous need Glenloch aroused in her.

Yes she could. She had not come this far to be
seduced by a notorious rake. She reached behind
her for one of the blankets on the bed and pulled it
over her shoulders. Somehow she managed to close
Laird Glenloch out, mortified by her behavior.
"Laird, please. I am not a . . . a light-skirt."

Brianna extricated herself from his grasp
and came off the bed. She went directly to the
fireplace, wrapping herself tightly against any
further sensual onslaught. Her legs still felt weak,
and there was a trembling awareness of him in
every pore of her body. But she would not do
this. She did not want a man in her life. Neither
Roddington, nor Glenloch, nor anyone else who
would use her and control her with little thought
for her own well-being.

By Margo Maguire

TAKEN BY THE LAIRD
WILD
TEMPTATION OF THE WARRIOR
A WARRIOR'S TAKING
THE PERFECT SEDUCTION
THE BRIDE HUNT

Taken
by the
Laird

Margo Maguire

AVON

An Imprint of HarperCollinsPublishers

This is a work of fiction. Names, characters, places, and incidents are products of the author's imagination or are used fictitiously and are not to be construed as real. Any resemblance to actual events, locales, organizations, or persons, living or dead, is entirely coincidental.

AVON BOOKS
An Imprint of HarperCollins*Publishers*
10 East 53rd Street
New York, New York 10022-5299

Copyright © 2009 by Margo Wider
ISBN 978-0-06-166788-6
www.avonromance.com

First Avon Books paperback printing: October 2009

Avon Trademark Reg. U.S. Pat. Off. and in Other Countries, Marca Registrada, Hecho en U.S.A.
HarperCollins® is a registered trademark of HarperCollins Publishers.

Printed in the U.S.A.

10 9 8 7 6 5 4 3 2 1

This book is dedicated to my scientist husband, Mike, the best brainstorming partner a writer could ever wish for . . . and also the guy who subscribes to the scientific journal which carried the article that inspired the Glenloch Ghost.

Taken
by the
LAIRD

Prologue

They that sow the wind shall reap the whirlwind.
SCOTTISH PROVERB

St. George's Church, London. December 1829.

A slow burn began to spread in Viscount Stamford's belly as he looked at the richly dressed crowd milling about the nave of the church. His wife should have arrived ten minutes ago with the damned bride. He could not imagine what was keeping her.

Arthur Crandall, Viscount Stamford, should be only minutes away from aligning himself irrevocably with the Marquess of Roddington and his powerful—and elderly—father, the Duke of Chalwyck.

It figured that his ward would cause some delay, the recalcitrant chit. She was a burr under his saddle, a pain in his arse. But she was far more comely than his own two daughters, a much more useful tool in his efforts to build the kind of alliances he had in mind. Brianna Munro was an attractive bit of chattel, far more suited than Catherine or Susan to trap this extraordinarily wealthy, but lazy, gambling gadabout—

"Where is the chit, Stamford?" the groom drawled. "I agreed to wed her, not grow old standing at the back of St. George's."

Stamford ignored the marquess's question and rubbed his bilious stomach through his waistcoat. "Who are all these people, Roddington?"

Roddington closed his cold, reptilian eyes and shrugged, his gesture a demonstration of complete ennui. "Merely a few of my intimates."

Stamford grimaced at the sight of all those syco-phants and hangers-on. Wastrels, all of them. He was quite familiar with Rotten Roddington's disgraceful reputation, but the marquess would one day take his father's place, and the daughter of a long-dead viscount could not be too choosy.

Nonetheless, Stamford's skin crawled at Roddington's proximity. The man was richly dressed, but did not cut the finest figure Stamford had ever seen. In fact, Stamford suspected the marquess wore a corset under his fine clothes, and perhaps even had his valet pour a concoction of walnut juice in his hair to keep it black. He was as vain as they came, and Stamford had to admit he was glad Roddington had never taken a fancy to his own two gels.

In any event, it had been an easy thing to put his winsome ward in Roddington's path, and then wait for the lecherous marquess to make his move. When Rod-dington cornered Brianna alone in the library, Stamford had made sure there were witnesses to her ruination.

Now the marquess and his father would become so closely allied to Stamford, the viscount would wield more social and political power than a country squire's son could ever have imagined. All those years of genteel poverty before inheriting Damien Munro's title and estates . . . of being thought second-rate at school. . .

Now everyone would know whom they were dealing with.

"I'm growing impatient, Stamford," said Roddington.

As was Stamford, and his stomach burned with irritability. As soon as this wedding was finished, he was going to have to pay a visit to the apothecary. At the same time, he hoped Roddington would make his irascible new wife pay for her inconvenient tardiness. He'd never cared for the brat. She was too independent and much too outspoken for a female, much like her dratted Scottish aunt.

But she had been useful in drawing potential suitors to the house, for neither Catherine nor Susan seemed to have the knack for it. Once Brianna's beaux arrived at Stamford House, it was no great challenge to remove the Munro gel and push the young men toward his daughters. Not that any of them had "taken" to each other. 'Twas something the viscount would deal with later, once his alliance with Roddington was cemented.

"Calm yourself, Roddington." Stamford reined in his own temper and opened the door of the church and looked out. "Likely some difficulty with a hem or a bonnet ribbon." *Dash it all, where was his wife?*

"She had better be biddable, Stamford. I will not have a shrew in my house."

"Just keep her away from her aunt in Scotland," Stamford replied. The two men went outside and stood looking down the street, Stamford with his hands on his hips, anxiously gazing through the misty rain. "Now, there's a true virago from whose ungovernable influence I removed my ward three years ago."

He did not bother to mention that he'd quite willingly given Brianna to her aunt Claire nearly a decade before, glad to be rid of the child who'd become his ward—his expense—upon her parents' death. He'd brought her back to London for a season or two when his own daughters failed to attract the caliber of suitors their family deserved.

"You mean that Dougal woman, up around Stonehaven?" Roddington asked.

Stamford turned his gaze to Roddington. "Don't tell me you know the old girl."

Roddington leaned against the doorjamb and narrowed his eyes as he looked down the street. No one would ever know the man's secrets, and Stamford could not help but shudder at the possibilities. "Bought some horses from her a few years back," the marquess said. "Didn't know she and your ward were connected."

Stamford had no chance to reply when a carriage turned a corner to rush down St. George's Street, stopping directly in front of the church. "About time," he muttered. He approached the carriage just as his wife flung open the door and scuttled down the step without waiting for assistance.

"Stamford!" she cried in a panicked hush. "She's gone!"

The heat in Stamford's belly turned to fire. "Gone?" he said much more calmly than he felt.

"Yes, gone—Brianna! *Your ward!*" Lady Stamford was as indignant as she was angry, flummoxed. "She padded her bed to make it appear she was sleeping. But she was not sleeping!" His wife grabbed his arm. "She was not even in the house!"

"Are you certain?"

"Of course I am certain! We tore every room apart looking for her! She must have left last night."

"Ridiculous. Who in her right mind would leave London in the dead of night?"

"A stubborn, headstrong Scot is who!"

Lady Stamford stiffened as Roddington stepped up to the viscount's side.

"Is there a problem?" the marquess asked.

"Of course not," Stamford snapped. "There *will* be a wedding today!"

Chapter 1

Flee as fast as you will,
your fortune will be at your tail.
SCOTTISH PROVERB

The Mearns, Scotland. December 1829.

Trudging along the coastal road in the misty rain, Brianna Munro felt as though she was walking on the edge of the world. As well it was. The rough waters of the North Sea crashed far below her on the left, and she could feel a storm coming. Heavy clouds had moved in from the east, bringing a bitter wind with them. Even if not for the late hour, it would soon be dark, and she was going to have to find shelter as she'd done the night before. Perhaps she should turn back to Stonehaven. There were inns there where she could stay until the storm passed, a much better refuge than an abandoned barn like the one in which she'd slept fitfully before starting out again this morn.

But Stonehaven was the second place her guardian

would look for her when he came searching. And she wanted to leave no trace of Brianna Munro.

She continued south, recalling the first time she'd traveled this road, but heading in the opposite direction, toward Killiedown Manor. Her aunt Claire had removed her from Lord Stamford's negligent care nine years before, and they'd stopped at a rarely inhabited castle. The place was mostly ruins and belonged to some high-born Englishman with Scottish ties, a nobleman who had not been in residence at the time of her visit. Brianna thought the place must have already passed from that elderly laird to a descendant.

It was the way of life . . . birth and death, and both wrought with pain. Brianna forced aside the memory of the fresh, desolate grave at the edge of the cliff at Killiedown Manor, and the wild, crashing sea below it. The site had always been Claire's favorite location on the manor . . . a fitting site for her earthly remains to spend eternity. Brianna wiped the tears from her face, the hot moisture that mingled with the cold mist that surrounded her.

There was no time to mourn, no time for regrets. Brianna's situation was dire, and she would honor Claire's memory by doing exactly what the older woman would have done. Bree had no choice but to act with boldness, defying every convention and pushing on, in spite of the fact that she'd lost the only person who'd ever stood up for her.

She kept moving south, wearing the clothes she'd bought from one of Killiedown's young grooms. She'd done it on impulse after the funeral, and with more than a little desperation, sure it was the only way to remain inconspicuous as she fled Claire's estate. For if Lord Stamford found her, he would surely drag her back to London and force her into the marriage he'd orchestrated through means both underhanded and immoral.

Everything was so very wrong. Brianna had already disregarded convention, defied her legal guardian, and run away to her aunt's home in Scotland. But on her arrival at Killiedown, she'd found Claire abed. Struggling for every breath. Dying.

It had hurt Bree to see her that way. Her vital, vibrant aunt had succumbed to a terrible ague that settled on her chest, robbing her of health. She had hardly been able to breathe by the time Brianna arrived at her bedside.

And Brianna would never forgive herself for allowing Lord Stamford to coerce her into staying in London for the winter. If only she'd known. If only Claire had sent word when she'd first become ill . . .

The cold, fine mist turned to rain, and Brianna shrank down into the oversized coat. The road veered slightly west, toward the village of Falkburn. But in such a cold mizzle, she would never make it there without succumbing to the same illness that had taken Claire's life.

She shifted her bundle of belongings to her other shoulder and stepped off the road into a long, bleak drive that led east, to the sea. The ruins of Castle Glenloch's ancient keep and its towers rose ominously in the mist, cold and unwelcoming, but Brianna knew it was her best hope for a quick, temporary refuge.

Brianna was certain she was unrecognizable, dressed as she was, in the old trews and tunic and coat, with her

hair tucked under a sloppy hat that did little to keep the
rain from soaking her face and running down her neck.
Stamford might question everyone who dwelled near
or traveled between Killiedown Manor and Glenloch,
but no one would have seen a lone female with fair skin
and hair.

A female who was presently chilled to the bone.

Her shivering increased at the promise of a dry
refuge out of the wind, but at the same time, she felt
heartened by the deserted look of the place. If her luck
held, no one need ever know she'd stopped there.

She plodded down the long drive between two tall
rows of barren trees that gave little shelter from the
wind. When the old castle loomed near, tall and majestic in spite of its decaying towers, Brianna saw no signs
of inhabitancy. Which made it perfect.

She quickened her approach, hoping she would be
able to find entry somewhere. The place was expansive, its old sections built of drab, gray stone, its back
toward the sea. It was a dark and brooding place, but
Brianna remembered hearing that parts of it had been
made modern and habitable by some recent laird. Not
that it mattered, for she would not stay long.

Hoping to remain unnoticed and anonymous, she did
not intend to approach the imposing main entrance. An
outside building would have to do if she could not find
a way in, or if the castle turned out to be inhabited. But
there was no light emanating from any of the windows,
and she really wanted to find a small room inside, where
she could build a fire and get herself warm.

The two tallest towers jutted up against the darkening sky. The one on her left was precariously tilted with age and decay, and though the other seemed more solid, it did not appear to be especially sound. Either one would have to do, as long as she could get inside. She hurried toward the ocean side of the building, to the low cliff on which the ancient towers stood.

Before long, she had managed to skirt around the dilapidated wall of the old bailey, and found herself standing at the base of the ancient north tower. There, she was not far above the sea-battered beach, where several small skiffs had been grounded and tied to posts in the sand. She hurried around the tower, looking for a door, not that she was going to find one unlocked. But a window might do, even if she had to break it.

With the sky darkening further to a deep, murky gray, she circled around the ancient tower, searching for an entry. But the walls of the room near its base must have collapsed eons ago, and any spaces where Bree might have crawled inside were hidden by brambles and wildly growing shrubs.

Besides, the thought of slipping was not appealing, for she might disturb something and cause the walls to give way completely. With even greater haste, she continued around the back of the castle, past doors and several windows that had been secured against illicit entry. She moved on toward the south tower and soon saw a promising opening that was nearly hidden by another dense thicket of brush.

These walls, too, seemed in poor condition, but when Bree saw a metal grate, positioned low in yet another disreputable-looking wall, her need to get out of the wet overcame her caution. She tested the metal lattice with freezing fingers, and it came loose. Pulling it away, she quickly crawled inside, then turned and carefully replaced the grate behind her, worried that one of the crumbling walls might collapse on her at any time.

Although there was little light inside, it was a relief to get out of the freezing rain. Brianna shoved the bundle of essentials that she carried ahead of her, then stood up and searched the shadows for a candle.

She found none, and complete darkness was rapidly encroaching.

The room was small and empty, and not much warmer than the outdoors. But a surprisingly solid wooden staircase led to a tiny landing and a door at the top, giving hope that she might be able to get inside and find the kitchen or scullery, where she could stay warm and dry for the night. Brianna climbed the steps, instinctively staying as quiet as she could, even though the castle seemed deserted. At the top of the staircase, she lost her nerve, but only momentarily. She knew she could not stay all night in that dark, chilly room, wearing her wet clothes, so her only choice was to breach the castle proper. Drawing out the dirk she'd strapped to her leg before leaving Killiedown, Brianna pushed open the door.

Someone was cheating Hugh Christie and the disagreeable partner he'd inherited from his father. To date, Hugh had taken the losses himself, unwilling to involve his London investor, a man Hugh preferred to avoid. But it could not go on any longer. He'd come to Glenloch to

find out who was stealing his smuggled French brandy
and selling it out from under him.

Besides, the situation in London had become sticky,
and Hugh had no intention of surrendering his bachelorhood. Not to Charlotte de Marche, the conniving
spinster who'd thought to ensnare him; not to anyone.
Far more cunning adversaries than Miss de Marche had
sought to trap him into marriage, and Hugh had learned
his painful lesson then. He'd married Lady Amelia
Norquist. What a disaster that had been.

No one in Falkburn knew he'd arrived at Glenloch,
not even his estate manager, Malcolm MacGowan. He'd
notified no one of his intention of coming to the castle,
so he was not expected there. Not that anyone would
have come up from Falkburn at dark. The servants
came only during daylight hours, and none—not even
his indomitable housekeeper, Sorcha Ramsay—would
stay through the night. Not with tales of Glenloch's ancient ghost floating about, rattling chains and frightening people.

Legend told of a benign, filmy creature that made
its appearance especially when trouble was afoot. As a
child, Hugh believed he might have crossed its path a
few times, but he knew better now. Tales of the ghost
were just stories told and perpetuated in order to keep
intruders away from the castle and its frequent caches
of smuggled goods.

Even so, Hugh didn't care for the possibility that his
late wife might have joined Glenloch's legendary Scottish bogle and was now haunting Glenloch's old halls.

It was three years since Amelia had killed herself at

Castle Glenloch, and all and sundry knew Hugh avoided the place as though it were cursed. As well it might be. Hugh and Amelia had never been happy there.

Hell, he'd never been able to make her happy anywhere.

But their incompatibility in marriage had naught to do with anything now. Amelia had been dead a long time, and Hugh's only interest in Glenloch was to learn why his free-trading profits had been diminishing every year since her death. There was only one possible explanation. Someone was pilfering his goods. And Hugh was going to see for himself who was doing it, and how.

He left the remodeled section of the castle and headed to the south wing and the ancient buttery, where his brandy came into the castle for storage before being diluted and shipped out. He followed an old, secret passageway, dark and silent but for the candle he carried and the quiet brush of his own footsteps. The air grew chilly as he moved farther away from the fire in the drawing room, but at least he would not need to go out into the wind and wet. The walls and roof in the old wings of Glenloch were intact, but just barely, making it an unlikely storage place. To Hugh's knowledge, customs agents had never broached the buttery in search of contraband.

Hugh did not expect to hear anything but his own breath as he approached the door, but when something moved stealthily on the stairs, he stopped still.

Dousing his candle, he moved to one side of the door, flattening his body against the wall. He held his breath as he waited in the dark, careful not to make any sound that might frighten the intruder away. He intended to make short work of this prowler, and likely gain the information he needed. He never expected it to be as easy as this.

The faint rasp of the door latch fairly screamed in Hugh's ears, and he braced himself for a physical confrontation. The door opened silently and a darker shadow emerged from it. He remained motionless as the fellow took a step into the room.

Hugh quickly lunged, and heard a grunt when he grabbed the intruder and wrestled him to the ground. The man struggled, and Hugh realized he was small . . . a lad, perhaps. He did not want to hurt him—at least, not yet—so he loosened his hold.

The boy made a sudden move, scissoring his legs round Hugh's hips, and quickly sprang up over him, leaning down, pressing his full weight against Hugh's chest. Hugh then felt the cold steel of a knife against his throat.

The intruder spoke. "Do not move, you . . ."

The lad was either very young, or . . . "You're a woman!"

"And who might *you* be?" she demanded.

"I'm the man who regrets going easy on you," he rasped. "Do you mind putting that thing away?"

"I *do* mind." Her breath was shaky and her hand unsteady. She was frightened, as well she ought to be, for she had to know she was no match for a man of his size or strength.

Hugh took care not to move suddenly—for she *did* hold the knife—and slowly inched his hand up to the level of his chest. "I'll do you no harm."

"Exactly."

"What have you against me, lass?" Besides a delectably soft feminine bottom, pressed against his groin.

"Y-you do not belong here!"

"But *you* do?" He took advantage of the uncertainty he heard in her voice and made a swift move, knocking the knife away as he rolled her to the floor. And then she was under him. He managed to gather both her hands in his, holding them securely above her head.

"Let me up, you oaf!" she cried, not at all uncertain now.

"Not until you give me some answers."

"I cannot breathe!"

He eased his weight off her somewhat, but held on to those ferocious hands of hers. No point in letting her get hold of the knife again. "What are you doing here?"

"I came in to get out of the rain," she said grudgingly. She was definitely soaked. He could smell the wind and rain on her, and the hint of warm, feminine skin. Her speech was refined, with barely a trace of Scots in her words, and her hands were smooth. Both signs were indicative of a gently bred woman.

"Where are you from?"

"Up away near Muchalls." He heard the lie in her words. She sounded more English than Scots.

"Who came with you?"

"N-no one." He felt the subtle roll of her throat as she

swallowed. She was small-boned and soft, and he felt a distinct stirring in the lower region of his body with the press of his chest against her breasts.

He refocused his thoughts. "Who are you?"

"Sir, you have me at your mercy. Please let me go. I've done naught but come in out of the cold and damp."

There was a breathless panic in her voice, and Hugh wished he could see her face and features more clearly. "'Tis clear you are a fugitive—"

"But not from the law!"

"No? What then? An angry husband?"

"Of course not!" she cried vehemently.

"Then who?"

"'Tis not your concern!"

"Ah, but it is," he said tightly. "I am laird here, and 'tis my house in which you trespass so cavalierly!"

She squirmed, and he stifled a groan when her pelvis pressed up against his groin. They could hardly remain there on the cold floor indefinitely. He had a far better idea for this audacious lass in her men's clothes.

"You are Laird Glenloch?" she croaked. "The Earl of Newbury?"

"Do not say we know each other." He did not think he could stand to face another conniving female.

"Not exactly. I am . . ." She swallowed again. "What are you doing here?"

"I own the place," he said. "Remember?"

"Yes, but . . ." She sighed resignedly. "Let me up, please."

"As soon as you tell me who you are and what you're doing here."

She stared up at him, hesitant, reluctant to speak.

"I'm waiting, lass."

"I am Br-Bridget. Bridget MacLaren," she said.

Her name did not stir a memory. But that was hardly surprising. If she was local, Hugh would not be likely to know her, for he had not spent any time at Glenloch in recent years. And, ever since Amelia's death, he made a general practice of casting a wide berth around society's doings. So Bridget MacLaren could be unfamiliar on that front, too. One would think the widower of a suicide, and a man who most assuredly deserved his reputation for fast living, would not be a prime catch. But alas . . . a goodly number of young, marriageable ladies in London, as well as a few whose prime had passed them by, still set their sights upon him.

Hugh judged that that did not seem to be the case here. He could think of no proper young lady who would go about in public wearing men's clothing, much less wielding a wicked knife as though she knew how to use it. And yet she was no raw Scottish lass . . .

Hugh lowered his head, dipping down toward this woman who excited him with her dirk and her unconventional clothes. Whoever Bridget MacLaren was, she was not at all commonplace. Her features were only slightly visible in the thickening shadows, but he could see that she kept her eyes upon his as he moved, bringing his mouth within an inch of hers.

"What are you doing here, Miss MacLaren, so far from Stonehaven?"

"Muchalls."

"Ah, yes. What are you doing so far from Muchalls,"

he said, unable to catch her up. He wondered why was she so well-prepared to defend herself with that dirk, if not expecting trouble. Perhaps she was involved in the theft of his goods. If that was true, Hugh knew better than to hope she would admit it outright.

She stiffened at their little interchange, giving rise to more questions. "'Tis rather too personal to say. I . . . I just stopped here to get out of the storm. But I . . ."

Reluctantly, Hugh eased his hold on Miss MacLaren and located her knife. Taking it in hand, he slid off her and reached for the candle he'd set on the floor nearby.

"But you . . . what?" Hugh lit the candle, observing her closely as she came to her feet. He'd been right about her build—she was not very tall, the top of her head only reaching the bottom of his chin. Her eyes, when she looked up at him, seemed translucent, the impossible blue of the Aegean Sea. Her skin was fair and her features nearly perfect, down to a slight dent in her delicately pointed chin. This one would draw attention in the finest London drawing rooms. But as he had never heard of her, she could not have been inside many of those.

". . . *but* I will find shelter elsewhere if—"

"You are dressed as a lad. Why? And what are you doing abroad without an escort?"

She turned away and pulled off her hat, letting a fall of pale blond hair cascade down her back. She slid one of her hands through the long waves, and scratched her head vigorously. "I am en route to Dundee."

"Alone," he said, wondering if it could possibly be so simple. She was soaking wet, and he wanted to believe she had truly entered the castle merely to get warm and dry. But he was no fool. There had to be more to it.

"Yes. Why not? I am perfectly capable of managing on my own."

Perhaps that was true, until she'd been confronted by a full-sized male who took exception to her. "Is that entirely proper, Miss MacLaren? Who are your connections? Your family?"

"I have no fam—"

She stopped abruptly when a strange sound—like the rustling of dried leaves—fluttered round their heads. Hugh was accustomed to all the odd noises in the castle, caused by shifting stone and old timber beams. But it startled the lass. She ducked and looked about her. "What was that?" she asked in a hushed tone.

Hugh decided not to regale her with all the blather about the Glenloch Ghost. He was not sure what she was up to, so he did not want to frighten her off just yet. At the same time, he had no interest in being caught alone with a gently bred woman. She might have denied having any family, but something about her words did not ring true. And if she had some familial connections she did not wish to mention, they would surely have expectations he had no intention of meeting.

Alternately, if she was involved in the theft of his valuable French brandy, then he wanted to keep her close. At least until he determined her methods and who her accomplices were.

"'Tis naught," he said of Glenloch's legendary harbinger of trouble. "A trick of the room. 'Tis always catching the sounds of the wind and rain."

*   *   *

With her nerves already on edge, Brianna looked up
to the shadowy ceiling and would have sworn she saw
something move there. She shivered and pulled closer
to Lord Newbury against the chill and the disquieting
sensations that seemed to fill the room. He touched
one hand to her lower back and Bree stiffened, unsure
whether her unease was due to the odd presence she'd
felt, or to Lord Newbury, Laird of Glenloch, himself.

She knew of him, of course. What young maiden of
the ton did not? He was one of the men she and Lord
Stamford's daughters had been warned against—a widower who was a rake and a charmer and a seducer of
the unwary. He was to be avoided at all costs, for he
would prove the ruination of any maiden who fell in
love with him. He had vowed never to wed again. Under
any circumstances.

True to all Brianna had heard of him, he had almost
kissed her. He had trapped her beneath him and lowered his head, his mouth nearly touching hers . . . Bree
did not wish to think of how she might have reacted to
his kiss. Like a wanton, she suspected, her body still
humming with an acute awareness of him, of the potent
masculinity she'd felt when he'd lain above her.

She'd seen him before, across one or two of the ton's
most fashionable ballrooms, though of course they had
never been introduced. Brianna had nearly melted at the
sight of the dangerous rake in formal attire, so dark and
handsome, while he clearly had no place in a genteel
setting. She remembered hearing tales of his pugilist
matches—savage contests among men with little regard

for the niceties of polite society. In spite of all that, Brianna could not deny the reckless sizzle of awareness that coursed through her, even as he stood yards away from her, on the far side of the fashionable ballrooms where she'd seen him.

Up close, he was altogether too tall, with shoulders impossibly broad. His black hair was unkempt and overly long, his face ruggedly hewn with a day or two's growth of whiskers. There was a crescent-shaped scar on his cheek, likely from his well-publicized exploits in the boxing ring. His touch and the gaze of his dark eyes unnerved her, but in a wholly different way than the effect the Marquess of Roddington had had on her. While Roddington had grabbed and squeezed, Newbury tantalized with barely a touch.

Brianna felt the need to flee again, but for a completely different reason this time.

"The castle seemed empty when I arrived," she said, feeling only slightly guilty for her deception. She could not tell him her true name. When Lord Stamford came searching for her, as she knew he would, she wanted to leave no one in Kincardineshire speaking the name of Brianna Munro.

"Were you expecting to meet someone?" His voice rumbled through her, even more deeply than when he lay on top of her. "A lover, perhaps?"

"No! Of course not." She intended to become as independent as her aunt Claire, to make a home for herself where she was not reliant upon anyone's largesse. No longer would she be the poor relation, living on the fringes of her guardian's family and subject to his whims. Once she came of age and inherited Claire's estate, she would be free of the machinations of that controlling, churlish man.

She would attend no more humiliating functions where young women were paraded before prospective husbands who stood back to evaluate and judge. As if they could learn anything important about her, just by looking.

Lord Newbury touched her chin and tipped it up, forcing her to look squarely at him. "Then what, may I ask once again, is a gentle lass doing, wandering about strange castles at this late hour, and in this weather?"

His cool fingertips sent shivers of impossible longing through her, for the elusive satisfaction of coming home. Of belonging somewhere. With someone.

Brianna suddenly remembered to breathe. The only place she'd ever belonged was Killiedown Manor with her aunt Claire. She pulled away and returned to the dark stairway to retrieve the bundle she'd dropped there.

"I didn't know quite where I would end up after my day's walk. I thought perhaps an inn." And as soon as the rain let up, she was going to get away from Glenloch and find one.

"There are no inns down this way—nothing at Falkburn, at least," Lord Newbury said, deflating her intentions. "Perhaps down at Inverbervie. Or Johnshaven."

She heard the wind whip brutally around the ancient stones of the building and knew she could not face going out again. Yet she could hardly stay here alone with a man of Lord Newbury's reputation, a man who muddled her senses with just a touch.

"You say you have no family?"

"No. None," she replied. And it was almost true. Arthur Crandall, Viscount Stamford, had been her father's heir, but he was so far removed he could hardly even be called a cousin. And his wife and daughters . . . Brianna shivered, the coldness of the Crandall women every bit as harsh as the bitter weather outside.

Newbury clenched his jaw and frowned, and Bree recognized how unwelcome she was here. She'd seen the very same expression often enough on Crandall faces during her early years in her guardian's household, and more recently when Claire managed to convince her to try a season or two in London.

As though Brianna cared about ensnaring a husband for herself. She wished Claire had relented and allowed her to come home after her first season and the fiasco with Bernard Malham, the young man who had proposed and then reneged when Lord Stamford disapproved of the match. But for some unfathomable reason, Claire had wanted Bree to stay on in London, to try again.

Brianna couldn't quite understand why Lord Stamford had tolerated her presence in his house, even though the entire family had made it clear they had no liking for her. And now, it could not have been clearer that Newbury did not want her at Glenloch, either. She hefted her bundle and started back toward the stairs. "I'm sorry for troubling you, my lord. I'll just—"

He stopped her. "What, go out into this storm?"

Bree raised her chin. "Well, yes. I do not care to put you out." There had to be a stable or barn somewhere nearby, and he need never know if she decided to make use of it.

Once again, she started to leave, but Lord Newbury took her bundle from her shoulder. "What kind of gentleman would allow a lovely young lady to go out in this?"

What kind, indeed? This time, she did not know how to read him. His tone was gracious enough, and he kept a perfectly polite smile upon his lips. But too much masculine power radiated from him for Brianna's peace of mind. Those hooded eyes held the promise of something dark and forbidden, of warm caresses and pleasures unlike any she had ever known, even with Bernard, the man who'd once purported to love her.

Brianna swallowed as she listened to the wind howling around the walls of the castle, and thought of her aunt, who wouldn't have thought twice about staying alone at Glenloch, whether its laird was a roué or the most trusted gentleman in Britain.

She decided she could deal with Laird Glenloch for one night. But Glenloch was not far enough away from Killiedown Manor, and it could not be a very long time before Viscount Stamford arrived here to look for her. Stamford was absolutely adamant that she marry George St. James, Marquess of Roddington. Brianna did not doubt the disturbing events in that secluded parlor had been orchestrated and calculated to force their marriage, for Lord Stamford was determined to forge a connection between himself and the most powerful peers of England. With his aspirations at stake, the viscount would spare no effort to find her.

Bree was having none of it. Roddington had behaved abominably, pure and simple, and she refused to tie herself to such an out-and-out rotter for the rest of her life. She did not care how wealthy he was or how much power his family wielded. Brianna had learned at a very young age that titles and wealth did not define a person's worth. Besides, she did not need a man—a tyrant who would use their marriage lines as a license to rule her life.

For some reason, Lord Stamford had declined to allow Catherine or Susan Crandall to have that honor.

"There are more habitable rooms this way," Newbury said, gesturing toward a long, dark passageway. "I daresay you'd like to get warm and dry."

"I wouldn't mind," Bree said, but neither of them moved. She eyed him warily while he held up the candle to look at her.

Bree knew she was nothing special. Susan and Catherine Crandall had informed her of it often enough, so she knew Lord Newbury was not overcome by her beauty. More likely he could not believe she was female, especially in her stable groom's get-up.

Feeling ridiculously lacking in attractive feminine charms, Bree pushed past him into the dark, chilly passageway ahead. She was well beyond worrying about her failings. In three seasons, she had received only one proposal, from Bernard Malham, the son of a Yorkshire baron. And when Lord Stamford had refused the match, Bernard had not tried to persuade her guardian of his worth, nor had he fought for their love. It had become perfectly clear to Brianna that only one heart had been deeply engaged in the affair. 'Twas her own, and it had broken.

Subsequently, she'd had no real interest in the dandies and fops who had nothing better to do than show a pretty leg at every dance and cotillion she attended. She'd gone through the motions required of her during the subsequent two seasons, but at the end of the day, all she'd wanted was to return to Killiedown, alone. Back to raising the sturdiest draft horses in all of Scotland with Claire, her heart protected and safe from risk.

Brianna felt Newbury behind her, allowing her to lead the way through the dark passage.

"Right here," he said, stopping her.

He put the candle down on the floor, then reached around her and touched the wall. Brianna heard a latch move, and a hidden door sprang open into a room that appeared similar to any conventional drawing room she might have visited in London.

But he did not move past her. He braced one hand against the wall beside her, blocking her way. "You have not yet explained why you are traveling alone, Miss MacLaren . . . in weather that would make a monk curse."

She felt his breath upon her, warm and smelling faintly of spirits. She bit her lip, and his eyes dropped to her mouth, catching the action in his gaze.

His eyes glittered nearly black in the flickering light, and Brianna could feel the heat of his body through her damp coat.

He inched closer, and she felt none of the loathing she'd experienced when Roddington had done the same. On the contrary.

"I'm waiting, Miss MacLaren."

Bree felt the throb of her pulse in her throat. No man would ever believe—many wouldn't even condemn—what Roddington had done to her, grabbing her breast and shoving his hand up her skirt. But even if Newbury happened to be the rare man who would, there was no point in telling him of Roddington's assault and the embarrassing scene that had ensued. He could do nothing.

"'Tis better if I do not say."

"But there we disagree," he said quietly. "If I am to harbor you in my house, I want some assurance that you are not a criminal."

"Do I look like a lawbreaker, my lord?" Brianna asked, shocked that he could entertain such a supposition.

Keeping his eyes on hers, Laird Glenloch touched her collar, then slid his fingers down the front edge of her coat, sending chills of potent awareness to Brianna's breast, tightening her nipples. She could barely breathe.

"I've never known a woman to wear men's clothes." His voice was low and intimate, his harmless words creating a reaction in her that was anything but innocent. He inched his fingers back up, halting just over her right breast. "'Twould be an effective disguise, but . . ."

"But?" she whispered.

"But the obvious," he said, caressing the side of her

unfettered breast. Then he slid his hand down to her waist and around to her hip. He pulled her against him. "You are clearly a woman."

"Oh," she said on the wisp of a breath. The press of his hard body against hers caused a potent reaction. Her bones turned to sawdust and her blood became some strange effervescent liquid bubbling through her veins.

She inhaled sharply, denying his effect on her. Pushing past him into the room, Brianna headed for the fire, hoping a servant would soon arrive to relieve the untenable tension coiling inside her. But no one came, and Laird Glenloch closed the door to the passageway. It became just another ornately painted panel in the wall, completely undetectable.

Brianna was distracted from the strange wall arrangement by the rain lashing viciously at the windows and the steam coming off her clothes. Feeling unnerved and out of her element, she leaned slightly forward toward the fire, relishing the welcome sensation of the heat on her hands and face. She was going to ignore what had just passed between them. By all accounts, this man was a master seducer. He'd known exactly what he was doing when he touched her.

"You have my word that I am no criminal. I have a very good reason for wearing these clothes," she said quietly, closing her eyes to savor the warmth of the fire. "But I cannot tell you."

"Cannot? Or will not?"

Brianna looked around and saw him eyeing her backside. She quickly straightened and faced him. "'Tis the same."

"'Tis hardly the same, Miss MacLaren."

"But it is. For if you knew anything more about me, you would be in peril."

"Why?" Hugh asked, unconcerned. He stood in the heart of a stone fortress with rooms and secret passages that could be made impervious to attack if they still lived in an age of knights and damsels in distress. But it was nearly 1830, and men were much more civilized these days.

The lass raised her head and continued. "Because my . . . my employer's husband is . . . well, he . . ."

"What about him? Did he make unwelcome advances?"

She nodded, her cheeks coloring at the mention of it.

It was obvious she did not wish to say more, but Hugh pressed her for information. He could think of no household near Muchalls where she might have been employed. More likely she was really from Stonehaven as he'd previously thought, or even Aberdeen, where there was any number of wealthy families. "You are a lady's maid, then? Or a governess?"

She hesitated for a fraction, then nodded again.

"For what family?"

"I cannot say, my lord."

"You mean you will not."

She shrugged. "It does not matter. I mean to make a fresh start. Far from—"

He waited for her to give something away, but she stopped herself before he could learn anything useful. "In Dundee?" he asked.

She swallowed, and his eyes were drawn to a small patch of her skin at her throat, exposed by the gap in her collar. He could almost taste her. "Yes. There are many fine houses there and I will surely be able to find employment."

"Without references?"

His question seemed to take her aback, but when she turned to the fire, all Hugh could do was stand and gape at her delectable bottom as she bent forward once again to warm herself at the fire. The effect of male clothes on a comely female was altogether unexpected. Had Hugh realized what simple trews could do for a pair of feminine legs, he might have persuaded a mistress or two to give it a go.

Trews or no, he didn't trust Miss MacLaren any more than he'd trust a pirate bearing a flag of truce. He felt fairly sure that her background could not be coarse. Her features were too refined, her hands much too soft to have hauled tubs of brandy from the beach, or hidden those crates in the secret passageways of the castle. But a gentlewoman, she was not. They did not wander the countryside alone.

She was hiding from someone, that much seemed clear. Perhaps her family had fallen on hard times and she had been forced into servitude. He understood that such women made excellent governesses, ladies' companions, and even maids. And women in those positions were vulnerable to the advances of an unscrupulous master.

Yet it was clear she was holding back information. Hugh was not entirely sure her tale of a lecherous em-

ployer was true, and he was not prepared to rule out the
possibility that she had something to do with the embez-
zlement of his liquor. Perhaps she was a distributor of
the brandy. A comely face and form would surely meet
with a warm welcome at every inn and tavern across
The Mearns where his liquor was sold. But even if that
were so, Hugh could not credit her ability to steal any of
his inventory without MacGowan knowing of it.

She seemed quite a capable sort, but not exactly the
rough-and-ready type he would expect a free-trading
woman to be. Her eyebrows were slightly darker than
her hair, gently arching over her stunning eyes. Her
lashes were also golden, the ends russet-tipped. Her
skin was pure ivory and her body abundantly curved,
even through her disguise. Hugh could easily understand how MacGowan might be swayed by her . . .
And at the same time, he did not doubt that some
wealthy Aberdeen gentleman might wish to lure her
into his bed.

But whether she was a free trader or a runaway servant, there were no easy answers to his questions. He let
out a deep breath and gave a slight bow. Whoever she
was, he was not going to turn her out into the inclement
night.

Keeping her with him felt more exciting than it
should.

"Miss MacLaren, we will leave our conversation
there while I go and find you a bedchamber."

"Oh no! I . . . can stay with the . . . Are there no . . ."
She glanced about the room, frowning. "My lord, have
you no servants?"

Keeping his eyes upon her, he shook his head. Deciding to test her as much as inform her of the situation. Staying alone with a bachelor would surely give a proper lass pause.

"No. My servants never come up to the castle after dark."

She swallowed visibly and gave him an equivocal answer. "I am sorry to be so much trouble."

"'Tis no trouble at all," he said, confirming her audacity, but learning nothing new about her.

Chapter 2

Necessity has nae law.
SCOTTISH PROVERB

The fire felt heavenly, but Brianna's clothes were soaked through. She needed to get out of them and into something dry, but that was out of the question. The few things she'd put in her satchel would hardly be wearable after being exposed to the rain. Nothing was impermeable to such a downpour.

She doubted she would ever feel warm again, but staying at Glenloch was not a good idea. She knew it down to the soles of her shoes, yet she had no other choice. She could not leave at this late hour or in this weather. And the option of returning to Killiedown to wait for her birthday and her inheritance was out of the question.

Brianna felt a renewed pang of grief over the loss of her aunt, her only other ally in the world. If only she'd known Claire was ill, she'd have returned to the manor well before this. Her three dismal years in London should have been enough, without returning for a round of winter soirees.

Now she would never see Claire again.

The wind renewed its assault on the castle, and Brianna shivered with the cold. Her teeth had started to chatter, and water dripped from her sodden jacket. She couldn't seem to get close enough to the fireplace.

At Killiedown, one of the servants would have already heated some bricks and put them into her bed to warm it. Her maid, the real Bridget MacLaren, would have helped her out of her wet things and rubbed her down with the softest woolen blankets this side of the River Dee. She would stoke the fire, and soon it would be toasty warm in her little bedchamber, and even cozier in her bed.

But Killiedown would never be the same without Claire. Bree took a shuddering breath and wiped away her tears. When Laird Glenloch returned to her, she needed to be in control of her wits. She could not allow her grief to cause her to err, for she sensed Glenloch's laird could be a dangerous man.

Not that he would harm her. Once he'd known she was female, he'd relaxed his struggle against her. Which was exactly the problem. Brianna was particularly vulnerable to this practiced roué, staying alone with him in his abode. He knew how to tantalize a woman with a well-placed touch and a glance of sincere appreciation. Even while being questioned, Bree had felt safe and comfortable with him, as though naught could make him lose patience with her and her incomplete answers to his questions.

She knew she should not have lied about her identity and her station, but she could not risk the possibility that he might alert Lord Stamford to her presence there.

Looking around, she wondered if he'd told the truth about his servants. An estate of Glenloch's size did not run itself, so surely there must be others about. Yet she'd seen no signs of life through the windows as she approached the castle. There were no signs of industry anywhere, except that this room, possibly the great hall at one time, would put any London drawing room to shame. Its thick carpets and beautifully upholstered fabrics on the chairs and settees made it a lush and comfortable room. The walls had been painted with an elaborate, continuous mural, and modern portraits hung on every wall. There was not a speck of dust to be seen on any of the highly polished tables.

It was a relief to be able to spend the night there, but Brianna had to be careful of becoming too relaxed. Her chosen shelter was warm and inviting, and the thought of a cozy bed was nearly too much to contemplate. But perhaps she'd be better off contemplating the horse Lord Newbury must have stabled on the grounds, and whether she could steal it during the night and ride somewhere far away.

But horse thieving would make her a criminal, and Bree refused to be that. Bad enough that she'd become a runaway and a liar.

The sooner she left Glenloch, the better, though it would be foolish to do anything but wait out the rain and hope that it let up by morning. Brianna was no coward. She could deal with Laird Glenloch tonight, and then leave again early in the morn on her own two feet. Dundee was her destination, and it was a large enough town that she should be able to remain there and evade Stamford until she reached her majority. Only two more months. Then she would be an independent woman.

Miss MacLaren could not possibly be acting without an accomplice, yet it seemed she'd arrived at the castle alone. Perhaps she'd intended to meet someone here, mistakenly believing the castle would be deserted. He wondered if she knew of the secret chamber that adjoined the buttery, the hidden area where his contraband brandy was stored.

Instinct caused him to dismiss his suspicions. He couldn't believe she was capable of hauling heavy tubs of brandy, and he knew her hands weren't tough enough to be driving a cart across the county in the harsh December weather. The explanation she'd given rang almost true, although Hugh sensed there was something more to it.

He figured he'd be able to discover the truth easily enough, and enjoy himself immensely as he did so.

His candle cast ominous shadows on the walls of the second-floor gallery. It was a long corridor, with cushioned benches and low tables comfortably arranged against the walls between the bedchamber doors. It was easy to believe that a ghost haunted these halls at night, and the very possibility of its appearance prevented the castle staff from living in.

Sometimes, Hugh felt nearly as skittish as the servants, avoiding the rooms the ghost was said to haunt. He shook his head in self-derision and proceeded to the end of the main gallery. He pushed open the door to the last room, a small chamber that had been meant for a nursery.

But he and Amelia had never had children. Amelia had never shown the slightest hint of a pregnancy. And though she eschewed his physical attentions as often as possible, Hugh believed they'd had relations enough times during their five-year marriage to have accomplished at least one pregnancy. He might have concluded she'd been barren, but in subsequent years, none of his mistresses had conceived, either. He knew each one had used some device to prevent pregnancy, but such things were notoriously unreliable.

Not that he wanted any Newbury bastards running about. But at least one conception might have reassured him.

He was sterile, so he planned to content himself with his money and his amusements, for he had no intention of marrying again. It had been bad enough the first time, and since he would never sire an heir, another marriage would be pointless. When he went to his grave, the title and all his estates would go to Sir John Hartford, his second cousin, once removed.

Hugh liked the fellow, actually. John was an amiable sort who could not believe Hugh intended to abstain from taking another wife, and never failed to encourage him to reconsider. The irony caused Hugh to shake his head. For, if Hugh married, then John would remain a country gentleman, supporting his four daughters off his farm. It was a hardscrabble existence, and without the yearly stipend Hugh sent him, the family would be in dire circumstances. John ought to be praying for Hugh's early demise.

And yet the man did nothing of the sort. He was entirely content with his lot. He cared deeply for his wife, and took great joy in his children. It defied all logic, for Hugh knew how elusive such sentiments could be. Hugh's own mother had absented herself from his presence for most of her life, and his own wife had never succumbed to feeling any gentle affection for him. The hell of it was that he had not required her undying love, but a bit of warmth would not have been amiss.

He entered the nursery and saw that the fire was laid and ready to be lit, and a stack of peat had been piled beside it. Hugh got down on one knee and reached into the fireplace. He lit the fire, then turned to assess the rest of the room. The window was shut tight against the storm, and the bed was piled with woolen blankets. Hugh could easily picture his puzzling intruder lying there, curled tight under the blanket against the bitter chill. Or better yet, lying with her heavenly bottom curled up against his lap after a bout of scorching loveplay.

She was a fiery maid, unlike his last few mistresses, who'd managed to grow dull and uninteresting inside a month of their intimate acquaintance. Hugh was certain that Bridget MacLaren would bring more than a bland, uninspired performance to the bedchamber. Such a woman would be wasted as a governess or lady's companion. She belonged in bed, with an appreciative lover.

Quietly, Hugh returned to the drawing room and

found that she had not moved from her place by the fire and was still trying to warm herself in spite of her wet clothes. The thought of getting her out of them tantalized him. Whoever this petite, knife-wielding warrior might be, she was vastly appealing. Her pale hair was beginning to dry in soft curls around her face, casting an alluring, halo-like glow about her. The rest of the blond mass trailed down her back, a spill of curls and waves that Hugh's fingers itched to touch. Her brown woolen coat concealed most of her curves, but he had felt them when they'd tussled at the top of the stairs. He knew her feminine assets were more than satisfactory.

Her brow was furrowed and her lips pursed as though she were deep in thought. He wondered if she was considering the brandy she intended to steal . . . or the rutting employer.

"You ought to take off those wet things. You'll never get warm this way," he said, startling her. Her head snapped up as she looked at him, her cheeks coloring with astonishment as well as indignation.

"If you think I'll disrobe for you—"

"Of course not, Miss MacLaren. What do you take me for? I've got a fire going in one of the bedchambers. You can stay there for the night."

"Oh. I . . . I apologize for jumping to the wrong conclusion." Her blush charmed him and her reaction gave weight to her tale of a randy employer. "Thank you, my lord."

"No offense taken," he said, smiling as he turned away. He would never take advantage of an unwilling woman, but he did not doubt his ability to bring this one around to his way of thinking. He reached down and picked up the bundle she'd carried with her, then led her up the stairs and down the long gallery to the nursery. There, he pushed open the door and allowed her to pass him.

"I daresay there are candles somewhere," he said, setting her possessions on the hearth. Her eyes were really quite remarkable—an ethereal blue and altogether too cautious. Perhaps the employer had tried to force her to undress, hence the presence of a knife and her willingness to use it. Hugh decided to give her a few moments alone.

"Lord Newbury . . ."

"Laird Glenloch while in Scotland," he corrected.

"Then I thank you, Laird."

He gave a slight nod and left her, but not for long.

In the flickering light of the fire, Brianna peeled off her wet clothes. She pulled one of the blankets off the bed and wrapped it around her, then stepped close to the hearth and opened her bundle. It was where she carried her money, but there were also two plain gowns and a chemise, two pairs of stockings, and one pair of shoes all rolled together in the satchel, inside an oilskin tarp. Only the shoes and one stocking at the very center of the package were dry.

Brianna was not worried. With the blazing fire and plenty of peat on hand, everything should be dry by morning. She would be able to leave.

In the meantime, she would be snug and warm here. The room was small, possibly a child's bedchamber, with a low desk and a narrow bed. She took her money out of her shoe and hid it under the mattress, then laid out her wet clothes, arranging them carefully, for maximum exposure to the fire. As she spread them out, an odd light shimmered from above, as though someone had suddenly lit a lamp above the door. But when Brianna looked up, there was no light. She glanced back at the bed to see if she had truly concealed her coins, or if they were somehow reflecting the firelight off the wall. But there was nothing to account for the strange radiance.

Dismissing the odd occurrence, she returned to the task of arranging her clothes by the fire, but suddenly felt a prickle of awareness. *Someone was watching her!* She whirled around, expecting to see Laird Glenloch, but the door remained closed and the flickering light had returned and was starting to gather into a discernable shape. Brianna blinked her eyes, then rubbed them to be sure she was not seeing things. *The bright, filmy form of a person could not be hovering at the door!*

And yet it seemed to beckon to her.

"What do you want?" Brianna whispered, feeling foolish and afraid all at once. Foolish because she could not possibly be talking to an apparition. Afraid because . . . what if it was real?

A knock at the door made Brianna jump. The figure disappeared as she yanked open the door, unnerved, forgetting that she was clad in just a thin, woolen blanket.

"You must be hungry after your long walk," said Laird Glenloch. He carried a plate of food and a glass of ale into the room and set it on the table beside the bed. Then he went to the writing table and opened the drawer. Drawing out two candles, he lit them both, leaving one on the table and placing the other next to the food.

Brianna clutched the blanket tightly, making sure the loose end was securely tucked under her arm. "My lord—"

"'Tis not much," Newbury said, turning to look at her. "Just a cold sausage pie and some cheese that I bought when I stopped at Marykirk." His gaze dropped to her shoulders and down to the upper curves of her breasts, and Brianna's skin began to tingle. She remembered the way his body had felt pressed against hers when he'd nearly kissed her, and wondered if he was thinking the same thing.

He stepped closer, and Brianna found herself unable to move away.

"You are very beautiful, Miss MacLaren."

His voice warmed her as much as the heat of his body. His deep tone was as rich as clotted cream, but far more dangerous. Bree could easily find herself leaning into his strong frame, seeking the comfort of his embrace.

But she knew better. She took an unsteady breath. "Laird Glenloch, you should not be here."

"'Tis late to be concerned about propriety, Miss MacLaren." He was so close she could smell his shaving soap, and see the reflection of the fire in his eyes. His jaw was ruggedly hewn, as though from a block of granite, and the scar on his cheek reminded her that he was not quite civilized.

"My actions tonight might not follow convention, my lord, but I assure you that I am otherwise a perfectly respectable lady."

"*Lady* Bridget, is it, then?" he asked, moving closer. With one long finger, he touched the hair that curled at the side of her face.

"No," she said quietly. "Plain Miss M-MacLaren."

"Hardly plain, Bridget, but not too high-toned, I hope?" His thumb grazed her chin, then slid across her lower lip.

"No," Bree whispered as his touch caused tiny shocks to course through her. "Not at all."

"But you are in need of protection. Assistance."

"No." Brianna gave a slight shake of her head. "I will leave in the morning."

"Perhaps I can convince you to stay awhile. Dundee can wait."

"Laird, I only came to . . ."

His hands slid down her arms, warming her, yet raising chills of awareness. His touch stunned her senses and made her brain go limp.

"I o-only came here to—"

He drew her toward him, his head dipping down, his mouth brushing hers. Brianna should have moved away, should have gathered some kind of self-control, put a stop to his gentle assault. She should have shoved him as hard as she'd done to Roddington.

But when he pressed her flush against his body and

deepened their kiss, his gifted mouth coaxed hers open. Brianna's heart tripped in her chest.

He tasted of brandy, and pure, scorching male.

Rationality deserted Brianna. She felt hot all over. Her nipples tightened and a raw sensation of pleasure pooled deep in her pelvis. The laird tipped her head slightly and sucked her tongue into his mouth, then skimmed his hands from her back to her sides, caressing the lower boundaries of her breasts with his thumbs, then cupping them fully. He made a low sound when he touched their tips, circling them with the pads of his thumbs, then lightly pulling the hardened pebbles between his fingers.

Barely aware of what she was doing, Brianna slid her hands up his chest and encircled his neck, slipping her fingers through the hair at his nape, surprised at the silky feel of it. She felt truly warm for the first time since leaving Killiedown, relaxed and secure for the first time in months.

Laird Glenloch inched her back toward the bed and stood before her, his hands inching around to her buttocks. Brianna felt the rasp of his waistcoat against her bare nipples and suddenly realized that her blanket was gone. Somehow, he'd managed to slide if off her, and now she stood fully naked before him, powerless— unwilling—to stop what he was doing.

His kisses were intoxicating, and his touch turned her knees to quivering reeds. She slid down onto the bed.

"That's it, lass," he said, caressing her, going down on one knee before her. "You were made for pleasure."

Brianna took a shuddering breath as he moved between her legs. She should have felt scandalously exposed. Should have slapped his face and made a grab for the blanket that lay pooled on the floor nearby. But he leaned forward and laved one of her breasts with his tongue, and pure, carnal sensation washed over her. A small voice in the back of her mind told her to resist, but she could neither ignore nor overcome the tremendous need Glenloch aroused in her.

Yes she could. She had not come this far to be seduced by a notorious rake. She reached behind her for one of the blankets on the bed and pulled it over her shoulders. Somehow she managed to close Laird Glenloch out, mortified by her behavior. "Laird, please. I am not a . . . a light-skirt."

Brianna extricated herself from his grasp and came off the bed. She went directly to the fireplace, wrapping herself tightly against any further sensual onslaught. Her legs still felt weak, and there was a trembling awareness of him in every pore of her body. But she would not do this. She did not want a man in her life. Neither Roddington, nor Glenloch, nor anyone else who would use her and control her with little thought for her own well-being.

Hugh scrubbed one hand across his face. He had not intended for things to progress so far. He'd only planned to soften her to the point of admitting her true business at Castle Glenloch. And if she was innocent of interfering with his smuggling operation, there would be no harm in making a lady's maid receptive to his advances.

But he'd lost control. And ended up walking out of her chamber sporting the most painful cockstand he could recall.

He dealt with it alone in a spectacularly unsatisfactory manner, then turned his attention to what he'd intended to do much earlier, when he'd first encountered the distracting, and oh so tempting, Bridget MacLaren. He returned to the secret door in the drawing room, determined to remove Bridget MacLaren from his thoughts, to eradicate her sweet taste from his lips and the weight of her breasts from his hands.

He muttered a low curse and worked the latch, then entered the passage leading to the stairs. Proceeding quickly down the steps, he arrived at the stone landing and checked the metal grate through which the brandy tubs were passed. 'Twas no doubt the way Bridget had entered. It was tight in the window frame, but the simple metal grille was not much of a barrier to the elements. She had not lied about the weather. It was hideous. Clearly, she had needed to find shelter somewhere, but it made no sense for her to be out walking alone, dressed as she was. She was entirely too intriguing.

Holding his lamp high, Hugh looked down at the stone floor. Wet tracks had pooled near the grate, but the footsteps proceeded directly to the stairs. It looked as though she had not attempted to find his secret cache.

Which meant naught. Perhaps she did not realize this was the place where the brandy was stored.

Castle Glenloch was the perfect place from which to run a smuggling operation. Riddled with secret doors and ancient passages, the towers looked as though they might collapse under a good wind, deterring any customs officer from investigating. And rumors of the Glenloch Ghost kept away the curious.

Hugh turned to the far wall and ran his hands along the uneven stones, searching for the catch that would release the hidden door. He rarely had any need to open this door, so it took some time to find it. But finally, his fingers located the small latch, hidden in a hollowed-out stone just above his head. It was a lever recessed into the stone wall, attached to a strong spring. When he pulled it up, the catch released and the door fell ajar. He pulled it all the way out, then entered the room. Tubs and ankers of brandy were stacked high against the walls with just a narrow aisle between them to walk through.

It was quite cold inside. Hugh cupped his hands at his mouth and blew into them as he counted each container, then left the secret room. Satisfied that he had the information he needed to start his investigation, he had nothing more to do down there. The next step would be to talk to MacGowan.

Hugh climbed the steps and exited the cold buttery, returning to the warmth of the drawing room. He tended the fire and poured himself a glass of his fine brandy, keeping his back to the prominent portrait of his father. Paintings of Jasper Christie were scattered throughout the castle, and Hugh generally avoided the rooms in which the old earl's dissipated visage looked down upon him from on high. Just as he'd done in life.

"Here's to you, old sod," Hugh said, raising his glass and tilting it irreverently in the direction of the portrait behind him. "No doubt you're enjoying this. Your incompetent son has failed once again, and allowed himself to be cheated, dolt that he is."

Hugh took a seat in the chair nearest the fire and swallowed a draught of brandy, enjoying the burn at the back of his throat. He considered how the thief might be getting away with his brandy and how his losses must be affecting the free traders in Falkburn. While Hugh could afford a decrease in profits, his people could not, and he felt a pang of regret at leaving it so long. He should have come up to Glenloch and put things to rights much sooner.

But then he would not have encountered Bridget MacLaren. He wondered if she'd fallen asleep yet. She'd be lying naked in the bed, for it was quite obvious that everything she owned was soaked through.

His body reacted markedly with the thought of her, despite the release he'd just experienced. She was the most fascinating creature he'd encountered in many a long month, with her dirk and her men's clothes. Her tale of running from a nobleman's advances was perfectly believable, but Hugh was not yet ready to absolve her from taking part in the operation that was stealing his brandy. He decided he was very much going to enjoy finding out the truth of the matter.

Mortification still burned Brianna the following morn when she awoke. She wanted to deny that she'd engaged in such shameless behavior with the master of Glenloch, and that she'd enjoyed it. She wished she could deny the sensual power Laird Glenloch wielded over her.

And yet she could not. She pressed her legs together to squeeze out the sensation of his touch, but it only made it worse. Her breasts still tingled where he'd nuzzled and sucked them, and her mouth felt swollen and bruised from his kisses.

Bernard's tame kisses had never created such a maelstrom of sensations, and she wondered if that had been part of his appeal—he'd never caused her to lose control.

She turned over and jerked the blankets up, over her shoulders. Glenloch was just a man, a roué whose only skills were those of a master seducer, a gambler, a sporting pugilist. Not a single one of his traits was admirable. She could—she *would*—resist his advances until she could get away.

But it might be some hours before that happened, for it was still raining. Brianna heard it dribbling down the windowpane, along with the howl of a stiff wind that chilled her in spite of the warmth of her room and the soft down of her covers.

She could not face it just yet.

If only Claire still lived, Brianna would not be in this predicament. Her aunt had been a beautiful, vital woman who'd swooped down on Stamford House nine years before to rescue Bree from a miserable existence with her guardian. Claire had been abroad at the time Brianna had been orphaned, and unaware of her niece's situation. But she'd rectified it the minute she returned, flouting convention to take Stamford's ward away to Killiedown.

And there they'd lived until Stamford's demand that Bree join his family in London for her first season. Brianna never believed those seasons had been provided for her benefit, else Stamford would have allowed her to wed Bernard, for he was a perfectly acceptable young man.

As recent events proved, Stamford was only interested in making a close alliance with a powerful family. And who was more powerful than the man who would become the Duke of Chalwyck?

It was a marriage that would never happen. Bree would move heaven and earth to stay out of Stamford's—and Rotten Roddington's—clutches until she reached her majority and was able to make her own decisions.

Brianna could not remember her mother at all, and her father was just a vague memory. But she recalled each and every miserable moment she had spent in Stamford House. Her subsequent years at Killiedown had been sheer heaven, and Bree would have been content to stay there forever.

And yet Claire had insisted that she comply with Lord Stamford's demand to return to London for a season. Brianna sensed that there was more to Claire's agreement than the fact that Stamford was Bree's legal guardian, and if he chose to press his cause, the law would have been on his side then, as it was now.

Claire had actually wanted Brianna to find herself

a husband and make a happy and suitable match, as her own parents had done. Which made absolutely no sense at all, for Claire herself had managed to form a perfectly satisfactory life, alone.

Brianna had gone to London under duress, feeling almost as lost she'd been in her early years. Somehow, she'd managed to persevere through that first season, puzzled and confused by the short-lived attentions of the young men of the ton who'd come to call on her, but then suddenly shifted their attentions to Lord Stamford's daughters.

Then she'd met her handsome, attentive Bernard. Brianna had been certain he'd loved her as she had him. And yet he'd given her up so easily. Their stolen kisses had signified nothing.

That debacle had taught Brianna exactly where she belonged. At Killiedown with Claire. And now her aunt was gone. Brianna still could not credit that she'd lost her aunt so quickly, and that she was now mistress of Killiedown Manor. She was bereft of the one person she cared for most.

Bree curled into a ball and wept. She'd never imagined this day would come, when she would have to go on without her beloved aunt. Claire would have objected to Stamford's disgraceful trap. She would have stood up for Brianna and defended her against such an outrageous trick. There never would have been any need for Bree to flee Killiedown and end up where she was.

She needed to get away from Glenloch before Lord Stamford made his way there, and equally important—

before there could be any more encounters in the dark with Laird Glenloch. Just the thought of his sinful caresses made her body flush in embarrassing places. No wonder he was known in polite circles as a libertine. And then there were the terrible rumors about his wife, conjecture that he'd made her so unhappy in her marriage that she'd ended her own life.

It was clear that Brianna would not make her escape from the castle by lying about and ruminating on her situation, so she dried her eyes and left the warm comfort of her bed. The clothes that were spread out by the fire were dry and warm, but for the coat she'd worn through the rain. It was made of a dense wool, so it was still damp and would need a few more hours by the fire to dry it.

Brianna debated about putting it on damp and slipping away from Glenloch, but when a sudden gust of wind drove the rain skittering across the window, she knew she could not face it. She would just have to deal with Laird Glenloch until the weather cleared.

She rearranged the coat so that it would dry evenly, then dressed in one of the two plain gowns she'd brought. She had neither a hairbrush nor hairpins, so she shook out her tangles as best she could, and simply tied her hair back with a narrow ribbon that she removed from the collar of her gown. Then she left the bedchamber in search of clean water to wash with, and some food with which to break her fast.

Brianna harbored a remote hope that the laird might have left the castle on some sort of estate business, for she had no idea how she was going to face him after the intimacies she'd so mistakenly allowed. How could she expect him to believe her tale of unwanted advances by her employer's husband when she'd allowed exactly the same from him—a complete stranger? 'Twas clear that he was everything she'd been warned against, and more.

The long gallery outside her bedchamber was dark and shadowy, with numerous closed doors and arched entrances to other corridors. Brianna went to the staircase and descended, arriving in a cavernous entryway. She looked around the open area to get her bearings and noticed the drawing room where she'd entered the night before. The sounds and smells of breakfast were to her left, and she headed in that direction, toward the delectable aromas of kippers frying in a skillet, and bread in the oven. She was so intent upon her goal, she ran straight into Laird Glenloch, who suddenly stepped out of a doorway in her path.

"Miss MacLaren," he said, catching her shoulders to help her regain her balance. His eyes were dark and sensual, his faint smile reminding her of the scandalous interlude that passed between them last night.

He was darkly handsome in his simple country attire, all tweed and leather, with the scent of his shaving soap about him. He looked seasoned beyond his years, his features angular, marred only by the crescent-shaped scar high on his cheek. His physique was utterly male, and Brianna was hard-pressed to forget the power of his touch and the deep desire he had kindled within her.

She moistened her lips and took a deep breath of resolution, aware that the forbidden sensations he roused in her could come to naught. "Good morning, Laird Glenloch."

His fingers drifted from her shoulders down to the middle of her back. "Are you hungry?"

Brianna swallowed and tried to speak lightly. "Yes. Quite."

"I am very glad to hear it," he said, his voice low and dangerous to her peace of mind. His head dipped, and he caught her lips with his own.

Brianna drew back. "Laird . . ." she said breathlessly. "'Tis unseemly t-to . . ."

"To act upon our attraction to each other?" He pulled her closer and feathered kisses down the side of her jaw to her throat, and Brianna forced herself to deny the sizzle of arousal that burned deep within her feminine core.

"Please," she said. "We cannot."

A door opened and an older woman with fading red hair came through it, carrying a tray. "Beggin' yer pardon, Laird," she said, pushing past them as though barely noticing their presence.

The laird released Brianna and followed the woman into a dining chamber. He turned and held out a hand to her. "Join me for breakfast, will you, Miss MacLaren?"

"No, Laird. Just a small bite in the kitchen will suffice."

"No—I insist."

Brianna clasped her hands at her waist, aware that she would touch him at her own peril. Her senses were humming with too much awareness of the man, yet he seemed barely affected, indicating that Brianna should go ahead, then following her through the door as though naught had just passed between them.

"Mrs. Ramsay, this is Miss Bridget MacLaren, who will be staying with us until the weather clears."

"Aye, Laird," the woman replied, her slight hesitation the only indication that she might remember Brianna from the one time she had visited Castle Glenloch with Claire several years before. But then Mrs. Ramsay gave a slight bob of her knees and the moment passed. "Let me know if there is aught ye need, miss."

Brianna blushed deeply, aware that Mrs. Ramsay had witnessed the kiss in the hall. She must think her a strumpet.

Laird Glenloch gestured for Brianna to enter the dining chamber ahead of him. Feeling flustered and ill at ease, she did so, and found two places set at one end of a long, polished table. She was determined to ignore her qualms about continued contact with him, and the poor opinion of his housekeeper. Bree was nothing if not practical, and knew she would need sustenance for her continued journey. And once she left, she would never see the Ramsay woman again. Whatever she might think hardly mattered.

Brianna took a seat and waited for Glenloch to take his own. He did so, and handed her the platter laden with kippers, eggs, and thickly buttered toast.

"'Tis too wet to travel today," said the laird.

"And cold as a stone," said the housekeeper as she returned with a pot of tea, which she poured into each of their cups. When it was done, she left them alone in the dining room.

Perhaps Lord Stamford would not be traveling in such bitter weather. Brianna's guardian was not one to sacrifice his comfort for any reason, but she knew he was quite anxious to accomplish the marriage he'd orchestrated. She tried to determine whether 'twould be safer to leave Glenloch or remain at the castle and risk further brazen advances from its laird.

During her three dull seasons in London, Bree had never met anyone like him. None of the swells who'd come calling could match this tall, dark nobleman with his seductive ways, not even Bernard Malham. Brianna could not help but wonder how she'd have felt if this laird had come to Stamford House to woo her as a legitimate suitor.

In spite of his scandalous ways, Lord Newbury—Laird Glenloch—was known to be a wealthy peer with more power and influence than most other noblemen in Britain. Perhaps Lord Stamford would have overlooked his faults, just as he'd overlooked Roddington's, to achieve a promising marital alliance with him.

The laird was vastly attractive, and Bree suspected that if he'd come to call, Lady Stamford would have sent her away on some errand, just as she'd done every other time an attractive young suitor had come to the house. Her guardian and his wife never intended to give her a choice in the matter.

In truth, Lord Stamford had orchestrated her "ruination" with Roddington to ensure a match with his powerful family. Brianna could only imagine how angry he must have been when he realized that Brianna was not coming to the church for the wedding.

She did not care. Let Lord Stamford marry one of his own daughters to the old lecher.

She looked up and saw Glenloch gazing intently at her.

"You said you have no relations."

"No. Only my aunt . . . who died recently."

His brow creased, and Brianna realized she shouldn't have mentioned it. Now he would probably ask questions she did not want to answer.

But he did not. "My sincere condolences," he said. "Your aunt was your only connection? The only one you could turn to when your employer's husband accosted you?"

Brianna had thought her tears had all been shed, but a fresh flood clogged her throat, and she could do nothing but nod.

"You were close."

She nodded again and bit her lower lip to keep it from trembling. She did not wish to discuss her situation, and so picked up her fork and started to eat, even though her appetite had waned with the reminder of all she had lost.

The silence lengthened, and Bree grew uncomfortable under Glenloch's scrutiny. "You are a long way from London, Laird," she finally said.

"There is always business, Miss MacLaren," he said gently, "at one estate or another."

His hands were large and strong-looking, his fingers blunt-tipped with nails pared short. Brianna had felt their strength and their tenderness, and she wondered which reflected the true character of the man. Lord

Roddington's hands had felt as soft as putty when he'd grabbed her hand and placed it on the front of his trews to prove his attraction to her.

Laird Glenloch had needed to do no such thing to demonstrate his desire.

"Are you cold, Miss MacLaren?" he asked, noting her shiver.

"Oh, uh . . . yes, I suppose so. I neglected to bring a shawl."

"'Tis clear you packed in haste," he said, and Brianna managed to refrain from looking down at her wrinkled dress. She knew she did not look particularly fashionable and hoped her attire supported the Banbury tale she'd told him. "Are you still disinclined to confide your troubles to me?"

Brianna bit her lip, aware that the less said, the better.

Glenloch gave a slight shake of his head. "We'll leave it, then." He turned toward the open door and called to the housekeeper, who returned to the dining room, wiping her hands upon her apron.

"Aye, Laird. What is it ye need?"

Brianna felt homesick as she witnessed the easy informality of Laird Glenloch's house. It was just so at Killiedown Manor, with servants who had been part of the household for nearly a generation and a genuine affinity between them. Brianna had told Claire's housekeeper that she would be back, to keep the fires burning, and she would return just as soon as she could—the day after she came of age.

Laird Glenloch spoke to Mrs. Ramsay. "Have someone fetch a shawl among Lady Glenloch's things and bring it down to Miss MacLaren."

"Ye know we doona like to go up to that chamber, Laird," the plain-speaking housekeeper replied.

"It will take but a moment," he said. "Send a maid for it. Or one of your grandsons. Are they here?"

The woman made a low sound of discontent, then turned away and called for someone named Ronan.

"I don't wish to put anyone to any trouble," Bree said.

"The servants have been working around the Glenloch Ghost for many a year. Don't worry about them," he said with a grin.

Chapter 3

Never show your teeth unless you can bite.
SCOTTISH PROVERB

"The Glenloch Ghost?"

"Aye," Hugh replied flatly. If Bridget Mac-Laren hadn't heard of it yet, she would soon encounter various tales of the phantom. Hugh had no control over the stories that were told all over the district, nor did he attempt to squelch them, for they served an important purpose. "'Tis said there's a filmy apparition that haunts the halls and galleries here."

"Then I did not imagine it."

He decided her engaging speech must have been tempered by southern regions. London, if he was not mistaken. Perhaps her family had had the wherewithal to send her to school there.

In the light of day, her eyes were larger than they'd seemed before, and the palest blue. He could not seem to take his eyes from the delicate arches above them, or the small dimple at the side of her mouth when she spoke. Her hair was slightly disheveled, as though she'd just arisen from a lover's bed, and—

Her words suddenly registered in his brain. "Imagine what?" he asked, his attention abruptly refocused. Dash it, he should never have left London so quickly. A visit to a former paramour might have taken the edge off his restlessness and helped to keep him from lusting so deeply after this woman.

"What did you see?"

"An odd light in my bedchamber, then a floating gray shape near the door. It seemed to take the form of a young woman."

"You jest."

"No, Laird. I assure you, I saw something."

"Alone?"

"Yes, of course I was alone."

"No, the ghost. Was it . . ." Good God, he could hardly believe he was questioning her about a myth. "Was it only one ghost, one figure?"

"I . . . I think so."

He stood. "Are you certain?"

"I cannot be absolutely sure, but it seemed to be only one."

Hugh felt reassured in spite of himself, knowing that Amelia's distraught spirit had not joined the old phantom. 'Twas ridiculous, he knew, and he shook off the absurd notion. "Well, don't worry. Our ghost has never hurt anyone in the centuries it's haunted Glenloch."

A young boy entered the room just then, carrying a woolen shawl in the deep russet color Amelia had favored. He brought it directly to Hugh, who put a hand on his shoulder, stopping him to look him over. "You're Ronan?"

"Aye, Laird. Ronan MacTavish."

"You were a mere bairn when I was here last." It had been three years, and Hugh could hardly believe this grandson of Mrs. Ramsay had even been walking then. "How many more MacTavishes are there?"

"I've got two brothers younger than me, Laird, and two older as well. All but the youngest are here, somewhere."

Hugh knew and trusted the lad's father, who was familiar with every aspect of the brandy trade. He would have to talk to Niall MacTavish, soon.

"How old are you, lad?"

"Six years." The boy puffed up his chest in a show of maturity.

Hugh gestured with the shawl the boy had retrieved. "And you're not afraid of Glenloch's ghost?"

"Nae, Laird. 'Tis only the lasses and old women who are scairt."

Hugh laughed. The lad was thin but sturdy. In a few years he and his brothers would join their father in the free trading. Hugh gave him a satisfied nod. "Is your grandmother keeping you busy?"

"Aye, Laird. I'm to stack bricks of peat in all the rooms ye like t' use."

"Ach, is that all?" Hugh asked. "A fine, strapping lad as yourself should have much bigger tasks than that, eh?"

"I have more, Laird," Ronan replied. "I'll be sweeping the kitchen and back halls after me gran's done wi' the cookin'."

"Then you'll be earning this, too," Hugh said. He

reached into his pocket and took out some coins, then handed them to the boy. "Give these to your mother."

Ronan's pale brown eyes lit up with excitement. "Thank ye, Laird. She'll be verra grateful to ye."

Hugh added another coin to the boy's hand. "Here's one to keep for yourself."

The boy smiled broadly, and before he scampered off, calling to his grandmother, he gave Hugh another gleeful thanks.

Hugh turned his attention back to Miss MacLaren and found her eyeing him quizzically. "He belongs to one of Mrs. Ramsay's daughters."

"I see," she said with a hint of bewildered admiration in her eyes, as though she could not quite credit that he could be kind or generous.

But times were difficult for Falkburn folk. The free trading eased their poverty, but even that was failing them now. Hugh's father wouldn't have given a moment's thought to their troubles, but Hugh had promised himself at an early age to do exactly the opposite of what Jasper would do in any given situation.

He stood and went to Brianna's chair. Draping the shawl over her shoulders, Hugh lifted her hair, allowing it to fall softly down her back. He lingered behind her, sliding his hands down her arms, thinking of all the ways he wanted her.

Later, when the servants had gone and they were alone together, he would finish what he'd begun the night before. There was no doubt she'd wanted him then. He'd not mistaken her ardor, and he looked forward to wooing her into his bed. An uncertain future in

Dundee could hardly compare with the arrangement he intended to offer her.

He was in need of a mistress, and a sweet governess or lady's maid was exactly the kind of lover that suited him, even though she might not yet be aware of it. This one was passionate and responsive, and would be freshly uninhibited once she let go of her nervousness. He'd tasted her desire, and he knew she was wary. But he did not doubt that he could convince her to stay at Glenloch with him. He looked forward to the next few days of becoming intimately acquainted with beautiful Bridget.

Hugh had already concluded that she had no involvement in the theft of his brandy. Her grief at the mention of her aunt had been quite real, and her story of an aggressive employer rang true.

He was quite content to be the man who offered her comfort and solace.

"Who is the ghost, Laird?" Bridget asked. "Or . . . who *was* she?"

Hugh was hesitant to tell the story, but he finally repeated what he'd always heard. "According to legend, she was the wife of an ancient Glenloch free trader. An unwilling, unhappy wife." A wife just like Amelia, no doubt. He put aside his suspicion that the ancient, legendary wife had also thrown herself from the parapet of the north tower to the ruins below.

"What does she want?"

Hugh shrugged and decided to tell her the truth. If she was going to stay with him at the castle, he did not want her jumping at every creak and odd reflection of light. "'Tis only a legend. There is no ghost."

Bridget shivered and drew the shawl tightly around her shoulders. "I saw it. Or something."

"'Tis not possible."

"I think it beckoned to me."

"Well, don't follow it," Hugh said, humoring her. He lowered his head, placing his mouth close to her ear. "This morn, you should follow me."

"Laird?"

"Through Glenloch. There is much to see in this ancient pile of stones." A tour was just the thing to keep her occupied while Mrs. Ramsay and her staff performed their duties. As they wandered through the castle, he could seduce her slowly, tantalizing her with the promise of pleasures to come. His task was to convince her that she need not run off to Dundee to find employment, but stay with him at Castle Glenloch. Perhaps he would even take her to Newbury Court in the spring.

It was a perfect solution for both of them. He wanted her fiercely, and she needed his protection. Besides, he did not care to return to London any time soon. Life had become too complicated there. They could remain at Castle Glenloch, or visit one of his country houses where he and Bridget MacLaren could enjoy each other without interruption or interference.

"Laird," said Mrs. Ramsay, intruding once again. "MacGowan is here fer ye."

Hugh had known he would have only one night to learn what he could about his brandy before being discovered by the servants. As of last night, he knew exactly how many tubs of undiluted brandy lined the walls in the secret chamber in the buttery.

He straightened up from Bridget's delectable scent and answered Mrs. Ramsay. "Send him to my study." Then he spoke to Bridget. "If you'll excuse me, I must see my estate manager, but I'll come and find you in your chamber in an hour."

"No! I mean, I'll just meet you . . . here."

"Afraid of me, Miss MacLaren?"

"Of course not," she replied quickly. " 'Tis only that I . . ."

"You plan on exploring on your own?"

She shrugged. "Perhaps. If you've a library, I might find something to read."

"Aye. Just next to the drawing room." She was a woman interested in books. A governess, then. He hid a small smile at the thought of pleasures to come. With a governess. She was going to be far more interesting than the well-practiced courtesans of his acquaintance.

Hugh left the dining chamber and went to the study where estate business had always been conducted. There, he found Malcolm MacGowan, a tall, burly man with hands the size of shovels and a perpetually irritable expression on his face. Hugh wondered how he would comport himself in the ring and decided he'd be a formidable adversary.

MacGowan combed his bright coppery hair over a receding hairline and grew thick muttonchop whiskers, perhaps to compensate for the lack on his pate. He was only five or six years older than Hugh's own thirty years, but had never married. From his early morning discussion with Mrs. Ramsay, Hugh had learned the man harbored a secret infatuation with a Stonehaven lass. "The fool doesn't know how lucky he is," Hugh muttered as he entered his study. 'Twas far better to leave one's emotions unattached and enjoy the moment with a willing lass.

"Laird," MacGowan said, rising from his seat by the fire. "We didna know ye were coming."

"Aye. It was an impulse. I left London rather abruptly."

MacGowan frowned. "Woman trouble, then?"

"You might say so," Hugh admitted, unsurprised that MacGowan knew of his reputation. The gossip sheets played fast and loose with his name so frequently that he was known for his supposed exploits all the way to Aberdeen.

The worst yet was what would soon be said about his encounter with Charlotte de Marche, although she'd brought it upon herself. Hugh had never expected her to corner him the way she'd done. He'd been polite, but not quite a gentleman, for that kind of fool would have allowed himself to be shackled as a result of the lady's bold advances.

From here on, he was going to take pains to stay clear of the ladies of the ton. Not a one was trustworthy.

"We've a shipment stored and waiting for dilution and distribution," MacGowan said.

"Ah?" Hugh remarked as though he did not already

know it. " 'Tis well-hidden in the buttery, I trust?"

"Aye. 'Tis a large shipment, too. Ye'll garner a tidy sum from it."

Hugh tried to discern if there was any dissembling in MacGowan's tone, any disappointment or annoyance in his manner. If MacGowan was the one responsible for Hugh's losses, he could not be pleased to have him there, in the midst of an operation.

This shipment would go a long way toward compensating for the deficits Hugh had had to live with over the past three years. Rather than dealing with his insufferable partner, he'd made up the differences himself, and given a higher percentage of the take to the Falkburn folk. 'Twas long past time he put a stop to it. "When does it go out?"

"We were hoping last night," said MacGowan. "And now tonight does no' look good, either. No' with more rain comin'."

"Tomorrow, then."

"Aye. It must be tomorrow, for another of Captain Benoit's ships will be comin' in late."

Hugh considered the news, frowning at the inefficiency of it. "Then you'd best get the brandy that's in the buttery diluted and out today, else where will you store the new shipment?"

"Mayhap in the barn, Laird? 'Tis winter and none o' the customs agents are likely to rouse themselves to poke into every wee cranny along the coast this time o' year."

"No," said Hugh. "They're too unpredictable. I'd rather not risk Berk Armstrong or Angus Kincaid finding it. Or worse yet—Mr. Pennycook. Get it out tonight. Regardless of the weather."

MacGowan nodded, though he was clearly not happy about it. His reaction only confirmed Hugh's suspicions, for the manager was his primary suspect in the thieving. No one else had access to the money Hugh sent, as well as all the information—the dates and times, numbers and distribution.

"You've yet to say why you've come here, Mac-Gowan," said Hugh, for the man had already admitted he had not known of Hugh's presence until his arrival at the castle.

"Oh . . . uh, just estate business," the man replied. "I come up every few days t' check on things."

"Very good of you, especially on a day like this."

"Weel, I always like t' know if anyone's been poking round the product."

Hugh crossed his arms over his chest and looked at MacGowan. He knew it was sometimes best to stay silent and let the situation play out, a direct contradiction to his father's ways. The old laird had been much more vocal, letting everyone know of his thoughts and plans . . . as well as his disdain. Hugh could not imagine the old man ever getting anything more than the most basic cooperation from those who worked for him.

Or from his son.

"I didna bring the books, since I didna know ye were here," said MacGowan.

Hugh waited, ignoring the harsh visage of his father, glaring down upon him through the dark oil pigment of the painting that hung on the wall behind MacGowan.

Jasper would have browbeaten the manager until he'd heard what he wanted to hear. Not necessarily the truth.

But Hugh was a patient man, and he waited as MacGowan pulled on one of his muttonchops and started to pace before the fire. The estate manager had never been a calm man, and Hugh knew better than to ask him outright if he was cheating Hugh, the way his father would have done.

"I can look over the books any time," Hugh said. "Our priority is to get the brandy let down, and out of the castle before tomorrow."

Hugh could dismiss his estate manager out of hand, but he wanted proof. And he wanted the names of all who were involved, especially if they were Falkburn men—the very ones he'd been supporting these past three years.

"Tell me, MacGowan," he asked, in spite of his belief that Miss MacLaren was not involved, "do we use any women as carriers?"

"Women? Nay, Laird. I doona believe so."

"You're sure?"

"I canna be entirely sure, nay. But I doubt it. I've no' heard of anyone giving o'er to a woman to sell the brandy. Why are ye thinking it, might I ask?"

"Just call me curious. Do you think you can find enough experienced men to let down the brandy tonight? And to carry it out?"

"Aye, Laird. Of course. We've none but the best in these parts."

*   *   *

The laird might think Glenloch's ghost was not real, but Brianna had seen it. Or seen *something*. She'd felt no danger from that strange flickering light, and as she returned to the bedchamber given her by Laird Glenloch, she kept her gaze high, so she might catch sight of it once again. If only she could speak to it . . . she knew it was an irrational thought, but . . . perhaps the phantom might carry a message to her aunt Claire.

She walked in on a housemaid who was doing up the bed. "Oh! Nearly done, miss," said the girl with a quick curtsy. She was obviously nervous and hurrying to complete her task in order to leave as quickly as possible. "I'm Fiona. Mrs. Ramsay told me to give ye a few extra blankets."

"I appreciate it. But I can finish here, Fiona."

"Oh, thank ye, miss. What with the ghost and all, I doona favor being up here."

"The ghost has done you some evil, then?"

Fiona shook her head. "Nay, I've ne'er even seen it. But I doona hold with bogles. Such creatures can do all sorts of harm. Can draw ye into their netherworld and trap ye—"

"Has such a thing happened to anyone?"

"Weel, perhaps some of the old laird's visitors were caught in the ghost's traps and followed it into the void," Fiona said. "But we—from the village—we know better than to come up and stay here through the night."

Bree said naught. She'd spent one night in Castle Glenloch and felt no threat. On the contrary, she'd slept better than she had any night in the week since she'd fled London, in spite of her encounter with Laird Glenloch.

"Ronan brought ye plenty of peat, miss. Enough to stay warm through the night."

"Thank him for me please, Fiona," said Brianna. "Don't worry about building up the fire. I'll stoke it so that you can go back downstairs."

The girl gave another quick curtsy and started to leave, but Brianna stopped her. "One thing . . . Where did Ronan find the shawl he brought me?"

"In Lady Glenloch's chamber at the far end of the gallery, just afore ye come to the north tower," the maid replied from the doorway. "Her Ladyship's things are right where she left them. Before she . . ." Fiona swallowed and wrapped her arms around herself. "Ach, 'tis a wonder she hasna joined Glenloch's ghost, dyin' as she did."

"How do you know she hasn't?"

"We doona," Fiona said. A loud keening sound rang out above them, and Fiona gave out a terrified squeal. "'Tis her! The bogle!"

"Fiona, 'tis the wind," Brianna said, but the girl ran from the room, and Bree heard her speedy footsteps all the way down the hall and the staircase.

It went silent in Bree's bedchamber, but for the crackle of the fire that was burning low, and she wondered if the noise had truly been the wind or the apparition she'd seen the previous night.

Or had she imagined it, as Laird Glenloch had hinted?

She thought about Fiona's words as well as the laird's concern that there was only one ghost haunting Glenloch, despite his dismissal of what she'd seen. But Brianna knew that she had not been imagining things. There had truly been a vague form of flickering light in this very chamber. And it had signaled her to follow it.

Brianna considered the possibility that Lady Glenloch's spirit had joined the castle's phantom. If the gossip was true, then Amelia Christie had been so terribly unhappy in her marriage that she'd ended her own life. Perhaps her sorrowful spirit now haunted Glenloch's rooms and galleries alongside the ancient specter described by the laird.

There was a distinctly brooding aspect to the castle. It appeared to Brianna that certain rooms had been restored and updated, and she had even found a modern water closet near the bedchamber Laird Glenloch had given her. But the rest was dark and derelict—a perfect setting to be haunted by Glenloch's restless spirits.

Bree laid a new brick on the fire, then turned to look up at the ceiling, hoping as well as dreading that the filmy apparition would reappear. She felt sure that spirits would communicate with one another, and . . . more than anything, Bree wished she could speak with Claire, just once more.

It was a ridiculous notion, she knew, and certainly not a good reason to remain at Glenloch, not when her coat had dried and she could leave. She *should* leave. She should run as fast as her feet would carry her through the cold rain. She believed there was a larger town not too far south of Falkburn, a place where there would be an inn.

Yet she was warm and secure at Glenloch, and she was not without wits. She could resist Laird Glenloch's seductive ways until the weather cleared sufficiently for her to go.

As she stood at the nursery window looking out on the low cliffs and the sea below her, she felt the warmth of the fire heating the room . . . and then something else. It had waited until Fiona had gone, and now Brianna felt it in the room. The ghost.

Slowly Bree turned, and saw the shimmering figure hovering above the bed. This time, Brianna was able to make out the shape of its voluminous gown and a veil arrangement on its head. Brianna was no expert on bygone fashions, but the ghost looked altogether medieval. "Who are you?" she asked it.

The ghost made no reply, but fluctuated, and seemed to float toward the open door.

Brianna rubbed her eyes, then looked up again, half expecting the thing to have disappeared. But the figure seemed to turn and face her, beckoning as she'd done the night before. Again, Bree felt no fear, though a sense of urgency filled her.

"Can you . . . Can you carry a message for me?" she asked in a hushed tone.

The ghost gave no indication that it understood Bree's request. "What is it?" Bree asked, disappointed. "Should I follow you?"

An infusion of color changed the appearance of the phantom, and Brianna approached it, ignoring Laird

Glenloch's admonition not to follow it. "Is there something you wish to show me?"

Perhaps if she went along with it, the thing would grant a request to communicate with Claire.

The shimmering light lost its shape, turning into a vague amorphous glow that moved slowly down the length of the gallery. Brianna walked behind it, passing closed doors and ancient furniture. She hesitated at the staircase that was at the halfway point, and listened to the eerie quiet below, wondering if the servants had already completed their work and left the castle.

The eerie glow of the ghost stopped at the far end of the gallery, near a set of thick oaken doors. It remained floating there, and Brianna watched it, bearing in mind Fiona's words. If Glenloch's specter made a practice of pulling people into some ethereal world that destroyed them, this might very well be the way it would do so.

Brianna wavered for a moment, but then sensed the phantom's urgency, along with some other emotion she could not identify. She took a deep breath and walked past the staircase, heading toward those large doors, but keeping a prudent distance from the ghost.

The shimmering light dissipated, and Brianna tried the latch, but found it locked. "The way is blocked," she said quietly.

But the phantom seemed undeterred, reappearing again just outside the last room they'd passed. Its door was also closed, but the phantom somehow slipped inside.

Brianna tried the door, and found it unlocked. She

pushed it open and stood under the lintel for a moment, then stepped inside.

The room was in shadows, and cold, in spite of the lush furnishings within. The wide bed was covered in a thick, rich brocade of blue and yellow. The bed curtains had been pulled aside and tied with golden tassels, as though waiting for its usual occupant to return. This was clearly the room Fiona had indicated belonged to Laird Glenloch's wife.

Brianna felt like an intruder. She should turn around and leave, but her curiosity got the better of her. She took another step into the room and stood at the foot of the bed where Lady Glenloch had slept, trying to understand how it was possible to be so despondent as to take one's own life.

Bree went to Amelia's richly carved, mahogany dressing table and touched the brush and ornate combs that lay there. She herself had felt a terrible, deep grief at the loss of her beloved aunt, and she was on the verge of being forced into an abhorrent marriage. And yet Brianna would never dream of doing herself in, of ending it all. She could not imagine what had driven Lady Glenloch to such despair.

Surely not her husband.

Now that Brianna had actually met the rakish Laird Glenloch, she did not understand how his wife could have felt so discontented. But her questions faded when the ghostly glow of the phantom returned, its light fluctuating like the unsteady light of a candle. It seemed to flatten against the wall above the table, then a few strange sparkles of light slid down, flowing almost like a stream of water, to disappear below. Bree tried to look down into the space where it disappeared, speculating that there was something the ghost wanted her to notice. But there was hardly any gap between the wall and the table.

Brianna touched the wall, then slid her hand down the same path the ghost's light had taken, stopping when her fingers met the rough side of the table.

She pushed the table aside and looked down at the floor. There was nothing. She started to move the table back, but caught sight of something that had caught on the rough edge of the table. She reached down and came up with a long gold chain with a locket attached.

She knew of married ladies who wore miniatures of their husbands or children in their lockets. Bree snapped it open, expecting to see a small picture of Laird Glenloch, but it was another man altogether. Brianna did not recognize him, but it was obviously not Laird Glenloch.

Perhaps it was a portrait of her father or a brother.

Or a paramour.

Brianna closed the locket in her hand and glanced about the room, looking for the ghost, for some explanation of what she held in her hand. But Bree had been left alone to wonder if the phantom's intent was to indicate something about Lady Glenloch's affections.

Feeling distinctly troubled, she quickly replaced the chain exactly where she found it and shoved the dressing table back against the wall. "Whatever she might have done, the woman is dead," Bree admonished the ghost, who must be hovering somewhere nearby. "'Tis not right to intrude on her privacy." Though Brianna could not imagine a wife who would cuckold Laird Glenloch.

He did not seem to be a brute, nor was he unkind. If Bree had been his wife—

She gathered the front of her shawl in her fist. She intended never to find herself in such a position, ever. There would be no marriage to Roddington or to anyone else. After Bernard's defection, she had decided to spend her life as Claire had done—as an independent woman, free to travel, or to raise her horses as she pleased. She might go to Greece and spend a few years there, in the village where Claire had lived before coming to London to take Brianna away from Lord Stamford.

Or maybe she'd go to France on an extended trip and see about buying some new stallions to improve the Killiedown stock.

Feeling like an intruder in the dead woman's room, Brianna exited, closing the door behind her. Where Lady Glenloch had placed her affections had naught to do with her, though Brianna wished she could be as immune to Laird Glenloch as his wife seemed to have been.

Brianna returned to her room and wondered how she was going to manage to avoid the laird's advances this evening, after the servants had all gone. She had never been so susceptible to any other man, not even Bernard Malham. And her reaction to him was bothersome. She could not allow herself to succumb.

"If you can help me," she whispered, hoping the ghost might be hovering somewhere nearby, "now would be a good time." For she knew the power of Laird Glenloch's touch, of his kiss.

But there was no reply, no strange flicker of light anywhere in sight. Brianna was on her own in this, and she could not leave until the weather cleared.

She collected her dry clothes into the oilcloth, being careful to place her money securely in the center of it. She'd brought enough to keep her in decent lodgings at Dundee for more than two months, and pay for a few extras, besides. Such as transportation back to Killiedown when it was time to go home. And perhaps a lawyer to help her claim her inheritance.

In the meantime, she could not allow herself to yield to Laird Glenloch's seductive charms. She knew 'twas unwise to spend time alone with such a gazetted rake, but there were no other options, not while the brutal weather persisted.

She turned her thoughts to the horses at Killiedown, rather than the sensation of Glenloch's strong hands on her shoulders, sliding down her arms. She managed to avoid shivering at the memory of his breath in her ear, stirring her as no man had ever done.

She considered the breed of horses Claire had developed over the past eight years, teaching Brianna everything she knew. Bree had loved their life up north of Stonehaven, and still could not understand Claire's insistence that Brianna go to London to find a husband. It had been a pointless exercise after Bernard's abandonment, and Bree had wanted nothing more than to return home.

Now Claire was dead, and Brianna found herself in a

perilous predicament here at Castle Glenloch. It would be even worse at Killiedown Manor, for Lord Stamford would surely go looking for her there. Fortunately, Bree had all she needed to survive in Dundee for two months, and when she was twenty-one, she could return to Claire's estate and resume the life she wanted.

But she had to get to Dundee first.

With a sigh of frustration, Brianna recognized there was nothing she could do about it now but wait for an opportune moment. If only the clouds would break, she could slip away unnoticed. Since they did not, she decided to go down to the library as she'd told Laird Glenloch she would do. Far better for him to find her there, rather than coming into her bedchamber again.

The library was smaller than she'd expected, with three walls lined from the floor to the ceiling with shelves full of books. A chess table was set with figures wrought of pale oak and dark mahogany, and there were two comfortable chairs with accompanying ottomans arranged on opposite sides of the fireplace. Directly in front of the fire was a long, lushly cushioned sofa.

But Bree did not feel like sitting. She lit the lamps and tended the fire, making the room warm and bright enough to stay, then looked through the window once again, in hopes that the rain had cleared. She knew Laird Glenloch did not intend to relent in his seduction, not if their encounter before breakfast was any indication.

Too restless to sit down and read, Brianna paced before the fire, her mind racing. Her skin felt hot and flushed, her young muscles anxious to move, to flee. She had to do something. She glanced out the window and looked at the sea beyond the cliff, and wondered how long she would need to resist the enthralling laird before she could make her escape.

Chapter 4

If you dinna see the bottom, dinna wade.
SCOTTISH PROVERB

Hugh came out of his bedchamber and stopped cold at the sight of Amelia's bedchamber door, standing slightly ajar. It was always kept closed, and yet—

He would not be surprised to find his late wife haunting the place. It would be just like Amelia to try to plague him in her distinctly disapproving yet passive manner. She'd never voiced her unhappiness or her disappointment in him, but neither had she failed to display her discontent in her eyes, every time she looked at him. Which was not often.

Not even when he bedded her.

She'd preferred to suffer in silence, wordlessly blaming him for all that was wrong with her marriage, her life.

Well, hell's bells, he blamed himself for that. He'd berated his inability to please her in bed, or to give her children. He was no stranger to criticism. His own father had denigrated him often enough—and included a few brutal beatings, besides—that Hugh refused to give anyone that kind of power over him ever again. He kept everyone, save his two oldest friends, at arm's length.

He didn't need anyone's approval, nor did he need the bad memories engendered by the sight of Amelia's open bedchamber. Taking hold of the door latch, he started to pull it closed. But he stopped and ducked his head inside the room for a quick look around. Shrouded in shadows, it was just the same as he remembered. Feminine fabrics and furnishings abounded, giving an aura of sensuous femininity.

Amelia had worn the same mantle of womanly sensuality. She'd dressed to please her admirers and smiled beguilingly. But once Hugh had married her, she'd turned as cold and unresponsive as one of Mrs. Ramsay's kippers.

Amelia's appeal had been a sham. Her feminine frailties and dainty sensibilities had all been for show. To bear children, a woman must be willing to conceive. Yet she'd had no taste for their marriage bed. Marital relations had occurred seldom between them, perhaps once a month during their five-year marriage. There'd been no fire between them, not even at the start. Hugh had convinced himself that that would change once he bedded her and they learned the pleasures of the bedchamber together. But she'd felt no fundamental attraction to him.

He jerked the door closed and shut Amelia out of his mind just as forcefully. There was a beautiful, intriguing woman awaiting him in his library, one who responded quite nicely to him, and he intended to woo her and bed her before much more time passed.

Descending the stairs on his way to the library, he heard voices near the main entrance of the castle. He detoured from his route and saw Mrs. Ramsay greeting Berk Armstrong, Stonehaven's official customs collector. Of all the Stonehaven customs officers, Armstrong was the least of Hugh's worries. He could be easily sidetracked.

Armstrong came inside, stomping his wet shoes on the rug in the entranceway just as Hugh reached the bottom of the stairs.

"What brings you all the way down to Glenloch in this weather?" Hugh asked, concerned by the man's appearance just now, when there were five hundred tubs of undiluted brandy in his cellar.

"Ach, Laird," said Armstrong, looking up at Hugh. "Mr. Kincaid got wind of a cutter putting in near yer cove two nights ago. A cutter bearing two guns. I came down to see about it."

"I wouldn't know, Armstrong," said Hugh, extending his arm in the direction of the kitchen. "I only arrived last night."

"In this muck?" the man asked as he allowed himself to be led toward the warmth and welcoming cooking aromas near the back of the castle. Hugh felt confident that the collector would never go near the old towers, not when they appeared to be one good breeze away from a full collapse.

"Aye, 'tis Scotland in December, eh?" Hugh wondered who in Falkburn would have mentioned Benoit's ship and betrayed their operation, for it profited everyone there. "Are you sure, Armstrong? Surely the weather would have discouraged any such vessel from plying our coast."

"Weel, no. We are no' sure." He laughed amicably. "But our surveyor, Mr. Kincaid, doesna like us to sit idle at Stonehaven. He's got Pennycook running up to Muchalls, and me down here. There's always something to investigate."

"I see," said Hugh, somewhat relieved. He had never met Mr. Kincaid, but the man sounded at least somewhat more competent than his subordinates. It would do to be wary of him.

"It might be a wild-goose chase, Laird, but when I saw the light in your windows, I thought I'd stop to warm m'self before going on to the village. If anyone saw anything, I'll find him in Falkburn, I expect."

"Quite possibly," said Hugh, going along with the man to the kitchen, annoyed by the delay in rejoining Bridget MacLaren. "But first you must refresh yourself. Tea, if you please, Mrs. Ramsay."

The housekeeper stood working alongside two maids, cleaning up after they'd prepared dishes that looked to Hugh as though they would last several days, at least. It seemed she was preparing for the possibility that the road from Falkburn would be an impassable mess upon the morrow. Hugh admitted she might be right, if the icy rain continued.

Hugh gestured for the customs man to take a seat on a bench at the old, scarred oak table, nestled in a corner of the big kitchen. "Oh, aye. And thank ye, but

I'll just stay a few moments before I continue on my way, Laird."

"'Tis no problem, Armstrong. You know you are welcome any day." 'Twas not entirely true, but Hugh would say naught to arouse the man's suspicions, not when there would be a good twenty men from Falkburn coming in tonight to let down the brandy and carry it away for distribution on the ponies MacGowan borrowed from farmers nearby.

Hugh was going to have to get word to MacGowan, for he had no intention of allowing Armstrong to stay at Glenloch tonight if the weather prevented his return to Stonehaven. MacGowan would have to host him at his own cottage and let Niall MacTavish handle the brandy shipment.

In any case, Hugh knew exactly how much liquor was hidden in the secret chamber. He did not need MacGowan's accounting skills for this batch.

"Thank ye, Laird," said Armstrong. "Eh, perhaps your servants saw the cutter."

"Feel free to ask them," Hugh replied, confident of the answer the man would get. He refused to believe that any of his servants would ever turn informer. They had too much to lose.

While Armstrong questioned Mrs. Ramsay and the others, Hugh drank his tea, outwardly calm, but inwardly anticipating his next encounter with Miss MacLaren. The dolt who'd tried to seduce her hadn't known what he was about, else he'd have succeeded in getting her into his bed. She was ripe for the picking, if her responses to him were any indication. She'd had an attack of principles, but Hugh did not doubt that he could overcome those.

She wanted him. He hardened at the thought of tasting her again. Of pulling a taut, rosy nipple into his mouth while he fondled her delectable backside. He sipped tea with Armstrong as the household staff prepared to leave the castle. Soon, he and the delectable Miss MacLaren would be alone.

"Ah, the rain has stopped," said the customs officer. "I'd best be on my way before it starts up again."

"I'll walk you out, Armstrong," Hugh said. "And why don't you plan to stay at MacGowan's cottage if the weather turns too evil for you to ride back to Stonehaven. I'll send him notice."

"That's very good of ye, Laird."

"Mrs. Ramsay, would you see to it, please?"

"Aye, Laird. I'll take it m'self since we're finished here and we'll be leaving presently."

Hugh was glad of the housekeeper's reply. He drew Armstrong away to the door where the man had entered, and saw him out. The weather was definitely clearer, but would not stay that way. It was still gray and cold. Not the kind of night one would want to be abroad.

The break in the clouds was exactly what Brianna was waiting for. It might last a couple of hours, enough time to get to Inverbervie if she hurried, away from Laird Glenloch and temptation. Her vague inkling that Glenloch's ghost wanted to show her something was no reason to stay, and she had one very good reason to get away.

Her weakness with regard to Laird Glenloch's advances.

Hurrying back to her room, she changed clothes, then quickly tied up the oilcloth. She met no one on her way back downstairs, and found the drawing room empty. Creeping quietly inside, she went straight to the wall panel that led to the hidden passageway, in order to avoid alerting anyone to her departure. She found the latch, and slipped out of the drawing room.

She'd forgotten to bring a lamp or even a candle, but managed to make her way carefully through the shadows to the stairs. She climbed down to the small room where she'd entered, and went down on her knees. Pushing out the grate, she crawled through it, getting her hands and knees muddy and wet. She brushed them off as best she could and moved through the overgrown shrubs, finally jumping off the shallow ledge that faced the beach.

Common sense would dictate that she return to the road and proceed south from there, but with every day that passed came the greater likelihood that Lord Stamford would come after her, traveling that very same road. And Brianna did not know what to expect from Laird Glenloch, although she thought there was a good chance he would come looking for her, too. The attraction that raged between them would not easily be extinguished.

It was the true reason Bree had to leave now, for she had no power to resist his advances. He made her feel lovely and wanted, and yet she was perfectly aware

that his pretty talk and sweet caresses were pure blath-
erskite. The man knew how to charm a woman, how
to fascinate her with his kisses and intimate touches,
making her lose all sense of self-preservation . . . of
decency.

The castle had been built on uneven land, with various levels and differing degrees of disrepair. She felt
fortunate not to have caused the collapse of the dilapidated southern tower with her tampering of the grate
and her scrambling through it. When she emerged on
the beach, her eyes were drawn to the north tower,
which was in even worse shape.

She had a distinctly disquieting impression that the
parapet of that dilapidated tower was the site from
which Lady Glenloch had jumped.

Stumbling in her haste to get away, she noticed a
rocky path that led down to the beach. No one would
find her if she walked the shoreline. She could follow
the beach for some distance, and when it became impassable, there would surely be some other way to continue south, even if she had to return to the road.

She headed down the path and soon landed on a wide
expanse of wet beach that was scattered with forma-
tions of large black rock. The three small boats she'd
seen earlier were still in place and secured against the
winter weather. She started past them, but stopped suddenly when it occurred to her that she might borrow
one of them.

She looked out into the cove and saw that the sea
was calm enough to navigate, especially if she stayed

close to the shore. Sea travel would be much faster than walking, and she might actually make it all the way to Montrose.

Brianna and Claire often used the same kind of skiff to get from Killiedown to Stonehaven, so she was familiar with the craft. But Bree did not relish the possibility of being out at sea if the rain returned, or if the sea became rough.

She eyed the boats and then looked back up at the castle. The cove was visible from many of the windows, but as soon as she cleared the point that jutted out to the south, she would pass unseen. Down to Montrose, or even as far as Arbroath. Did she dare?

Her situation was dire enough to warrant the risk. She chewed on one nail and thought about her choices. Lord Stamford would have even more difficulty tracing her if she traveled by water, and she surely needed to get away from Glenloch and its laird. He was an indulgence she could not afford, a diversion from the safe, circumspect path she'd chosen.

Without allowing any further doubts, Brianna dropped to her knees beside the closest skiff and used her dirk to cut it loose from the stakes. She replaced the knife, then righted the boat and made sure there were oars, then dragged it down to the sea, jumping in just as the water lapped onto the scuffed, ill-fitting boots she'd bought from Killiedown's groom.

Hugh smiled with supreme male confidence even though he did not find his blond beauty in the library. Clearly, if she was waiting for him in the bedchamber, he could take it as a signal that she was willing to entertain him there. Intimately. He was already aroused when he climbed the staircase and walked down the long gallery to her room, anticipating the intimate lessons they would share. He thought about her sweet, feminine taste and the feel of her smooth skin under his knowing touch.

He knocked at her door and waited, then softly called her name. When she did not answer, Hugh thought perhaps she was asleep and decided he would wake her with gentle kisses. Taking care to unlatch the door quietly, he stepped inside and saw that she was not there— not in the bed, not in the chair at the writing table.

She might be reticent, but he could not believe such an intrepid lass would hide from him, not a woman who dressed in men's clothes and carried her own dirk for protection. Something outside the window caught his attention. 'Twas movement on the beach, which Hugh would have dismissed, since MacTavish's men were due to arrive soon to dilute the brandy and move it out tonight. But this was not MacTavish's gang. It was one person, putting one of his tub boats into the water. A sudden gust blew off the culprit's hat, revealing a mass of golden hair.

'Twas Bridget MacLaren, stealing the boat!

Instantly, Hugh whipped out of her room and scrambled down the staircase. The quickest path to the beach was through the buttery, but would require crawling through the wet grass and mud outside the grate. Instead of going there, he headed to a rear door of the castle, where he'd just let Armstrong out. Grabbing his greatcoat, he flew outside, hurrying around to the old buttery to find the path to the beach.

In a moment he was descending it, but the tub boat had already floated out of sight.

He swore viciously and went to one of the remaining boats, tearing at the ropes holding it securely to the ground. The ropes were wet, and he cursed the wicked little dirk Bridget had obviously used to cut the ropes holding the boat she'd taken. Hugh finally managed to untie the knots, freeing one of the remaining boats and flipping it over to shove it down to the water, just as the rain started again.

There was no question of leaving her to fend for herself in a tiny skiff during a winter storm in the North Sea. She must be mad. Or desperate.

What in hell had she thought he would do to her?

A fine drizzle fell, enough to drip down the neck of his coat as he jumped into the boat and started rowing. The wind increased as did the surf, and Hugh had to battle against the waves as they lapped against his skiff. Bridget was not going to be able to control her own craft if the storm got any worse or the wind picked up.

He rowed furiously and cleared the southern point of the cove, then caught sight of her, far ahead. She was struggling, and drifting too far from the shore. The cold drizzle turned to rain, and Hugh knew that if she did not turn in toward land, there was a good chance she would be swept into the current and carried away.

Hugh doubled his efforts to reach her, working frantically, straining against the heavy waves and his biting anger. 'Twould not serve him now. "Bridget!" he shouted, turning to face her. "Row toward shore! Go on! Toward shore!"

It looked as though she was trying to do exactly that, but the waves were too high, splashing into the hull, soaking her. Hugh knew she would soon be too cold to hold the oars. Her hands would freeze and she would be paralyzed with shivering. He had to get to her soon, or she would be drawn out to sea and there would be naught that he could do.

Hugh's own situation was not much different. The sky darkened further, and his worst fears were realized as the wind sharpened and the rain started coming down in sheets. The waves splashed high, crashing into his small craft and jarring the oars from his hands. He risked turning once again to see how Bridget fared, and realized that she was losing the battle against the wind and waves.

He roared his frustration and pulled harder and faster, cutting through the water with a superhuman effort. He heard a cry behind him, and glanced briefly, afraid to see what was amiss. He was only marginally reassured to see her still in the boat, but struggling to hold on to one oar. "Hang on! I'm coming!" he shouted.

They had drifted far south of Glenloch, but nowhere near Inverbervie. The beach between the two was mostly deserted, though there were a few places where kelpers put in to shore. Some of them had small crofts near the beach, and if they survived this reckless adventure, he and Bridget might find one where they could wait out the rain before heading back to Glenloch.

If he didn't kill her first.

Hugh could not believe she'd been foolish enough to try to get away by sea on a vile day like this. He sped toward the irresponsible wench, using all his strength to pull the boat in her direction, sweating under his coat despite the frigid conditions. He could no longer feel his hands.

"I'm sinking!" she cried.

"I'm almost there!" he shouted, wishing it were true, for he still had some distance to cover. Rushing madly to get to her, he let the rain batter his head and eyes without stopping to wipe it away. He ignored the frigid water sliding down the back of his neck and onto his back, and the ominously growing puddle at his feet.

With one last burst of strength, he finally came alongside her and grabbed the edge of her boat. "Is there any rope in there?"

"N-no!" she cried. She looked terrified, but her fear did not stanch his anger.

"Then we'll leave the boat. Come to me." He spoke as calmly as he could, in spite of their dire circumstances. One wrong move and his boat would tip and they would both go under. Hugh knew they would not survive it.

"What should I do?" she cried.

"Take my hands and lever yourself over the side. Try to land in the middle of the skiff."

"I can't!"

"Aye, you can!" He grabbed hold of her hands and she raised her bottom, eyeing his boat.

"We'll tip over!"

"No, I'll lean away and counterbalance you. *Now*, Bridget! Move!"

He pulled her and she fell into the puddle at the bottom of his boat. Hugh managed to move at the same time, throwing his weight against the opposite side. The boat wobbled crazily in the water, but they managed to stay upright.

Bridget pulled herself up onto her knees in front of him and held on to the edges of the boat. Hugh did not stop to ask her why she'd been so intent upon getting away from Glenloch that she'd had to steal one of his boats to do it. She was rightly fearful, but not cowed by his icy stare, and he went right to work before the storm could get any worse, before his own strength failed.

The wind became brutal and he had to fight it to get them back to shore. The current pulled them farther south, but he managed to stay on course for the most part, dragging them relentlessly toward the land. Her lips matched the blue of her eyes, and her teeth were chattering uncontrollably. Hugh's hands were beyond numb, and he feared his eyelashes had turned to icicles.

When they were only a few yards from land, Hugh saw a large upright rock, an obsidian obelisk that was used as a landmark by kelpers and fishermen and free traders all along the southeastern coast. He made for the obelisk, hoping his memory of a nearby kelper's croft was accurate. He would hate like hell to get out of the water, only to freeze in the elements on land.

The oars went aground and Hugh jumped out, landing in a few inches of water. He pulled the boat in as far as he could, and Bridget climbed out after him, half falling out of the boat. He helped her gain her feet, and they somehow managed to pull the boat from the water. He put his arm about her waist and dragged her along with him as he followed a path away from the water, trudging through wind, rain, and mucky sand, to find the shelter he only half remembered. They had to get warm, soon.

"This way," he said. "Hang on to me."

Brianna felt like a fool. She was vastly grateful that Laird Glenloch had come after her, but she'd endangered his life as well as her own. She should apologize, but what would she say? How could she possibly justify what she'd done?

No doubt he thought her a lackwit, though it had seemed such a good idea at the time.

"Move your arse, Miss MacLaren," he said rudely, provoking her indignation. "We've a distance to go."

"You've no need to be vulgar, Laird Glenloch."

"You think not?" he retorted angrily. "I didn't risk my neck for you only to freeze to death out here."

"You needn't have come!"

"No? And where would you be if I had not?"

The answer loomed between them as Brianna doubled her speed. She tripped and would have fallen, but for Glenloch's quick move to hold her up.

She was not happy when he kept his tight grasp on her arm and helped her up the path, but her sodden, ill-fitting boots were awkward on the rocky ground. She knew his anger was fully warranted, even if she did not care to admit it aloud.

She was freezing, shivering so badly she did not believe she could form the words of an apology, even if she knew what excuse to give him.

They got to the top of the ledge beyond the shore when she saw it, a small stone croft, set among the rocks on the beach. It was a primitive building with a low, thatched roof that did not look promising, but they made their way toward it, since any small shelter would be better than full exposure to the elements.

A small boat lay behind it in the wet sand, tipped bottom up, just as Glenloch's boats had been. Bree hardly noticed it, not when her arms and legs were stiff with cold, and her eyes burning with the frozen salt water of the sea. Glenloch released her when they reached the door, and he tried to open it, but failed since it was either jammed or locked. Cursing under his breath, he backed away, then crashed his shoulder into it.

The door flew open and he pushed her inside, shoving the door closed behind them. The place smelled. It was dark and there were no windows, but at least it was dry inside, and protected from the wind. Laird Glenloch stepped over to the hearth and knelt before it. When he spoke, his tone was curt and gruff. "Look for a tinderbox."

Brianna's eyes adjusted to the dark, and she saw that there was a table, one chair, and a low pallet of straw near a fireplace. She located flint and steel, but her hands were shaking too badly to strike them to-

gether to make sparks. She handed them to the laird,
who found something to use as a char cloth and quickly
lit the small chunk of peat that rested on the grate. Once
the fire was burning, he stood, turning to survey their
surroundings.

"Get those clothes off," he said.

Chapter 5

Hearts may agree though heads differ.
SCOTTISH PROVERB

"I-I—"

"Do not even think to argue with me," Hugh said, the anger in his voice broaching no discussion, no disagreement. He picked up the chair and bashed it against the floor, breaking it into pieces, then fed it to the fire. "Get them off so we can both get warm." His expression was dark and dangerous, and Brianna did not dare deny him.

With shaking hands, she worked at her ties and fastenings. The heat of the fire penetrated the room, and she could no longer see her breath. What she *could* see was Laird Glenloch, pulling off his greatcoat, then the rest of his clothes. She eyed one disreputable, thin blanket of plaid lying in a heap on the pallet, the wool looking far too insubstantial to ward off the cold.

"Only a fool would go into the water on a day like this," he growled.

"I could not st-stay." She bristled at his tone, even though she fully recognized how foolish she'd been.

They'd barely managed to get out of the water, and it remained to be seen whether they would survive her wild escapade.

"Only a scatterwit—"

"I am no scatterwit, sir!"

"Hmmph," he muttered. He unbuttoned the placket of his shirt and pulled it over his head, tossing it to the floor near the hearth. "'Tis December. In Scotland, in case you hadn't noticed. The North Sea."

"Your mockery is unwelcome, Laird." There was no need to go on about it.

He started to unfasten his trews and Bree averted her eyes. "So is good sense, apparently."

"I have *plenty* of good sense," Brianna retorted, fuming at his despicable attitude. She somehow managed to get her own sodden breeches down her legs, then stepped out of them and threw them angrily in the direction of the fire. "But I needed to get away from Glenloch."

"Why? Were you anxious to get away with the plate? Or the brandy?"

"I am no thief! Nor am I a drinker," she retorted, so angry she did not even notice she was nearly naked.

"Well, whatever it was you took, 'tis lying at the bottom of the sea by now."

Brianna clutched her chest. "Oh no! My dresses, my money!"

"Ha," he said without mirth.

"'Twas all I had!" she shouted, turning all her anger, her frustration, and the vestiges of her terror on him. "All that was to keep me until—"

She stopped short, unwilling to tell him her true purpose.

"Until . . . ?"

"Until I got to Dundee."

"Ah, right." His voice dripped with sarcasm. "You want me to believe you intended to walk all the way to Dundee."

"I have a very good reason," she snapped.

"Which is irrelevant now. Get the rest of your clothes off and come over here."

She bristled at his words. "There is only one blanket."

"Aye. So we'll share." He came to her, and before she realized what he was doing he'd ripped her shirt from her shoulders, then grabbed her, pulling her against him.

"No, we will not share!" she cried indignantly.

He ignored her and yanked the blanket off the pallet, wrapping them together in the dry wool even as he hauled her down to the straw mattress with him. Brianna sputtered her protests against the frigid skin of his neck, but he paid her no heed, dragging her naked body as close to his as was physically possible. They shivered together, and Brianna struggled to shove away from him.

"Be still!" Glenloch rasped, grabbing her bottom and pressing her hard against him.

She froze when her hips met his.

He made a low sound deep in the back of his throat, and Brianna felt his body change. Time seemed to stop as every nerve ending in her body shifted from her outrage and funneled directly to the stirring she felt below. She pressed her eyes closed and tried to resist it. Yet when he began to stroke her buttocks, his pelvis rubbed hers in a way that heated her from her inside out. Brianna could neither withdraw nor protest.

His breathing became harsh, and his shuddering diminished. Brianna felt enveloped by him, by his size and his growing heat. She pressed her cold nose into the crook of his neck while his hand slid up her back to cup her nape, and then trailed back down.

Brianna's breath caught in her throat and she felt him swallow, hard.

"I should throttle you," he whispered against her hair, "but Christ, if you are not the most exciting woman I've ever encountered."

He shifted and pressed Brianna into the straw mattress, turning so that he rose slightly above her, drawing her into a close embrace. He slid one of his densely muscled legs between hers, and Brianna made a whimper at the sensation of his direct touch on her feminine flesh.

"Aye, lass, 'twill be good between us."

"No," she whispered. "I left Glenloch because of this. Because you . . . B-because I don't want . . ." But dear heaven, she did. She wanted more of his touch, more of his kisses. She could no longer deny that she wanted to feel the heat and exhilaration of his embrace.

His head descended and his mouth captured hers in a searing kiss. He pressed his tongue against the barrier of her lips, and Bree opened on a sigh, allowing him in. He speared her with his tongue, and Brianna felt as though she were being consumed. There was a fire in him, and it burned away her logic, her sensibility. His touch robbed her of self-control, and she responded with abandon. She encircled his waist with her arms, then skimmed her hands down to his bare buttocks.

"Yes. Ach, touch me."

His body was hard, yet the skin below his waist was smooth. Bree was fascinated by the contrasting textures of his body, hard and firm, but at the same time, smooth as the finest silk. The rasp of the hair on his legs brought a groan to her lips.

When he nuzzled her neck at the sensitive corner of her jaw, she sighed with pleasure, then arched her back at the touch of his hand at her breast. She moaned when he circled her nipple with the tips of his cool fingers. She willed him to touch it, to put his mouth on it and suckle as he'd done the night before.

He finally lowered his head and licked the hard peak, and Bree shuddered with arousal. Their bodies separated slightly with his movement, and she touched his chest, slipping her fingers through his coarse hair until she found his nipples. He groaned when she caressed them, and moved his hand down her belly, his destination her most private parts.

Brianna let out a harsh breath when he touched her, fondling some hidden place that responded exactly the way flint sparked when struck by steel. She grabbed the straw on either side of her and opened for him, afraid he might stop, stunned and mystified by her body's reaction to his touch.

"Ah, lass, you're wet for me."

He kissed her mouth again, and used one finger to enter her while his thumb kept up the same caresses that made her wild for something more. A deeper touch, a stronger stroke. "Please," she cried.

"I need to be inside you," he rasped, shifting to move between her legs. He took hold of her hand and placed it on his hard member, then guided it to the spot his own fingers had just abandoned.

She pressed the velvet tip of his erection to the private place that hungered for him. "Now," she whispered, her need replacing what little bit of good sense she still possessed. "Now, please."

He pushed into her, moving slowly, gently breaching her maiden's sheath until he could hold back no longer. He plunged deeply, then held still for a moment, trembling above her, lowering his forehead to hers. He swallowed thickly. "Are you all right?"

Bree did not know. "Yes," she said, moving against him with a whimper, anxious to feel more of the building sensations. "I-I . . . need . . ."

He slid back, and a powerful tightening pooled in Bree's lower extremities. Her muscles felt as though they would explode, and when he pushed back in, her body moved with the rhythm he set. The friction of their bodies stoked a deep, primal pleasure in her, and when a sudden exquisite spasm overtook her, she shuddered with primitive gratification, the repeated contraction of her muscles pulling her into some perfect netherworld.

The laird continued to move, sliding in and out of her with increasing speed until he stopped suddenly, groaning deeply and trembling violently with the climax of his own pleasure.

"'Tis a far better method of getting warm than arguing, is it not?" Hugh said, using a glib tone, rather than expressing his wonder.

He'd shared the bed of many a skilled lover, but no one had ever roused his passions as Bridget MacLaren had done. Every untutored touch and caress had raised his arousal to a higher level, until he'd felt as though his entire being had been caught in a maelstrom of sensation.

If he'd had any question about making her his paramour, it had been answered. Beyond belief.

He kept them tightly covered with the old blanket as he shifted positions, keeping her in his arms. She cuddled against him, her head resting on his chest, her hand trailing precariously close to his spent erection. She touched him, sliding his cock into her hand even as she pressed her mouth against one of his nipples. Hugh did not think it possible, but his entire body responded at once. He nearly came off the pallet as she swirled her tongue around his exquisitely sensitive nipple, then drew it into her mouth, sucking.

She was too inexperienced to understand the profound effect she had on him, and as he became erect and ready again, he forced himself to remember that she had only just lost her maidenhead. She could not possibly take him again. But yet. . .

He let out a ragged puff of breath. "Lass, you don't know what you do to me."

He looked at her in the flickering firelight and she met his gaze, without interrupting her intimate explorations. Her eyes reflected the same amazement that coursed through him at her touch.

"So this is why they don't tell us . . ." she whispered, moving to straddle his leg, pressing her feminine mound against him. She sighed and shuddered with pleasure.

"Tell you what?" he asked, stifling a groan.

"How it feels," she replied, her fingers skimming over the swollen head of his cock. His member grew apace with her intimate touch, and her eyes slid closed.

He took her mouth in a wild kiss as he eased her onto her back, twining his legs with hers. Christ, he wanted her again. Now.

" 'Tis too soon for you, lass," he said, torn between trying to cool his ardor and delving into her again, as she clearly wished.

He'd had only one experience with a virgin—his wife. And Hugh had subsequently wondered if he had botched that first time, for she'd shied away from their marriage bed ever after. And yet with Bridget the experience could not have been any more stunning. What she'd lacked in skill, she'd more than made up for in a hot, sensual keenness to feel it all. To take every thrust of his hips and give back every inch with a fervor that still took his breath away.

Hugh should have felt at least a pang of guilt for bedding this innocent, but he'd been powerless to arrest the momentum of their attraction. And now he could not regret his actions. He slid down to press his mouth against the fullness of her breasts, laving each one with his tongue. He could not remember ever feeling such a fierce arousal so quickly after climaxing, yet her touch made him mad for more. He craved the sensation of sliding into her tight sheath, of feeling her tighten around him.

He licked and sucked her nipples, and she writhed beneath him until he felt nearly mad with his own need. Yet he held back, pressing his hand against her mound, stroking the sensitive nub that lay hidden in her folds. She held his head in place and made small panting sounds as he pleasured her.

"I want . . . Oh!" She was breathless but demanding. "Oh, Hugh, I . . . Please. Can we . . ."

"Come for me, Bridget. Let go, sweet." He was entirely focused on her pleasure, caring only that she come apart at his touch, in his arms. He wanted to see the amazement on her face and in her eyes.

He altered the rhythm of his touch and she suddenly cried out, clamping her thighs around his hand. "That's it, sweet. You were made for this. For pleasure."

She pulled him down for her kiss as shudders wracked her body.

And Hugh was very glad indeed that he'd seen her from the nursery window, taking the skiff out to sea.

Brianna felt a well of emotion fill her chest as Hugh tightened his arms around her. It was the oddest feeling . . . as though she could breathe freely for the first time in years. She'd felt some degree of peace during her years at Killiedown with Claire, but nothing like this. Nothing like the calm and secure sensation that filled her now.

His embrace turned into a brief hug and he withdrew from her, suddenly leaving her alone on the pallet. In truth, they were much warmer now, and so was the croft. He moved quickly to the hearth and added a few more pieces of wood to the fire, then spread out their clothes to dry.

Bree turned to watch the flex of his long legs as he moved quickly and efficiently, to appreciate the dense muscles of his chest and shoulders as he tended the fire, and to study the curious male part of him that had just been inside her. It was still hard and large, and Brianna knew it did not normally jut out from his body as it did now. She wondered if it was painful.

Inexperienced as she might be, Brianna knew he had felt the same sensations created by their joining as she had. But he'd pleasured her a second time without reaching his own climax, no longer angry, but concerned for her well-being.

She gathered the blanket around her shoulders, feeling warm and sated, perhaps a little bit sore. And more vulnerable than she'd felt since coming to Scotland with her aunt Claire nine years before.

She'd turned onto a dangerous path, and it involved more than just giving up her virginity. She'd let down the defenses she'd built so desperately during her early years and again when Bernard had deserted her. She needed them now—she needed to keep some control.

If she did not, she would have nothing.

And yet it was difficult to hold back that part of herself she'd always protected. She was anxious for him to return so she could do something akin to what he'd done to give her pleasure. Perhaps he need not enter her to reach fulfillment. She was eager to learn, in spite of social convention and all the arguments against it.

Bree did not want to think. She knew this man was an avowed bachelor and a dedicated rake. He'd seduced her without difficulty, but Brianna had made her own vow to elude the shackles of marriage. She'd lost her ignorance as well as her innocence this day, and acquired what she believed could be only a mere inkling of the pleasures to be gained in sharing a bed with a man. With a skilled lover—a paramour—whose regard would last only as long as their bedplay kept him interested.

Brianna pressed her eyes closed and tried to suppress the need he'd aroused in her. Her situation had not changed, in spite of what had happened between them. She still needed to go into hiding, else Stamford and Roddington were going to find her with Laird Glenloch and. . .

The thought eluded her when he pulled the door of the croft open a crack. Brianna smelled the rain outside and felt the bite of the wind just before he closed it tight again and latched the door. Moving quickly, he returned to their narrow bed, and Bree moved aside and lifted the blanket for him. He climbed onto the pallet and drew her into his arms.

"'Tis still raining."

She nodded against him and tangled her legs with his. With a naked man. Her lover. And that strange rush of emotion flooded her chest again. "I know," she said, her voice a whisper of uncertainty.

"We have no amenities, Bridget," he said. "We'll have to make do with what we find inside."

"Oh," she said, realizing what he meant. "How will we . . ."

He ran his fingers across her shoulder and down the center of her back to her buttocks, raising goose bumps on her skin. Her nipples pebbled. "We are beyond secrets, I think. And since we cannot go outside . . . There is a bucket in the corner."

She found herself blushing. "Ah . . . Perhaps the rain will let up soon and we can leave," she said, even though it was the last thing she wanted. Just a few hours more, in her handsome lover's arms. And then. . .

"Our clothes are still wet. They'll take all night to dry."

"Have we enough wood for the fire?"

"If we ration it carefully, we'll be all right. And we've a chipped clay cup. I've set it outside to collect rainwater for drinking."

"Did you know this place was here?" she asked, running her foot up the back of his leg.

"Aye. We're still on Glenloch land." He closed his eyes and sighed.

"Are you still angry?" Bree asked, pressing hot, openmouthed kisses to his neck.

"Aye," he whispered as she moved down his body. "Furious."

* * *

She remained asleep when Hugh got up again and stoked the fire. He rearranged their clothes and turned back to look at her, sleeping contentedly on the straw pallet. He could not remember a more eager or spontaneous lover. She made up for her naïveté with ingenuity, just as he'd hoped, and his body reacted sharply in anticipation of their next sensual encounter.

He would not mind staying closed away here with her for a week, but they were going to run out of fuel for the fire before too long, and they would eventually need to eat. Besides those issues of survival, he had not forgotten his primary purpose for coming to Glenloch. Niall MacTavish and his crew would arrive to let down the brandy and cart it out tonight to make room for the next shipment. He'd hoped to be there to oversee the proceedings and talk to MacTavish about it.

Bridget did not awaken when he slid back into their bed and drew her into his arms. It was the first time he would spend an entire night with a woman, even his own wife. In spite of his intimate relations with Amelia being less than satisfactory, Hugh had never strayed. He might have been a fool for it, but he'd taken his vows seriously, refusing to follow the example of his father, a philanderer who had not a faithful bone in his body. His indiscretions had driven Hugh's mother to her own lovers, and caused untold damage to the young innocents who'd succumbed to Jasper's charms.

Amelia might have shied away from their marital relations, but Hugh would not insult—or possibly hurt—her by keeping a mistress or frequenting any of the popular but debauched "gentlemen's" clubs around London as his father and his peers did. Hugh had lived a monk's existence with Amelia, though little good it had done either of them.

Which was one very good reason never to marry again. Since it was impossible to try out a wife before marrying her, Hugh knew it was best to abstain from the institution altogether. His cousin John Hartford was a worthy heir, and there was every chance he would eventually sire a boy to inherit Hugh's titles and all his entailed properties.

He would also see to it that Bridget was taken care of when their affair was over. He was feeling particularly generous toward her after their amazing night together. He didn't want her ever to feel powerless again, to need to run and hide from the next opportunistic employer she encountered, who would use her and discard her when he lost interest.

Hugh could not foresee losing his desire for Bridget in the very near future. Only a fool would turn away from one so beautiful and so giving. Even now he wanted her, after making love all through the night.

Hugh had not forgotten that she'd been virginal and might experience second thoughts and regrets in the light of day. He would need to handle her carefully, need to make her the promises that would keep her in his bed.

She opened her eyes lazily and smiled. "Is it morning yet?"

"Just dawn."

She stretched. "Do you know if it's still raining?"

"Some," he replied. "But not as hard as before. It might stop long enough for us to go back."

"I'd rather stay here," she said.

The same thought had crossed his own mind, but Hugh had not expected her to say it. Feeling slightly off balance, he said, "I imagine hunger will finally drive us out."

"But not too soon, I hope." She laid one hand on his chest. "Do you ever wish you could go far away where no one would ever find you?"

He gazed down at the wistful expression on her face and thought again about the bastard who'd driven her out into the cold. "Aye. Just now, in fact."

Hugh allowed himself to relax. He felt sated in a way that had never happened before, and he had not even needed to engage in any coercion. He'd made her no promises, nor did she seem inclined to wheedle any out of him. "Our clothes are not entirely dry yet."

"No, I suppose not. It took more than a night to dry my coat the last time, Hugh."

He slid his fingers across the smooth skin of her shoulders and felt her shiver.

"Do you mind if I call you Hugh?"

"When I'm inside you, you might call me anything you like."

"But only then?" she whispered.

"No, I like hearing the sound on your lips. No one ever calls me by my given name."

"What about your parents? What did your mother call you?"

He avoided thinking about them as much as possible, especially his father, with his cruel streak and the blatant debauchery and mistresses that had driven his mother away. Hugh was not even certain he was Jasper's true offspring. "I was born with three or four other titles, but she was partial to Glenloch."

"That's what she called you?"

"Generally," he replied, wondering why her distant attitude should bother him now. It had never occurred to him before to be troubled by it, by the impersonality of the woman who'd borne him. "My mother tried to be a very conventional person." At least in public.

"Mine was not," Bridget said. "Nor was my aunt."

"Nor are you, I think."

"I hope not," she said quietly. "I should like to be exactly like them—like my mother and her sister."

"Tell me about them." And he would be spared the aggravation of thinking about his own parents.

"I don't remember my mother at all. She died when I was very young. But my aunt . . . She was very beautiful, and unlike anyone I've ever known. She traveled. Alone, if you can believe it, to exotic places," said Bridget. "And I'm fairly certain she had a lover in Greece."

"But you're not sure."

She frowned slightly. "'Twas not something we ever discussed. After all, she tried to raise me as a . . . a respectable woman."

Hugh knew he had to steer her away from that topic, before her conscience came into play. "So you don't really know about the Greek lover."

"No, but . . ." She bit her lip and seemed to be deep in thought.

Hugh realized that her aunt must have been a woman of means at one time, if she'd traveled to Greece. He wondered what misfortune had sent Bridget to work for her living.

"But she left him to come here," Hugh said.

She nodded. "When she learned of my father's death, she knew I'd been left alone."

"How old were you?"

"I don't really remember. About six, I suppose."

"And your aunt came for you?"

"Eventually. My father had been gone at least three years before the bad news found her. It took many more months for her to get back."

"What did you do in the meantime? How did you live?" Hugh found he did not care to think of Bridget as a child, having to manage alone until her aunt arrived. He wondered what she had done, how she had survived.

She slid her leg over his. "'Tis a long and dull tale. I'd much rather talk about your ghost. When did it first appear at Glenloch?"

"You know 'tis not real." He spoke just as something loud slammed against one of the croft's walls.

"See?"

"See what?"

"'Twas the ghost, contradicting you," she mused.

He shook his head. "Not bloody likely. When you hear such sounds at the castle, they are merely the creaking and settling of that pile of ancient stones."

"So you say. But there is something. I've seen it."

He allowed her to stay on the subject of the Glenloch Ghost, for he'd caught her fleeting expression of sorrow when speaking of her aunt.

He wanted to know more about her, but perhaps later. "As far as I know, there has always been talk of a ghost at Glenloch. For centuries, at least."

"How many years has the castle stood?"

"Centuries. 'Twas built in William Wallace's time."

"Do you think she—the ghost—was one of the original inhabitants?"

"I suppose there is no point in my repeating that there is no ghost?"

"None at all. Who was she? Do any of the legends give her name?"

"There are no records of those times, so we'll never know exactly who the tales are about."

"Hmmm . . ."

"What?"

"'Tis possible the ghost itself could tell us."

Chapter 6

There's naething got by delay,
but dirt and long nails.
SCOTTISH PROVERB

Hugh laughed, enjoying the soft graze of her body against his. "'Tis not very likely, Bridget, since the thing is a figment of the very active Scottish imagination."

Bridget was quiet for a moment, then changed the subject again. "Your housekeeper will wonder where you are. And me, too, I suppose."

"She might."

"What will you tell her?"

"Naught. Where I go and what I do is none of her concern."

"She has known you a long time."

"Aye. Since I was born," said Hugh.

"She and the other servants truly do not go into the castle after dark?"

He nodded. "They're fearful."

"But you stay there, and I did . . . Doesn't it occur

to them that naught has happened to you over the years?"

"They might have come to that conclusion, but then Amelia threw herself from the roof."

She propped herself up on her forearm and looked at him, her eyes full of sympathy and compassion. "I am so sorry. I . . . I'd heard."

"No doubt all Kincardineshire knew of her suicide."

"Aye. Such tales seem to have legs."

"The servants are not convinced that the Glenloch Ghost had naught to do with it."

"They think the ghost pushed her?"

"It's a thought that's crossed their minds."

"But—"

"But what, Miss MacLaren?" he asked, wondering if she would repeat the usual cant about Amelia having been a happy woman with every advantage and absolutely no reason to kill herself.

"The ghost I saw would never have done such a thing," she said, surprising him.

She seemed so adamant, he could almost believe she'd seen the specter. "How would you know?"

"I'm not quite sure," she said as she slid down and touched her lips to his chest. "It just didn't seem . . . It's much too ethereal."

"Ethereal," he rasped when her tongue circled his nipple.

"Aye. Without substance. How would such a being ever manage to push her?"

Hugh closed his eyes and swallowed. "How, indeed, Miss MacLaren."

"The servants should try not to be so terrified of it." Her hands found his erection and she traveled farther down his body, her tight nipples burning a path down to his waist, and below.

"And you are not?" he croaked.

"I'm a great deal more terrified of you, Laird," she said.

And Hugh could not find his voice to answer her.

They slept again, and when Brianna awoke, Hugh was partially dressed, leaning up against a wall for balance. He pulled on his boots while she observed him surreptitiously, admiring the breadth of his shoulders and the long, lean lines of his body.

She renewed her vow never to give in to Stamford's wishes that she marry Roddington. The man was a repulsive toad, and she could not imagine sharing even the slightest intimacy with him. Hugh was the only. . .

The fleeting thought that had escaped her the night before returned. *Roddington wouldn't want her, now that she'd shared the bed of another man.* She was no longer an innocent virgin, the respectable bride her aunt had raised. Her reputation was shredded. If Stamford found her now, she would not be required to marry the marquess, not when he knew she'd spent hours, *days*, alone in Hugh's company. She would not be required to marry Roddington.

It was a relief, but at the same time, worrisome.

"Ah, you're awake," said Hugh.

Bree sat up, holding the blanket in front of her, though it was much too late for modesty. "Good morning again."

He came and sat down beside her. "'Tis more like noon, or even later. And it's stopped raining."

"'Tis good news."

"Depending on how you look at it." He leaned close and took hold of an edge of the blanket, tugging it down, baring her body as he feathered light kisses against her mouth.

He cupped her breasts in his hands, and a familiar pleasurable pressure mounted between her legs. A soft moan emanated from the back of her throat, and she lay back, pulling Hugh down with her. She reached for the placket of his trews and started on the buttons, gratified to feel his arousal, hard and hot, ready for her.

"Hurry, Hugh," she said, breathlessly. She wanted him now. She wanted to feel the hard completion of his body inside hers.

He clearly felt the same, for he shoved his trews out of the way and moved quickly between her legs, entering her with a groan of intense pleasure. He moved out again quickly, then began a sharp rhythm that took Brianna to the edge in only a few strokes. She shattered, her spasms squeezing him, her pleasure engulfing her at the same moment that he reached his own climax. Hovering over her, he quaked and trembled, then lowered his forehead to hers, breathing heavily.

"Are you always so insatiable?" he asked.

"I . . . I'm not . . . I don't know. I-I've only . . ." she spluttered before she could collect her thoughts. His lovemaking turned her brain to pap, her only coherent idea that she wanted to stay with him in the primitive little croft.

Their simple existence there eliminated all her worries, but only temporarily. Once they left, Bree would have to carry out her plan to go away and stay out of her guardian's control until she reached her majority. Only then would she be able to return to Killiedown Manor.

Yet the thought of leaving Hugh caused her chest to burn. The thought of going away, perhaps never to see him again, was crushing. "I did not know . . ." she whispered, hardly able to find her voice. "This is all so . . ."

"New," he said. "Aye. You are perfect, lass."

He kissed her once lightly, then drew away and refastened his trews while Brianna rose from the bed, feeling as though the ground had been pulled out from under her. All she wanted in the world was to live at Killiedown and raise her horses.

There was absolutely no future with Hugh, so her path was clear.

She watched as he finished dressing and wondered if he truly thought she was perfect. Likely it was something he said to every woman who shared his bed, although their night together came close to that description for her.

"I'll wait for you outside." He stepped out, giving her a moment's privacy to wash as well as she could with the water he'd collected in the cup. She dressed quickly, then put on her coat and started for the door, but stopped suddenly. As she turned back to look at the intimate space she'd shared with him, an ache of longing washed over her.

She squelched her foolishness, but just before she made her exit, grabbed the plaid blanket from their pallet, folded it, and wrapped it around her shoulders. She tied it against her chest like a shawl, the only reminder she would have of their one night together.

The sky was heavy with clouds, but at least it was not raining. Or snowing. Brianna shuddered, aware that the break in the weather would also allow Stamford to resume his travel. She knew she should go south now. Every instinct screamed for her to go away and lose herself someplace where Lord Stamford could never find her.

And yet she could not face leaving Hugh. She did not know how she was going to bid farewell to his dark gaze and the intimate touch of his hands and mouth, or his body inside hers.

He looked large and forbidding in his greatcoat, his visage made dangerous by the crescent scar on his cheekbone. But Brianna had known the tenderness of his touch. He'd risked his life to save her from the roiling sea, even though she had not deserved it, not when she'd acted so stupidly.

She put her hand on his forearm and looked up at him. "Thank you for coming for me. In the boat."

He dragged her up against him. "Promise me you'll never do anything so foolish again."

Her only desire at that moment was to please him. She nodded. "Never."

"We've a distance to go before it gets dark," he said, releasing her. "And I don't like the look of those clouds."

"Might we walk on the beach?" she asked, hoping to avoid the route Stamford would surely take. No doubt he'd already been up to Killiedown and Aberdeen. Perhaps he was in Stonehaven now, and would soon be on this very same road.

"'Twill be much easier—and faster—this way." He took her hand and placed it in the crook of his arm, and started walking on the road that lay directly west of their croft.

Brianna quickly glanced south, but did not possess the resolve to take her leave of him now. Nor did she think he would let her go. She felt his hunger and the promise of pleasures to come once they reached the castle.

She could do naught but give them one more night.

A wicked wind blew in from the north and bruised their faces as they walked, but at least they met no one on their way to Glenloch.

"You know it will be difficult to secure employment in Dundee," he said after they'd covered some distance in silence.

"Perhaps," Bree replied, her heart dropping as he spoke of such practical matters. While she'd been thinking he must be recalling every intimate move they'd made together, he'd brought up her departure to Dundee as though naught had occurred between them. As though anticipating her departure.

"We'll talk about it when we get back," he said in an

offhand way, and Brianna's breath caught somewhere deep in her chest. She should have realized he was well-practiced at dealing with lovers taken and eventually cast off.

It was not going to happen that way for him this time. She would be at no man's mercy. Yet her decent clothes and all her money were resting at the bottom of the sea. She could not survive in Dundee now, without money—as Hugh had just reminded her—and little chance of employment. Killiedown was out of the question, for there was too good a chance that Lord Stamford would return there when he failed to find her anywhere else.

And he would be furious. She'd felt the back of his hand a number of times in the early years before Claire had come and taken her from his house, and Brianna did not doubt that she would feel it again if he caught her before she had the authority to evict him from her life. She could only imagine how angry he must have been when she did not arrive for her wedding at St. George's. He'd have felt humiliated and foolish, too—a man who had no control over his ward.

Bree had known her defiance would have consequences. Yet she'd been certain that if she arrived at Killiedown and informed Claire of Stamford's intentions, her aunt would have stepped in and dealt with the man herself. Now she'd put Hugh between Roddington and his promised, innocent bride.

If Hugh ever discovered her real identity and that she'd betrayed a marquess with him, he would not simply be angry—he would want nothing more to do with her.

Brianna shook off her sense of foreboding. She clutched the shawl to her breast and kept moving, her future uncertain. She'd let down her defenses temporarily, but she knew how to rebuild them. She'd managed to do it many times before.

Chapter 7

A woman is at the best when she's openly bad.
SCOTTISH PROVERB.

Hugh was loath to end their little adventure. As perilous as it had been, it had been equally enjoyable. Even more so.

"I owe you an apology."

She looked up at him, her beautiful eyes cloudy with puzzlement.

"Not for taking your maidenhead, I assure you," he said, enjoying the expression of pure embarrassment that crossed her face. "But for being the cause of your flight from Glenloch. You must not have understood you had a choice."

"I'm afraid I behaved like a silly society miss," she replied.

He laughed. "What do you know of society misses?"

"Oh! Hardly anything at all. Just that they can be . . . er . . ."

"Missish?"

"Exactly!"

"Which is something you are clearly not," he said, feeling very glad of it. He stepped in front of her and walked backward as she continued forward. "And I hope it means you will share my bed again tonight."

"Laird, I'm not sure I—"

"*Laird?* What happened to Hugh?"

"I-I should not . . ."

"Aye, you should," he said, stopping in front of her, catching her hands in his. He pressed a light kiss to her mouth, sorry they had to lose the close intimacy of their comfortable, isolated nest in the kelper's croft.

They resumed walking, and Hugh took her hand again, feeling much different than he had a few days ago when he'd ridden from London to get away from the oppressive females there. Bridget MacLaren was nothing like those lying, conniving chits. She was a breath of fresh air, spirited and full of heart.

He supposed he should apologize for taking her virginity. But he could not regret it. He could so easily envision a continued liaison with this fiery, passionate woman. He gave a quick squeeze of her hand and glanced ahead. Glenloch's towers were visible in the distance, but they would be lucky to arrive at the castle before dark, which came early in winter this far north.

He wondered if MacTavish's men had gotten the brandy out of the buttery to make room for the new shipment. If the weather held, one of Captain Benoit's cutters would be just outside the cove at midnight. Plenty of time to make love to Bridget MacLaren before he hit the beach with the Falkburn free traders. This night, he would work alongside them and assess the operation for himself.

Berk Armstrong might be a problem, but worse was the possibility that someone had actually informed him of Benoit's ship holding fast near the cove. Everyone in Falkburn benefited from the free trade. Only a fool would betray them to the Stonehaven customs officers.

And only a fool would think he could get away with stealing from the Laird of Glenloch. He had the initial information he needed to find out how it was being done. There had been five hundred tubs of brandy in the buttery the night before. Once it was let down and the caramel color added, it would yield ten or twelve gallons of drinkable brandy from every tub.

Hugh wanted an accounting of every gallon, almost as much as he wanted Bridget MacLaren in his bed.

It was full dark when they arrived at Glenloch, and he could see Mrs. Ramsay leaving with her young MacTavish grandsons and the two female servants who worked for her in the castle. None of them would dare ask where he'd been or what he was about, but Hugh was uninterested in dealing with the questioning glances they were sure to give him. Besides, it never hurt for their laird's actions to be somewhat beyond their ken. "We'll go around to the buttery," he said to Bridget.

They went down toward the sea and the grate through which his tubs of brandy would be passed, the same place where Bridget had come into the castle. Hugh looked to the water for any sign of a ship, but there was none. And no one in the tower to signal it. It was still early, though. He knew that Benoit rarely arrived before midnight.

Bridget had been quiet for the last mile of their walk, but she turned to him after they'd scrambled through the grate. "I'm famished."

"Aye. Food first." Then he had plans for later.

Brianna followed Hugh up the steps, then through a passageway and into the scullery. The room was still warm so soon after the servants' departure, but she and Hugh were chilled and they kept their coats on as he stoked the fire. Bree stood close to the hearth and let the heat penetrate to her bones while Hugh found a plate of oatcakes, which they quickly devoured. He went about opening doors to adjoining rooms and corridors, obviously looking for something.

"There used to be a . . ." he muttered. "Ah, here it is." Brianna looked on as he dragged an iron tub from a small alcove and placed it in front of the fire. Then he went back and collected a wooden bucket from the same place.

Using the bucket he'd found, he filled the bath from the copper boiler at the back of the stove. Brianna soaked up the heat while she watched him perform the task, considering what he had in mind. Arousal surged through her, with more heat than the fireplace could possibly project when she realized he meant for her to bathe there—probably with him.

When the tub was full, he located a cake of soap and placed it on the tub's edge, then returned to Bree and started to unfasten the buttons of her coat. His eyes seemed much darker in the flickering firelight than they had in the muted daylight of their walk back to Glenloch.

"A bath, Laird?"

"I did not treat you well last night." He slipped the coat from her shoulders and let it fall to the floor. "I would have preferred to see to your comfort . . . your first time . . ."

"I have no complaints."

He nipped her lower lip and pulled it gently into his mouth.

Brianna shuddered and slipped her arms around his neck. He unfastened the buttons at her throat, then broke their kiss to pull the shirt over her head.

"You are so beautiful," he said, taking both her hands in his and stepping back slightly to gaze at her.

"You needn't ply me with empty compliments," she said, embarrassed by his bold perusal.

"Never was a compliment so far from empty." He released her hands and feathered the backs of his hands over her nipples, letting out a tremulous breath as he did so.

Brianna could almost believe he meant it, contrary to all of Lady Stamford's criticisms. Brianna knew her hair was unruly, her chin too pointed, and her eyes too wide. But none of those flaws seemed to matter to Hugh.

He suddenly changed course and began to disrobe, dropping his clothes in a pile beside the tub. "Take them off, Bridget. Your trews."

She held the edge of the bath as she did so, and as soon as the last article of clothing hit the floor, Hugh swooped down and lifted her into his arms and then stepped into the water. He sat down, turning her on his lap as he lifted her hair and pressed light kisses to the back and sides of her neck.

With her back against him, he cupped her breasts and gently swirled their tips between his thumb and fingers. She felt his erection pressing against her lower back, hot and insistent, teasing her and making her wait.

He took the plain-smelling soap into his hands and worked up a lather, then rubbed it all over her, starting at her neck and working down, teasing her breasts, then working his way to her nether regions. His hands had learned her well, for he tantalized her with his touch, promising future delights.

When she could stand it no more, she turned to face him, kneeling between his legs. Her position put her slightly above him, and she leaned down to kiss him as she took his arousal in her hand. He made a low growl, and Bree began to stroke him. She lowered her head as she kissed his chest, and took one of his nipples into her mouth.

Whirling her tongue around the hardened peak, she blindly found the soap and bathed him in turn, repeating each of his actions, kissing and licking him as she rinsed him. He made a strangled sound when she twined her slick fingers around his hard member, and when he rose up from the water, Bree leaned forward and pressed a kiss to its tip.

"God, yes!" His voice cut to a rasp of raw need. Brianna laved the thick head with her tongue, then drew it into her mouth. He trembled and put his hands on her head, holding his body perfectly still as she pleasured him.

His heated reaction aroused her beyond belief. Her own legs trembled, and she felt hot and needy, desperate for him to touch her, to join his body to hers. And yet she did not want to stop what she was doing. He began to move with her, imitating the rhythm he used when he was inside her, except that now he was inside her mouth.

He suddenly withdrew and stepped out of the tub. Before Bree knew what he was doing, he'd draped his greatcoat around her shoulders and lifted her out of the tub. "Not another minute, lass. I want you now."

He carried her from the scullery and walked through yet another dark passageway, finding his way flawlessly in the shadows. Without hesitation, he climbed a back staircase and turned to walk down a dark gallery that she recognized. He took her into the room across from Amelia's and set her down beside the massive bed inside.

Quickly going to the fireplace, he lit the peat, never giving her a chance to feel the chill of the room. He returned to her, taking her mouth in a kiss that seared her to her toes. He cupped her face in his hands. "You are a marvel, Bridget MacLaren. More than any man could dream of."

Brianna did not believe it, but she did not dispute it. The fire in the grate caught, and as he pulled down the blankets on the bed and removed his greatcoat from her shoulders, Bree felt another twinge of guilt for keeping her identity from him. He would not be pleased to know who she was, but she intended to be gone before he could learn the truth, before there could be any consequences to him.

His mouth descended on her nipple, and she shivered with pleasure, momentarily forgetting all about the deceptions they told each other.

Hugh put on fresh clothes in the glowing light of the peat fire. Bridget was sound asleep, turning and pulling the blanket over her shoulder as he took up his greatcoat and slipped it on.

She amazed him.

He could not imagine Bridget MacLaren being weighed down by hopelessness or despair. She would not lie still as Amelia had done, and allow circumstances to destroy her, but take action to change that which troubled her. She had more audacity than any woman he'd ever met, but not the dishonest kind shown by Charlotte de Marche. If only Charlotte had shown a sliver of the backbone Bridget possessed, Hugh might not have been quite so ready to flee London and her trap. He might even have considered allowing the woman to leg-shackle him.

He took a lingering look at the woman in his bed. Even now, he hardened at the thought of her body nestled tightly against his after making love. Naught was going to keep him from returning to their bed as soon as the brandy shipment was unloaded and stored in the buttery room. He took pleasure in the anticipation of holding her until morning.

Feeling full of supremely satisfied energy, Hugh

walked to the nursery and looked through the window overlooking the beach, just as the heavy clouds opened up and partially exposed the half moon shimmering high above the sea.

There were no lights down below, but Hugh knew MacGowan's gang would be gathering shortly to unload the shipment, if they were not on the beach already. He strained his eyes to see if he could pinpoint a cutter out in the cove, but saw nothing on the water. It was likely lying outside British waters, waiting for the free traders' signal from the tower nearer midnight.

Hugh lit a lamp and walked down to the drawing room, then let himself out through the panel to the secret passageway. He closed it carefully behind him and started for the stairs, stopping when he heard voices.

Moving forward to the top of the steps, he saw MacGowan in the meager candlelight, talking to another man. They pushed open the door to the secret storage room and propped it open with a rock.

"Laird," said MacGowan as Hugh started down the steps. "We'd heard ye were away."

Hugh came down to the floor of the buttery where he and Bridget had come through only hours before. His body tightened at the mere thought of her. Fortunately, she was safe in his bed and knew naught of the danger they all might be in. If Kincaid had more than just suspicions, he might well have sent out riders to watch the coast, to watch Glenloch.

He glanced at the sky and hoped its ominous clouds would keep any intruders away. "Did you get yesterday's brandy moved out?" he asked MacGowan.

"Aye. MacTavish saw to it with Coll Murdoch's help."

"Is that Murdoch with you?" Hugh asked as MacGowan's companion looked up. The man had gone bald in the three years since Hugh had been back to Glenloch.

"Aye, Laird. Greetings to ye."

He turned to MacGowan. "Did Armstrong go up to your cottage yesterday?"

MacGowan answered. "Aye. I stayed up there with him while MacTavish and Murdoch took care of the letting down and shipping out." He held the candle up and stepped into the secret room. It was empty.

Hugh wondered if Murdoch was in it with Mac-Gowan. Or if he was right in thinking MacGowan was involved at all. He hoped the evidence he needed would turn up in the next few days. He would deal with it swiftly, and then be free to enjoy Bridget MacLaren for the rest of the winter without any distractions. Her employer's husband's loss was Hugh's gain.

"What of Armstrong's suspicions, MacGowan? How did he know there was a cutter out here a few nights ago?"

"I doona know, Laird. Kincaid is a canny one. He might be playing with us, sending Armstrong out to see if anyone would snitch."

"Or someone might have informed."

"'Tis always possible, but no' likely, is it?"

"You saw Armstrong go back to Stonehaven?"

"Ach, aye. He was no' happy with stayin' at my place.

He wanted the comfort of his own hearth. Lit out of there as soon as the rain cleared this noon."

"Looks like snow comin' tonight," said Murdoch as he slid through the grate.

Hugh would not mind snow, for it would be a further deterrent to the customs officers. As long as it came after they brought the brandy inside and got it hidden away, Hugh would be content.

Three Falkburn women came through the grate and scooted into the buttery. They positioned themselves to receive the containers of brandy when they were handed in, but as they took their places, one of them suddenly noticed Hugh. She took in a sharp breath and curtsied, and the other two followed suit.

"Laird, we didna know ye were here!"

"Just lending a hand is all," he said, feigning innocence. And ignorance.

"MacTavish is about to give the signal, Laird," said MacGowan, making his way through the grate.

Hugh followed the manger outside. "I'll go down to the beach with you, MacGowan."

"Just like the old days when ye were a lad, eh?" said Murdoch when they were all clear of the castle.

"Exactly," said Hugh. But there wasn't going to be any pilfering this time.

At least fifty people had gathered on the beach below the castle, able-bodied men and women from Falkburn. Hugh took a glance up at the tunnel lantern shining from the parapet of the south tower above them, then he looked toward the sea. The cutter gave no signal back, but Hugh knew Benoit would be sending stout boats to shore, now laden with the liquor for which MacGowan had already paid with Hugh's gold.

The weather was cold, and the clouds thicker than ever. A light flurry of snow drifted down as they worked quietly and efficiently, carrying the full tubs of brandy to the castle, passing them through the grate to the women who waited inside. They had a rotating system, carrying the tubs carefully in turn to the secret room where they stacked them.

It was years since Hugh had participated in this aspect of the trade—not since his father was alive and had stood watching from the south parapet with his debauched partner, the Marquess of Roddington. The two had quickly tired of the common tableaux and returned to their depraved amusements.

Later, Jasper had derided Hugh for joining the peasants in their labor, but Hugh had kept silent. Far better for him to show the townspeople that he knew and understood every aspect of their free-trade process, than to join two of the most contemptible peers of the realm in their diversions. Hugh hadn't even stayed at the castle that night. He'd made the hour-long ride to Stonehaven and spent the night at an inn rather than pass a night under the same roof as his father.

After Jasper's death, Hugh had wrought dramatic changes in every one of his estates, and the servants no longer had any reason to fear their lord. He'd striven for fairness in all his dealings, and avoided Roddington at all cost, which was the main reason Hugh been making up for their losses instead of speaking to him of the problem. The less contact he had with Rotten Roddington, the better, though 'twas high time he severed their partnership once and for all.

Lookouts were posted in strategic places along the road and at the edge of the castle, but as the night progressed, Hugh did not think any of the customs agents would appear tonight. Armstrong had braved the rain the day before, and he would likely have no interest in risking being caught in another storm. And since Armstrong had already checked on the rumor of a cutter in the cove, neither Kincaid nor Pennycook would have any reason to venture out from Stonehaven in the cold. Hugh believed there would be no surprises tonight.

Bree woke alone, in need of the water closet. She tossed back the covers and slid out of bed naked, wondering where Hugh had gone. She dreaded going into the cold corridor, so she looked for the greatcoat he had dropped when they'd come up to his bedchamber, but it was gone, too. Likely he had used it to keep warm while he took care of his own needs.

Remnants of the meal they'd shared were growing stale on a plate beside the bed, and the fire had burned low.

Never having taken a lover before, Bree did not know what the etiquette of the situation required. Should she wait until he returned? Pick up the plate and carry it down to the scullery and retrieve her clothes?

Since it went against the grain to sit and wait for something to happen, Brianna pulled a blanket from the bed and wrapped it around her shoulders, then went to the door. From there, she took only a moment in the water closet, and when she returned to the hall, a shimmering glow drew her attention. The ghost appeared as a vaguely feminine form, and as before, Bree felt no fear. Instead, she felt drawn to the young woman whose spirit walked the castle.

Hugh denied its existence, and it suddenly occurred to Brianna that this might not be the ancient specter at all. Perhaps it was Amelia's troubled spirit that haunted these halls now. Since everyone who came into the castle gave the ghost a wide berth, and no one seemed to have seen it, how would they know if it was their old familiar bogle?

She followed the translucent form to the end of the gallery, into the room where she'd slept her first night at Glenloch. The ghost gestured toward the window, and Bree stepped up to it and looked out. A light snow was falling, and the half moon cast an eerily brilliant light on the clouds surrounding it and the water below.

There was a ship in Glenloch's cove, and Brianna could see shadowy figures on the beach. "Smugglers!" she whispered, and realized Hugh must know about it. That's where he must be.

Bree turned toward the ghost, but it was gone.

The bitter cold in the hall suddenly seeped into her bones, and she hurried down to the scullery where they'd left her clothes. Dressing quickly, she pulled on her boots and hat, and found her way outside, hoping she could blend in with the free traders below. Her aunt had participated in a profitable operation from Killiedown, importing tea and spirits. Bree knew how it worked, that as many hands as possible would make short work of the shipment.

The thought of seeing Hugh now, of working beside him, excited her. She wanted to stand with him among the others, knowing more about him than anyone else, even though she was perfectly aware that the intimacies they'd shared were merely expressions of a strong physical attraction. It was no different than what passed between a man and his mistress. Bree had no claim to the avowed bachelor, nor did she want one. She craved her freedom.

Nonetheless, she was determined to enjoy and relish the closeness and sense of well-being she felt with him, even if it was temporary.

For tonight, she was content to stay at Glenloch.

Laborers from Falkburn carried pairs of tubs—half ankers that held about four gallons each—to a point beyond the beach where the castle rose up from a short, rocky ledge. There, each pair was lifted up to the ledge where they were received by yet another group of Falkburn workers who conveyed them, one man to the next, until they reached the grate to the buttery. At that point, someone slid them inside, and the women in the buttery carried them to the secret chamber where they stacked them.

It was quiet, dark work, for each one knew 'twas important to avoid drawing unwanted attention to their efforts. Hugh felt invigorated by his exertions, and more at ease than he'd felt in many a year. Working in the cold and dark, he could not recall why he'd ever thought he preferred to stay away from Glenloch in favor of his aimless pursuits in London.

His mistresses' talents paled compared to the adventure of sharing Bridget MacLaren's bed, and the allure of his boxing matches and gaming clubs had no hold over him here. His few days at Glenloch had been filled with more exhilaration than he'd felt . . . perhaps ever.

Anticipating his return to his warm bed and the soft, sweet body of his lover, he worked with nimble energy alongside the others until the silence was broken by MacGowan's harsh whisper. "You there!"

He had grabbed a newcomer, a lad by the looks—
Good Christ, it was Bridget!

Hugh put down the tubs he'd hauled from the quay and scrambled up the beach to intercept his estate agent before he could do her any damage. "Leave her be," he said.

"But Laird, I doona know who—"

"I know her."

Bridget skipped down to him smiling broadly, and the earth seemed to open up at Hugh's feet, threatening to swallow him whole. The impact of her presence, of her beautiful, beaming face, was more vitalizing than it should be.

She placed her hand upon his arm, and the heat of her touch shot through him in spite of the barrier of his greatcoat. "I've come to help."

He drew her aside. "Bridget, sweet, you don't have to—"

"Aye, I do." She went up on her toes and whispered

in his ear. "'Tis dull and lonely in that big bed without you."

He swallowed and shoved away the erotic thoughts that could only distract him from the task at hand. "Come, then."

They went down to the water together and he rejoined his gang.

Bridget took a set of tubs from the quay and carefully lifted the straps over her shoulders, positioning one tub against her back and one to rest against her chest.

"You are no stranger to this," Hugh said, marveling that she was strong enough to carry the weight of those gallons.

"No," she said, keeping her voice down as every competent smuggler would do. "My aunt . . . She used to run tea, among other goods."

"Up near Muchalls." It should not have surprised him, for Bridget had called her unconventional. She was following her aunt's example—taking him for her lover, involving herself in his free-trade dealings. He wondered again about Bridget's background and wished he'd gotten more details. He felt a pang of wariness at the realization that he still knew hardly anything about her.

"Aye," Bridget replied, saying no more, and Hugh did not ask her. But he would later. They worked together, side-by-side while Hugh counted the minutes before he could to take her back to bed. By his calculations, they'd transported only a couple hundred pair of tubs, and there would be many more before they were finished. Bridget worked tirelessly, her eyes frequently meeting his as they worked, flirting with him, distracting him with the promise of intimate delights to come.

Hugh could not let arousal interfere with his observations. He kept an eye on MacGowan as well as every other member of the crew who worked on the beach, unable to dismiss the suspicion that MacGowan was the swindler. The only question was why the man would risk it.

MacGowan was well-paid, and had to know that if Hugh ever caught on to what he was doing, he'd be sacked. He would lose his income from the brandy trade as well as his post as estate manager. He would be left with naught.

Hugh had not given the man any indication that he knew something was amiss. Perhaps MacGowan believed Hugh would continue to neglect Glenloch and the free trading indefinitely and he could go on reaping his illicit profits.

It continued to snow—just a few big flakes that melted when they landed, but they lent a pale, watery light to the beach. Hugh looked at Bridget, bundled in her dark woolen coat, with her hat pulled low on her head, and deemed himself very fortunate that he'd decided to come to Scotland just at this moment. Otherwise, he'd have missed the experience of wrestling her to the floor on the night he'd arrived. He wouldn't have felt the exhilaration of pulling her out of her sinking skiff and taking her away to the kelper's cottage. He would never have felt the fierce anger or the wild excitement of making love to her all through the night.

Instead, she might have been well on her way to

Dundee by now. Or her employer's husband could have found her.

He felt a deep wave of possessiveness. She belonged to him, at least for the time being. No other man was going to touch her while she was under his protection.

There was an eerie stillness to the morning. Brianna lay on her side in Hugh's snug bed without moving, her back against his chest, his hand cupping her breast. She could feel his heartbeat and his deep, regular breaths blowing the hair next to her ear.

She felt a misplaced sense of contentment, of being at peace, at home. She braced herself against the sure knowledge that she had to leave. Now, before she got in any deeper. And before he learned her true identity.

A man like Hugh would not turn her over to Stamford or Roddington. He would be angry, for certain. And he would walk away, cold and betrayed. Brianna did not think she could face his abandonment. She needed to leave Glenloch first, before he learned of her deception and withdrew.

She eased out of the bed, somehow managing not to disturb him. Quietly drawing her shirt over her head, she went to the window and moved the thick curtain a fraction of an inch to look out on the quiet morning. It was still snowing, but more heavily now than when they'd gone to bed, hours before. It blanketed the ground, and muted every normal sound that Bree was accustomed to hearing.

Looking over the different levels of roof and eaves,

Bree saw that they were covered with at least eight inches of the stuff. The road, which should have been visible from the window, was nonexistent.

It was impassable. She could not leave.

Even though Brianna felt a keen sense of relief to know that no one could travel in this weather, she also knew that no good could come of her staying at Glenloch.

She'd been concerned about the servants finding her in his bed, but there were no sounds from below, no permeating aroma of breakfast cooking. Of course the servants had not ventured from their homes in Falkburn. They were likely closed up in their own small crofts and cottages, taking care of their animals and trying to keep warm as they waited for the snow to abate before digging themselves out.

Letting the curtain fall back, Bree turned to the bed and saw that Hugh was just barely awake, his dark eyes watching her. She felt her entire body blush at his perusal, aware that she could not possibly compare to his fancy women in London—to the beautiful opera dancers and courtesans with whom his name was so often associated in the scandal sheets.

"Come back to bed," he said, his voice a deep, sensual rasp that sent shivers of desire down Brianna's back. She felt wholly naked before him, even though she wore a shirt that covered all her essential parts. But her feet and legs were bare, and she did not even want to consider what a mess her hair must be. She was exactly the disaster Susan and Catherine Crandall claimed she was.

She returned to the bed and climbed in, leaving the shirt on. "The snow has gotten deep."

"Aye. It was coming down hard by the time we finished last night."

"No, I mean really deep. There must be nearly a foot on the ground now."

He gathered her into his arms and nuzzled her neck. "So much the better. Mrs. Ramsay will stay at home today and I'll have you all to myself, then."

"I cannot stay," she said.

"You are safe and warm here. And there isn't a vengeful gentleman in the entire county who would be out today. Nor will you be, lass."

"The roads will be buried," she mused aloud, agreeing with him as he slid one of his legs between hers and settled in to sleep. 'Twas as though all was settled between them as well. Brianna wondered how he thought she could possibly fit into his life. She'd supposedly run from a repugnant seducer, and yet replaced him immediately with Hugh. There was no logic in it, except possibly his belief that he was a more worthy—and more skilled—lover than the man from whom she'd run.

His skill was not something Bree would deny. She couldn't imagine wanting any other man more than she desired the Laird of Glenloch, and she wondered how her aunt had felt when she'd had to leave her Greek lover.

Claire had never given any indication that she regretted her decision to return to England for Brianna, to take her to Killiedown Manor and raise her there, far from the pernicious Crandall family. And yet she'd spent the following seven years living a celibate life, providing a perfect example of robust Scottish purity and fortitude. Of course she had never expressed any regret at changing her life for her niece.

Claire Dougal had been. . .

Bree's progression of thoughts about her aunt came to an abrupt halt when she remembered Claire's frequent trips to Aberdeen. Claire had explained away those visits in vague terms, saying she had business to attend to in the city. Brianna had been very young then and had assumed the trips related to Claire's own free-trading interests, possibly meeting with her smuggling collaborator, Captain Benoit. But now that Bree understood the pleasures and the sheer comfort of sharing a man's bed, she wondered if there was more to those meetings with Benoit. An intimate liaison was something Claire would have wanted to keep secret.

"Sleep, lass. You were out late last night and worked hard. You'll need your rest for what I have in mind for later."

"Mmm." She closed her eyes and snuggled into his body, her thoughts racing, trying to recall the way Claire behaved each time she'd returned from Aberdeen. As though her muscles and bones were made of pudding? Had she smiled and gazed into thin air the way Bree found herself doing, now that she'd shared Hugh's bed?

Yes. Claire had been besotted with a lover.

And yet she had not married him. Her life at Killiedown had been enough.

Brianna wondered if Captain Benoit had learned of

Claire's death, and whether he would mourn her. She could not believe her beautiful, vibrant aunt had been just one of many women on the coast of Scotland whom he'd wooed and bedded. Surely the French captain had cared for her, even if Claire would not wed him.

When it occurred to her that perhaps it was Benoit who had declined to marry, Brianna's heart ached for her aunt.

She allowed herself to drift to sleep in Hugh's arms, though her sorrowful thoughts kept her from resting peacefully.

Chapter 8

Happy is the wooing tha's no lang o' doing.
SCOTTISH PROVERB

Hugh emptied the water and cleared away the bath from the scullery, feeling as though the pieces of his life were finally falling into place. His free-trading business was under control for the first time in ages, and he wasn't dealing with the asinine rumors and innuendos that seemed to follow him in London, no matter what he did.

The scandal sheets had never mentioned his part in helping one of his old friends thwart a killer. There were no reports of his generous donations to the orphans' charities sponsored by the elderly Lady Sutton, or his attendance at various intellectual gatherings in Town. As far as polite society was concerned, Hugh spent all his time and money on actresses, gambling hells, and pugilists' matches. The gossip wasn't even half true and he was glad to be away from it.

While Bridget dressed, he braved drifts of snow to go out to the stable, where he fed and watered his horse, and surveyed the area where they had unloaded and carried his brandy to the castle.

The snow was as deep as Bridget said and had obscured all the footprints. There was no sign that any activity had occurred in the wee hours of the night. If any of the customs men arrived to visit the site, he would see no traces of the smuggling operation.

Once again, Hugh had made a count of the tubs that were brought ashore, and he intended to be present when MacGowan and his men diluted the brandy before carting it away for sale. He knew what he paid for each of the tubs, and they would be much more valuable after they were diluted and sold to the inns and taverns throughout the county. And yet his free-trade income had dropped in the past year by more than a third.

Whoever was cheating him could not be happy that Hugh was at Glenloch now, observing every stage of the process. MacGowan had not said or done anything untoward last night, but of course he would not. If he was the one, he would have to hope that Hugh would soon be on his way and business could resume the way it had done for the past three years.

Hugh returned to the castle, realizing he'd forgotten how agreeable a heavy, Scottish winter storm could be. There was food in his larder, wood or peat stacked beside every fireplace, and a beautiful, fiery woman to grace his bed.

She was trapped at Glenloch for now, but she'd stated quite clearly her intention to go. Hugh found he was loath to bid her farewell, and he knew he would have to do some convincing to entice her to stay. His desire for her wasn't nearly sated.

He found Bridget in the library, wearing her traveling clothes, obviously the only clothes she had. She'd already lit the lamps, and was starting a fire in the grate. It was the perfect place to spend the morning together.

He came up behind her and slid his hands around her waist. It would be some time before he tired of her. "Much as I enjoy looking at your delicious bottom in those trews," he said, "I think there must be some gowns somewhere in the castle to replace the ones you lost . . . if you would prefer."

She turned and looked up at him over her shoulder. "Oh aye. I would much prefer it. I know my attire is truly awful—"

"Ah, but you're wrong," he interjected. "You look luscious, now, but especially when you're wearing naught."

Her eyelashes fluttered down with embarrassment at his frank words, and he realized he must still tread lightly with this innocent governess. "You flatter me, Laird. I'm quite sure I—"

"Not at all." He pushed her hair away from her neck and kissed her there. "Surely I was not the first man who ever showed a strong attraction to you. Your employer's husband, for example."

He felt her tremble, and he drew her back into his embrace. She was much better off here, with him. Her talents were wasted in the schoolroom.

"I-I never thought . . ."

"You have naught to fear from him here," Hugh

said. He slipped his hands up her rib cage, brushing his
thumbs against the lower curves of her breasts. "Do you
not believe I can protect you?"

"No, I m-mean, yes. I am sure you can. Besides, who
would travel in this weather?"

"The clothes are in my late wife's bedchamber."

She inhaled sharply. "Then perhaps I'll just wear
what I have. I would not wish to—"

"Do not concern yourself," he said, stepping away.
"Whatever is stored up there is only going to waste."

He could see that she remained hesitant. "You don't
believe they're tainted, do you? None of the servants
would take them because of Amelia's . . . cause of
death."

"No. I don't believe they're tainted. I just feel . . . very
sorry for her. She must have been unbearably sad."

"'Twas nothing she ever spoke of to me."

"I don't understand."

"I was not privy to her thoughts. Amelia and I
spoke rarely." He recalled the cold silences that always
stretched between them. "She wasn't expecting me
when I arrived at Glenloch the night before her death.
She was clearly not happy to see me, so I absented
myself the next day with business in Falkburn. Only
the servants and an old friend of my father happened to
be here at Glenloch when she fell. I learned of it soon
after it happened."

Hugh walked to one of the bookcases. It was just like
Amelia to spite herself in order to demonstrate what a
dreadful husband he'd been. He had failed at pleasing
her, in any way.

He felt Bridget's questioning gaze, and took a book down from a shelf. He opened it to a random page and glanced over it as though their conversation carried little weight.

"It must have been terrible."

Amelia could have lived in London while Hugh stayed at Newbury Court. Or she could have taken any one of his other houses while he remained in London. She had not needed to take her life to escape him.

"Aye," Hugh said, eager to change the subject. "Did you see anything here that struck your fancy?"

"Books?"

"Aye. Does not a governess enjoy books? Or did I mistake you, and you are—*were*—a lady's maid?"

"I saw nothing suitable for young children," she said, avoiding the question altogether as she sat down at the chess table. When she started to rearrange a number of the pieces, he saw that they'd been placed incorrectly on the board. Probably by one of the maids after dusting.

"You play?"

She nodded. "A little."

"Shall we have a game?" he asked.

She smiled and his blood thickened.

"I'll see if I can figure out how to make tea and get us some breakfast," he said, "while you go up and find something to wear. Her bedchamber is across from the one you and I shared last night."

It was nigh impossible to keep up her lie! More than once, Brianna had nearly slipped, because she'd gone too far with her deceptions. She knew now that if she'd told Hugh her situation at the very start, he'd have helped her. But it was much too late for that. Now she was stuck having to perpetuate the falsehoods she'd told. She did not think he would be very forgiving if she told him the truth now.

And she would not blame him for being angry with her.

Little had she known what would happen when she'd detoured from the road to Dundee. She hadn't expected to encounter anyone at Glenloch, much less the laird himself, which was her only excuse for lying so grievously. She'd been completely unprepared for him.

And now she was his mistress.

The enormity of what she'd done gave her pause. First, to have jilted Lord Roddington—a duke's son and heir—at the altar. Now this.

Her life had been transformed into something unrecognizable. She never should have agreed to go to London with the Crandalls for the winter. If she'd stayed with Claire, Bree might have been able to nurse her back to good health. Right now, they could have been sitting together in Killiedown's small parlor, reading or discussing the bloodlines of their herd.

But Claire was gone, and so was Brianna's life as she knew it.

Perhaps worst of all was her relief that she could not leave Glenloch just yet. She should be trying to figure a way to get to Dundee as fast as possible, and yet she found herself eagerly anticipating the hours she and Hugh would be spending alone. Held captive by the snow, no servants would intrude on them, nor would Lord Stamford arrive to shatter the peace.

Brianna did not want Hugh to suffer any ill consequences because of her actions. She didn't know how much trouble Stamford or Roddington could cause him, but when her guardian arrived, Bree needed to be far away from Glenloch. Even though her liaison with Hugh would make her an unsuitable marchioness for Roddington, Brianna would not put Hugh into the middle of the mess she'd made.

No doubt Lord Roddington would be incensed to learn his fiancée had been intimate with another man, but not because he cared anything for her. She'd found him to be a pompous, preening, self-important skirt chaser, and knew his pride would be badly stung. Bree did not want to think about consequences to the man who had trespassed on what Roddington would see as his property.

With any luck at all, she would be far from Glenloch when Lord Stamford arrived, and tales of a lass named Bridget MacLaren would mean naught to him.

Bree left Hugh and went up to Amelia's bedchamber. She stepped inside and stood still in the cold, silent room, rubbing her hands up and down her arms, sensing an overarching loneliness. Not even a fire in the grate or lit candles would make this room cheerful and bright, and Brianna did not care to stay there any longer than absolutely necessary.

The first of the two wardrobes was stuck shut with three years of disuse. With a forceful yank, Brianna managed to pull it open. She reached inside and sorted through the clothing that lay folded neatly on the shelves, and chose a simple green muslin morning gown with long, contrasting white sleeves. Holding it up against her, Bree saw that it laced up the back, so no matter what her difference in size from Amelia, Bree could make the bodice fit. But the length was sure to be a problem, for Brianna was nowhere near as tall as Amelia had been.

She took a chemise from a drawer at the bottom of the wardrobe, then borrowed Amelia's brush and the two combs she found on the dressing table. She glanced at the dead woman's shoes and saw that they were much too large. Resigned to wearing the battered and ill-fitting boots she'd bought from Killiedown's groom, she hurried out of the room.

Bree stopped short when she noticed a faintly shimmering form hovering near the door of Hugh's bedchamber.

"What?" She looked down at the items she carried, feeling suddenly guilty for having taken them. "I shouldn't, I suppose, but . . ."

The figure disappeared, leaving Bree feeling vaguely unsettled and annoyed. "What else should Laird Glenloch do with these clothes?" she asked no one. "The servants won't take them."

Still muttering to herself, she went exploring, in search of a needle and thread to alter the length of the gown. She eventually found what she needed and returned to Hugh's bedchamber to make quick work of the hem.

* * *

Hugh was just about to go looking for Bridget when she finally appeared in the library. She wore a gown he could not recall having seen on his wife, which was not very surprising, since she avoided his company whenever possible, and he spent a lot of time at his clubs. He concentrated on Bridget, rather than the sharp twinge of guilt that threatened to destroy his mood.

She'd done something to her hair. It was smooth now, but not exactly flat, and she'd arranged it in an intricate style of twists at the back of her head. Soft, wheat-yellow tendrils curled near her ears and at her nape, at just the places where he liked to kiss her. She looked as regal as a duchess, only far more accessible.

"I'm sorry for the delay," she said, going right to the teapot he'd placed on a table in front of the sofa. "The gown was too long for me. I'd have tripped on the hem if I hadn't shortened it."

"Oh aye. Amelia was nearly as tall as me. I'd forgotten." It was true. He could hardly picture her anymore, and he thought of her as little as possible. He watched as Bridget sat down and poured, her surprisingly strong hands performing the task with grace.

"Thank you for putting it that way," she said.

"What do you mean?"

"I am much too short," she remarked. "I've been faulted for my lack of height on enough occasions to know it's true."

He came around and sat beside her on the sofa, disturbed at the thought of such a petty criticism against her. "You are not short at all." He lifted her chin with his finger and looked into her eyes. "You fit me well, don't you agree?"

Deep pink flushed her high cheekbones and she looked away. "If you say so, Laird."

"Aye," he said quietly, letting his finger drop to the modest neckline of her gown. He ran it lightly across her collarbone. "You are perfect." He'd said it before, and he meant it. Perfectly beautiful, perfect in bed, perfectly unattached.

She gave a short laugh. "Oh, hardly."

"You don't believe that you please me?" he asked, moving his hand to her waist. If she was a pure erotic fantasy in her trews and tunic, she was equally alluring dressed in this feminine confection of green and white. "Whoever you are, you fascinate me."

He saw uncertainty in her eyes. "Whoever I am?"

"Aye. In whatever guise you choose to appear, I want you, lass. Fiercely."

He touched his mouth to hers and kissed her lightly, belying the immense arousal he felt. He needed to draw back, else he would take her back to bed before she had a chance to break her fast.

"You're not Scots, are you?"

She turned her attention to the table and the tray of oatcakes and dried fruit he'd brought in. "No. I was born in England, but my mother was Scots."

"But you've lived here. I can hear it in your words," he said, subtly seeking whatever information he could glean from her.

She nodded. "I spent my early years in England with my parents. But after my father died, I was sent up to Edinburgh."

"Where you awaited your aunt to return from Greece?"

She shook her head. "No. I was too young to remember her then. And, in any event, I wouldn't have known she was coming for me."

He supposed not. "How did you fare in Edinburgh?"

"My mother had some distant relations there. They . . . they took me in, one family after another," she said with a false brightness to her voice. She looked down, and a muscle in her jaw contracted. "I was one more mouth to feed—certainly an unwelcome one."

Hugh felt a wave of irritation for her father, who might well have been a gentleman to have sired a daughter like Bridget. A very lax gentleman, who had not planned better for his child. Frowning, he asked, "Did your father not provide for you before he died?"

"Yes, of course he did," she said quietly. "But I was very young, and those who had control over my fate were only too happy to leave me to my own devices."

Hugh felt his own jaw clench, and he made a point of relaxing it. He wanted to know more, to know everything. But she was not exactly forthcoming. She would not say the name of the employer who had tried to accost her, and she did not seem eager to tell him of her early years.

"Which accounts for it, then," he said more lightly than he felt.

"For what?"

"Your independence. You've had no one to rely upon but yourself, have you?"

"I had my aunt . . ." she said.

"But you had to seek employment for your keep." He leaned forward and cupped her cheek in his hand. "She must not have had the means to support you."

She shrugged, clearly disinclined to discuss the matter any further. Obviously, neither her father nor her aunt had possessed the wealth to keep her, and so she'd been required to hire herself out as a governess.

Her situation was not at all unusual. Many young women were respectably employed in households all over Britain. But when Hugh and Bridget parted, he intended to settle enough money on her that she need not seek employment ever again. He did not believe he could stand to think of her wrestling away from yet another insufferable employer in her future.

"You are not a careful player, I see," said Hugh, leaning forward to study the chessboard. Brianna had enjoyed modest success at chess, simply because her play was rash and unpredictable. Her opponents never knew what to expect from her.

"Are you saying I'm reckless?"

"Sometimes 'tis best to have a strategy in mind before you take action." He'd clasped his hands loosely together, and they hung between his knees. They were strong, as were the muscles in his arms and shoulders. Last night, he'd carried as many barrels of brandy as the burliest hands.

"But sometimes 'tis necessary to act quickly," she said.

"And hope for the best? Hmmm . . ."

Brianna smiled wryly at the undercurrent of meaning. He was chastising her once again for her rash flight from Glenloch as he moved his bishop, giving her access to his king.

Brianna's docile smile turned into a broad grin when she placed his king in check.

"You needn't look so happy about it," he growled, pondering his next move.

"Oh, but I do." She laughed. "I have a feeling 'tis not often that the Earl of Newbury, Laird Glenloch, is bested at anything."

"I'm not beaten yet," he said, moving his queen. "Check."

When he looked up and smiled at her, Bree's heart seemed to stop, and not because of the game. Her mouth went dry and her throat closed.

"Try to maneuver out of this one," he said.

She didn't know if she could. *'Tis lust, pure and simple*, she told herself a little bit desperately. Her heart was not involved in the least. It couldn't be. It was merely the strength of his personality and the powerful attraction raging between them that confused her senses. He was a master of flirtation and seduction, and Bree knew this game was only a prelude to the lovemaking they would soon share.

The only question was where. Would he seduce her in the library? Or take her back upstairs to his big, comfortable bed?

He moved suddenly and took her hand, drawing her up to her feet. "Where is your coat?"

"In the scullery," she said, glad of the distraction.

Keeping hold of her hand, he led her to the back kitchen, where they located their coats hanging on hooks on the wall. He took hers down and draped it over her shoulders, then shoved his arms into the sleeves of his own.

"Come on."

"Where are we going?"

"Following an impulse," he replied. "You should know about those."

"I nearly won."

"Aye. Nearly." He laughed and took her outside, through a door that was far from the buttery where they'd hidden his smuggled brandy.

The sky was still full of thick, dark clouds, but the snowfall had slowed to a few wispy flakes. Brianna lifted her hem and walked toward the sea, noting that the snow came up well above her ankles. Her recently dried boots became wet again, but she did not care.

She turned and saw Hugh bend down and pick up a handful of snow. He walked toward her, forming it into a ball.

"No!" She laughed. "You don't intend . . ."

But he did. She quickly recognized the wicked gleam in his eyes and reached down for her own handful while making a run for it. She saw the remnants of a low stone wall emerging from the deep snow, and darted for it, crouching behind it as she formed her own missile.

"Throw yours, and it'll mean war!" she cried in good humor.

"I'm counting on it," he said, his voice coming closer.

Bree stood and ducked, just as his snowball came at her. She quickly threw hers, hitting him square in the chest.

He kept coming toward her, and Bree squealed and ran through the snow, her speed hampered by her wet boots and her voluminous skirts. "'Tis not fair! I should have changed clothes first!"

She felt a ball of snow hit her back. It was obvious he was holding back, for it was not a vicious hit. "I'll get you for that!"

"Try!"

She grabbed another handful and formed it into a ball as she ran, then turned and pelted him with it. But she lost her footing and fell, landing on her bottom in the soft snow.

Laughing, she started to scramble away, but he caught up to her, turned her onto her back, and pinned her down. He dipped his head close, his lips only an inch from hers. "You're not cold, are you, lass?"

She gazed into his eyes and saw the heat of desire in their depths.

"No!" she said, shoving him off her and rising to her feet. The game was on. She ran as fast as she could, skidding past snowdrifts, dodging and throwing snowballs at him, and laughing until tears filled her eyes.

She felt him close on her heels and knew he would soon catch up to her. Bree looked forward to it, but not too soon. Their merry chase invigorated her and dispelled the disturbing inklings of her heart. She did not want to think about what Hugh was coming to mean to her, or of her imminent departure from Glenloch. This was pure fun, with nary a troubling thought to vex her.

She rounded the corner of the castle and flattened her body against the wall, waiting silently for him to follow. When he did, she let him pass, then crouched down to make another snow missile. He turned before she was finished, and grinned as he lunged at her, missing her as she darted away.

She squealed when he caught an edge of her coat and struggled against his capture.

"You are all mine, wench!" He lowered one shoulder and tossed her over it, holding on to her legs as her head dangled down his back. "It's time to go inside."

Chapter 9

They did not make it past the scullery the first time
Hugh made love to her. But he managed to get her
up to his bedchamber for their second go. And their
third.

She dozed now, curled against his chest, where she
belonged. A wisp of her hair tickled Hugh's chin and
he smoothed it away, much too content and satisfied to
consider her intention to leave as soon as the weather
cleared.

He did not want her to go.

And why should she be so anxious to go into hiding
at Dundee, without any of her belongings, when she
could stay at Glenloch, with him?

Hugh had not yet suggested that she stay, although
his actions surely spoke volumes. She could not possibly
mistake his desire for her.

He intended to remain at Glenloch at least a month,
and he could think of no better way to pass his leisure
time there than with Bridget MacLaren. He wanted to

make love with this woman in every room of the castle, and sleep every night through with her in his arms.

Her chess game was a reflection of her personality, he thought. Intelligent but daring, deliberate and delightfully impetuous. She charmed him with her resilience during their short tenure in the primitive croft, intrigued him by her sudden appearance and assistance the previous night, unloading the boats, and captivated him with her playfulness in the snow. She renewed him.

It occurred to him that if Amelia had been half as hardy and amenable as Bridget MacLaren, their marriage might have succeeded.

The thought of it took his breath away. Hugh's opinion on marriage had been very clear since long before Amelia's death. He wanted naught to do with it ever again.

Bridget sighed against his chest, and Hugh reflected on what she'd told him about herself. She'd been vague about her father and the lack of arrangements he'd made for her upon his death. She had said the bare minimum about her employment, and he still didn't actually know if she'd been a governess or a lady's maid. He hadn't learned the name of her employer, or whether she had any connections in Dundee. In spite of the lack of information, he realized how completely entwined they were, so much that he could hardly tell where he ended and she began.

He extricated himself slightly and decided her reticence was perfectly satisfactory. It helped to keep an appropriate distance between them. With limits and no expectations. If he could convince her to stay at Glenloch all winter, they would enjoy each other for a time, and part ways when he tired of her.

Or she tired of him.

He felt disgruntled at that unwelcome notion. Looking down at her sleeping face, he recognized that she was unlike any of his previous mistresses. She was no practiced flirt, angling for attention and gifts. Bridget MacLaren was unspoiled and unpredictable. If she'd been a nobleman's daughter, she'd have been presented at court and to society. And they would have deemed her an Original.

Hugh deemed her ideal—for his purposes. Where an Original would have been sought after by the young wife-hunting bucks of the ton, Hugh did not intend to do anything more than slake his lust with her.

The dress Brianna had hemmed was definitely worse for the wear. If only she'd understood Hugh's plans when they'd gone out into the snow, she might have changed into her groom's clothes. Now, she would have to remain in his bed, allowing the gown she'd taken from Amelia's room to dry, or put on the old trews.

Hugh must have laid the gown out by the fire before he left, but the lower half had been well-saturated by their snow games. It would be some time before it would be ready to wear.

She lay back and gazed absently at the shadows on the ceiling, caused by the fire in the grate. There was a pleasant soreness in her shoulders and legs, as though she'd spent hours riding her favorite mare through the countryside.

And yet it had been just a man.

She thought of the wedding she'd abandoned and wondered why a woman was not allowed to wed a man of her own choosing, one who appealed to her. A man who made her laugh and caused her knees to quake with his heated glances. A man who made her heart clench in her breast at his intimate touch.

A man like the Laird of Glenloch.

Brianna closed her eyes and put her foolish thoughts aside.

She managed not to sigh as she climbed out of his bed and found her chemise draped on a chair. She drew it over her head, then pulled on her coat and stepped out of Hugh's bedchamber. There were plenty more gowns in Amelia's room across the hall. Bree went inside and saw the familiar ghostly form the instant she opened the door. Its filmy shape hovered beside the bed, and signaled for Brianna to join her there.

Bree let the door close behind her and went toward the hazy light that seemed to move aside when she came near. "What is it?"

The wavering light flickered near the head of the bed, then drifted toward the wall. Bree followed what seemed to be insistent gestures, but they meant nothing to her. Her inability to understand what the Glenloch Ghost wanted frustrated her, for it had a truly urgent air about its movements.

"Who is the man in the locket?" she asked.

Her question went unanswered. Likely the ghost was not Amelia and did not know who he was, or maybe the pendant was only part of what the ghost wanted her to understand. The miniature in the locket seemed a clear indication that Amelia had been involved with a man other than her own husband.

Brianna wondered if Hugh had known. By his own admission, he and his wife had not been close. Many fashionable couples did not reside together. Brianna certainly would not have lived in the same house with Lord Roddington if their marriage had taken place. She could not fathom the depth of Amelia's unhappiness with Hugh and wondered if she'd chosen her moment to jump from the parapet *because* he'd been nearby and she could punish him that way.

If that was the case, 'twas no wonder he'd made a very public vow never to wed again.

It was freezing in Amelia's chamber, so Bree quickly chose another gown and hurried back to Hugh's room. If the apparition had something more to tell her, it would have to do it in the warmth of Hugh's bedchamber.

She added more peat to the fire, then covered her legs with her shawl and sat down near the fireplace with a needle and thread.

The ghost did not reappear, and Bree wondered if there were limits to where it could wander. The servants did not seem to fear its presence on the lower levels, but only in the upper rooms and galleries. Amelia's possessions were intact, and Bree was sure the locket had not been found because the servants wanted no contact with the dead woman's things.

And yet Brianna felt no uneasiness in Amelia's room or any other part of the castle. Glenloch had become her refuge when every other aspect of her life had failed her, and she was going to find it difficult to leave when the weather finally cleared.

The castle might be her safe haven, but Hugh had become her sanctuary. He could have no idea how consoling it was to lie in his arms, to feel his sheltering strength around her. As lovely as these moments together were, Brianna was quite aware that her respite at Glenloch was temporary. And she knew she would never again feel the same contentment. Or the same desire.

She could not imagine any other man attracting her the way Hugh Christie did, with his dark, brooding looks and his mischievous streak.

As though her thoughts could make him materialize, he arrived at the door.

"You're awake," he said.

She nodded. "I found another dress to wear."

"I shouldn't have caused you to ruin the other one."

"It wasn't your fault. Entirely."

"No." He grinned. "Like hell it wasn't." He crouched next to her chair. "I shouldn't have caused you more work."

"Oh. This. 'Tis nothing."

His eyes glittered darkly in the firelight, and she followed her impulse to lean over and kiss him.

He cupped her chin in his big hand and Bree closed her eyes, enjoying his warmth and his show of affection. His touch did not portend an intention to take her to bed, or to draw her into a discussion or game. 'Twas just a simple moment in time, a touching of lips with warmth and affection, and the promise of more to come.

Brianna had never known anyone like him. He

seemed a rake clear to the tips of his boots, and yet he'd
shown kindness to Mrs. Ramsay's grandson, and actually taken part in the unloading of his smuggled goods.
He'd risked his life to rescue her, a stranger, from her
sinking boat, and become the most generous lover she
could ever have imagined. He possessed a depth that
Brianna did not understand.

Nor would she, after she left Glenloch as she
planned.

"Do you know you always turn your back to your father's portraits?" Bridget asked as she sat opposite him
in his study. It was well past dark, and she had heated
the fish stew left by the servants while he'd sliced the
bread. They carried their bowls into the small, intimate
room to eat.

Hugh had never thought of his study as intimate
before, but it seemed that intimacy occurred everywhere
Bridget happened to be. He did not want to speak of his
father, not with Bridget, who was so fresh and open.
Jasper had been a liar and a lecher, and Hugh was glad
Bridget had never had occasion to encounter him.

The bastard would have done his utmost to corrupt
her, as he'd tried with every other woman he perceived
as vulnerable. His style had featured the seduction of
innocents—not opera dancers or lusty widows who understood a rake's motives and would have known how
to get what they wanted from him.

But Jasper had never played fair.

"I don't care to face him, ever again," he said simply.
"We were oil and water."

She frowned. "Why don't you take down his portraits, then? There are so many."

Hugh wasn't normally a superstitious man, but some small part of him felt that if he kept the paintings on the walls, Jasper's ghost would stay away. It didn't hurt anything to keep them there. "I don't spend a lot of time at Glenloch, so it doesn't matter much."

"Are you in London when you're not here at Glenloch?" she asked. Her hair was loose, and fell in soft waves down her back. Her eyes seemed darker somehow, though the glimmer of the firelight reflected brightly in them.

"Aye, I live in London most of the time, but I have a number of other estates," he replied. "And you? Who was your employer in Stonehaven? Or Aberdeen?"

She bent to her bowl and resumed eating instead of answering.

Hugh changed seats, moving his own bowl and sitting beside her on the cushioned settee. At the moment, he didn't give a damn where Jasper's eyes were focused. "Why do you want to protect him?"

She did not look up. "There's naught to be done about him. I've moved on."

"To Glenloch."

She stopped chewing and put down her spoon. "Only for now."

So she still meant to leave. "Why did you choose Dundee?"

"'Tis closer than Edinburgh, so I'll be able to walk the distance. And it's big enough that I should be able to disappear there."

He didn't like to think of Bridget alone in Dundee, with no family, no friends. "That's what you mean to do? Hide for the rest of your life?"

"No, only until . . ." She gave a quick shake of her head. "Just for the time being."

There was a tiny bread crumb on her lower lip. Hugh touched it with one finger, then put his finger into his mouth. "Stay."

Her eyes flared beneath her puzzled brow.

"Stay at Glenloch with me." It surprised him, how much he wanted to spend every evening like this one, sequestered here with her against the harsh winter weather of the eastern coast, playing chess in the afternoons, slaking their hot, passionate lust with each other every night, and making sweet, lazy love every morning.

She looked away. "Laird, I'm not . . ."

He hooked a finger under her chin and turned her to face him. "'Tis good between us, is it not?" he asked, lowering his head to kiss her.

She swallowed hard just before he touched her lips with his own. The kiss started slow, but she slipped her fingers into the hair at his nape and pulled him closer, inviting him in when his tongue invaded her mouth. He deepened the kiss, tasting her and wanting more.

Her hands were small, but the sensations she created at the back of his neck made his cock huge. He drew her onto his lap and she turned to face him, shoving her skirts away to straddle him. A deep, harsh sound came from his throat when his erection met her heat, and he broke their kiss to catch his breath, pressing his forehead against hers. Slowing down.

He wanted to be inside her so much it hurt.

She opened his shirt and tugged it over his head, then feathered light kisses on his neck and throat, soon moving down to his chest. Showing an ardor that matched his own, she teased his nipples with her fingers, and then bent to torture them with her tongue. He managed to loosen her bodice and lower it, baring her beautiful breasts with their hard, pale pink tips. Brianna straightened, and Hugh pressed his face to the cleft between them.

She gave out a thoroughly erotic sigh, and Hugh delighted in her pure, feminine reaction to his ministrations. He groaned at the sensual bounce of her full globes as she pushed her bodice down to her waist and touched her nipples with her own fingertips.

He watched her pleasure herself, her hair curling wildly about her face as her eyes closed in bliss.

"Ahhh, lass. You make me mad with desire." He reached down and opened his trews, but she was the one who drew out his hard length, caressing him, curling her fingers around him.

"Oh, aye, Laird. I don't want to wait," she whispered, raising her hips and moving her skirts. Sliding down onto him.

He nearly exploded. "Jesus, God."

Slowly, she drew him deep inside, clearly enjoying the torture she made him suffer. Hugh held back, letting her take the lead, allowing her to move at her own pace, seeing to her own pleasure. She put her hands

on his shoulders and leaned forward, clearly demanding that he give his attention to her breasts. Her pretty
nipples stood out as hard peaks, and he groaned as he
took one into his mouth, and stretched out his legs to
force himself to slow his own arousal. He wanted her
to do the moving, sliding as she would, pleasuring him
as she pleased herself.

"Christ, you are a greedy wench," he rasped, happy
to give her whatever she demanded.

Hugh sucked her deeply, and let her tease him with
her slow, tortuous movements, but suddenly he could
take no more. He shifted positions, turning her so that
she was beneath him. He plunged deeply, creating a
perfect fit.

She wrapped her legs around his waist and cried out
breathlessly, "More, Hugh!"

As deep as he went, he wanted—*needed*—to be
closer. With his hands braced on the settee he kissed her
deeply, battling her tongue with his own as he slid out
of her wet heat, then back in. He moved hard and fast,
listening to her harsh breathing, drawing out her pleasure as well as his own. She made him feel powerful,
like a wild Pict warrior with painted skin and braided
hair. Like a Glenloch ancestor who had worn armor
and ridden an enormous destrier into battle. Hugh was
the only one with the power to excite her this way, to
draw every dram of pleasure from her, and relish what
she offered him.

Every move, every slide of his flesh against hers
caused her to tremble. Her breathing quickened when
he increased his rhythm, and her warm sheath tightened

around him. He knew she was close. "Come for me, lass. Come apart."

She made a breathy, exquisitely feminine sound that sliced directly through the center of his chest, and when she spasmed and reached her climax, he spilled his seed inside her, shaking as he came in unison with her.

And as he held her shuddering body against his own, he realized she had not answered his invitation to stay with him at Glenloch.

It must have been the wind that woke Brianna during the night. She rose from the bed and went to check the window, but it was closed tightly. Adding more peat to the fire, she was about to return to the bed when she noticed a light shining under the door. The ghost, no doubt. It had not been the wind at all, but the urgency that always seemed to emanate from Glenloch's phantom.

She drew her chemise over her head and wrapped her shawl around her shoulders as she slipped her feet into her boots. A moment later, she stepped quietly into the hall, careful not to awaken Hugh.

"Why don't you just come in and wake me?" Bree whispered, shivering in the cold corridor. "Or . . . can you *not* come into this room?"

Of course the ghost did not reply, but Brianna had a suspicion that must be it. If the servants did not fear seeing it below stairs, it likely meant that it never appeared down there. Perhaps it *could* not.

"Well"—she yawned—"'tis the middle of the night, I've got a blister on my heel, and I—"

The ghost flitted down the gallery, toward the corridor opposite the staircase. Its filmy light shifted, and beckoned for Brianna to follow it.

"What is it?"

It was cold away from the fire, and Brianna could easily return to Hugh's bedchamber and warm herself against the heat of his body. But Glenloch's ghost clearly had some purpose in mind. And Bree was curious.

She walked down the hall to the place where the glowing figure waited, watching as it made a change in its form, flattening to slip through the space beneath the closest door. Brianna followed, opening the door and looking inside.

It was dark, but for the faint light that shimmered off the ghost. Bree went inside and saw a table with a lamp on it. Locating a tinderbox on the mantel, she lit the lamp, then picked it up and looked around.

'Twas a bedchamber, much larger than Hugh's, with two adjoining doors. The bed was huge and looked as though it had been made for a king. Like Amelia's, it was draped in a rich, dark brocade, its curtains tied at each of the four posts, as though waiting for its occupant to arrive and close them against the chill of the room. Obviously, it was the master's bedchamber, and Brianna made note of the fact that Hugh had chosen not to use it. He didn't want even that much similarity to his father.

There were two large wardrobes standing across from the bed, and a cheval mirror in the corner between them, tilted to accommodate a tall viewer. A man. Yet it was carved in a more opulent style than anything Hugh used in his own bedchamber.

Brianna opened the first adjoining door and looked into what must be the valet's quarters. There was a plain, narrow bed against the far wall, with a large chest at its foot. She saw nothing of interest there, so she withdrew and walked across to the door to the other adjoining room. Expecting to find the mistress's chamber, she was puzzled to see the room devoid of furniture. The only furnishing inside was a dark rug on the floor in front of the fireplace.

"'Tis odd," she said softly. Since every other room had been left with its furniture intact, this did not make any sense. She wondered if Hugh had ordered it stripped, or if it had always been empty. It should be the lady's bedchamber. His mother's perhaps. He had said little about her, and now she wondered. . .

Brianna returned to the master's room and saw that the ghost was gone. There was no sign of any other-worldly light, and Bree could not help but wonder if she'd dreamed seeing it.

She hugged her shawl to her chest and glanced around again, trying to understand if there was some purpose to her visit here. Opening each of the ward-robes, she wrinkled her nose at the stale smell of the men's clothes stored inside. It must have been some time since the old laird had used them, and she wondered how long Hugh's father had been gone.

Probably not long, for his animosity seemed quite fresh.

Shivering, she returned the lamp to the table and started to extinguish it, but stopped short at the sight of several long strips of leather lying on the table, beside two large squares of black cloth. She pushed them apart with her fingers, curious about their purpose. Bindings and a blindfold?

"Is this a whip?" she breathed as her mind reeled. An empty bedchamber and a whip . . . She could think of only one thing it could signify.

Hugh had said he and his father had not gotten along, but he had not elaborated. If the old laird had used the whip on his son . . . She picked up the leather strips and saw that they were crinkled some distance from each end as though tied. They *must* be bindings.

Jasper Christie had tied his son—and perhaps others—to use that whip on them. He'd been a brute. 'Twas no wonder Hugh avoided looking at his father's portraits. No matter how long the old laird had been dead, she doubted Hugh would ever forgive him for his brutality.

Feeling outraged on his behalf, she looked for other evidence of wrongdoing, finding nothing but shoes and more clothing. The room had been left to molder as it was, a testament to Hugh's disdain for his father.

The coldness of the room went beyond a normal chill, and seeped into Brianna's bones. A queer sensation penetrated her lower back, causing a bone-deep shiver. Extinguishing the lamp, she fled, feeling as though she was escaping something dreadful.

She hurried back to the bedchamber and let herself

inside, quickly shucking her boots and climbing back into the bed. Hugh rolled toward her and gathered her into his arms, drawing in a sharp breath.

"Have you packed yourself in snow, sweet?" he asked sleepily.

"No, I, er . . . just had to get up."

"Come close. I'll warm you."

She pressed her face into the crook of his neck and let his warmth suffuse her as she embraced him, realizing it was small comfort against what must have been a miserable, horrific childhood.

Bridget was a puzzle to Hugh. She liked to read, but her choice of books surprised him. She did not favor the handful of novels he'd taken down from the library shelves for her, but chose a book on animal husbandry.

"Are you planning to take up farming?" he asked her when they retreated into his study.

"No, I just . . . My aunt had a farm and we . . . Well, it just interests me."

"You're blushing just as I must have done years ago, when I was caught with a book of naughty pictures given me by my school friends." He drew her down to the sofa beside him, the place where he'd recently experienced the most amazing sex of his life. His reaction to the way she used her mouth on him had excited *her*, a powerful aphrodisiac in itself.

She laughed, and the sound went through him like warm honey mixed with fine Scottish whisky. "Tell me about school. Where did you go?"

"St. Paul's in London."

"And your friends got hold of naughty pictures?"

"Well, they were older, much more experienced."

She frowned. "How much older?"

"Well, there was Tony Maddox, who was at least three years older than me, and Daniel Bryant who must be two years my elder."

She laughed, and the dimple beside her mouth captivated him. He was already looking forward to tasting it again. "Ah, I see . . . they were much older men."

"I was tall for my age. I don't think they realized how much younger I was."

"Ah. Are you still friendly with them? Or were they banished from your august presence for such an immoral infraction?"

He thought fondly of his old friends. "No, on the contrary. I spent a few holidays with Tony at his grandmother's estate."

"You did not go home?"

"God, no. Not if I could help it."

He did not want to think about the subsequent years when he'd had no choice—after Tony had been lost on safari and his father had returned to England alone. He had spent many an hour trying to think of ways that he might sail to Africa himself to find Tony. But eventually, he'd had to give up and accept that his boyhood hero was dead.

He had gone to Daniel's family home a few times, but most holidays he'd been subjected to Jasper's harsh and cheerless control in London, or his mother's wan indifference at Newbury Court. Sometimes he'd come with his father to Glenloch if he had estate business to attend to.

"You do not use the master's bedchamber."

"No." His tone did not invite any discussion, but Brianna surged forward in spite of it.

"I . . . happened to go inside it. The ghost—"

He rolled his eyes. "I told you—"

"I've seen it. 'Tis not just a legend."

Hugh sighed, unwilling to argue. As long as she did not flee in fear as the servants did, then he would be free to enjoy her. To breathe in her sweet scent and dally with the hair at her nape.

"The ghost . . . it showed me a whip."

Hugh's hand stilled. God, he'd thought the servants would have burned everything they found in that room, for they'd loathed Jasper as much as Hugh had.

"Did he use it on you?"

"'Tis ancient history. My father was beneath contempt, and I rarely think of him anymore."

"Only when you're faced with one of his portraits."

He rose suddenly, absolutely unwilling to speak of those days. "Tell me of the dirk you carry," he said. "Would you have used it on me?"

"Only if I thought you were going to harm me. When you attacked me on that first day, I was afraid you were a vagrant."

Relieved that she was willing to change the subject, he returned to her and took her hand, drawing her up from the sofa. He should teach her to use the knife properly, but at the same time, he didn't care to think of her leaving his protection and needing to know how to defend herself. Far worse would be the knowledge that she might find some trouble and have no way to protect herself.

"I did not find it too difficult to take it from you," he said quietly, bending to touch his mouth to the sensitive corner of her jaw.

"Pray, don't remind me," she said breathlessly. "I'll be on better guard next time I'm accosted in the dark."

"I look forward to it," he said.

"What? You plan to accost me?"

"Next chance I get," he said. His mouth went dry and he realized it was true. He could barely refrain from taking her into his arms even now, just after making love to her there, on the sofa. It had been some of the most satisfying lovemaking they'd yet shared.

Since her introduction to the pleasures of the bedroom, she'd become insatiable, welcoming his touch and all his advances. He did not foresee a time when he would tire of this woman.

But he wanted a distraction now. Her curiosity about Jasper was still in her eyes, but he wanted no more talk about him.

"We might try to go out walking today," he said, noting the bright sunlight shining through the library windows. She had not said she would stay with him, and with the clearing weather, she could leave today if she chose. He intended to convince her otherwise.

"On the beach?" she asked.

"Aye, if you like," he replied, letting out the breath

he'd been holding. "Although the snow might still be too deep."

"I'll go get my coat," she said.

Brianna collected it from Hugh's bedchamber. She started for the door, stopping short when the sight through the window caught her attention. She could see the road from her vantage point. The sun shone brightly on it, and it struck her all at once that it might be passable now.

She sat down hard on the bed and pressed one hand to her chest, taking a tremulous breath. *What was she doing here?*

Her one-night detour had turned into many. She'd allowed herself to be seduced by the most proficient rake of the ton. Worse, she was halfway to falling in love with him.

She had vowed never to marry. All she'd wanted was to return home to Claire and Killiedown, where she would never again be subject to the whims of another. Of a guardian who would deny her marriage to the man she loved, and force her to wed the disgusting ravisher of respectable young ladies whom Bree had taken pains to avoid through every season.

With Claire gone, Brianna lived for her independence, for the moment she would turn twenty-one, never to be reliant upon anyone again. A few days with a rakehell like Laird Glenloch had not changed that.

Yet she could not remember the last time she'd thought of the Killiedown stables or whether their horsemaster had seen fit to stay on in Claire's absence.

Time seemed to have stopped at Glenloch while she and Hugh were blanketed in snow, insulated from the rest of the world.

Brianna knew it would not continue. Hugh might want her to stay with him for a few weeks, and she was oh so tempted. He drew her like a bee to honey, but he was not interested in permanence any more than she was. He'd let it be known to all and sundry that he intended to remain a bachelor, that one marriage and one unhappy wife had been enough for him.

The hollow feeling in Brianna's chest expanded. She would be a fool to stay any longer, to let herself become any more attached to him.

She'd almost forgotten how important it was to keep at least a small part of herself separate, never becoming too comfortable, too secure. Life at Killiedown had made her careless. She'd found security there, and permanence, never believing her social seasons in London would result in being forced to marry against her will.

A feeling of panic rose in her breast when she thought of the day when Hugh tired of her and sent her away. 'Twas a separation she did not think she could bear.

Turning to the window, she looked out, blinking away her foolish tears. She could not allow anything to cloud her vision of the road that lay before her. Somehow, she was going to find the strength to do what she must, which could only mean taking her leave of Glenloch.

She wiped her eyes when she saw a group of people walking through the snow toward the castle, from the direction of Falkburn. The servants, she thought, or perhaps free traders, come to take Hugh's brandy out of storage.

She had to go. She had to get away from Glenloch and Hugh before—

Brianna suddenly realized she could not make a clean break, for her money now rested at the bottom of the sea. She could not survive in Dundee without money. Nor could she stay.

She was going to have to ask Hugh to lend her some. Or perhaps he would pay her—just as he had the rest of the laborers—for her part in unloading the contraband.

Still, it would not be enough. She had to find lodgings in Dundee, or perhaps Perth, and somehow survive another two months. Work would not be easy to find, especially without references, and wearing her old boots and ill-fitting gowns. She leaned her forehead against the cold pane of glass. She was going to have to ask Hugh for a loan.

He was not in love with her. Hugh simply didn't believe in it. But he could not ignore the niggling suspicion that he might be able to tolerate Bridget MacLaren indefinitely. He could actually foresee keeping her with him even when he returned to London, and not in separate residences, either. Hang society and what it would say about any arrangements he made with her.

Never before had he been so content with the lack of a valet and the other servants. Mrs. Ramsay had left plenty of food, and he and Bridget had managed to keep the fires burning in the two rooms they used most—the library and his bedchamber.

He hardly recognized himself, looking forward to a simple outing with her, to listening to her laugh as they cavorted in the snow down near the beach. She brought back memories of the enjoyment he used to take in simple things. He looked forward to a clearing in the weather so that he could teach her to ride. He did not doubt she'd be a spirited horsewoman.

He was waiting near the scullery for her when Mrs. Ramsay arrived with Fiona and Ronan, and two young men with shovels, all stomping snow off their boots as they came inside. The invasion of these few servants into the quiet world he and Bridget had been sharing felt like the worst ballroom crush he'd ever experienced.

"Ach, Laird, ye survived the storm! I stewed over yer whereabouts—no' that 'tis any concern o' mine, but then MacTavish said he'd seen ye," Mrs. Ramsay remarked as she put down her basket and instructed the others to place the ones they carried on the table, too. To Hugh, they seemed to have brought enough food to feed a large house party for a week. "I'm verra glad t' see you well and sound," the housekeeper added, going right to the stove to check its status.

"We're fine," he said.

She looked up sharply. "Miss Munro is still here?"

"Miss MacLaren," he corrected her. "Aye."

Mrs. Ramsay pursed her lips and went about starting the fires in the stoves. "If ye say so."

"What?" Hugh asked, annoyed by the housekeeper's patronizing tone. "What do you mean?"

"'Tis no' Miss MacLaren ye've been entertaining here."

What did *she* know? "Then pray tell me who she is," he said, leaning against the table's edge.

"The lass came here once maybe five years ago, with her aunt—Lady Claire Dougal."

"You're mistaken," he said, although the mention of an aunt—of Claire Dougal in particular—sent a frisson of unease through him. Lady Claire was a daughter of Lord Drummond. Which would make Bridget . . .

Dread pooled in the pit of his stomach. He had *not* deflowered the granddaughter of an earl. She would surely have mentioned . . .

Christ!

"Ach, well," said Mrs. Ramsay. "If ye like to think so."

Chapter 10

A lie has nae legs, but scandal has wings.
SCOTTISH PROVERB

"**H**ow would you remember such a visit?" he scoffed halfheartedly.

"Who would forget such a face?" Mrs. Ramsay said. "She still has tha' bonny dimple aside of her mouth, and those eyes. Never saw tha' pale a blue, jus' like Lady Claire's."

And her strikingly blond hair that grew nearly white at her nape and her temples. Places he'd kissed while he was inside her.

She'd lied to him. He'd known from the start that she was no peasant lass, but never had he considered the possibility that the granddaughter of a peer would be wandering down the coastal road alone, dressed as a young boy, with only a pathetic little dirk for protection.

He wondered if her family was, even now, bearing down on Glenloch, prepared to drag him to the altar with her. God knew he would be doing the same if it had been his daughter, found sequestered with a bachelor of questionable reputation.

He shoved his fingers through his hair and swore. It had been years since anyone had betrayed him to this extent. Amelia's death had struck him the same way—the ultimate betrayal, a need to punish him for her unhappiness for the duration of his life.

And now he would be forced to wed the woman who'd been sharing his bed, apparently without qualms.

He stopped short. Perhaps not. She'd told him her only family was her aunt, who had recently died. He recalled everything Bridget had told him—about her employer's husband, and her intent to go to Dundee. If that was a lie, too, then why had she been so fixed upon anonymity—even as far as taking a false name?

It could only mean that someone else was after her.

He went into the study and looked up at his father's smirking portrait. "Aye," he muttered. "You are right again. I'm a perfect idiot."

Turning his back on the picture, he waited for her, holding on to the mantel as though it could somehow give him the solid stance he needed to confront her. But his knees felt surprisingly unsteady when he heard her come down the steps and into the room. She stopped abruptly, and he realized his rigid posture must have signaled something was wrong.

He turned slowly to face her.

He saw uncertainty in her eyes. She bit her lower lip, and Hugh felt an immediate, intense tightening of his groin. In spite of her lies, he still wanted her.

"I m-must speak to you, Hugh," she finally said, her voice low and subdued.

He clenched his teeth and waited, aware that she

could not yet know what he'd been told about her. She came to him then, and put her hand on his forearm. "I . . . I cannot stay any longer." Her throat moved as she swallowed thickly. "I saw the servants arriving. If they can get through, then I can, too. I . . . must leave."

It was not what he expected.

"And go to Dundee?"

She nodded.

"Why, Bridget? Who is after you?" he asked, in spite of himself. He knew he should just let her go, get on with the investigation of his free-trade accounts, and be relieved to have escaped the marriage shackles that were sure to follow if anyone learned of their sexual liaison.

"I-I told you."

"But it wasn't true, was it?"

"What?" Brianna croaked. "How did you know?" Her heart sank at the realization that he somehow knew she was a bald-faced liar. She'd had no choice about leaving Glenloch, but not this way. She did not want Hugh to think badly of her, and yet he would.

"Mrs. Ramsay remembered you," he said coldly.

Dismay filled her. She had never anticipated this turn. Tears clogged her eyes again and she turned away, unwilling to let him see them. She went to the window and put her hands on the sill, swallowing hard. "I did not think she would. It was years ago that I was here."

"Then it's true?" he said. "You're Lord Drummond's granddaughter?"

She nodded. "On my mother's side. My father was Damien Munro, Viscount Stamford."

"Who is after you, Bridget? Or is that really your name?"

She shuddered, remembering all the times she wished he'd called out her true name when they'd made love. Now he would think of Brianna Munro with disdain, as the woman who had blatantly deceived him. She turned to him. "'Tis Brianna. I'm sorry. I-I could not tell you."

"Why?" His voice was low and dangerous. "Why could you not tell me the truth?"

"My guardian is my father's heir—a distant cousin, many times removed. He has no liking for me, perhaps because I remind him of the years when he possessed no title. But he is a truly despicable man"—she turned to face him, her despair changing to righteous anger—"who has sold me in marriage to the most self-indulgent, debauched, disgusting libertine known to God or man. I refuse to wed him."

Two spots of color dotted the arc of his cheeks as he listened to her litany of reasons. "And so you ran."

"What else was I to do? Lord Stamford *owns* me. And if I'd told you my true circumstances, you'd have been compelled to take me back to him."

Hugh scrubbed one hand over his face and made a low sound that reminded her of their lovemaking. Only this time, it was a growl of disparagement, and not pleasure, and her knees went weak with regret—but not for having run from Roddington. For the situation that had compelled her to lie.

"There will be no consequence to you, Laird Glenloch." She braced her feet solidly on the floor, keeping her back straight. She might not have a great deal of height, but she had her pride. She had done what was necessary to survive. "I will leave today. Now."

"You cannot. The roads are nowhere near clear."

She moistened her lips and ignored the ache pushing up on her breastbone. "I'll manage. No one but your housekeeper knows that Brianna Munro was here—and I'm sure you can convince her to remain silent if Lord Stamford comes looking for me."

"Christ, Brianna, the man will be incensed," he said, and Bree's heart leaped at the sound of her name, and how it slid past his lips. His voice rumbled through her chest and expanded her heart with longing. If only she had felt safe in telling him the truth when she first arrived, perhaps everything would be different now. "Stamford will want blood if he finds you here."

"I realize that. I never intended to stay . . . You know I tried to leave . . ." Her throat closed when she remembered her flight in the tub boat and his daring rescue. *Oh heavens, why did this have to be so difficult?*

She bolstered her resolve, crossing her arms over her chest as though she were in complete control. "I'm ready to go . . . but for one thing. I need to ask you . . ." *God, how could she ask him?*

"Ask me what?"

"For a loan," she said in a rush of words.

He blew out a harsh breath, and Brianna forced herself to deny the yearning that he would open his arms and pull her into them. She knew better than to hope

for the warm, masculine strength and comfort she knew
he could give. Yet she'd allowed herself to crave it. To
crave *him*.

She tipped up her chin, making her stance seem as
sturdy and robust as she could. She'd never been a wa-
tering pot in her life, and yet one stupid tear coursed
down her face, threatening to undermine everything her
posture said. She brushed it away quickly. "You owe
me payment for helping the other night—for unloading
your tubs of brandy."

"Is that so?"

"You know it is. I worked as hard as any of those
night runners down in your cove."

He did not reply, but after a moment's hesitation, he
went to his desk and opened a drawer, and took out a
heavy metal box. Still without looking at her, he removed a key from his pocket and unlocked the box,
then turned it toward her. "Take what you need."

Inside was a large cache of money—notes as well as
coin. Brianna felt incensed by his nonchalant yielding
of the treasure within. As though he could not have
cared less what she chose to do.

Glad that anger replaced her anguish, she turned on
her heel and started for the door, but he beat her to it,
taking her elbow in his hand and turning her to face
him.

"What do you think you'll be able to accomplish with
no money and no resources?" he growled.

She yanked away. "I'll figure something out."

"Jesus, Brianna." He shoved his fingers through his

hair, something she'd done ever so gently, countless times in the past few days. "A woman alone on a Scottish road? What can you possibly be thinking?"

"I've got my dirk."

"And God knows how effective you are with it. You cannot go alone."

She forced her voice to remain steady. "Look, just give me what you owe me and I'll—"

He took her hand and drew her out of the study and dragged her into the corridor and up the staircase behind him. She tried to pull away, but he held fast until they reached his bedchamber and went inside.

"Sit down."

"No."

"Christ, can naught be easy with you?"

She put her hands on her hips and averted her eyes as he changed clothes, putting on heavier trews and a thick, knit waistcoat underneath his coat. He meant to take her himself.

Her relief was unfounded. She knew all he wanted was to be rid of her, not to be her devoted escort.

"What makes you think you can hide long enough for your guardian to forget about you?" he asked.

"I only need until February." Her voice was unsteady, but she refused to allow tears to clog her throat again. She lowered her head and busied herself with the buttons of her jacket.

"What happens in February?"

"My birthday. I'll come of age and then—"

"And then Stamford will have no sway."

She nodded. "I'll inherit Killiedown Manor—my aunt's estate—and live there just as I did during our years together."

He seemed to wince. "As a spinster."

"I have as little interest in marrying as you do."

He made another disparaging sound and took her across the hall to Amelia's room. Without ceremony, he pushed open the door and went directly to one of her wardrobes. He took out a heavy woolen coat and dragged it over Bree's shoulders, over the layers she already wore. A vertical line slashed between his brows as he pulled the collar together and started to fasten it under her chin.

"Please don't."

"Don't what? Don't let you walk all the way to Dundee alone with blisters on your feet from those abominable boots?"

In silence, she slid her arms through the sleeves of the heavy coat and let him fasten the too-long garment for her. At least his mood seemed to have changed from acute anger to mere exasperation. Bree allowed herself a moment to savor the brush of his fingers, likely the last time he would touch her.

"The carriage won't make it through the snow, and I don't have a sleigh," he said. "And since I've only the one horse, we'll ride together."

A shiver started at the small of Brianna's back at the thought of the close quarters they would share on the road to Dundee. "You can't mean to take me all the way there."

He stood still, gazing down at her mouth as if memorizing its taste and the way she'd responded to him. She wanted to rise up on her toes and kiss him, just to remind him.

"I don't see that I have any choice."

"Of course you have a choice." She swallowed and forged ahead. "There's no point in unnecessary chivalry, Hugh. I've been managing on my own for—"

A bright flicker distracted her, and Brianna turned to see the ghost taking shape behind Hugh in the space beside Amelia's bed. "Look, it's floating up the wall."

Hugh took hold of Brianna's hand and pulled her out of the room before the ghost actually took shape. "Time to get out of here."

"'Tis harmless, and I think it wants to show us something."

"I have no interest in delaying. We're finished here," he said, closing the door tightly. He seemed more irritated than afraid.

"It's real, I'll have you know," Bree said. "And Amelia's spirit never appears with the ghost, if that's what worries you." He ignored her words, pulling her alongside him, stopping short when Fiona made her appearance at the top of the stairs.

"Laird, the customs men are here!" she called out in a quiet voice.

"God damn it," he said. "Wait here for me. Do not even think about leaving without me."

Christ almighty, he did not need this! Not now.

Hugh followed the maid down the stairs and out the scullery door at the back of the castle, avoiding the area where his brandy was stored as though it were infested with vermin.

Angus Kincaid and Berk Armstrong were walking in the snow on the beach with a crew of their men. The underlings were clearing snow with shovels, then Kincaid and Armstrong took the long poles they carried and shoved them deep into the sand of the beach. Looking for buried contraband.

"Armstrong!"

The man looked up at Hugh's voice and started walking toward him.

"Laird, good day to ye."

To hell with the greetings. "What are you doing here?"

"Weel, we got word again of another ship in the cove a couple of nights ago."

"When would that have been? The night of the storm?"

"Aye, Laird."

Hugh made a derogatory sound. "Is there a free trader in all the North Sea who would risk sailing on such a night?"

"We've heard of one," said Kincaid, a small, unpleasant man with a full, graying beard that he'd trimmed to a sharp point at his chin. "A man called Benoit."

"Benoit, you say? A Frenchman, I suppose?"

"Aye," Kincaid said, sneering. "A daring fool, from all that's said of him. Trades illegally up and down the coast from Aberdeen to St. Andrews."

"And you think he's buried his goods here? On my land?" Hugh demanded.

" 'Tis always a possibility, Laird," said Armstrong.

"Not likely, though, without my knowing of it."

Kincaid gave Hugh a hard look, but Hugh returned it, hoping the men understood whom they were dealing with, and that any accusations would have serious consequences. "But go ahead and see what you can find." He turned to leave them. "Let me know if anything turns up."

"Ye can be sure we will, Laird," said Kincaid.

'Twas the worst possible timing. He could not leave Glenloch with Brianna Munro while the customs men poked around his property. He didn't want them talking to Mrs. Ramsay or any of the other servants, not while a thousand tubs of uncut brandy stood stacked in half ankers in the secret room near the buttery. And yet he could not allow Miss Munro to stay.

What he ought to do was see that she was returned to her guardian, Viscount Stamford, but he knew the man. And a more fawning, parsimonious mushroom was not to be found within or without the echelons of society. The man dangled after every peer of consequence, hoping to gain influence just by association. Hugh could not imagine Brianna at his mercy.

Brianna sat on the edge of the bed of the nursery, her arms wrapped tightly around herself. She thought of running, but Hugh would have been after her before she could make it a half mile down the road. Not that he was so set on keeping her. She would not delude herself about that. But she knew he would take it amiss if she left when he'd told her to stay and wait for him.

She shivered with a sudden sense of cold, and looked up to see the ghost hovering nearby. "If you've a suggestion about what I should do, then out with it."

The apparition did naught but float there, just above the floor, its shape only vaguely human.

"What is it, then?" she demanded, not even sure what she was seeing. Hugh denied the existence of the ghost, and no one else had ever seen it. Perhaps her anger and frustration were making her see things. Perhaps she was going mad. "What do you want to show me?" she asked, exasperated.

The filmy consistency of the ghost seemed to ripple in place, and Bree lost all patience. "I cannot read your mind. I don't know what you want!"

Nor did she care. She did not want to know. She just needed to get away from the discontented spirit, away from Glenloch and the ache in her heart, and the knowledge that she would never feel for another man what she felt for Hugh.

She started for the door to make her escape, but stopped when she felt the cold prickle of unease on the back of her neck. It was the oddest feeling, as though Glenloch's phantom had actually slipped its icy fingers around the back of her neck. If this was all some kind of illusion, then she did not understand reality.

Brianna swallowed and turned in resignation. "What do you want from me?"

The room looked exactly the same as it had on her first night at Glenloch, except for the plaid blanket from the kelper's croft that was folded neatly at the foot of the bed. Brianna knew it must have been a child's room at one time, else the furniture would have been larger and there would have been hangings on the walls similar to those she'd seen in other parts of the castle.

The filmy light still shimmered in the center of the room.

Brianna stepped back inside and looked around, since her illusion clearly wanted to show her something. She opened the small wardrobe, worried that she might discover another whip or some other indication of Hugh's bleak childhood. She took a breath of relief when she found it empty. There was nothing on the shelves, and the drawers were empty.

"What now?"

The writing desk was empty, too, but for an additional half-burned candle in the middle drawer. Bree shut it, but heard the rustle of paper inside as she did so.

"Is this it? Is this what you want me to see?"

She unbuttoned Amelia's heavy coat and tossed it onto the bed. Turning back to the drawer, she pulled it open again and removed it all the way. She placed it on the desk and reached into the empty space, pulling out the crumpled foolscap she found there.

It was a child's drawing of a sailing ship, so detailed that it even showed a map of the African coastline along its right edge. Bree could not understand why the ghost wanted her to find it.

She sat on the bed and looked down at the smoothed-out picture in her hands. Hugh must have drawn it years ago, during one of his visits at Glenloch with his father. He'd barely mentioned his mother, only telling Bree that she'd called him Glenloch.

"Glenloch," she said quietly, the word sounded very cold when applied to the man whose bed she'd shared. Bree could never call him that. To her, he would always be Hugh, the brave hero who'd come to her rescue at sea, the generous lover who'd given her untold pleasure in his bed.

She dropped the drawing onto the bed and stood. Was this what the ghost had wanted? For Brianna to slow her thoughts and curb her anger long enough to think about the man with whom she'd spent the last several days?

"I've done naught *but* think about him, Ghost!"

Bree admitted his anger was justified. She'd lied to him and put him in an untenable position. The only thing she could do to prevent even more trouble was to disappear. She could get away from Glenloch before Lord Stamford learned that they'd spent days alone together.

For if her guardian did not find her here, he would have no grounds to force Hugh to wed her.

She wondered if there was a way to get around Hugh and leave without him. He might be occupied for some time with the customs men. But he had his horse, she reminded herself, and could make much faster time than Bree would be able to do on foot. Perhaps she could hide somewhere on Glenloch property, and when he left the estate to find her, she could flee in the opposite direction.

Brianna put a halt to her impulsive train of thought, for it was just as bad as the plan that had taken her out to sea in the small tub boat. The weather was still brutally cold, and if she found herself caught in it, she might freeze to death. And she would deserve it this time.

She sat down hard on the bed and allowed herself to face the truth. She did not really want to escape. In fact, Brianna almost wished she had agreed to stay at Glenloch with Hugh.

But he wouldn't have asked her if he'd known who she was. Nor would he have taken her to his bed. Every aspect of their association would have been entirely different.

Yet Bree would not have changed anything, except for the misery she felt now, with her departure at hand. She'd tried to leave before, but that time, she hadn't felt anything like the anguish that coursed through her now.

Her eyes lit once again on the crumpled picture of the sailboat lying on the bed. "It explains nothing," she said aloud, even though she was alone.

As alone as Hugh must have felt, she supposed. He'd mentioned the holidays he'd spent with friends rather than with his family. And he'd grown up to marry in typical aristocratic fashion, to a woman with whom he'd shared no closeness. Likely they'd wed for family alliances rather than any liking for each other.

And yet . . . Had Hugh cared for his wife? He'd sworn off marriage after her death. Perhaps because it had devastated him, rather than freeing him. Brianna had not thought of that possibility before. He might have loved Amelia.

Bree had not mistaken the expression of deep emotion crossing his features, or the regret in his voice when he spoke of his late wife.

She picked up the picture. Taking it to the desk, she smoothed it out on the wooden surface and tamped down the pang of jealousy that twisted in her chest when she thought of what Hugh might have felt for his wife.

She had no right to any such feelings. But that did not keep her from having them.

Hugh went to the stable and saddled his horse with every confidence that Brianna Munro would not have the ballocks to leave Glenloch when he'd specifically told her to stay put. As much as he wanted to go right back up to his bedchamber and confront her with her lies, he needed to deal with Armstrong and Kincaid. He decided to make a show of disinterest, leaving the castle while the customs men poked about.

They would find naught, of course. And Mrs. Ramsay knew better than to give them admittance to any part of the castle other than the kitchens. As further insurance, she and the other servants had instructions to keep everyone away from the ruins, for these were said to be dangerous areas with walls and floors that might collapse at any time.

Such tales, along with rumors of a ghost, had always worked before. And the lairds of Glenloch had allowed the exterior of the castle to remain in its run-down condition in order to add authenticity to the claim.

He mounted his horse and rode down to the beach. "Make sure to have Mrs. Ramsay brew you some tea before you go on your way," he said to the men.

"Aye, and thank ye, Laird!" Armstrong called out while Kincaid continued to scowl and stab at the ground.

Hugh's mood was dark as he rode to MacGowan's cottage. He'd known something was not quite right about Brianna Munro's story, but he'd never guessed. Good God . . . the granddaughter of an earl. The daughter of a viscount. *Stamford's* ward! He didn't even want to consider who the jilted bridegroom might be. The man could call him out and be justified by it.

Brianna was doubly naïve if she really believed their liaison would cause no consequence to him. If Stamford ever got wind of it . . . He shuddered to think of it. Her guardian was one of the worst social climbers, exactly like Charlotte de Marche and the rest of her ilk, who would like nothing better than to entrap him in marriage. To his ward, in Stamford's case.

Hugh had avoided such shackles assiduously for the past three years, and by God, he was going to steer clear of them now. He would just put the customs men off their suspicions of contraband at Glenloch by leaving the estate and heading toward his manager's cottage. It was time he had a frank conversation with MacGowan, anyway.

He had been to the man's house only twice or thrice in his life, for the custom had always been for the lairds of Glenloch to conduct estate business in the castle's study. MacGowan greeted him with surprise and admitted him to his front parlor, a comfortable sitting room that served as an office, with a tidy desk at one end.

MacGowan offered him a seat and a cup of tea, which Hugh declined.

"Laird, I'd have come up to the castle if I'd known ye needed t' see me."

"Kincaid and Armstrong are poking about the beach," Hugh said without preamble. He was in no mood for niceties in light of . . . everything.

The manager paled. "The brandy is still up at the castle."

Hugh nodded, very much aware that the weather had prevented removal of the liquor.

"And it has yet to be let down."

"Tonight would seem to be a good time," said Hugh. "The sooner the better."

MacGowan frowned. "I'm no' sure of that, Laird. Mr. Kincaid's customs office is in an uproar over the sightings of Benoit's ships."

"You're saying Kincaid will send riders all the way down to Glenloch even when the roads are barely passable?"

"They're passable enough on horseback."

Hugh had found that to be true, though he still hoped the customs office would not bother sending riders out after dark. "None of them showed up the other night when we took in the last shipment."

"Ach, weel, mayhap because I did what I could to lead Armstrong astray when ye sent him here for shelter."

Hugh raised a brow.

"I told him we'd heard rumors of a smuggler's ship seen down closer to Inverbervie."

"Well done, MacGowan," Hugh said, watching the man carefully for signs of deception.

"I'm thinkin' we might want to wait awhile before we dilute this shipment and get it out to market," MacGowan replied carefully.

"I'll consider it. In the meantime, perhaps you can tell me why my free-trading income has been dropping steadily these past couple of years."

"Laird?"

"I'd like a look at your balance sheets, MacGowan. You've got them here, haven't you?"

"Of course."

He had not shaved, so there was a thick growth of red whiskers on his neck. Even so, Hugh noticed his throat reddening as he swallowed thickly. Guiltily?

The man took out a large, bound ledger and set it on the table between them. He opened it to the first page. "Here 'tis. Every shipment since your grandfather started the trade."

Hugh turned the pages until he came to his father's tenure and saw the partners he'd brought in to expand their business. Of those investors, only Roddington was left, and Hugh wanted to know why. There were other operations Roddington would be better suited to, with partners who did not despise him.

"Times are difficult, Laird. A tub of brandy doesna fetch what it used to."

Interesting. "In other words, we are no longer doubling our outlay, as we once did?" Hugh asked.

"Not here in the Mearns," MacGowan said. His face was flushed with color, and he opened and closed his big fists as he moved nervously about the room. "I've had t' find men t' carry it as far south as Kirkaldy and Edinburgh. But even so, we're down more than half."

Hugh did a quick mental calculation. "You've been cutting Falkburn's percentage?"

"Weel, aye." MacGowan nodded. "T' make up some o' yer losses, I had t' do it."

"Who are these distributing men you've brought in?"

"They've mostly come from Stonehaven. The Falkburn men won't do it."

He closed MacGowan's book and picked up his gloves. "I've decided to arrange for a crew to go up to Glenloch later today. MacTavish will let you know when the brandy is diluted and ready to be shipped."

Feeling unsatisfied by the conversation, Hugh left the manager's cottage and walked his horse down the road to the village to get more information. He encountered Niall MacTavish—Sorcha Ramsay's son-in-law—shoveling a path near the vicarage.

"Hello, Laird. I was planning on comin' up to see ye at Glenloch later. I'd like a word, if ye doona mind."

"Let's walk to Tullis's place."

"Aye, Laird." MacTavish put up his shovel and they walked together through the snow-covered village. The paths between cottages had already been cleared, making it easy to reach the center of the small town. Hugh led the way to the public house, where MacTavish followed him inside. Together, they stepped up to the bar, where Osgar Tullis greeted him and drew two glasses of ale from a cask, placing them on the scarred wooden surface of the bar.

MacTavish spoke. "I thought ye should know Guthrie saw Gordon Pennycook going into MacGowan's cottage a bit over a week ago."

Chapter 11

Fresh fish and unwelcome visitors, stink before they are three days auld.
SCOTTISH PROVERB

The hairs on the back of Hugh's neck prickled. MacGowan hadn't mentioned any such visit, even though Hugh had told him of the customs men exploring the sand around the castle. "You think Pennycook knows we're free trading at Glenloch?"

"Weel, I wouldna know about that. But Sorcha thinks MacGowan fancies one of Pennycook's daughters."

"What?" Hugh asked, dismayed. His manager had to know better. Attention from any customs agent was not something to be encouraged.

"My wife's mother is seldom wrong. The woman hears everything," MacTavish said, scratching the back of his neck in bewilderment, "though I doona know how."

'Twas a chilling thought, though Hugh did not believe MacGowan would risk his own income by betraying the business to a customs agent. Perhaps he hoped to cull favor from the girl's father with bribes. Many a customs agent was known to accept inducements to turn a blind eye. And Pennycook was not one of the agents who had come to Glenloch today to search in the sand for illegal goods.

"Armstrong told me someone reported seeing a cutter in Glenloch's cove," he said.

"Aye," Tullis remarked. "Mayhap he's just pokin' where he thinks he might hit a vein."

"Actually, he's poking down at the beach even as we speak."

A young woman came to refill their glasses as the Scots muttered quiet curses of alarm under their breath. She was a pretty lass with wispy blond hair who looked up at Hugh with a promising flirtation in her eyes.

He could have her if he chose. When he finished with these men, he could accept her invitation and make his way to one of the upper rooms of the house. There, they could engage in a lusty interlude that would leave him . . .

Dissatisfied?

No, it could not be. The lass was a likely enough bed partner and Hugh's appetites were sufficiently healthy. He knew how to give as much pleasure as he took, and he prided himself on his stamina. If she was willing to give, then he was willing to take. But not today.

She leaned forward, and the bounty of her assets nearly overflowed the neckline of her gown. And yet Hugh felt not even the slightest stirring of desire.

He clenched his jaw and turned his attention to the matter of his brandy business. Once he got Brianna Munro away from Glenloch, he'd be free to return and sample the maiden's charms.

"Could there be an informer in Falkburn?" he asked.

"Ye jest, Laird," said Tullis. "With the pitiful harvest pulled in this autumn, no' a one of us can afford to lose our free-tradin' income."

"MacGowan's been bringing in his own crews to carry out the brandy," said MacTavish.

"And he's brought in batsmen from Stonehaven and Aberdeen," Tullis added. "Real thugs they are, too."

"Aye, a bad lot," MacTavish added.

"We've never needed batsmen before," said Hugh, disturbed by this news.

"Nae, and we still doona. Kincaid and his lot have never given us any serious attention."

Word of Hugh's presence in the public house must have spread, for soon a small crowd had gathered around him. As Tullis brought out a cask of brandy and began filling glasses, the men spoke of bad crops and the free-trade income they'd been counting on for their labors. They had no intrinsic right to Hugh's profits, but for three generations, the brandy trade had been a necessary supplement to their income. Hugh had not begrudged them fair pay for their work, but his neglect felt far too much like his father's disregard.

It would end now.

The men drank and told their tales of woe to their laird. Hugh kept up with the lot of them, drinking and half listening while he watched the barmaid tend tables. She was a sure thing. Her smiles were directed exclusively toward him, and he should have felt more than a mild interest. He should be roaring with lust at such a blatant invitation and take her to a private room even now, and have his way with her.

But Hugh's body was not cooperating. Clearly he'd had too much to drink. His speech started to slur and the floor began to ripple under his feet. 'Twas past time he returned to Glenloch to deal with Brianna Munro, for the room was swimming before his eyes.

"Laird," MacTavish said with a grin. "Are ye all right?"

"Fine. Jus' fine," Hugh said, pulling on his greatcoat with more awkwardness than he liked.

Taking MacTavish aside, he talked to him about distribution. "There's something I'm still not clear on. MacGowan tells me there's little profit to be made here in the Mearns."

"Laird, I canna believe any Scotsman's taste for brandy has faded in the past two or three years," MacTavish replied. "All we know is what MacGowan tells us."

"It used to be Falkburn men who carried our brandy out," said Hugh. "Who were they?"

"Guthrie, Currie, and MacLaren," he said, startling Hugh with the mention of the false name Brianna Munro had used. He staggered as the sudden image of her face . . . and her mouth . . . blazed through his brain. He turned to look at the barmaid, trying to dispel the memory of Brianna's enticing feminine scent and the taste of her pink-tipped nipples. He tried to avoid thinking of the particular sound she made when he was inside her, just before her climax. . .

But he failed miserably.

She was such an audacious woman, Hugh could

almost imagine her climbing into one of their wagons and driving the brandy herself to all the taverns across the Mearns. Her rough trews would tighten across her bottom as she pulled herself up, tempting him with the secrets of her luscious body.

When she looked down at him, her cheek would dimple with her intrepid smile, and she would pull her ugly hat down over her hair to obscure her femininity. As if that was even possible. He'd known she was a woman within seconds of encountering her.

Hugh let out a long breath and walked unsteadily to the door, his brain hazy and his gait wobbly. He had to find some way to eliminate his craving for Brianna Munro, and it wasn't going to happen through drink. For the brandy he'd consumed that afternoon had only made it worse.

He made a disparaging sound and took hold of MacTavish's arm. "Have th' men prepare to get their horses and carts ready," he said, his tongue thick with inebriation. "They can let down the brandy and take it ever' place that used t' buy from us."

If it turned out to be a catastrophe, it could hardly be any worse than hosting a viscount's very marriageable daughter alone at Glenloch.

It went against Brianna's nature to sit idly, and she found it next to impossible to wait patiently for Hugh's return.

To take her away.

Considering what he intended for her was almost as upsetting as it would be to return to Killiedown and wait for Lord Stamford to arrive. Hugh surely thought of himself as a gentleman, roué that he was, but Bree did not think he would take her back to her guardian as a gentleman ought to do. Given their circumstances, he would not want Lord Stamford to know they'd spent any time alone together.

But he would want her as far from Glenloch—and himself—as possible.

Dundee was still a likely destination, but as Brianna glanced out the window, she realized that it was getting late. Perhaps even too late to start out on a journey that was likely to take several hours, even when the roads were clear. It meant another night at Glenloch.

No doubt Hugh would want to leave first thing in the morning. Brianna could not imagine what he intended to do with her, once they arrived at their destination. He might find her a room somewhere and leave her there with enough money to survive. Or possibly pass her on to a friend or acquaintance and ask them to look after her.

Her temper flared at the thought of either option. Neither he nor any other man had the right to dictate what she would do once she left Glenloch. And if she wanted to leave without him, it was her own concern and none of his. She could go any time she wished, without waiting for permission from him or anyone else.

Still wearing the old, worn clothes she'd arrived in, she hastened down to the study where the old laird's portrait glared down upon the room, and went to the desk. She pulled open the top drawer and looked down at the money box Hugh had shown her. She was well past the days when anyone could claim authority over her and shift her from one household to another, ridding themselves of her when she became inconvenient.

The Laird of Glenloch owed her money. It was just a few shillings, to be sure, and not enough to survive on. But he'd offered her as much as she wanted. There was no reason that she shouldn't take it now and go.

Except that her dratted conscience wouldn't allow it. Tears of frustration burned the backs of her eyes and she rubbed them away, turning to the window to compose herself. The sea was fairly calm and the customs men were gone. There was nothing to keep her there, nothing but Hugh's order . . . as well as her lack of transportation and the weather.

Movement in one of the windows caught Bree's attention and she turned in time to catch sight of Hugh, walking his horse to the stable. He seemed unsteady on his feet, and since Brianna did not know where he'd been all day, she felt a twinge of worry, of concern that something was seriously amiss.

The servants were already gone for the day, so there was no one to see to him. No one to deal with whatever was wrong with Hugh. Brianna pulled up her collar and held her coat tightly around her. She made her way to the door closest to the stable and stepped outside. The MacTavish boys had shoveled paths earlier in the day, so she followed one of them across the expansive bailey until she reached the stable doors.

It was nearly dusk, which contributed to the deep darkness inside. Brianna stood still for a moment, allowing her eyes to adjust. "Laird Glenloch?"

She heard a crash.

"Hugh?" she called, running forward.

He groaned, and she almost tripped over him on the straw-strewn ground. "What's wrong? Are you hurt?" she asked as she crouched down beside him and reached for him.

"Ever'thing's wrong." He sounded odd.

"Where does it hurt?"

He grabbed her hand and pressed it to his chest. "Here."

Panic welled in Brianna's chest at the possibility of a serious injury. "Let me get a lamp so I can see," she cried.

She started to rise, but he would not release her hand. Instead, he pulled her sprawling down onto him.

"This can't be good— What are you doing?" she demanded as he slid one arm around her and trapped her against him.

She pushed against his chest, but he was much stronger, even in his incapacity. "Come to me, lass."

"What? You are not hurt?"

"I want you, Miss Munro." His speech was slurred.

"You're drunk!"

"Verily. Come 'ere."

Tears gathered in her eyes as she straddled him and felt his potent arousal. He did not really want her. 'Twas only the liquor muddling his brain and doing his talking, for he'd been quite clear about his contempt for her.

"No. You need to get off this cold floor and into the—"

He moved suddenly, coming up to capture her lips

with his own, and she was powerless to resist. She felt a tear course down her cheek as she opened for him and felt his tongue seeking hers. This changed naught, for as soon as he was sober again, he would remember that he wanted her gone.

Which was exactly what Brianna wanted. She had always meant for her time at Glenloch, and everything that had passed between her and Hugh, to be temporary. Less than temporary. But as he kissed her as though the world would crumble if he could not get closer to her, she melted against him.

He broke the kiss and started nuzzling her neck, pulling the edges of her coat apart to kiss her throat. Shifting her position, he slid lower and pulled her shirt out of her trews, then took her breasts in his hands. "Ah, God," he murmured.

And Bree was powerless to do anything but let him touch her, let him draw her into the sensual haze he created. It was just this last time, she told herself. Tomorrow she would go, and never look back.

He took one of her nipples into his mouth and sucked, drawing a cry of pleasure from her. Bree lowered herself down and skimmed her fingers to the fastenings of his trews. She opened them and drew him out, savoring the steely heat of his erection. He felt like part of her already, but Bree wanted him inside her, wanted to feel the pleasure that hard length could give her.

Hugh tried to disrobe her, but failed miserably. Brianna did it herself, glad of his thick coat beneath them and the straw insulation on the ground. She hardly noticed the cold air that whirled up, under her coat.

She shivered, and he cupped her buttocks in his warm hands, plunging deeply into her. "Yes," he said quietly, shuddering as he started moving in a way that assured pleasure for both of them.

Brianna's breath caught, but she tamped down the weight of emotion that rose up in her chest. Keeping control was the only way to protect herself from the anguish of leaving.

She moved with him, oblivious to her own sighs of sweet satisfaction while he teased and tormented her with the ebb and flow of his body. Their pace quickened, and she quivered with the intensity of their joining. She let her mind go empty of everything but the contact between them, the bond she would never again share.

Hugh's head was pounding. He opened his eyes a crack, and the light coming in through the windows blistered his eyeballs. *What the hell was wrong?* He turned slightly and saw a mussed blond head right beside him.

Jesus, what had he done?

Not gotten Brianna Munro out of his life, obviously. *Good God.*

At the very moment he had customs men breathing down his neck and the presence of Brianna Munro jeopardizing his carefree life, he'd been sufficiently lackwitted to spend his afternoon dipping much too deeply into Tullis's brandy. For God's sake, he'd become ape-drunk instead of returning to the castle and spiriting Brianna away.

He vaguely remembered his inauspicious return, riding into the stable and half falling from his horse. Brianna must have seen him wobbling. She'd gone out to help him, and he'd actually pulled her down to the floor of the stable with him. Even in a stupor, he'd wanted her. What a bungling fool he'd been.

Thoroughly disgusted with his reckless, barbaric behavior—his actions dramatically undermining his true intentions—Hugh slipped out of the bed and stood stock-still while a vicious wave of nausea passed. He went to the washstand and bathed his face in the cool water, then braced his hands on the wooden stand at either side of the basin.

What a disaster.

The bed creaked and he steadfastly avoided looking in that direction. Some of yesterday's anger returned, and he cultivated it as he picked up a towel and dried his face. She'd known he wanted to be rid of her and yet she allowed—

Christ, he'd taken her on the stable floor.

He heard her slide to the edge of the bed and sit up. "I'll be ready to go as soon as I'm dressed."

He did not turn to her or even reply to her statement. Remaining at the washstand, he listened to her gather her things and leave the room.

Only then did he allow himself a shaky sigh. Brianna Munro was not the one who'd been foxed when he returned from Falkburn. Dash it all, she could have—*should have*—stopped his advances, could have left him to his own devices in the stable and returned to the castle without him.

He muttered another curse and dragged on some clothes. The inside of his head felt as though a band of crazed tinkers were pounding furiously to get out. He could barely remember what had happened with Brianna, so of course he didn't know if MacTavish and the Falkburn men had come into the castle and prepared his brandy for shipment as planned. He tamped down another burst of nausea at the thought of the potent liquor, and realized he did not know exactly where he was going to take Brianna.

Dundee was where she'd wanted to go, and he tried to remember whether he had any connections there . . . decent people who would take her in and keep their mouths shut. There had to be someone. Or perhaps in Kirkaldy.

He pulled on his boots and left his bedchamber, just as Brianna came out of the nursery. She said naught, and kept her eyes down as they met at the top of the stairs. He went to take her arm, but she avoided his touch.

He grumbled under his breath as they descended to the landing and stopped when they heard voices and stomping feet just inside the main entrance. Hugh looked across the expanse of the main entry, and wished someone would just pull out a pistol and shoot him. Or that Glenloch's ghost would come and drag him away to the netherworld so feared by the servants.

For coming into his own private refuge were Viscount Stamford and the Marquess of Roddington, who stood suddenly still when they caught sight of the woman beside him.

Chapter 12

A guilty conscience self accuses.
SCOTTISH PROVERB

Hugh did not think his emotions could have become any more raw, but when he saw Stamford standing there, he felt as though he'd fallen headfirst into a black pit of doom. There was no possible way to avoid the man now. And by the expression on his face, Hugh knew he'd already caught sight of his ward.

An appalling thought shuddered through his mind, and he spoke to Brianna under his breath. "I'll be damned. Do not tell me Roddington is your fiancé."

Brianna did not answer him, and when he looked down at her, she seemed to have shrunk into her coat and hat as though it might be an effective manner in which to hide from her guardian and the mangy blackguard who stood beside him.

Dash it, he hated seeing her appear so vulnerable, hated knowing that Roddington must have committed—and been caught at—some reprehensible act that compelled him to marry her.

"Bloody hell," said Stamford, his face a mask of raw surprise. "If it ain't the prime article herself!"

"Eh? What?" Roddington asked, tossing his hat to Mrs. Ramsay.

"Your little bloody whore," Stamford said, holding his gaze on Brianna. "Surprised the chit isn't up at Killiedown, hiding behind the Dougal woman's skirts."

Hugh's hand fisted in her sleeve at Stamford's words. "Go back upstairs," he said to her.

She hesitated, and he could feel her indecision, radiating off her like a wave. He hoped she was not considering trying to run away now. "I'll deal with this."

She finally complied, and when she was halfway up the steps, Hugh started toward Stamford and Roddington. If only he had taken Brianna away the day before, rather than delaying in Falkburn and allowing himself to become inebriated, he would not be facing this mess today.

Now he was trapped.

"Newbury," said Stamford. "I see you are . . . *in possession* of my ward."

Roddington said naught, but the smirk on his face spoke volumes. Hugh considered his best strategy, but telling Stamford Brianna had just arrived at Glenloch— implying they had not spent any solitary time together— meant he would be throwing her to the worst kind of wolf in all of Britain, a man just like Jasper. In any case, they were unlikely to believe such a story, given the condition of the roads.

"How did you manage to travel in this?" he asked.

"We were not far. Heading for Killiedown Manor,

but got delayed in Johnshaven," Stamford replied, removing his gloves as they met midway. "But there is some urgency to our search for Miss Munro."

Hugh crossed his arms over his chest and kept his face expressionless as he tried to figure some way to keep Brianna from Roddington for two measly months. If he could just spirit her away somewhere . . .

The roads being what they were, that was going to prove difficult, if not impossible. Stamford and Roddington might have managed to get from Johnshaven to Glenloch, but it couldn't have been easy. Which meant that Stamford was desperate.

"What's the urgency?" he asked.

"The little cow is meant to marry Roddington," he said with indignation. "She humiliated us all by absconding on the morning of the wedding."

Hugh suppressed a grudging smile. "Absconding?"

"She ran away in the dark of night," said Stamford.

As she was wont to do, Hugh mused with a contradictorily admiring disapproval. She was nothing if not daring. "Are you saying she never arrived at the church?"

Stamford let out a low, condemnatory sound, but did not answer, leading Hugh to believe that that was exactly what had happened. Brianna had managed to escape Stamford's house and leave London before anyone knew she'd gone. He didn't know whether to congratulate her or throttle her. London was a seriously dangerous place after dark, especially for an unescorted woman.

Roddington moved to the fireplace in the drawing

room as though he were an honored guest in Glenloch's hall, with no interest in the dull conversation that would determine Brianna's fate. Hugh had not seen him since Jasper's death, nearly three years before.

It had been jarring to see the indolent bastard at the graveside, one of the few who'd attended the funeral. No other members of Jasper's contemptible Cerberus Club had attended, and Hugh had wondered about Roddington's presence there. The marquess had never cared about anything but his own pleasures, his own plots and games. It made little sense for the bastard to have bothered attending services for a man whose own son would have preferred to avoid them.

Yet it should not have surprised Hugh to see Roddington there. The man had been hand in glove with Jasper in those days, closer even than old school chums, despite their age difference. They'd belonged to a despicable club whose members engaged in a level of debauchery that made Hugh cringe even now, not that he was any sort of prig. But he had an aversion to activities that took advantage of those who could not fend for themselves. Jasper had made great sport of that.

The thought of what Roddington might have done to Brianna to result in their engagement turned Hugh's stomach, and he would have liked nothing better than to toss the two rascals out on their arses. But that was no solution to the problem.

Hugh followed Stamford into the drawing room where Roddington already stood warming his arse by the fire. The man was little more than ten years older than Hugh, but he had aged badly since Hugh had seen him last. He looked closer to fifty than forty, a decidedly sad dog. 'Twas no wonder Brianna had absented herself from the church and run, even if she did not know about her fiancé's involvement with the Cerberus Club. Frowning, he wondered how her aunt's death had figured into her flight.

'Twas likely Brianna, bold as she was, had gone to Lady Claire for her protection, because she would be powerless to stand up against Stamford and Roddington alone. Hugh clenched his teeth together. Stamford would have bullied her, and Roddington would have—

Christ, if the bastard had touched her—

"You've had a pretty time of it, eh, Christie?" Roddington asked, using Hugh's surname rather than his title.

He stepped away from the fire and Hugh scowled, his mood turning deadly. "What do you mean?"

"All alone with the curvy little Munro doxy," he taunted. But Hugh was going to keep his anger in check, no matter what the marquess said, no matter what he suspected the brute must have done.

"I want an accounting, Newbury," Stamford demanded. "And so does Roddington—the, er, injured party."

"Lud," Roddington muttered, turning to glower at the viscount. "I'm out of it now, Stamford. Soiled goods and all that. Don't have to marry the chit now."

"*What?* We've come all the—" Stamford threw his hands up in the air, then turned and shot an angry glare at Hugh. "'Tis *your* doing, Newbury! And *you* will wed her!"

A lethal rage simmered just below Hugh's deceptively calm surface, and when he spoke, his voice was low and dangerous. "You are deranged, Stamford."

Who was this flea-minted viscount to demand anything—much less Hugh's freedom? Hugh had no intention of becoming shackled in any way, to anyone. He could not possibly be held responsible for his actions with a woman who claimed she had no connections, who'd actually needed his protection . . .

Hugh berated himself for allowing lust to cloud his judgment, seducing a virgin who would hardly know what was happening to her until it was too late. Christ, she'd been an innocent, his father's typical victim of choice, someone who didn't have the experience necessary to understand the consequences of her actions.

It was a small comfort that he hadn't tied her in leather bindings against her will, or fed her any opium to make her compliant, the way Jasper and his cronies had been known to do.

But it did not alter the fact that he had made love to a viscount's virgin daughter.

Hugh did not remember ever feeling so furious or so powerless. He wanted to throttle Stamford for what he'd planned for Brianna, and then wring his neck for even suggesting that Hugh recant his bachelor's vow.

"Send someone for the vicar," Stamford said, his voice low and resolute.

"You give no orders here, Viscount," Hugh said in a deprecating tone, intentionally citing Stamford's lower rank. "Nor are we in England."

"What? Oh. Yes, well, this may be Scotland, but if

you refuse to wed the gel, you'll never be able to show
your face in London, boy," Stamford said. "Your reputation will be in shreds."

No more than Brianna's.

Hugh's blood turned to a roiling cauldron of disgust.
The walls seemed to close in, and it felt as though the
air was being sucked out of the room. Between the
nausea and his aching head, he could hardly breathe.
He was too preoccupied by his fury to notice Roddington stepping away, wandering in what seemed to be an
aimless manner to the other side of the room.

No man would ever wed Brianna if Stamford let
it be known that she had spent days and nights alone
with him—with a man of his reputation—at Glenloch.
She might think she wanted to remain unmarried, only
to retire alone to Killiedown, but she was young. Her
hopes and aspirations would surely change, as would
her need for a man's attentions.

For Hugh knew that Brianna Munro was not a woman
who could ever be content with a solitary, celibate life.

Society was not about to accept a "ruined" woman
into its midst. The ton would be absolutely correct in assuming that she'd been intimate with him, and it would
destroy her life. Her friends would shun her, and she
would never again be invited into respectable homes.
Her future would be bleak.

He jabbed his fingers through his hair and turned
away from Stamford, catching sight of Roddington
starting up the staircase.

"*Hold, Roddington, if you value your life!*" Hugh
turned back to Stamford, the only possible decision

made. "Go down to Inverbervie and take rooms there for the night. Miss Munro and I will wed on the morrow. Here at Glenloch. Noon."

"What about the aunt?" said Stamford. "You'll need to send someone for her."

"That won't be necessary," Hugh said without offering any further explanation. The fewer questions and even fewer answers, the better.

Hugh stood fast in the main entryway and watched as the two reprobates gathered their coats, gloves, and hats, and left the castle. Then he went down to the corridor near the scullery, where he jammed his own arms through the sleeves of his greatcoat and slammed out one of the rear doors of the building. He headed for the stable, to the scene of yesterday's drunken blunder.

Brianna's knees gave out, and she sat right down on the floor at the top of the stairs. If Roddington's approach on the first step of the staircase had not been enough to stun her, Hugh's words had done it. In one breath, he'd both thwarted Roddington from coming after her and committed himself to marrying her.

She felt light-headed and shaky, even as indignation coursed through her. Who had given Hugh Christie leave to decide her fate? He had not asked her opinion or her preferences, making the decision as though she was naught but a speck of dust on the banister.

Feeling as wobbly as a new colt, she rose to her feet and stood, her thoughts flying madly. She had no intention of acquiescing to their demands—to *any* of them. Laird Glenloch was just as overbearing and unreasonable as Stamford. He was a man, which caused him to believe he had the right to dictate every aspect of her life. *How dare he?*

She descended the stairs and went to his study. The money box still sat in the drawer where she left it when she'd gone out to him in the stable the day before. When he'd staggered in, Brianna hadn't considered the possibility that he was drunk, or that he would ravish her willing body in the stable. He'd been insatiable, even after they'd returned to the castle, finally collapsing only a few hours before dawn.

He'd bedded her again, even after learning who she was. He should have stayed sober and taken her to Dundee instead!

She estimated what she would need for food and a modest lodging for two months in Perth. Going to Dundee was just inviting Laird Glenloch to come and find her, and she did not want to see him ever again, not when his intention was to trap them in a marriage they would both abhor.

Her chin trembled, but now was no time for tears. She'd learned long ago how to protect her heart, how to wall off her emotions. Laird Glenloch didn't want her any more than Bernard Malham had. Less, even, by the sound of his grudging commitment to marry her.

She did not belong at Castle Glenloch any more than she had fit in at Stamford House. Killiedown was the only place Bree had ever been able to call home. Claire had suspended her own exciting travels to create a life there for Brianna. Together, they'd built up the farm and their breeding program. Killiedown's draft horses were unequaled in all of Britain. She and Claire had been completely happy.

And yet Claire had sent her to London for three seasons.

You deserve a chance for a husband and your own family to love, Claire had said the night before their departure for that first London season. But Brianna had dismissed her words, certain her aunt had been mistaken. Claire had been perfectly content without a husband—

But had she?

Brianna wondered if Claire would have wed her free-trading captain if he'd asked. She considered the possibility that her aunt would have preferred a husband in her bed to a lover she visited occasionally in Aberdeen, a man she'd had to keep secret from her niece and all her tenants.

Brianna sat down in Hugh's chair. Dropping her chin to her chest in misery, she tried to understand what was so bloody brilliant about having a husband. And yet she knew, somehow. A husband should be the man who warmed not only her bed . . . he should warm her heart and her soul. A husband would provide companionship, and children, and a clear sense of belonging. To some-one. *With* someone.

It was possible that Claire's own experience had been the reason she'd insisted that Bree go to London. Per-haps she regretted her own lack of a mate, and wanted to be sure that Brianna did not suffer the same lack.

It hurt Brianna to think it might be true, and that she might have missed signs of her aunt's restlessness. It seemed so very clear that Claire had given up her lover in Greece, and now Brianna realized her aunt had limited her contact with the sea captain to make sure her niece was content at Killiedown.

Would it be a mistake for Brianna to do the same thing, just to keep her independence at Killiedown? Marriage to Hugh would not provide any of the warmth or companionship Claire had wanted for her. It would be a marriage of *inconvenient* convenience, for she knew his thoughts on marrying again. He did not want another wife.

She stood abruptly and tried to decide what to do. Traveling to Perth on snow-covered roads would be arduous, and Brianna did not believe she could get there—or hide somewhere en route—before Hugh discovered she was gone and came after her. He'd stated his intention to marry her, and she did not believe he would easily renege on his word.

With the portrait of Hugh's father at her back, Brianna had the most disconcerting feeling that he was looking directly at her. Wondering if Hugh had ever felt this eerie sensation, Bree turned slowly toward him, and faced the old laird's harsh visage.

His gaze was nothing like his son's, the lines about his mouth and eyes self-indulgent at the least, with a hint of wickedness in them. "You do not frighten me, Laird," she whispered. "Not even with your leather strips and the whip you kept in the master's bedchamber."

She turned her back on the portrait and fixed her gaze on the window where she'd seen Hugh the day before.

He was there now, coming out of the stable on horse-back. He was tall and formidable in his seat—so different from the way he'd looked the day before—his shoulders broad, his greatcoat spread out behind him. A shudder of pure physical awareness shot through Brianna as she watched him. His eyes were shaded by his hat, but she had the distinct feeling he could see her through the window.

He turned abruptly, handling the gelding with mastery and care as he kicked his heels and plodded through the snow in the direction of Falkburn, no doubt to get drunk again.

Chapter 13

They that dance must pay the fiddler.
SCOTTISH PROVERB

There was no need for Hugh to make the hour-long ride to Stonehaven for a lawyer to draw up a marriage certificate. MacGowan handled all the rest of Glenloch's business, and the man was perfectly capable of making a document that Hugh and Brianna could sign when it was done.

He rode up to MacGowan's cottage and quickly gained entry.

"Laird, I hope all is well," the man said as Hugh entered. "The brandy—"

"I took care of it, MacGowan. I'm here on an entirely different matter." Hugh did not remove his coat, but told the man what he wanted, then turned his back to the window of the parlor while MacGowan wrote the marriage lines according to his wishes. There would be no reading of banns, no special license. Here in Scotland, they only needed witnesses to their declaration. Mrs. Ramsay and her son-in-law, Niall MacTavish, would do.

He and Brianna would exchange vows at noon the following day, which would give Stamford and Rodding-ton enough time to arrive and witness the marriage's validity. Fortunately, there were far fewer formalities and much less fanfare than he'd have had to endure in England. A veritable leg-shackling was easy enough to accomplish north of the border. Once done, he would send the two reprobates on their way, far from Glenloch. And with luck, they would never cross his path again.

"Laird," MacGowan said as he waited for the ink to dry, "I thought ye'd vowed nev—" He took note of Hugh's obdurate expression and changed his tack. "Will ye be stayin' at Glenloch fer the winter, then?"

"I haven't decided." There was no point in letting MacGowan in on his plans, especially when those plans included finding out how the man was cheating him.

When the document was ready, MacGowan rolled it and tied it with a simple piece of string. Hugh clenched his teeth and eyed the thing, his fate sealed.

He led his horse down the short path to Falkburn, then stopped at MacTavish's cottage. The door opened on his arrival, and Niall stepped outside. "Laird," he said. "We missed seein' ye last night, down in the buttery."

"Er, too much brandy at Tullis's."

MacTavish gave a rueful grin. "Aye. I'm feelin' fair jug-bitten m'self."

"Is the brandy set to be transported?"

"No' yet, Laird. We let down maybe half."

Hugh nodded. "We can finish it tonight." He didn't want to keep so much brandy about, especially with Kincaid so interested in probing the area.

"Aye, Laird," he replied. "We'll be there.

"One last thing, MacTavish. I'd like you to come up to Glenloch tomorrow morning."

"Laird?"

"To witness my wedding."

Turning abruptly to mount his horse, Hugh took no notice of MacTavish's astonished expression. And since he'd dealt with his reasons for coming into Falkburn, he had no reason to delay his return to Glenloch—and his future wife—any further. He muttered a silent curse at the way his body reacted to the thought of her, and his vivid memory of the way her smooth skin slid against his. He should be thinking about throttling her, not bedding her.

Brianna could not escape the sensation of being trapped. She'd run from one objectionable marriage only to land in another.

And yet 'twas not quite the same situation. Hugh was not at all repulsive, as Roddington was. The thought of his touch, of sharing his bed, of bearing his children, did not make her freeze up with distaste. It heated her from the inside out, in spite of his obvious displeasure in the situation.

Bree took satisfaction that her marriage to Hugh would not benefit Stamford in the way he'd intended to profit from a liaison with Roddington's family. Far from it. Brianna doubted there would ever be any courtesy from Hugh toward Stamford, although her guardian would not realize that yet. No doubt he believed Hugh was much like himself and most every other man of the ton, who could be intimidated and then manipulated.

But Brianna had little doubt that Hugh was unlike anyone with whom Stamford had ever dealt.

It was little comfort, though. His opposition to marriage had not changed, yet he would soon be bound to Brianna in a way he'd never intended.

Nor had she. But she knew it was inevitable.

She'd given up on her thoughts of taking some of his money and running away again. Retreating to the nursery that felt like her own sanctuary, she hooked her thumbs into her trews and started pacing. Her fate was unavoidable, but she had no intention of presenting herself as a pathetic, unappealing bride. She was going to show Laird Glenloch—show them all—that the soon-to-be Lady Glenloch was no longer anyone's poor relation.

Ignoring the filmy wisp that hovered near the door of her room, she marched down the hall to Amelia's bedchamber, carrying a lamp with her. She opened the door and stepped inside, finding the room nearly as cold as the temperature must be outside.

Ignoring the chill as well as the wisp of a ghost that was now hovering near the bed, Brianna went to Amelia's wardrobe and started going through the clothes she'd overlooked before. She remembered seeing gowns for every season, each one more elaborate than the next. In the drawers were lace chemises and delicate hosiery. Bree found gloves and hair ornaments and jars of fine cosmetics.

She picked a gown of gros de Naples in azure blue, with white fur trim bordering the deep neckline and cuffs. A scalloped flounce of white fur danced a few inches from the skirt's hem, and tiny, pearl buttons marched in two decorative rows from the center of the neckline to either side of her waist, bracketing her breasts.

The second wardrobe held shoes and outerwear. Coats and pelisses lay on the shelves, each folded neatly, with tissue paper and rose-scented sachets among the folds, just as though Amelia would soon return.

Brianna was loath to dismiss the woman or her woes, but after tomorrow, there would be only one Lady Glenloch present in Hugh's mind and memory.

She tried some of Amelia's shoes, but none fit her well enough to wear. Admitting defeat on that front, she borrowed the prettiest chemise, the finest stockings she'd ever seen, and a pair of garters, then left the room and went in search of a competent needlewoman. Or two.

'Twas nearly noon, and Hugh had not seen Brianna since the previous day, when he'd declared his intent to wed her. He knew she was still in the castle, for she'd been closeted with Mrs. Ramsay and one of the maids all the past evening, and again through the morn.

The marriage document lay upon a highly polished table in the library, safe inside Hugh's richly tooled leather portfolio, but he avoided looking at it. Soon enough, the time would come when he'd be compelled to sign it.

"Laird, I've been told yer lady kept my wife's mother and Fiona busy up here after dark last night," said Niall

MacTavish, standing next to Hugh in the library, his hat off, and wearing his best coat. "'Tis a wonder they stayed to prepare the lady's gown, what wi' the Glenloch Ghost about."

The library was one of the few formal rooms in which Hugh's father's portrait did not stare out at him with those malicious eyes.

He and Brianna could have exchanged vows anywhere, even at the stable, or down by the tub boats on the beach. But this room had always been Hugh's haven at Glenloch. His father had eschewed the books here, making it the perfect retreat. And it was the location where Hugh and Brianna had shared the most intense sensual experience of his life. 'Twould help him to keep in mind the prime advantage of marriage to Brianna Munro.

"Aye. I was as surprised as you," he said to Niall.

"Sorcha said yer lady insisted on being prepared as a proper bride. She convinced them they had naught to fear from the ghost."

Hugh did not bother to disabuse Niall or any of the servants about the ghost, for it had always served Glenloch well to have tales of the ghost widely believed. He clasped his hands behind his back and stared straight ahead, hardly able to believe this was happening to him. He'd done everything in his power to avoid remarriage, and yet here he stood, obligated by one of the most debauched Englishmen and his toadying cohort to yet another arranged marriage.

He had not wanted a marriage of any sort, arranged or otherwise. But at least this way, Roddington would never have Brianna. Stamford was a fool and a bastard for promising Brianna to the marquess, and Hugh barely suppressed a shudder at the thought of that debauched scoundrel touching her.

Hugh heard voices at the main entrance and knew Stamford had arrived. "MacTavish, would you go and ask Mrs. Ramsay to see what's keeping the bride? You might as well bring Stamford and Roddington back to the library with you when you return."

As Niall MacTavish left the room, Hugh rubbed one hand over his freshly shaven face. He smoothed back his hair, straightened his neck cloth, then his waistcoat and coat. Feeling more restless—Christ, more *nervous*—than he had in years, he stepped out of the library to see for himself what was delaying Brianna.

At that moment, his bride started down the stairs with Sorcha Ramsay and one of the housemaids following close behind her.

Hugh's breath caught at the sight of her, an enchantress from some made-up tale. She wore a gown of ice blue, with an enticing neckline accented by a trimming of soft, white fur. Cunning little buttons progressed from the cleft between her breasts down to her waist, creating what would surely make a very interesting opening. Later.

She'd done something simple and elegant to her hair, and a faint sparkle flashed from some tiny ornaments she'd placed strategically in her pale locks. Her skin was flawless, her lips moist and pink, and a few curling wisps of her hair touched her ears and the nape of her neck. Hugh felt a tightening in his groin at the thought of pressing his lips to those places. Of tasting her.

She descended the staircase regally, barely looking at him as she arrived at the foot of the staircase and placed her hand on his, to venture into the library beside him. Mrs. Ramsay and her son-in-law followed them, and soon everyone was assembled in the library. Stamford and Ramsay took seats near the chess table, while Mac-Tavish came to stand beside Hugh.

Just as Hugh was about to begin, Malcolm MacGowan arrived, uninvited and unannounced.

"Laird." The estate manager came to the doorway, carrying the free-trade ledger. Hugh stifled his annoyance and opened his own leather-bound portfolio, removing the thick sheaf of vellum on which the manager had written Hugh's vows.

"Come in then," Hugh said to MacGowan. "Just another witness."

Hugh returned to Brianna and faced her. He'd read the simple words often enough last night while pondering his fate, so he was able to speak them without referring to the vellum. In simple terms, he took her as his wife and gave himself as her husband. He made no additional promises.

When it was Brianna's turn, she started to speak, but stopped to clear her throat. Then she looked up at him, and the bottom fell out of Hugh's stomach. Her eyes were twin mirrors of his own feelings at the moment—betrayal and hurt, resignation and a hint of defiance. When she spoke, her voice was clear, and loud enough for all to hear.

"I, Brianna Elizabeth Munro, take you, Hugh

Dùghlas Christie, as my husband." Her throat and neck were unadorned, but she could not have looked more dignified or noble. Her bare skin was exquisite, and he knew how soft it felt beneath his rough hands. She looked up at him, but turned her gaze slightly, to some point past his shoulder, as she spoke, as though she could not bear to face him.

She moistened her lips and continued. "Before God and these witnesses I vow to take you as my husband with all your faults and all your strengths, as I offer myself to you as wife, with my own imperfections as well as my skills . . ." She took a deep breath, as though she needed some fortification to say the words. ". . . from . . . from this day forward."

His knees went rubbery when he listened to her short speech, so much more profound than his own, and spoken without reference to any notes. He swallowed hard at the magnitude of her vow.

He knew better than most that there was no guarantee of happiness or satisfaction, and he wondered if Brianna Munro's indomitable spirit could withstand the truth of his inadequacy. This marriage would fail, too, for he did not know how to give a wife the kind of attention she craved. Worst of all, he would never give her children, never give her true contentment.

All were silent for a moment. Not a sound broke the stillness of the room until the fire cracked and sparked loudly. Then Hugh remembered the ring.

He reached into his waistcoat pocket and took out the golden circle of alternating diamonds and garnets he'd found among his mother's possessions when she died.

He'd never seen fit to give it to Amelia, but he wanted Brianna to wear it.

He took her hand in his and slid it onto her finger, then lifted her hand and pressed his lips to its back. "A gift for you, wife."

She took a shuddering breath and blinked back tears, still not looking at him. They were tears of regret, most likely, but she whispered a polite thanks while Roddington muttered a few deprecating words that were just barely audible in the quiet room.

Hugh spoke. "You've worn out your welcome, Roddington."

"I'm just as glad to be rid of the chit," he drawled, stretching his legs out before him, "but you ought to try to avoid losing another wife the way you lost—"

"Shut up, Roddington," Stamford rasped, aware that Hugh could very well call him out for such a remark.

Hugh chose to ignore it, for the day was bad enough without adding violence to it. He walked to the desk and took a pen and bottle of ink from a drawer. Sliding it across the desk to Mrs. Ramsay, he handed the pen to MacTavish. The two witnesses affixed their rough signatures to the document, then Brianna and Hugh signed, and all the legalities were met.

Hugh carefully placed it, along with the sheaf with his own vows, into the leather brief.

It was done. He was a husband again.

Brianna did not delude herself into thinking Hugh cared anything for her beyond his enjoyment of her in bed. His eyes had darkened at Roddington's words, but fortunately, he had not acted upon them. For her emotions already seemed to be teetering on the edge of a bleak abyss, and she didn't think she could bear one more ordeal.

Twirling the stunning ring Hugh had given her around her finger, Bree knew she had just become his possession. She had given up her right to an independent life, her right to her inheritance. By law, Hugh would become owner and master of Killiedown Manor. Nothing belonged to a wife, unless some special provision was made by her father or guardian. She was quite sure Lord Stamford had done no such thing.

It was a struggle for Brianna to stay on her feet and keep a mask of neutrality on her face while Hugh ushered her guardian and former fiancé out of the room. From what she could hear, he was practically tossing them out of the castle, promising to do the marquess some damage if he ever returned.

"M'lady, my good wishes to ye," Mr. MacTavish said warmly with a quick bow.

She felt no such warmth from the other man—the beefy estate manager who'd been so rough with her the night they'd unloaded Hugh's brandy shipment. Brianna doubted he'd have added his own good wishes had MacTavish not done so before leaving. But they were boorish, at best.

"Ach, lass, ye look fashed," said Mrs. Ramsay, who'd not only removed her ubiquitous apron, she'd combed her hair and worn a very good dress for the occasion. Two things that had not changed were her stern features and her authoritative manner. "Come and sit here while

I get you a draught of something to restore ye."

Brianna allowed herself to be led by Mrs. Ramsay's steady hand to the sofa near the fire, while Mr. MacTavish poured her a glass of brandy. "I'm sure the laird will return shortly," he said, "and then ye'll feel better."

Perhaps, but Brianna doubted it.

"Drink up lass, er . . . m'lady," said Mrs. Ramsay.

She took a sip, and the liquor burned her tongue and all the way down her throat. She told herself that the tears that filled her eyes were merely due to the strong brandy she was unaccustomed to drinking. She blinked them away and found herself perusing every corner of the room, all the places where Hugh had made love to her.

And she wondered how long Castle Glenloch would be her home.

Hugh's free-trading business might keep him in Scotland until spring. But then what? Would he expect her to remain at Glenloch after he tired of her and returned to his usual pursuits in London?

A sickening weight settled in the pit of her stomach at the thought of Hugh resuming his roguish life in town. If she believed every bit of gossip she'd ever heard about him, he had a mistress or two down in London who would be awaiting his return.

"The ring you wear belonged to the laird's mother," said Mrs. Ramsay when they were alone.

Brianna curbed her glum thoughts and looked up at the housekeeper. "Did you know her well?"

"She didna spend much time at Glenloch," the woman replied with a brief shake of her head. "Like the rest of us, she didna like hearin' the ghost."

"What of Laird Glenloch's wife?" she asked, addressing the question she had burned to ask as they'd worked on her wedding dress. "Did you know her?"

The woman's brows creased together and she clasped her hands at her waist. "No, m'lady. I doona think anyone really knew her. She was a quiet one. Kept to herself."

Brianna wanted to ask for details about Amelia and the day she'd jumped to her death, but it seemed much too awkward to speak of, and the housekeeper did not seem inclined to discuss it. "'Tis very sad."

"Aye," said Mrs. Ramsay. "Will there be anything else?"

"Thank you, no," Bree replied as she stood. She felt steadier now, and went to the table where her marriage lines lay inside a beautiful leather folder. Opening it, she looked at the words that bound her to Hugh and to Glenloch, and at the signatures that made it all legal in Scotland. 'Twas final.

Startled at the sound of Hugh's voice right behind her, she whirled around to face him.

"We might have avoided all this had you been honest with me from the start," he said.

The anger she'd anticipated and managed to avoid all the previous day was clear in his tone.

"You are not the only one who is trapped, Laird Glenloch."

He gazed at her, his eyes so dark, his cheeks slightly flushed, and yet the scar on his cheek seemed blanched white. "Just so. But I made a perfectly unsatisfactory spouse the first time around." He reached behind her and closed the portfolio. "Do not expect any improvement this time."

He took the documents and strode out of the room.

If he were in London, Hugh would have gone to his sporting club and challenged someone to a boxing match. Striking out in the ring would be the only way to rid himself of the wild-eyed frustration that permeated every pore of his body. Naught but a colossal beating—either given or taken—could dispel the degree of dissatisfaction he felt.

And the fear.

He walked up to his bedchamber and placed the portfolio inside a drawer in his wardrobe, underneath his clean shirts. He did not want to look at it for a very long time, if ever again. So much for his vow of permanent bachelorhood. He was married now to Brianna Munro, and naught could change that. He'd become responsible for her, just as he'd been responsible for Amelia.

He did not see how this could work out well for either of them.

He changed out of the clothes he'd worn during their brief but all-too-final marriage ceremony, and left the room. Amelia's door was ajar again, and he stepped across the hall to close it, deciding all at once that he was going to have it cleared out—Amelia's furniture and all her belongings removed, once and for all.

He pushed open the door and looked inside. A few of Amelia's dresses lay in disarray upon the bed, likely from Brianna's search for something she could tailor to fit her. He wished she had chosen something less appealing than the azure confection she'd worn to say her vows. It would have made it far easier to despise her for ensnaring him in yet another marital debacle.

To be fair, he could not really blame Brianna for their situation. She seemed to have as great an aversion to marriage as he did. And it was quite true that she'd tried to leave Glenloch the very day after she'd arrived. And they would have left for Dundee before Stamford's and Roddington's arrival had he not gotten himself half sprung in Falkburn instead.

Hugh glanced around the room, reluctant to go inside, for if there was any restless spirit in Glenloch, 'twould reside there. But naught had happened the last time he'd gone in with Brianna, no rattling of windowpanes, no ghostly presence.

He scrubbed one hand across his face and walked to the open wardrobe where most of Amelia's clothing was still stacked neatly on its shelves. His marriage to his first wife had been just as inauspicious as his new one, arranged by their fathers when Amelia was only eighteen and he barely twenty. Hugh had been too young—and too naïve—to understand that her shyness and their differences in temperament would make them forever incompatible. Perhaps if they'd had children, things would have been different.

This time he had known better, and yet he'd allowed it to happen all over again. He decided that Brianna would never use this room, this bedchamber where Amelia had spent so many hours avoiding him. In fact, he was going to have Mrs. Ramsay lock it and throw away the key.

He went inside and closed the door of the wardrobe, stopping suddenly when he felt a cold, clear sensation of being watched. He turned and looked around, but saw naught, in spite of the shiver of dread that coursed up his spine. It would be just like Amelia to begin haunting him now that he had remarried. He shuddered and exited the room, then went downstairs, deliberately avoiding the library as he headed for the door. He did not want another interchange with his chilly, distant wife. His past was full of those.

He went out to the stable and discovered young Ronan MacTavish, shoveling out the horse's stall. "I'll do that," he said, taking the implement from him. "Run back to the castle and see if your grandmother has any other jobs for you. I'll finish out here."

"Aye, Laird!"

Hugh started immediately, working off his anger and frustration by shoveling and making sure the stall was clean, then taking care of the gelding. He brushed the animal to a fine sheen, then checked each of its hooves. He was on the last one when Brianna's voice startled him.

"I'd like to talk to you," she said.

He dropped the horse's fetlock and came out of the stall.

He was dirty and sweaty, but she had not changed out of her wedding clothes, though she wore a heavy woolen shawl across her shoulders. She was still so beautiful she took his breath away.

He tossed the hoof pick onto the worktable and gave her his attention.

She looked down at the floor and then quickly back to his eyes as she flushed pink, obviously remembering their impetuous coupling in the straw. "I'd like to go up to Killiedown Manor."

"Killiedown?"

She nodded. "My aunt's estate—my home."

He had not expected her to want to leave now. With solid deliberation, he closed the distance between them and crossed his arms over his chest.

She took a step back, a telling move.

"I do not wish to quarrel, *wife*. But this is your home. You are now Lady Newbury. Or Lady Glenloch, if you prefer."

He reached out and touched a wisp of her hair. She swallowed audibly. "I realize that. But m-my belongings are at Killiedown. All my clothes, and . . ." She raised her hem a few inches and stuck out one booted foot. It was the boot she'd worn with her old trews and rough coat. "I would like to get some of my own shoes . . . that don't give me blisters."

It was nearly Hugh's undoing. She'd looked as majestic as a queen in her altered gown, and yet her feet had been clad in her rough boys' boots.

He cleared his throat, but his voice sounded gruff, nonetheless. "We'll go in a few days. I've got a shipment to dilute and move out first, and I want to supervise every stage personally."

She gave a questioning frown, and he realized she did not know that anything was amiss.

"There have been some irregularities in Glenloch's

free trade of late. I want to see that everything is done correctly."

"What kind of irregularities?"

Her interest didn't surprise him, not when he remembered her mentioning that her aunt had been a free trader. Lady Claire, of all people. "MacGowan's been transporting the brandy away from the Mearns, and using some Stonehaven ruffians to do it."

"What of the locals? Will the Falkburn folk not do it?"

"No, they'd be happy to do it, but MacGowan tells them there's no market for brandy in these parts."

She made a sound of surprise. "That doesn't seem likely, does it?"

"Not particularly."

"Does all this mean you'll be leaving Glenloch for the distribution?"

"Are you anxious to see me gone?"

She bit her lower lip.

"Because I'm not going to be anywhere tonight but in our marriage bed."

Though she was wearing only a woolen shawl, Brianna felt overheated when she returned to the castle. Hugh meant to consummate their marriage that night—as though it had not been consummated before. Many times.

Yet theirs was not a real marriage. They'd said the words that bound them to each other, but Brianna doubted that Hugh intended to be any kind of a husband. Nor did she want one. She only wanted her life at Killiedown back. She wanted to study her breeding lines and choose strong mares and stallions here and in Ireland, and on the continent.

If she could just get to Killiedown, Brianna was sure she could convince Hugh that she belonged there, and not at Glenloch. He could leave her at her home up north, near Muchalls, and go about his life as he pleased, without giving her a thought.

She let herself in through the door nearest the scullery and started for the staircase in search of refuge in her own bedchamber, but was waylaid by Mrs. Ramsay.

"Ye'll be wantin' a special wedding supper," she said, "so we've—"

"That will not be necessary, Mrs. Ramsay."

"Beggin' yer pardon, m'lady, but I think ye're mistaken."

Brianna stopped in her tracks. Mrs. Ramsay and Fiona had stayed until just past dark to help her alter Amelia's gown, and the housekeeper had said little during the hours they'd spent together. Brianna assumed it was fear of attracting the ghost that kept the two women silent. Today, Mrs. Ramsay seemed to have no such qualms.

She wiped her wet hands on her apron. "Ye may have marrit under . . . difficult circumstances, and ye've done yer auntie proud. But I've known yer husband since he was a wee bairn. I know that he can be a verra persuadin' man."

Brianna felt a blush rise from her chest to her cheeks,

for it must have been obvious to all that Hugh had persuaded her into his bed. And Mrs. Ramsay was absolving her of blame for her downfall.

"M'lady, ye've done everything jus' right thus far. Ye made a beautiful bride, and ye're Lady Glenloch now. Doona repent this day."

How could she not? Hugh was not particularly enamored or committed to her. He had married her out of obligation, and nothing more. Glenloch would be yet another temporary home for Bree. Soon Hugh would leave Scotland without a backward glance.

But he intended to have a wedding night.

"You're right, Mrs. Ramsay," Brianna said, suppressing a sigh. It did not matter. "Thank you."

"All will be ready when we leave today. Ye'll only need t' light the candles."

It was hours until suppertime, and Brianna was not sure Hugh would come inside, even then. She might have to choke down Mrs. Ramsay's special meal by herself while she thought about the life she might have led if Bernard had not withdrawn his offer of marriage at Lord Stamford's objection. Or how her life might have played out if she'd been able to escape her guardian until February.

Brianna missed Claire desperately and wished once again that she'd known of her aunt's illness. She'd have hurried back to Killiedown the moment she heard of it, and not left her side until she was well. Bree knew she would forever feel the pain of remorse for her neglect.

She wondered if Hugh felt guilt or regret over Amelia's tragic death. Her suicide must have been a blow to him, even though he'd admitted they were not close.

Brianna considered whether any society husbands and wives were ever close. Lord Stamford and his wife were not, and during Brianna's seasons in London, she'd heard of several illicit affaires being conducted between married men and widows, between adventurous wives and their paramours.

It was all exceedingly distasteful, and she did not care to be a part of any of it. Especially as the spurned wife.

Brianna's stomach clenched. Had that been the reason for Amelia's suicide? The thought of it chilled her. Had Hugh left his wife here at Glenloch for months on end, to wander these haunted halls all alone?

Feeling unsure what to do with herself and her dismal thoughts, Brianna went into the library and took a book from one of the shelves. She took it upstairs and went into the nursery, the only place—besides the library and Hugh's bedchamber—where she felt comfortable. She supposed she ought to change out of her gown and into the plainer dress, but it was her wedding day, and even though her husband had not seen fit to stay with her and admire it, she was going to keep it on.

She built up the fire in the grate, then pulled a chair close to it. Unfolding the plaid blanket at the foot of the bed to wrap it around her shoulders, Brianna looked out the window that faced the sea.

It was calmer than it had been in days, the water almost smooth, and it reflected the deep, dark, gray hue of the sky. Brianna shivered at the sight of those frigid depths and pulled the plaid tight around her shoulders.

She remembered how cold that water was, and marveled that she had not killed herself as well as Hugh in her attempt to leave.

If only—

There was something in the water. It did not seem to be a boat, and when the clouds cleared slightly, she could see what it was.

A body.

Chapter 14

He's as welcome as water in a holed ship.
SCOTTISH PROVERB

Hugh finished in the stable, but no matter how hard he worked, he couldn't dispel his agitation. He felt as though he could unload one of Captain Benoit's ships single-handed. Too bad they were not expecting another shipment in the near future.

He pulled on his jacket, and when he opened the stable door, he saw Brianna running frantically toward him, with the servants right behind her.

Hugh's heart immediately jumped into his throat, but he quickly calmed himself. Brianna was all right, else she would not be running so determinedly.

"Hugh!"

He hurried out to meet her, taking her by the arms, noting that she wore their plaid blanket around her shoulders. "What is it? What's happened?"

"There's a"—she swallowed and caught her breath—"a body. In the cove. In the water. Drowned, I think."

Immediately, he started for the beach. "Go back to the castle," he called to her and the others.

But they ignored his order and followed him across the lawn and around to the sand. He started to run when he caught sight of something in the water. It did not look like a body from where he stood, and he sincerely hoped Brianna was wrong.

But when he came to the edge of the surf, he saw it. A man, floating facedown, about twenty feet out.

"Christ," he muttered. Nothing like this had ever happened at Glenloch before, discounting Amelia's death. And he did not need this now, not while more than a thousand gallons of undiluted, uncolored brandy was lying in tubs inside the castle.

His remaining tub boats were tied to a stake, and Hugh went to them, marveling that this was no less than the second occasion this winter that he'd had to get into one of these small skiffs. It was not one of his preferred activities.

He made no explanation, for what he was doing was obvious. And he tried to ignore the speculation he heard from the servants, who stood shivering in the cold as they wondered who the poor drowned sot was. They would soon know.

"Ronan, run into the stable and get me a length of rope," he said, then dragged one of the boats to the water's edge, glad that he was wearing his oldest boots.

"I hope 'tis no' Artie Stewart," said Fiona. "His poor wife—"

"Hush, Fiona. We doona know if 'tis Artie," Mrs.

Ramsay admonished, but she was standing on her toes and craning her neck to try to see whoever was floating in the water.

Ronan returned with the rope, and Hugh sent him to Falkburn to fetch his father, as well as Malcolm MacGowan and a few more men. Then he pushed off into the water.

Brianna watched him jump into the boat and start paddling at a much more relaxed pace than when he'd come after her, to rescue her. If he had failed then, it might have been both of them floating in the cove.

When he reached the body, he moved with firm deliberation. Clearly, there was no reason for undue haste, nothing to be done for the person.

Hugh reached over the side of his boat and slid a circle of rope around the victim's body. He then looped the opposite end around a clip in the boat, sat back down, and started rowing, dragging the body behind.

It took only a few moments for him to return to the shore, where he jumped from the boat and pulled it in as far as he could, though the weight of the body seemed to work against him.

" 'Tis not a pretty sight," he said to the women when he'd gotten the boat as far in as he could. He climbed back into the hull and went to the rear where the body still drifted, and pulled it closer to shore.

Holding on to the rope, he jumped out of the boat again and looked up at Bree. "In fact, 'twould probably be best if you all went back to the castle."

"Laird, 'tis likely one of our own," said Mrs. Ramsay. "We'll stay."

"This fellow is not exactly one of our own," he responded, pulling the body from the water. "'Tis Angus Kincaid."

Brianna did not recognize the name, but she caught sight of the man's tangled hair and his gray, bloated face just before she turned abruptly and walked a few steps away. Mr. Kincaid's terrible fate was a bit too close to what might have happened to her, and she felt a surge of nausea at the thought of it.

"What d'ye think happened to him, Laird?" asked Mrs. Ramsay.

"By the look of that gash on his forehead, I'd guess he was given a good bash on the head and thrown into the water."

Bree could not imagine who would do such a thing.

"Who is Mr. Kincaid?" she asked.

"He is the customs surveyor from Stonehaven," Mrs. Ramsay replied.

"He was here a couple of days ago, inspecting the cove and the beach for signs of free trading," Hugh said.

Brianna's breath caught. "Do you think . . . Who would have done this to him?"

"He was not the most popular man in the Mearns," said Mrs. Ramsay.

"Easy to understand why, having met him the other day," Hugh remarked.

"Aye. He had a sour temperament, Laird, t' be sure."

Free traders would be inclined to do him harm, Brianna thought, especially if he was getting close to a valuable shipment. "Would one of those Stonehaven ruffians have done it?"

"'Tis possible," said Hugh.

Brianna turned to face the water, keeping her eyes averted from the dead man while Hugh detached the rope from the tub boat. From the corner of her eyes, she could see him pulling the body onto the shore.

When he'd pulled the man far enough in to be sure he wouldn't be sucked back into the surf, he came and took her by the arm. "You're freezing out here. Come back inside." He turned to the housekeeper and the others. "The rest of you, come, too. Nothing more can happen to Mr. Kincaid now."

They went inside, all of them going directly to the kitchen, where it was warmest. Meal preparations were in progress, with pots boiling on the stove, bowls and plates on the table, and cupboard doors standing open. Brianna knew Mrs. Ramsay was in the midst of preparing a massive feast that was unlikely to be consumed tonight. As laird, Hugh would surely have some official duty with regard to Mr. Kincaid.

He let go of Brianna's arm, and she shuddered and pulled the plaid more tightly around her.

"We'll have to send someone to Stonehaven for the magistrate. And a coroner, I imagine," Hugh said.

Mrs. Ramsay clucked her tongue and rubbed her hands together. "Laird, 'tis a world o' trouble we doona need. Will a magistrate want t' come out here to the castle, do ye think?"

Brianna glanced at Hugh. "There's brandy in the storage room, isn't there?"

"Aye. But we're going to get it diluted and out of Glenloch as soon as possible."

She heard Mrs. Ramsay's sigh of relief.

"When MacTavish and the others get here, we'll put Mr. Kincaid in the barn," Hugh said, obviously making his plans as he spoke. "Then we can organize a gang from Falkburn to let down the liquor and get it out tonight. Perhaps 'twould be best if MacGowan and I took Mr. Kincaid into Stonehaven in the morning and had a talk with the magistrate."

"Do you think Mr. Kincaid found anything?" Bree asked. "Is that why he was killed?"

"I don't know," Hugh replied. "He might have. Or he could have been killed merely because he was an ill-tempered little man who was digging into places where he should not."

Everyone knew that free traders were not a particularly peaceful lot. If anyone got in their way, there could be trouble, with killings on both sides of the customs table. But news of any such altercations would surely have reached Glenloch.

"Aye, Laird. 'Tis a good plan," said Mrs. Ramsay. "But your wedding supper . . ."

"Will have to wait," he said as Mrs. Ramsay's son-in-law arrived with another man. They came inside and warmed themselves in the kitchen before going out to collect Mr. Kincaid's body.

"Where's MacGowan?" Hugh asked.

"He went up t' Stonehaven earlier today," said Mac-

Tavish. "I doubt he'll return before the morn."

Hugh frowned, clearly puzzled by the news. "What business has he in Stonehaven?"

MacTavish shook his head. "I doona know, Laird. Only tha' he left just after ye and yer lady said yer vows."

Hugh's expression darkened and he left the kitchen with the other men, without bothering to speak privately to Brianna. But she knew he was thinking about those Stonehaven ruffians he'd mentioned earlier.

When he was gone, Bree felt adrift. Mr. Kincaid's death was a terrible occurrence, but it had little to do with her. And now that she knew that the brandy was going out tonight, she would ask Hugh again in the morn to take her home to Killiedown Manor, since it was not far past Stonehaven.

Hugh started to leave, but his eyes alighted on the tub in which he and Brianna had bathed together. He felt his throat go dry as he recalled their incredibly sensuous encounter.

He'd told her they would share a bed tonight, and he meant it, especially now, as he thought of the worn plaid she wore draped around her shoulders. It was almost as though the threadbare blanket served as a reminder of the closeness they'd shared in the croft on the beach.

He wanted her in his arms, in spite of the noose that had been slowly choking him since Stamford's arrival at the castle. He would deal with her request to return to Killiedown later. He had to get the brandy out as soon as possible, for there was every chance that the investigation into Kincaid's death would bring the authorities to Glenloch.

Castle Glenloch had always remained above suspicion, but Hugh would never dismiss the possibility of someone looking toward the dilapidated-looking wing where the buttery was located. He knew he would need to use his status and every bit of influence he could muster to keep any magistrate away from Glenloch and Falkburn.

Kincaid's death would surely be attributed to free traders in the area, and Hugh hoped he could direct the authorities toward a belief the man had been injured somehow, or even killed at sea and fallen overboard. It was an explanation that made complete sense.

The Stonehaven customs office did not usually run coastal patrols during inclement weather, but with the rumors of a smuggler's ship in the Glenloch vicinity, Kincaid might have taken one out to investigate. And it was entirely possible that there *had* been a mishap on board his ship that resulted in his death. If that was the case, the authorities would already know about it and there would be no further investigation. Just a cursory inquest.

Hugh could only hope.

"Lady Glenloch, we'll just finish here, and store everything for the morrow," said Mrs. Ramsay. "No reason ye canna have yer wedding supper then."

Brianna gave a nod and retreated to the library. She settled in to read, trying not to reflect on the irrevocable change that had occurred in her life today. Nor did she want to think about Hugh and his men moving that poor man's body into the barn. She had never met the customs man, but it was just one more violent death here at Glenloch.

Brianna wondered if people would start calling the place cursed. It was already haunted, whether Hugh wanted to believe it or not, and after Amelia's terrible death and the discovery of Mr. Kincaid's body in the cove, she could easily imagine that bizarre tales of untimely death would quickly spread.

It had been some time since she'd seen Glenloch's ghost, and Bree began to wonder if she'd ever really been visited by the troubled spirit. According to Mrs. Ramsay and Fiona, no one else had ever laid eyes on it, and Bree knew the suspicious creaking and unearthly howls that were heard about the castle could easily be attributed to the wind. Or to the settling of the building's old beams and timbers. Perhaps she'd been dreaming all those times that she'd seen the hazy light. Or her grief over losing Claire had made her imagine things.

And yet the ghost had led her to certain discoveries in Amelia's room and the master's bedchamber that she wouldn't have seen otherwise. It *had* to be real.

Brianna finally turned her attention to the book in her lap, but her concentration was poor. Mrs. Ramsay came into the room with a tray, and Brianna realized it was already dark. She had not seen Hugh since he'd left to deal with Mr. Kincaid.

"I brought ye this, m'lady. Something to tide you o'er until the laird returns." The housekeeper placed it on the table, and Brianna thanked her.

"I'll see ye in the morn, then," she said as she left.

Brianna was not much interested in the food, but she drank the tea and wondered if Hugh had gathered a crew to work on diluting the brandy. It would take some time to let down so many tubs, and she knew it was essential to get the brandy away from the castle as soon as possible.

Carrying a lamp from the library, she went to the drawing room and slid back the panel that led to the stairs down to the buttery. Quietly, she slipped inside and crept to the top of the steps. 'Twas well-lit at the bottom, so a thick blanket had been tacked across the grille to prevent any lamplight from escaping. She could hear movement and quiet voices down there.

They were definitely working.

Brianna might have participated in the unloading of this shipment, but she was quite sure Hugh would not appreciate her arrival now, into the midst of his activities. She retraced her steps back to the drawing room and closed the panel. When she turned, her gaze caught on the portrait of the old laird.

She decided that Hugh must resemble his mother, for he did not look at all like his sire. But besides the difference in their features, there was a strength in Hugh that Brianna did not detect in the portrait. The old laird's expression was one of superiority and arrogance. And perhaps a hint of cruelty in his narrow eyes. She shuddered at the thought of the whip she'd found in the man's bedchamber, and wondered if he had made a habit of using it on his only son.

If Brianna had planned on staying at Glenloch beyond the next day or two, she would have seen to it that all these portraits of Hugh's father were removed. He never looked up at the old man's countenance, and there was no need for him to be constantly reminded of the cruelty and discord between them.

But she was not staying, and as Hugh had told her, he did not spend very much time here, anyway.

She extinguished the lamps and went up the stairs to the bedchamber she thought of as her own, the nursery where she'd first seen the Glenloch Ghost. There was no hazy form in the room, no sense of the phantom anywhere nearby, so Brianna wrapped herself in the plaid she'd shared with Hugh in the kelper's croft, and lay down on the bed, quickly drifting into an uneasy sleep.

Wearily, Hugh climbed the stairs to his bedchamber. They'd gotten the brandy diluted and loaded onto carts, then he and the men had shoveled the residual snow over the tracks outside the grille, and all the way to the road. They'd wanted to leave no trace of their night's activities, in case a customs agent or even the magistrate cared to make a visit to Glenloch.

He went inside his room and stood stock-still at the cold, dark emptiness that greeted him. There was no fire in the grate, and the bed was empty, undisturbed.

Brianna was gone and Hugh was stunned by the way her absence hit him, square in the solar plexus.

He sat down heavily and drew in a deep breath before summoning the energy to go after her. She'd wanted to go to Killiedown . . .

No, she wouldn't have left. She was somewhere in

the castle, and Hugh had a good idea where he would find her. He stood and headed down the long gallery toward the old nursery.

It was late, and she was sure to be asleep. He eased the door open and saw her in the firelight, lying on her side, wrapped in the old plaid. Hugh's relief was palpable, but so was his fatigue. He built up the fire and then removed his shoes and eased onto the bed beside Brianna, pulling a heavy woolen blanket over them.

Curling his body around hers, Hugh put one arm around her and breathed in her scent as he fell into an exhausted sleep.

Brianna awoke sometime later, when the fire had burned low and she felt the heat of her husband's body behind her. The pink light of dawn streamed in through the windows, but Brianna had no desire to get up and look through them. The last time she'd done so, she'd seen a nightmare—Kincaid's body floating in the water.

She must have been sleeping quite soundly for Hugh to have climbed into the bed without waking her. They were both dressed, but he'd pulled a blanket over them. Brianna felt each of his breaths, deep and even in her ear, and knew that he was still sound asleep. She closed her eyes again and allowed herself these few moments of quiet peace in his arms, glad that he had not left with Mr. MacTavish to take his brandy out across the Mearns for distribution. He could take her to Killiedown instead, since he was going in that direction, anyway.

She tried not to think of their leave-taking once she

was home, but could not put it from her mind. Their farewell would be painful, but Brianna knew she had to make her break now, before their separation had the power to shred her heart.

She got up and untangled herself from the blankets and his arms. The russet shawl was on the chair, and she wrapped it around her shoulders.

"Morning already?" His voice sounded particularly deep and husky.

She moistened her lips and started for the door. "Just dawn. You must have worked late."

"Miss me?" He sat up and swung his legs out of bed.

"Hardly."

He came to her just as she took hold of the latch. Standing behind her, he spoke quietly in her ear. "I missed *you*, wife. I had intended to spend most of our night inside you."

His words wrenched the air from Brianna's lungs. But they were only words, and he'd mastered the ones that made her breathless and melted her bones. He knew exactly what he was doing. "I'll be ready to leave for Stonehaven as soon as you are."

He pushed the door closed before she could go through it, trapping her between his body and the heavy wooden door.

"What are you talking about?" His voice sounded even deeper, and a great deal more dangerous than she'd ever heard it before.

"Stonehaven is on a direct path to Killiedown Manor," she said, turning to face him. "There's no reason for you to go all the way to Stonehaven with Mr. Kincaid's body, and then have to come all the way back here, only to collect me and make the trip all over again."

A muscle in his jaw clenched, but Brianna stood her ground. "'Tis entirely reasonable," she said.

"What if I'm not ready to take you?"

Brianna slipped out of his reach. "You don't want a wife any more than I want a husband. We were both trapped into this situation—this marriage. You were obliged by custom to marry me, and I had no other choice. But that doesn't mean we must stay together and make each other miserable."

The scar on Hugh's cheek turned white as it seemed to do when he was annoyed. He opened the door and stepped out of the nursery before her. "No," he said, turning to look at her. "I don't want you with me when we go to the magistrate."

"Hugh—"

"'Tis better this way. I'll take you when I get back."

He left the room, and Brianna stood motionless, gazing absently into the fireplace, disturbingly relieved by the delay in her departure.

Hugh felt much too distracted to deal with official business, but he had no choice. He had to get Angus Kincaid's body up to Stonehaven this morning. He could not delay or there would be even more questions.

He went to his bedchamber to change clothes, and when he emerged a few minutes later, he noticed that Amelia's bedroom door was ajar again. He pulled it closed and listened to hear it latch tight, then returned to the nursery where he'd spent the night with Brianna.

She was wonderfully rumpled and her hair was now a mass of loose curls around her face and shoulders. She had just washed her face, and before she had a chance to raise the towel and dry it, he crossed the room and took her into his arms.

Giving her no chance to protest, he took possession of her lips in an openmouthed kiss that left no doubt about his plans for her when he returned. She fisted her hands in the fabric of his coat, though whether she was pulling him close or trying to repel him, Hugh could not be certain. All he knew was that she shuddered and opened for him when he pulled her tight against his raging erection.

He wanted her now, but there wasn't time. He wasn't going to cheat them out of a spectacular bout of drawn-out lovemaking and pleasure.

He released her and left the room without a word.

The servants were just arriving when Hugh left the castle. He went into the stable, but found his horse gone. Taking a detour to the barn, he found Niall MacTavish inside, already hitching the gelding to the wagon. "I stopped at MacGowan's place, but he wasna there," MacTavish said.

"I'd be very interested in knowing what he's been up to these past couple of days," said Hugh, wondering if it was such an easy transition to go from stealing contraband brandy to committing murder.

"Aye," MacTavish replied, his somber expression indicating that he was considering the same question. They climbed in and headed north.

They made the arduous trip across the snowy road,

and had to stop numerous times to use the shovels Mac-Tavish had thought to bring, to dig themselves out of deep drifts of snow.

"I'm thinkin' maybe Mr. Pennycook is involved."

"How so?" Hugh asked.

"Weel, if MacGowan is smitten with his daughter, mayhap he's been trying to cull the man's favor. Make him more receptive to a proposal."

"With bribery? Or by cutting Pennycook into his new arrangement with the Stonehaven batsmen and distributors?"

"Either, Laird. Or both."

"You're probably right."

"And if Mr. Kincaid got wind of their collusion . . ."

"Which Kincaid might well have done, for he strikes me as a very thorough man."

"Aye. He'd ha' been a direct threat t' MacGowan's interests."

"With both the brandy trade and Pennycook's daughter."

It seemed a likely theory, but that's all it was. Conjecture.

"Let's take Mr. Kincaid directly to the customs office," Hugh said when they finally arrived in town. "I believe we should turn here."

Hugh had been to Stonehaven only a few times, and though he knew the office was at the harbor, he needed to stop and ask for its exact direction. They soon arrived at a long, low building on the wharf, and Berk Armstrong came outside only moments after they drove up and jumped down from the wagon.

"Laird Glenloch! 'Tis a surprise to see ye here!"

Hugh saw Pennycook's grim visage looking out at them through one of the windows, but could read neither guilt nor innocence in his expression. The man soon came out to stand beside Armstrong.

"We've some bad news," Hugh said, approaching the two men at the front of the building.

The lackadaisical Mr. Armstrong seemed not to grasp the import of Hugh's words, but Pennycook shoved past him and gestured toward the tarp-covered wagon bed. Hugh wondered if it was a guilty man's ploy, to act the curious party when he knew full well what was in the wagon.

"What've ye got there?"

"We found Mr. Kincaid floating in the sea yesterday afternoon," Hugh replied. "He was some distance north of Glenloch, but my wife happened to catch sight of him from one of our windows."

"Mr. Kincaid!" Armstrong cried with genuine dismay, coming toward the wagon behind Pennycook. "Why, it canna be!"

"I assure you, Mr. Armstrong, 'tis most definitely your surveyor."

Pennycook was more reserved in his reaction, turning his gaze from the cargo in the back of the wagon. "Yer wife, Laird?" he asked.

"Aye. I've recently wed," he said, discounting Pennycook's ignorance of his marriage. The only way the man would have known Hugh had married was if he'd spoken to MacGowan. And if Hugh's theory was correct, Pennycook wouldn't care to have that association known. "My bride happened to look down from one of the upper rooms of the castle when she saw something floating in the water."

"And ye're absolutely sure 'tis Kincaid."

Hugh was unimpressed by the man's apparent doubt, nodding while MacTavish untied the tarp and pulled it back, to verify Kincaid's identity for the two men. Pennycook remained in place, standing stiffly, a few steps from the wagon, with his arms crossed over his chest. Armstrong went directly to it and looked, flinching at the sight of the dead man and the jagged cut on his forehead.

Hugh had to admit it was a gruesome sight, for Kincaid's skin was a pasty gray color, and the wound black. But his nose and fingers appeared to be intact, leading him to think the man had not been in the water very long.

"Has he any family?" Hugh asked.

"Nae," said Armstrong. "His auld mother passed on a few years ago. Since then, he's been alone."

"The magistrate will have to be notified," said MacTavish.

Armstrong seemed unable to take his gaze from the body, but Pennycook barely looked. Hugh watched the man's reactions, but could not swear to any conclusion. Either the man was particularly squeamish, or this death had been no surprise to him. Hugh had been wagering upon the latter, but how the man fit into the picture, he was unsure as yet, and he still didn't know what part MacGowan had played, if any.

"Perchance, would either of you know if Mr. Kincaid

was recently out in a ship patrolling the coastline?" he asked.

Armstrong shook his head. "We've had no customs ships out since the snow."

"When did you see him last, then?"

"Yesterday morn," Armstrong replied. "Isn't that right, Mr. Pennycook? Mr. Kincaid spilled his tea on his trews and had to leave to go home for another pair."

Hugh looked at Pennycook, who pursed his lips and gave a curt nod. "Aye." Then he turned and went back inside the customs office.

"Perhaps you could send someone for the magistrate?" Hugh asked Armstrong.

"Oh, aye, Laird. Right away."

As soon as Armstrong had gone back into the office, Hugh turned to MacTavish. "I had a feeling we might see MacGowan here at the office."

"So did I, Laird. But if he's courtin' the Pennycook lass . . ."

"Did you sense anything wrong with Pennycook's reaction to seeing Kincaid?"

"Aye, Laird. The man wasna at all surprised."

"That's what I thought, too," said Hugh. "Do you know where Pennycook's house is?"

"Only a general idea," MacTavish replied.

"It'll have to do," said Hugh. "Take a walk in that direction and see if you can catch sight of him. So much the better if he doesn't see you."

"Aye."

"We'll meet at the Queens Hotel in an hour."

MacTavish pulled his hat down low and started off,

away from the harbor as Hugh went inside the customs office to wait and see if MacGowan happened to be inside.

If not, he would just wait for the magistrate.

The day was long and ever so dull. Brianna had never spent so much idle time, and she wondered what she might have been doing had she been home at Kil-liedown. She'd have had numerous chores to perform, mostly out in the stable.

But there were Claire's things—her clothes and shoes that should be given to the poor in Muchalls. Claire would have wanted that, and it was up to Brianna to take care of it. Yet here she was, a useless fixture in a house that was not her home, waiting for a husband who had not disagreed that staying together would make them both miserable.

Thoughts of past, temporary homes teased at the edges of Brianna's memory, and she pushed them away, unwilling to think about them after all this time. She'd had six good years with Claire, and had never worried about being sent away. Her aunt had promised that Kil-liedown Manor would always be her home.

A loud crash sounded somewhere above her, causing her to rise abruptly from her chair in the library. She went to the staircase to see if she could discover what was amiss. Suddenly, Mrs. Ramsay and the two maids had joined Brianna at the bottom of the stairs, and were looking up the steps with frightened eyes.

"'Tis the ghost," cried Fiona.

"Aye, lass," said Mrs. Ramsay, wiping her hands on

her apron, turning to Brianna. "You'd best come back to the scullery with us."

"Does anyone know what it wants?" Brianna asked.

"Who will ever know what it wants?" Mrs. Ramsay said. "'Tis a troubled soul, who must torment the living."

It might be troubled, but Brianna had never felt tormented by it. Bree had felt its urgency, its determination to show her something, even though she could not figure out what it was. Everything had been so vague. A locket, the whip, the picture of the sailing boat. She did not know if they were all connected, or if each one carried some separate message.

Brianna started up the steps, but Mrs. Ramsay caught her arm, clearly bothered by her mistress's intent. "M'lady, I doona think 'tis safe. Ye'd best wait fer Laird Glenloch to return."

"I don't think so," Bree replied. Mrs. Ramsay might have ruled Glenloch for many years without a master in residence, but as long as Brianna was here, she was the woman in charge. "'Twas likely only the wind."

Mrs. Ramsay tried to deter her once again, but Brianna gave her a reassuring smile and proceeded.

Holding her shawl tightly around her shoulders, she ascended the stairs. It was mid-afternoon, and though the light was fading, the windows at the opposite ends of the main gallery provided adequate light for her to see her way. She glanced across the floor, expecting to see a pile of broken rubble, but there was nothing, no indication of what had crashed.

The filmy light of the ghost was conspicuously absent.

Brianna walked past all the rooms along the main gallery, including those where the ghost had led her. Then she looked inside the rooms she had not explored. They were just unoccupied, unremarkable bedchambers, and none of them had any breakage that Brianna could see. She closed each door behind her and headed down to Amelia's room, where it seemed the ghost most often visited.

Brianna pushed opened the door and stood just under the lintel of the bedchamber, looking inside. The entire floor was cold, but Amelia's chamber seemed chillier than any other room. On quick glance, naught seemed to be out of place. The room looked just as it had the first time Brianna had entered, except that no phantom was hovering about.

Bree exited the room, and the door slammed shut behind her. Only then did she see the hazy light of the ghost, hovering in front of the heavy doors that led to the tower adjacent to Amelia's bedchamber.

The ghost vanished as suddenly as it appeared.

Goose bumps came up on Brianna's arms, and she turned around and went back in the direction she'd come from. There was no reason to stay up there, waiting for the phantom to reappear, for none of its actions seemed to have any purpose, in spite of the urgency she always felt from it.

Brianna hesitated. The ghost had never led her into danger . . . There was obviously something it wanted her to see, for why else would it have drawn her up there to investigate? Perhaps there was something about the tower itself.

Intending only to collect a lamp from Hugh's bedchamber across the gallery, she went inside and was hit with a sharp pang of loneliness. She would sleep there only one more night, and then it would be time to go home. Killiedown seemed so very distant now, its bedchambers cold and empty.

She picked up the linen sheet from the bed where they'd slept together and pressed it to her face. Hugh's scent was on it, and Brianna closed her eyes and inhaled deeply, memorizing all that she could about him . . . the texture of his hair, his thick lashes, the scar on his cheek, his big hands with their roughened knuckles . . .

And how those hands had felt when he feathered his fingers across her breasts.

She swallowed back a foolish yearning for what could never be. He had promised to take her to Killiedown Manor, and there was little doubt that he understood her reluctance to remain at Glenloch. He must also realize that she belonged at Killiedown. Brianna did not think he would invoke his husbandly right to Claire's property, but would allow her to keep possession of Killiedown, and see to it that the deeds for all of Claire's properties were put into Brianna's name. Alone.

At yet she did not find that conclusion comforting in the least.

She took a deep breath and pressed a hand to her stomach. Claire had provided well for her, and everything would be better once she was home. Until then, she needed a diversion from her cheerless thoughts.

She lit a lamp, then carried it out to the gallery, looking both ways for signs of the filmy apparition that had led her there in the first place. Other than the eerie silence, there was nothing out of the ordinary.

Brianna crossed to the doors that barred her way from the tower adjacent to Amelia's bedchamber, and found them unlocked this time, when she was certain they'd been locked before.

Puzzled by the change, she cautiously pushed one open and stepped inside the cold, bare tower, onto a landing of sorts. Lifting the lamp, she could see the rough stone walls that had been mortared in place several centuries before. A circular stone staircase hugged the wall, climbing as far as the top, and descending all the way down to the ground. Brianna cringed at the near certainty that Amelia must have climbed that very staircase to the parapet at the top of the tower.

She swallowed her unease and quickly turned to look through the narrow window that overlooked the north road, the route Hugh would soon travel.

The road was empty and looked quite desolate with the bare trees in the fields to the west, and the new falling snow. 'Twas only a few flurries now, but Brianna knew the snowfall could become much heavier, and Hugh might not be able to get back to Glenloch.

She walked down a few steps and looked out the window that faced the opposite tower at the south end of the castle, and the buttery at its base. The snow in the area appeared undisturbed, and Brianna could see no sign that there'd been any activity there the night before. The free traders had covered their tracks well.

She felt entirely isolated, but told herself the feeling that crept up her spine was not loneliness, but merely uneasiness, caused by the prospect of spending the night alone, with only the Glenloch Ghost for company. Shaking off the disquieting notion, she climbed back up to the landing and left the tower, wondering what possible reason the ghost had had for bringing her there, and whether it was connected to any of the other things it had shown her.

Perhaps the phantom wanted Bree to recommend that the tower be taken down so that when it collapsed—as it surely would one day—no one would be hurt. She would be gone when it happened, so it wasn't really any of her concern. But she would not want to learn someday that Ronan or some other innocent had been injured by falling debris.

She pulled closed the door to Amelia's bedchamber and returned to the main floor of the castle.

Chapter 15

Do what you ought and come what will.
SCOTTISH PROVERB

Magistrate Lachann Sinclair was a tall, blond fellow with fresh good looks, much younger than Hugh had anticipated. And he was no fool.

The magistrate had a number of questions that Hugh answered honestly, adding what he thought was pertinent information. There was no reason that Sinclair should not know about the strong southerly current that ran just north of the castle, a current that would have drawn Kincaid quickly from a more northerly site, drawing his attention from Glenloch as the site of the man's demise.

Sinclair took Hugh's statement, and then went outside and looked at the body, still lying covered in the wagon. He returned a few minutes later and sat down at a long wooden worktable in a room with two large windows that faced the harbor. He indicated that Hugh should take a seat across from him.

"It looks as though Mr. Kincaid took a bump on the head and then . . ." He looked directly at Hugh.

"What? Fell into the sea? Or was pushed."

"What of the docks here?" Hugh asked. "Is there any chance he might have gashed his head somehow, then fallen into the water?"

"There's nearly always someone about," said Mr. Armstrong.

The magistrate agreed. "I don't see how such an accident could have occurred without someone witnessing it, Laird," he said. "I believe someone must have hit him and thrown him over. Mischief, pure and simple."

"Free traders," said Armstrong, solemnly.

Pennycook snapped irritably at him. "Well, who else would it be, Berk?"

"We'll need to have the coroner take a look at him, and there'll be an inquest," said Sinclair. "Laird, I'll need to have you come back for it. And Lady Glenloch as well."

"No," Hugh responded, feeling unexpectedly protective of Brianna. "I will not expose my wife to any questioning." Especially not from the all-too-attractive Mr. Sinclair.

"Laird, I'll need to ask her what she saw."

"I just told you what she saw," Hugh replied, keeping his voice low and even. "Lady Glenloch is not available for any inquest."

Sinclair shuffled the papers on the table before him. "What if I were to come down to Glenloch and speak with her personally? In your presence, of course."

Even worse. "I see no need for it. I'll not have my wife disturbed any further. Seeing that dead man was bad enough—"

"Laird Glenloch, I assure you my questioning will be short and to the point. There is no need for concern."

Hugh suddenly heard himself sounding like a jealous husband. Which was absurd. He stood up and went to the window. "Fine. If you can keep it short. And delicate."

"Aye, Laird. Thank you. I can ride down tomorrow, if that suits."

Hugh gave a quick nod, then Sinclair glanced at Armstrong and Pennycook. "If one of you would drive Laird Glenloch's wagon to the coroner?"

While that was done, Hugh arranged to return later to collect his horse. He decided to leave the wagon in Stonehaven, for it was much too cumbersome for the trip back to Glenloch over the snowy roads.

He left the customs office and walked toward the livery with the intention of buying another horse. Brianna would soon need one, although he had no intention of taking her back to Killiedown Manor just yet. If his prized bachelorhood had been taken from him, he intended to get at least one more night's pleasure from its loss.

Taking a direct route to the livery, Hugh did not need to veer far from the harbor. He neared the Ship's Inn, but stopped suddenly at the sight that greeted him. He quickly turned back and hastened away in the direction from which he'd come. Then he turned a corner in order to conceal his presence from the man he'd seen coming out of the inn.

'Twas Roddington.

Hugh wondered what the likelihood was that Roddington just happened to be in Stonehaven on the day after Kincaid had been murdered. Hugh had verified that Kincaid hadn't been on board a patrol ship, nor was it likely that he had fallen accidentally into the sea without witnesses. There could be only one way for him to have received that wound on his head. It had been no simple accident.

In spite of Roddington's presence and his long history of deviousness and malevolence merely for its diversionary value, Hugh could not dismiss his suspicion that MacGowan was involved in some way, too. But putting together the pieces was not going to be easy, not if he wanted to keep secret his duty-free brandy business.

MacGowan and Roddington had a connection in Glenloch's free trade, exclusive of Hugh, just as he'd wanted it. And now he wondered how nefarious their link had become. Hugh puzzled over possibilities, wondering if Stamford was here as well, or if Brianna's guardian had already left the area.

Hugh watched as Roddington climbed into a hired coach with a driver and two footmen, who would surely find it necessary to clear drifts of snow off the road. He continued to wait through some delay, and then suddenly, Malcolm MacGowan stepped out of the building with the innkeeper. The estate manager climbed into the coach with Roddington as the innkeeper handed a small bag to one of the footmen, then returned inside his establishment.

Hugh was dumbfounded. He'd come to believe that MacGowan and Pennycook were the villains here, but

Roddington's presence put an entirely different twist on the matter. He could not help but wonder if Malcolm MacGowan had some history with Jasper, other than the obvious, and that possibility turned his stomach.

If Hugh had been on horseback, he might have followed the two as they drove away, but since he was on foot, he approached the inn and went inside. The innkeeper greeted Hugh immediately.

"I beg your pardon," Hugh said, swallowing his distaste as he spoke, "but I believe I just missed meeting an old friend. The Marquess of Roddington."

"Oh, aye, my lord," the man replied. "He jus' drove away."

"I might catch him if I hurry. Where is he bound?"

"Dundee," the innkeeper said. "Though the roads are no' good, the marquess said he had urgent business there."

"Ah, then I will not be meeting him, for my path leads elsewhere."

"If he returns, shall I tell him you called?"

"Aye," said Hugh. "Tell him Lord Stamford was looking for him."

"What did ye see up there?" asked Mrs. Ramsay when Brianna returned to the main floor of the castle. The servants were putting on coats and gathering their things as they made ready to return to their homes in Falkburn.

"I couldn't find anything broken. But I didn't go up to the attic." She didn't mention the unlocked tower doors.

"Best to stay away from there," the housekeeper replied. "'Tis the ghost's favored place."

Bree had not found that to be true, but she didn't suppose any of the servants spent enough time on the upper floors to know.

"'Tis nearly dark," said Mrs. Ramsay. "We'll be goin' now, m'lady. P'rhaps 'twould be best if ye came into Falkburn with us to await the laird."

"No, I'm sure he'll be back soon. Besides, I'm not afraid."

"Oh, but—"

"No, really. I'll be fine here," she said, pulling on her old coat. "And Laird Glenloch won't be much longer, I'm sure."

Mrs. Ramsay gave a questioning glance to Brianna's coat. "M'lady?"

"I'm going outside for a bit."

"But—"

"Just for some air. A short walk. I won't go far."

"But 'tis almost dark, m'lady."

Brianna ignored Fiona's worried entreaty and went to the main entrance of the castle. She let herself out the front door and walked a few yards down the drive, under the canopy of tall, barren trees that grew on either side. The drive had been cleared of snow, but would soon be covered again if the flurries continued at the present rate.

She did not want to think about the possibility of Hugh being waylaid in Stonehaven, and reminded herself of the kiss he'd given her before leaving. If that could be any indication, he would make certain to return to Glenloch tonight. And though Brianna knew she should try for indifference, she sincerely hoped he did.

Turning to look up at Glenloch, Brianna saw the windows of Hugh's bedchamber in the newer section of the castle, added many decades after the original keep and castle towers had been built.

Uninterested in the different kinds of stone and mortar that were used, or the particulars of Glenloch's unique architecture, Brianna circled around the building until she came to the north tower. A thin, jagged crack scored its length from the ground to its peak, and the high, crenellated parapet was worse than decrepit. Large chunks of stone were gone, and had fallen in huge pieces that were lying on the ground at her feet.

Staying in close proximity was obviously dangerous, for the tower looked as though more stone might fall from it at any moment. And Brianna thought it might split in two with a strong wind. She took several steps back while gazing at the ancient structure, at the curved, moss-covered stone façade and the tall, narrow arrow loops that were strategically placed at every level.

She studied the low building that abutted the base of the tower, likely an ancient pantry or kitchen that had been added sometime after the original tower. She had avoided it on her arrival at Glenloch, for its stone walls had collapsed, and the entire broken-down structure seemed impenetrable, overgrown as it was with a thicket of brambles. Its condition appeared only slightly worse than that of the buttery in the south tower, but Brianna guessed the smuggler's room would have been reinforced internally over the years, keeping it intact for the free trading.

Skirting a wide berth around the decaying building, Brianna walked around the north tower, viewing it from this new vantage point, trying to see if she could get a glimmer of what the ghost might have been trying to show her. But there was nothing special there that she could see. This part of Castle Glenloch looked just like any number of castle ruins she'd seen in Scotland and England. She could not imagine what—

Amelia's bedchamber window was in a newer section of the castle, but it was adjacent to the old tower. If Amelia had climbed the north tower on the day she'd died . . . Perhaps that was why those interior doors were kept locked.

Brianna knew very little of the details surrounding the late Lady Glenloch's death, and she had avoided dwelling upon thoughts of it. The poor woman's terrible sorrow, and the despair that had driven her to take her own life were just too disturbing.

If Brianna had had any inklings about Amelia's fall, she'd thought it had occurred from the south tower, which was more accessible than the one closer to her own bedchamber. But having been inside that tower and seeing those steps, now she did not know.

Bree gazed up at the ragged parapet of the north tower and tried to understand what point the ghost was making in reminding her of Amelia's tragic death. It had happened several years before, and had naught to do with Brianna—especially since she would be leaving Glenloch on the morrow.

She concluded there was naught to be learned from Lady Glenloch's death, nothing new that the ghost could show her. Quite possibly, all the other things it had uncovered and shown Brianna were meaningless, too, though its aura of urgency persisted. Brianna tried, but could not dismiss the feeling that she was missing something important.

Bothered by her unsettling thoughts, Bree hurried around the back of the castle toward the scullery door, stopping abruptly when she caught sight of the stable yard. Hugh was just coming in, riding his gelding and leading a second saddled horse alongside him.

A profound wave of relief struck Brianna at the sight of him. He was tall and strong, and more powerful than any man she'd ever met. Even Glenloch's ghost stayed away from him, and yet Brianna could not.

Hugh dismounted when he saw her and walked toward her, and she resisted the urge to run to him, to enfold herself in his capable arms. She would not allow herself to dwell upon the promise she'd felt in his kiss that morn, for 'twas all too fleeting a pledge. A mere portent of one last night to be spent in his bed.

"You didn't bring the wagon," she said.

Hugh gave a shake of his head, keeping his eyes upon her, their heat and desire unrelenting. Brianna felt her knees weaken under his perusal.

"It would have taken hours longer to get home," he said, his words full of meaning. "I bought a horse for MacTavish to ride instead."

She stepped up to the mare and patted its forehead as she composed herself. She did what was so familiar to her, assessing the qualities of a horse, determining its breeding value. "'Tis still a sturdy beast," she said more calmly than she felt, "though she's past her prime for breeding."

"Aye. But the price was right, and we needed another mount for MacTavish—as well as for you. For when we travel up to Killiedown."

Bree swallowed a surprising wave of disappointment. If only he had said he had no intention of taking her to Killiedown . . . that he wanted her to stay . . .

'Twas too ridiculous a thought to entertain. She was a most inconvenient wife, and he was the husband she'd never planned for, never wanted.

Hugh turned the horses and started for the stable. "I believe our wedding supper awaits. I'll meet you inside after I see to the horses."

Hugh had been engaged to Amelia for six months before they married, and yet he'd hardly known her when they met at the altar of St. George's. He'd been young and hadn't had the slightest idea what to do to make a wife happy. Hell, he'd have settled for the smallest form of contentment from her, but even that had not been possible, especially when it became clear that he would never make her a mother.

That particular failure set Hugh up for additional derision from his father, who had ridiculed him for his lack of mastery over his wife, and his lack of potency in the bedchamber. As though Jasper had enjoyed so much success. Hugh's mother had borne only one child, and her husband had spent the rest of his life punishing her as well as his son for his many dissatisfactions with them.

The old laird had been a bloody varlet, something Hugh had vowed never to become.

He took care of the horses as he thought of his new wife, a woman he knew far better than he'd known Amelia on their wedding day. Finishing in the stable, he collected the package he'd brought from Stonehaven and closed up the stable. He went up to the castle, looking forward to his next hours with Brianna far more than he should. He let himself in through the scullery entrance and smelled the mingling scents of their supper, but he was not hungry for the food left by Mrs. Ramsay.

He left his greatcoat on a hook, then went in search of Brianna. She was in the dining chamber, looking as demure as a proper wife, dressed in her green gown, her hair gathered into an uncharacteristically neat chignon at her nape, bending to light the candles on the long table.

Hugh found that he wanted his impetuous lass in trews back, with her wild hair and wicked smiles, the one who'd surrendered to him in a fiery yielding of anger, need, and passion.

Without making a sound, he climbed the stairs and went to his bedchamber. He pulled off his shirt, then his boots, then went to the washbasin and cleansed away the miles from his face and body. As he took a clean shirt from his wardrobe, he noticed the portfolio that contained his marriage lines. So much for hiding it away.

Taking the leather folder from the drawer, Hugh

took it to the desk and opened it, looking over the marriage lines MacGowan had written, as well as the vows Hugh had said. But there was something missing. He sat down and took out a fresh sheet of vellum from the desk drawer, then dipped his pen into the ink.

"The Marriage Vows of Brianna Munro Christie," he wrote.

He sat quietly for a moment with his eyes closed, remembering the words Brianna had recited before witnesses, with obvious trepidation, in a slightly breathless voice.

He looked down at the vellum and started another line. "*Before God and these witnesses I vow to take you as my husband . . .*"

It surprised him that he was able to remember her words so clearly, those vows that were so much more elaborate than his own.

He went on writing, finishing the words that had bound her to him. "*. . . with all your faults and all your strengths, as I offer myself to you as wife, with my own imperfections as well as my skills from this day forward.*"

He laid the pen aside and sat still, waiting for the ink to dry. There was nothing particularly romantic about writing the document. It was just something he should have done—actually Brianna should have done it—right after they'd exchanged vows. For the record.

Brianna felt foolish waiting for Hugh in the big, empty dining room, so she retreated to the smaller, cozier library. She heard him come downstairs, and when he entered the room, he was wearing clean clothes and had combed his thick, black hair. He looked almost civilized.

Brianna suppressed her shiver of awareness that he was not. That mouth and those hands could elicit the most primal responses in her, and she wondered if she would always crave his touch. When she was a woman Claire's age, would she ache for the touch of the lover she'd long since left? Long for the sweet moments of quiet in his arms?

"The magistrate from Stonehaven plans on coming to Glenloch to question you about Angus Kincaid's death," Hugh said, placing the package he carried on the mantel.

"When?" she asked, tamping down the desire that welled up at the base of her spine and inside her chest.

"Tomorrow," he replied. "Which means our trip to Killiedown will have to be delayed another day."

Brianna swallowed and gazed into Hugh's glittering dark eyes, aware that he intended for them to have the wedding night they'd missed the night before. Her stomach roiled as desire and caution warred inside her. She was not sure how she was going to get through the wedding supper.

"There will be an inquest into Mr. Kincaid's death," said Hugh, crouching to add peat to the library fireplace, "for 'twas obviously no accident."

"Then Mr. Kincaid did not fall from a patrolling ship?"

Hugh looked over his shoulder at her. "There've been no sea patrols of late, so no. He was killed and then thrown into the surf."

"Who would have done it?"

He stood and brushed off his hands. "That's what the inquest will try to determine."

"And must I testify there, too?"

"No," he said, setting his jaw, and Brianna had the distinct impression that his refusal was meant to shield her somehow. "I told the magistrate he could question you here."

"I see."

"So he plans to come here on the morrow," Hugh said. "I know you are anxious to leave Glenloch . . . But perhaps this will help to mitigate your delay."

He took the package he'd brought in, and set it on a table next to the sofa. "Sit down," he said, taking her arm.

More than her curiosity about the package, Bree felt a rush of pleasure at his touch. She sat on the sofa and he took a seat right beside her, then handed her the package he'd brought. "Open it."

The box, wrapped in plain paper and tied with a thin string, fit easily on her lap. She pulled off the string and unfolded the paper, then looked up at him. But his expression was closed, giving her no indication of his reason for bringing her a gift . . . if, in fact that's what it was. Perhaps it was something entirely practical.

She opened the box and her breath caught.

"Oh my."

Inside was a pair of delicate ivory slippers made of

butter-soft leather. As Brianna touched one of them, a surge of something beyond mere gratitude went through her, and she felt a sudden burning behind her eyes. "These are . . . They're beautiful."

He stood up and walked to the fireplace. "You should try them on," he said, his voice detached. " 'Tis merely a pair of ready-made shoes, the only ones in Stonehaven that looked as though they might fit you."

She wondered if that meant he'd scoured every shop in town, but quickly decided that would not have been the case, for his business in Stonehaven had been quite clear and he would not have bothered to delay his return home by . . . shopping. Nonetheless, Brianna was grateful for the gift and bent down to unlace the boots she'd been wearing since her flight from Killiedown.

She knew better than to make anything of this. Hugh had been quite aware of her desire to get out of the ugly, ill-fitting boots she wore.

"Thank you."

He shrugged. " 'Tis a practical matter. Your return to Killiedown is delayed, and those boots are ill-fitting. I've seen your blisters."

She swallowed thickly and bent down, but had trouble with the tattered lace of one of the old boots. Hugh muttered something under his breath and came to her, kneeling on one knee before her. "I'll do it," he said impatiently.

He took her foot in his hand and untied the knot, then slipped the boot off. Moving slowly and deliberately, he held her stocking-clad foot while he took one of the slippers from the box and slid it on. "A little too large, I think."

His voice was husky, his eyes heavy-lidded.

"Hardly at all," Brianna replied, softly. " 'Tis a fine fit."

He took his time removing the boot from her other foot, and Brianna felt his hand trailing up the back of her leg, settling on her calf. She closed her eyes at the heavenly sensation of his touch, and waited for him to put the remaining shoe on.

But he did not. He eased her skirt up to her knees and leaned forward to press a kiss to the top of her thigh.

Brianna could not breathe as he slid both his hands up the backs of her legs. She held on to the cushions on either side of her and waited anxiously as he moved between her legs and reached up to cup her jaw in his hand. He drew her down to him, touching his mouth to hers softly, gently, as though she were as fragile as a china teacup.

He feathered kisses across her lips, then down to the sensitive skin just below her ear. Bree let her head drop back as he kissed her jaw and throat, then moved down to the neckline of her gown. She felt him unlacing the bodice, then shuddered with arousal when he opened her gown and buried his face between her breasts.

He turned and took one achingly hard nipple into his mouth, and Brianna sighed with pleasure. His hand found its way under her skirt again and slid upward to the point where Brianna needed him most, and her bones melted at his touch.

"Yes, Hugh," she whispered. "Please."

She cupped his head in her hands and relished the attention he laved upon each breast. She quickened at the intense sensation of his fingers penetrating her, sliding across her moist flesh, and wanted more.

"Just as soft as I remembered," he said, lifting his head to look into her eyes.

The intimacy of the moment, of his gaze on hers as he pleasured her, was nearly unbearable. Brianna drew him up for her kiss, and their mouths melded together in a heated coupling that took her breath away. Hugh laid her down on the sofa and came over her, sucking her tongue deep into his mouth. Brianna felt him unfastening his trews, and she tore at his shirt buttons, wanting to feel his chest against her naked, sensitive breasts.

He broke away long enough to pull his shirt over his head, then pushed her legs apart as he covered her. With his hands bracketing either side of her head, he entered her in one quick thrust, then held perfectly still, his eyes darker than Brianna had ever seen them. She skimmed her hands up his chest and around to his nape, pulling him down to her, face to face, chest to chest.

Arching her back, she made a low sound of pleasure at the sensation of his rough chest hair against her sensitive breasts, and he groaned and moved inside her. 'Twas a slow rhythm at first, but as Brianna dug her fingertips into his back, he increased the pace. She made a hushed, primal sound at the back of her throat and met every one of his drives with more than just her body.

She feared her entire heart and soul were involved.

With that realization, her climax came over her, driving her to a height of sensation she had not experienced before. Spasms of pure bliss originated in her feminine center and spread throughout her body. Her muscles and bones seemed to melt, and when Brianna felt Hugh's spasm within her, and his body trembling above her, she peaked again with an even greater force than before.

It was some time before their passionate shudders ended. When it was over, Hugh rolled to his side, with Brianna caught between his body and the back cushions of the sofa. Their faces were mere inches apart, and when he tucked back the lock of her hair that had come loose, she closed her eyes, aware that it was beyond unwise to reflect on how warm or how sheltered she felt.

Hugh knew Brianna had experienced nothing more than the moment, else she'd have kept her gaze locked with his when he moved inside her, while he pleasured her and brought her to her climax.

He hadn't, either. 'Twas just the passion of the moment that had tricked him into imagining a depth of emotion that plainly did not exist. He'd known very few couples who ever attained profound connections with each other, and it was unrealistic to expect such a bond to occur with Brianna. Hell, they'd known each other barely a week, and she had deceived him for most of the duration.

"I can hear your stomach," he said to her, more than ready to put some space between them. "You must be hungry."

She nodded. "I waited for you."

"Ah. The wedding supper." He hadn't planned on

taking her here on the sofa. He'd intended to give her the shoes, and thought they would then sup together, enjoying Mrs. Ramsay's meal and a glass of wine before retiring to his bedchamber. To consummate the marriage.

And yet it was made clear once again that restraint was impossible with this exquisite woman. Especially when most of his thoughts on the return trip to Glenloch had been of her plump breasts filling his hands, her sleek legs wrapped around his waist, and her breathy sighs while he was deep inside her.

He was already partly aroused again, but he contained the urge to make love to her once again and sat up. He located his clothes on the floor nearby and stood to pull on his trews while Brianna lay sated, watching him.

Slowing his movements, he allowed her to look her fill of him . . . the man who would soon be her husband in name only.

It was a relief, really, to know that she was just as anxious to return to Killiedown as he was to take her there. His bachelor freedom was far more appealing than the thought of living through the disappointments and sorrows of another marriage, through the perfunctory marital coupling and the frustration of failing to conceive, month after month.

He looked at Brianna—superbly dazed and disheveled as she started to hold her bodice together—and suspected that marital coupling with this woman would never be perfunctory. 'Twould eventually be disappointing as they failed to bring about a pregnancy, but lovemaking would never be an obligatory performance.

He took her hand and assisted her to sit up. She stood and turned her back to him as she fastened her laces, and Hugh found himself swallowing an annoying wave of frustration at the knowledge that he would never see her grow large with his child under her breast.

'Twas a fool's dissatisfaction, for Hugh knew naught of being a father, and his example for such a role had been terribly flawed. Far better for Sir John Hartford and all his progeny—hopefully a male heir, one day—to inherit the Newbury lands.

They had not spoken all night, not even during the two times Hugh woke her, or the instance when she'd done the same to him. For there was naught to be said between them.

'Twas late in the morn when Brianna awoke for the day and found Hugh, freshly shaved and fully dressed, waiting for her. She drew the linen sheet up to her chest and sat up. "Have you been up long?"

"Long enough. Here." He draped a deep red dressing gown of soft wool around her shoulders, then took her hand. "I've got something for you."

He led her down to the nursery, and when he pushed open the door, Brianna saw a fire blazing in the grate. In front of it was a large copper bathtub full of steaming water waiting for her.

She fairly melted with delight and gratitude.

"Let's not let it get cold," Hugh said. He slipped the dressing gown from her shoulders and let it drop to the floor.

Standing fully naked before him, Brianna cupped his

face in her hands and kissed him lightly, as a courtesan might do to a generous benefactor. And, as delightful as the setting was, Bree knew better than to form any deeper attachment to this charming little room or the warm, intimate bedchamber at the far end of the gallery.

Or to Laird Glenloch himself. She put a seductive smile on her face. "Thank you. 'Twas very thoughtful."

He touched her chin, then skimmed his hand down to her throat and the center of her chest. A muscle in his jaw clenched, and he took her hand and assisted her as she stepped into the tub.

And then he left.

Hugh shouldn't have been surprised at how quickly his cock had roared to life when he held Brianna's hand and steadied her when she stepped naked into the hot water. She never failed to arouse him.

He saw that he'd abraded the skin of her throat and breasts with his whiskers, and it crossed his mind that he should make a point of shaving before they went to bed—

Except that such an accommodation would hardly be necessary, since Stonehaven's magistrate would be coming to Glenloch today. Hugh could not imagine the man allowing anything to delay his questions for Brianna, not when the murder of a Stonehaven official was at issue. And afterward, Hugh would take her to Killiedown as he'd promised.

The first things he saw when he went down to the library were the shoes he'd bought her. They had been a purely practical acquisition, for her old boots fit her ill, and Amelia's shoes could not be any better.

The purchase meant naught. Hugh knew it was unwise to become too accustomed to any one lover. Hopes and expectations always followed—none of which he intended to fulfill. He told himself 'twould actually be a relief when he returned Brianna to Killiedown Manor, and went back to his town house in London where there was any number of available bed partners from which to choose.

But he did not know when he would be able to leave Glenloch. There could no longer be any doubt that Malcolm MacGowan was guilty of embezzling the Glenloch brandy and taking potential income away from the Falkburn folk. It followed that he was also responsible for Kincaid's death.

But what part did Roddington play in all this?

Hugh hoped MacGowan had left the district forever. If the man had any sense, he would have gone as far away as possible, instead of staying to be brought up on murder charges. Perhaps his meeting with Roddington had been by chance, and the marquess had recognized him and offered to take him out of the district.

As much as Hugh would like to believe that, he did not think so. Roddington did naught for anyone without a price. If the two had met in Stonehaven, there had to have been a reason, and Hugh knew he wasn't going to like it if he ever discovered what it was.

The marquess might not have been directly involved in Kincaid's murder, but his association with MacGowan was suspect. Hugh had made no secret of his disdain . . . no, of his hatred for the marquess. He'd banished the iniquitous scoundrel from all his estates, extending no invitations, and avoiding the man if they both happened to be in town.

MacGowan and Roddington were scheming together, and it suddenly occurred to Hugh that it must have been going on for some time. While Hugh had been making up the difference in Roddington's profits, there was every likelihood that the scoundrel had been stealing those very profits from him. He'd been double-dipping.

Hugh felt angry and frustrated enough to terminate Glenloch's brandy trading altogether. And now that smuggling had become even more perilous than before, with customs agents poking nearby, and batsmen from Stonehaven, the people of Falkburn might be better off without the danger, too.

Yet they needed the income. Hugh could manage well without it, but he could not take it away from them.

There was no question that MacGowan and Roddington were out of it now. And Hugh decided he could put Niall MacTavish in charge of the operation. MacTavish could manage it well, in spite of his rudimentary reading and writing skills. No one would get anything past MacTavish, for he was an intelligent man and knew every aspect of the trade. And there was no doubt his first loyalty was to Hugh.

But even with MacTavish in charge, Hugh could not leave the district while Roddington was still at large. He'd have thought the marquess would have hastened back to his usual, preferred, Cerberus amusements in London, having escaped the marriage that had been forced upon him.

Yet that was not the case. And Hugh's suspicious

mind could not accept that Roddington and MacGowan had run across each other at the hotel by coincidence. Something was very wrong. And the murder of the customs surveyor only made it worse.

Hugh heard a rider approaching the castle. Safely assuming it would be Mr. Sinclair, he put Brianna's shoes into the box and set it on one of the steps to be carried upstairs with a maid. Then he returned to the library to await the man.

Mrs. Ramsay went to the door and let in the guest, calling for one of her grandsons to come and take charge of his horse. Then she brought the man to Hugh. A moment later, Lachann Sinclair was coming toward him with his hand extended. "Laird Glenloch."

Hugh rose to meet the magistrate, and indicated a chair near his own. He intended to use his usual subtle manner to lead the man to certain conclusions, and direct him as far as possible from suspicions of free trading in Falkburn.

"Have a seat and warm yourself, Mr. Sinclair." He looked at the housekeeper, who awaited instructions. "I believe you are preparing luncheon, Mrs. Ramsay?"

"Aye, Laird."

"Set a place for the magistrate, will you? And see if Lady Glenloch is ready to join us."

Mrs. Ramsay gave him a quick bend of the knee and left the library to summon Brianna. Hugh turned to Sinclair.

"Thank you," said the magistrate. "'Twas a long ride through the snow." He was well-dressed in a heavy woolen suit with a dark blue waistcoat and neck cloth, and his strikingly handsome face was ruddy with the cold. "'Tis a clear sky, but bitter cold today."

"I haven't been out, so I'll take your word on it, Sinclair."

The man looked around the room. "I've never been to Glenloch," he remarked. "'Tis an impressive place."

"Aye. More a fortress than a home, though."

"'Tis said it's haunted."

Hugh believed Sinclair was referring to the ancient ghost—not Amelia—so he gave a nod. "There are noises that would make one believe so . . . The townspeople are a superstitious lot."

"Aren't we all?" Sinclair remarked with a sociable laugh.

"Tell me, have you any more information regarding Mr. Kincaid's death?"

Sinclair sobered. "Alas, no. It looks as though he was hit with a shovel, for the wound was more than a simple blow. Something broke the skin . . . Ah, well, you saw it yourself. It looked to the coroner like the edge of a shovel."

Hugh nodded. "Have you any better idea of what might have happened to the man?"

The magistrate leaned forward. "Free traders, more than likely. Kincaid was investigating reports of a cutter down in these parts. We're guessing he must have interrupted a shipment and run afoul of a batsman or two."

"We've heard rumors as well . . . of smuggling ships up a ways north of here."

"You mentioned a strong current in your cove. In which direction does it flow?"

"From north to south. And it's swift."

"So Kincaid's body might have been dumped north of here and drifted south by the time Lady Glenloch saw it."

"That would be my guess. He might even have been killed in Stonehaven and his body drifted this far."

Sinclair paused to consider that possibility. "Have you heard anything else about the smuggling trade?"

"I have a concern that my estate manager, Malcolm MacGowan, is involved." He did not mention Roddington. The marquess was a master at escaping blame, only to turn suspicion on an accuser. It was dangerous enough for Hugh to implicate his former manager.

"MacGowan, you say?" Sinclair asked, taking a pencil and a small ledger book full of scribbled pages from his pocket. Hugh watched him write MacGowan's name on the first blank sheet.

"Yes. Malcolm. A tall, stocky, red-haired man."

Sinclair looked up at Hugh. "We've no dearth of those, Laird."

"No, you're right," Hugh said, although he knew of no other who was brazen enough to cheat his employer. "I discovered some disturbing inconsistencies in the records this particular man sent me in London and was forced to come up here in this dreadful weather to see about them."

"And were you satisfied with what you found?" Sinclair asked.

"Not exactly," said Hugh, prevaricating. "I believe the man has been stealing from me for quite some time."

"Might you elaborate, Laird Glenloch?"

" 'Tis rather personal, Sinclair," Hugh said. "But I will tell you that he and I had a bit of an altercation. I felt it necessary to tell him of my dissatisfaction, and upon further examination of the records, I intended to dismiss him from his post."

" 'Twas serious, then."

"I would say so. But the point of the matter is that MacGowan has disappeared from Falkburn."

"Do you suspect foul play?"

"Not against him, no. But he left the village only a few hours before my wife first saw Mr. Kincaid in the water." Long enough for MacGowan to have ridden to Stonehaven.

Sinclair frowned.

"And there were whispers of the man's involvement with free traders and Stonehaven batsmen."

Mr. Sinclair placed his book on his knee. " 'Tis what I feared."

The conversation was going exactly as Hugh had hoped, with Hugh playing the magistrate like a finely crafted pianoforte. Each note was emerging just as it should. But then Brianna entered the room, and Sinclair stood abruptly at the sight of her.

"Bria— er, Miss M-Munro!" he said, obviously startled by her arrival, and quite obviously a close acquaintance.

Chapter 16

Feather by feather, the goose is plucked.
SCOTTISH PROVERB

Hugh narrowed his eyes and went to her side. Taking her hand and placing it in the crook of his arm, he demonstrated his dominion. "Mr. Sinclair, my wife, Lady Glenloch. But apparently you know each other?"

Brianna slipped away from Hugh and extended both hands to the magistrate. "Lachann Sinclair? It's been a very long time!" she cried, taking his hands in hers.

"A good three years, I would say. Ever since you went off to London and became too busy for your Scottish country friends." The image of a dog slavering over a bone came to Hugh's mind, the kind he'd like to kick from the room.

"You've grown up!" she said, as though he was the only lad ever to have reached manhood.

"You are more beautiful than when you left us, if that is even possible."

She smiled prettily at the man, and with the way Sinclair gazed down at her, Hugh thought he might have to crush the magistrate's throat.

"You are too kind."

"But Lady Glenloch now?"

She blushed but did not answer as Mrs. Ramsay came to the doorway and interrupted the nauseating interchange. "Laird, luncheon is served."

Brianna slid her arm through Sinclair's and walked beside him to the dining room. Hugh followed, resisting the urge to rush ahead and grab Brianna, and escort her there himself.

He managed to exercise excellent restraint. What difference did it make that she'd had an admirer in Stonehaven? Muchalls was not very far north of Stonehaven, so Killiedown must be fairly close to town. The social interactions Brianna and Claire enjoyed were likely split between Aberdeen and Stonehaven. Of course she'd known him. Of course he'd desired her. What sensible man wouldn't?

But it occurred to Hugh that she had not gone to him, or to anyone else in Stonehaven for assistance when she'd fled from her wedding to Roddington.

Sinclair assisted Brianna with her chair, then found his own seat across from her while Hugh took the end, to sit between them. And ended up subjecting himself to their reminiscences of past events.

"Society became worse than dull in Stonehaven after you went down to London," Sinclair said. "Even Lady Claire seemed to shun us while you were away."

"I am sorry to hear that," Brianna said. "I believe she had close . . . friends in Aberdeen whom she liked to visit while I was away from home."

Home. It was a good reminder for Hugh. Her home was Killiedown Manor, and he was going to take her there later. Or perhaps it would be best to wait until the morrow, when they would be able to leave early.

And then everyone in the district would learn that Laird Glenloch and his wife were estranged, and she would become prey to every handsome—as well as every randy—buck on the eastern coast.

"'Tis understandable," said Sinclair. "And now the most beautiful lass in Kincardineshire has returned to us as Lady Glenloch. 'Tis hard to believe."

Hugh unclenched his teeth. "Why might that be?"

"Oh, no reason at all—just that every bachelor in Stonehaven will be crushed to learn that you are . . . taken."

Brianna flashed a look at Hugh, but quickly turned to her soup. Hugh inhaled a deep breath and took the moment to return to the discussion that had been interrupted by Brianna's arrival in the library.

"About Malcolm MacGowan," he said, most definitely intending to prejudice the magistrate, as well as divert the conversation from the darling of Stonehaven.

"Ah, yes."

"No one here or in Falkburn has seen him since the day Mr. Kincaid washed ashore."

Sinclair looked across the table at Brianna, and when Hugh noticed her sudden pallor, he realized he was being the worst possible cad, and never should have brought up such an indelicate subject. At lunch, no less. He clenched his teeth with the knowledge that his brain must have become addled by the syrupy conversation thus far.

And yet he'd felt out of sorts ever since he'd left their bed that morn and come downstairs. It could only be due to lack of sleep.

"I have some questions for you, Miss Munro—er, my lady. But perhaps I'll wait until after the meal."

Brianna nodded. "Yes. Thank you."

They proceeded to engage in small talk, on subjects regarding Stonehaven's social mavens and a few of their mutual friends. Hugh learned that Lachann Sinclair had read law in London, had become magistrate two years before, and had dealt with only one other case of murder in his district.

Hugh thought there might be yet another, if the damned magistrate didn't stop ogling Brianna's décolletage.

Hugh looked as though he was prepared to murder someone, and Brianna did not understand why. The conversation was progressing exactly as it should, with Lachann being directed away from the free trading at Glenloch, toward Mr. MacGowan.

It was strange to see Lachann again, after her seasons in London. He was comely in his way, with coloring similar to her own, and fine gentlemanly features. But she felt no connection to him, and his magnetism could not compare to Hugh's.

They returned to the library after luncheon, and Brianna sat on the sofa where Hugh had made love to her the night before. She suppressed a shiver at the thought of it, of the worrisome intimacy she'd felt then, and again during the night.

She knew such intense feelings could only hurt her. She'd learned more than enough about attachments that caused too much pain, and she wanted nothing more to do with them. 'Twas far better to banter with Lachann, the young man who'd flirted with her in good fun during her adolescence, than to allow herself to be distracted by the dark, brooding man who stood a few feet away, looking out the library window.

"Now I fear I must come to the business at hand, Lady Glenloch," he said. "Will you tell me how you happened to notice Mr. Kincaid's body?"

"I was upstairs in one of the bedchambers," she said, not at all pleased at having to recall what she'd seen. She swallowed and continued. "When I happened to look out the window, I saw something in the water."

"At that time, could you tell what it was?"

"Not really. It was too far away, and there was no sun to speak of."

"Did you ever imagine it might be a body?"

"Not until the clouds cleared and I was able to see better. Then, I admit, it did occur to me."

"Once you suspected it might be a person floating there, what did you do?"

"I ran out to the stable, where my husband was."
Her husband. The words fell so easily from her tongue, and yet Hugh did not come to her then, or even turn toward her.

But Lachann turned his attention to him. "What did you do, Laird?"

"I went to the beach immediately, of course." He came to stand by the table where they'd signed their marriage document and crossed his arms over his chest. "By that point, the body had drifted quite close, and we could see what it was."

"Were you able to reach it from shore?"

"No," said Brianna. She hesitated, biting her lip in dismay. "My husband had to get into a boat and . . ." She swallowed.

"It was several yards out, so I had to row out to it and drag it back to shore."

Lachann asked the same questions again, but in different ways as he took down notes in his small book.

"My lady, would you mind showing me the window through which you first saw the body?"

"Of course."

"I'll take him," Hugh said. "'Twas the nursery, was it not?"

Brianna nodded, but Lachann was not satisfied with the arrangement. "If you don't mind, Laird, I'd like Lady Glenloch to point out exactly where she first saw the body."

'Twas clear that Hugh was not pleased, but he led the way to the staircase, then stepped aside for Brianna to precede him. Lachann followed, and they climbed the stairs, then walked down the long gallery to the nursery. A low-pitched howl sounded somewhere nearby, and Lachann stopped abruptly.

"'Tis the ghost, Laird?" he said. "Where does it

haunt? Does anyone know what it looks like?"

"I've never seen it," Hugh said as he pushed open the door to the nursery, obviously uninterested and unconvinced by the ghost's disturbance.

"That sounded rather alarming," said Lachann.

"The wind."

Even as Hugh said it, Brianna knew he was wrong, but she did not challenge his words as they entered the room.

The tub had not yet been removed, and it stood full of cold water, before the fire that had died down almost to naught. The dressing gown Hugh had given her lay draped across the bed, and the room had an air of intimacy Brianna had no wish to share with Lachann Sinclair.

She went directly to the window and pointed in a northerly direction. "It was there—just barely in sight."

"'Tis a wonder you saw it," said Lachann.

"I believe Mr. Kincaid was . . . wearing red. He was not difficult to see."

"Ah." He stepped back from the window and started for the door, subtly pausing to peruse the room. He made no remark, but Brianna felt her face heat with embarrassment. Without thinking, she slipped her hand into the bend of Hugh's arm.

"Have you seen enough, Sinclair?" Hugh asked, and Brianna blushed at his choice of words. Lachann had seen more than enough.

"Aye, Laird. Thank you."

They returned to the foot of the stairs near the main entryway, and Hugh called for Mrs. Ramsay to bring Lachann's coat and to have one of the lads bring his horse to the front. He was clearly anxious to be rid of the man.

Perhaps so that they could be on their way to Killiedown?

Lachann could take her. Claire's estate was not too much farther north of Stonehaven, and Brianna did not think Lachann would mind escorting her there.

Yet the thought of it was sobering. She was not yet ready to leave Glenloch. Of course she wanted to return home, but Hugh had indicated they would leave the day after the magistrate's visit. 'Twas what she had prepared herself to do.

Besides, she could not go while there were unanswered questions about the customs agent's death. And there was something unresolved about the ghost. Bree knew it had been trying to tell her something the previous afternoon, and she had decided to pursue it today. Perhaps she would finally understand the meaning of those hidden items and why the poor thing persisted in haunting Glenloch's halls and rooms. She wondered why it had howled just now when they were in the nursery, and not shown itself to the master of Glenloch himself.

Lachann rode away, and Brianna returned to the library with Hugh. "What will you do about Mr. MacGowan?"

"Nothing. I just hope your Mr. Sinclair will locate him and deal with him."

"*My* Mr. Sinclair?"

He took an iron poker in hand and prodded the peat in the fireplace. "He is clearly enamored of you."

The willful streak that she usually managed to keep submerged, surfaced. "Do you think so?"

He did not turn to her, nor did he reply. Instead, he gave the fire far more attention than was strictly necessary, and Brianna realized he was bothered by the possibility that Lachann was attracted to her.

He muttered something low and menacing, and Brianna decided it would be best to allow the subject to drop.

"Where do you think Mr. MacGowan went?" she asked.

"I have no idea." He finally stood and brushed off his hands. "Perhaps he's decided to leave Britain on one of Captain Benoit's ships."

She sat down and gave him a questioning glance.

"He'll know he's wanted for murder, won't he? So perhaps he's already found a ship to take him to France," said Hugh.

"He has connections there?"

"Only with Captain Benoit, I believe. But he might prove himself of value to the captain on that end."

Brianna sat down. "Will you return to London now? I mean, after I go to Killiedown?"

He answered her flatly. "Not yet. I must stay here and decide what to do about the brandy trade before I go."

He'd been irate before, and now he seemed so cold and indifferent that it was difficult for Brianna to rec-

oncile this man with the one who'd so thoughtfully ordered a hot bath for her—in the nursery, no less, where
its preparation would not disturb her sleep.

Bree could almost believe he'd been angry with
Lachann Sinclair over her old friend's flattering attentions. Perhaps even jealous. The very idea put her quite
off balance.

"I'm thinking of leaving MacTavish in control of
the business. He can write and cipher well enough to
manage it."

Brianna decided Hugh could not have been jealous
at all, but merely out of sorts with all the recent com-
plications he'd had to deal with. Once those issues were
settled, he would be free to go.

"You seem to have been all the crack in Stonehaven,"
he said suddenly. "What made you leave?"

"My aunt thought I should go to London for a season
or two."

"To find a husband."

Brianna looked at him curiously, for his tone had
changed once again. "That's what she thought. That
even though it would require staying with Lord Stamford for a few months of the year, I should have a chance
to make as good a marriage as my mother had done."

"And what did you think?" His eyes disarmed her,
dark and speculative.

She looked directly into those eyes. "I fell in love.
It was my first season, and Bernard Malham was the
handsomest suitor any young lady could desire."

His eyes flared with the use of that word.

Desire. She wondered if that was all there was between them.

"And yet you did not marry him."

"Lord Stamford would not give his consent. He was uninterested in aligning any of us with an insignificant Northumbrian baron." She swallowed, and lowered her voice. "And with my guardian's refusal, my young man chose someone else." She reached down and adjusted one of her new shoes. "At least he waited a few days before becoming engaged to her."

He let go a long, deep breath, and started to leave the room. But he stopped at the doorway and scratched the back of his head, turning around to ask her, "What happened between you and Roddington?"

Brianna was taken aback by the question. "Roddington? What do you mean?"

The bloody marquess had not left the district, and now Hugh could not get him out of his mind. He could not even begin to consider what might happen when the bastard learned that Brianna was alone at Killiedown, and he had no doubt that would happen. Brianna would renew her acquaintances in Muchalls and Stonehaven, with Sinclair and others. Word of her presence would spread.

Sinclair might be infatuated with her, but Hugh knew the man couldn't protect her.

"I mean, what happened to make Roddington agree to marry you? I used to know the damned bounder fairly well—far better than I ever cared to. So I know that something must have occurred—some incident—

that gave Stamford the leverage to make him marry you." Hugh knew better than to ask this. He'd hated hearing about the baron who'd disappointed her, and knew that what he learned about Roddington's actions was going to enrage him.

He kept to a prudent distance, staying near the doorway to ask the question, hoping the space between them would help him to keep his emotions in check. "Did he . . . Did he hurt you?"

She swallowed, and her brow furrowed slightly before answering. "Not seriously," she finally replied.

"Not *seriously*? What did he do to you?"

She picked at one of her fingernails. "Hardly anything."

"Brianna, what?" He found himself going to her in spite of his best intentions, and taking a seat beside her. "What did he do?"

She looked away. "Lord Stamford had taken us to a house party in Kensington. One evening after supper, he sent me to fetch one of his daughters from a parlor at the back of the house, but Catherine was not there."

"I assume Roddington was."

She nodded, and paused before continuing. "I thought only to be courteous and exchange greetings, then quickly take my leave. But he would not let me go. I am not sure how he did it, but he cornered me. He got around me somehow and shoved me back against a wall and . . , and . . ."

Her voice quavered, giving Hugh more than just a vague impetus to make the ride to Dundee right now, to find the bastard, and to call him out. Better yet, to drag him into a boxing ring. Someone needed to interdict Rotten Roddington's practice of seeking out the most innocent, vulnerable prey he could find, and teach him a lesson at the same time.

"Before I could stop him or even call for help, the marquess . . . He had one hand up my skirt and the other on my breast."

Hugh saw red, but managed to keep a relatively calm, even voice. "Then I suppose someone came into the room and found you that way. *Compromised.*"

"Yes. *Ruined*, to use Lady Stamford's word. She and two of her friends discovered us, and made such a fuss that half the party came running as though the house was afire. My guardian's wife made it sound as though the marquess and I had had an assignation." She looked up quickly, her features reflecting the anger and frustration she must have felt. "But nothing could have been farther from the truth! He squeezed me until I bruised . . ."

Hugh's jaw tightened.

"And then he acted as if I were some sort of . . . of . . ."

She was too innocent to know the word she was looking for, and Hugh did not doubt that Stamford and his wife were every bit as guilty of putting her in Roddington's path as the marquess had been for assaulting her. They'd sacrificed Brianna to their aspirations for a marital connection to the future Duke of Chalwyck, refusing the insignificant young man she'd loved.

"You are not that, Brianna," he said quietly. "They victimized you, intentionally."

She looked down at the edge of the thumbnail she'd torn away. "I know. But I should have known better."

"How could you? Besides, you escaped their intrigues, did you not?"

"I could not marry him, Hugh. He is . . ." She shuddered. "There is something rather twisted about him. I had to flee, no matter what the consequences."

And Hugh was ashamed to admit that he'd put her in exactly the same compromised situation her first night at Glenloch. 'Twas no wonder she'd run from him at her first opportunity.

Though he was not "twisted," as Roddington was, Hugh feared he was not much better than the damned marquess.

They left the library and parted company awkwardly, with Brianna feeling relieved that they would not be leaving for Killiedown just yet, but puzzled by all that had gone unsaid.

Hugh left the castle to go into Falkburn to meet with Mr. MacTavish, and Brianna still could not shake the notion that he'd been jealous of Lachann Sinclair. And she sensed that he had not been pleased to learn that she'd fallen in love during her first season.

Feeling restless after the conversation in the library, Brianna went into his study and watched out the window as he came out of the stable, riding his gelding toward the Falkburn road. She wondered how long he'd

known Roddington, and whether the marquess would
have become as loathsome a father as Hugh's had been.
She shuddered at the knowledge that she might have
become mother to his offspring, and thanked God that
she had escaped that fate.

The intimidating portrait of the old laird glared down
at Bree from its place of honor on the wall. She wished
that her husband would dispose of it and all the others
like it, just as he'd expelled Roddington's odious presence from their house.

But he would not speak of his father, and even tried
to behave as though he was unaffected by all the pictures of the loathsome man. Turning her back on the
portrait as Hugh always did, Brianna left the room and
retrieved her coat, then went outside to look at the north
tower again. The ghost had surely been trying to show
her something, and Brianna could not give up trying to
figure out what it was.

This time, she approached the building much more
closely, climbing past the snowdrifts to look into the
ruins. There was a hollow space inside the old pantry,
but Brianna could barely see into it, for precious little
light penetrated through the cracked walls. She backed
away and skirted around the snow-covered shrubs,
then went to the opposite side of the ancient room.
Peeking in through a gap in the stone wall, she was finally able to discern some shadowy forms in the ruins,
but could not see clearly enough to make out any of
the objects inside. She doubted there was anything
notable there.

Shivering with the cold, Bree retreated into the castle, wondering once again if the ghost's intent had not really been to show her something specific. Perhaps it only meant to make her to stop and think, as she had done before, when she'd found Hugh's drawing of the sailboat.

Bree hung up her coat and went upstairs. She stopped in the nursery to retrieve her shawl, but took the plaid blanket from the croft instead, folding it and draping it around her shoulders.

Then she went to Amelia's room.

She had not thought there would be any reason to return there, for she had no use for any more of Amelia's clothes. But the ghost had led Brianna there more than once. If Glenloch's ghost wanted her to reflect upon something . . . What could it be?

Hugh's jealousy during lunch?

He *had* been jealous. It was quite clear that he hadn't enjoyed learning that Brianna had been sought-after in Stonehaven, or that her first love had been denied. She was not sure what it meant, but she felt an unexpected inkling of hope.

He might not want her to go at all.

It was worse than troubling to realize that she did not wish to leave, either. Not that she felt attached to Castle Glenloch. It was Hugh. She wanted to stay with her husband, wherever he might be.

Brianna felt her heart drop to the pit of her stomach. Perhaps Hugh had only been acting in a territorial manner with Lachann, as a stallion would do around other males when his mate was near. It might have been a purely instinctual reaction. And yet she did not want to believe it. He cared for her more than he wanted to admit.

Perhaps his reticence was because of Amelia, Bree thought as she stepped into the woman's room. It was entirely possible that Hugh had loved her, and she'd betrayed him with her suicide.

If Brianna's heart could have dropped any further, it would have done so then. The pain of being moved from one home to another when she became the inconvenient poor relation paled compared to what Hugh must have felt at Amelia's death. She remembered finding the locket that had been lost—or perhaps hidden—down the side of the dressing table. Slipping her hand into the narrow gap between the table and the wall, she drew it out, took the pendant in hand, and opened it.

She ran her thumb over the edges of the locket and the miniature of the young man, snagging it on a tiny catch at the bottom of the oval. The front of the pendant swung open. Behind it, Brianna found a small lock of hair. 'Twas the same light brown hair as the man in the picture.

She sat on the ornately sculpted chair in front of the dressing table and gazed down at the locket, wondering who the young man was, and how important he must have been to Amelia. A lock of hair gave every indication that he was more important than her husband.

It must be a significant find, since the ghost had shown it to Brianna. But Bree did not know what to make of the revelation, or what to do with it.

* * *

Hugh was relieved to be away from the castle. Away from Brianna and everything she made him feel. Life was so much simpler when he was not wasting his time comparing himself to Roddington, or worrying about her safety when he eventually left her at Killiedown. Alone, without protection.

Good Christ, could he even leave her there alone? If he allowed himself to face the truth, he would have to admit it was no longer what he wanted. Before he'd known who she was, he'd asked her to stay at Glenloch with him, at least for a while. Now he feared he might want Brianna to stay with him always.

Yet that was a disaster in the making. She would eventually hope for a real future with him, with all the trappings of an actual family. Births, christenings, ponies, school holidays. Hugh knew he would be no more successful in providing her with children than he'd been with Amelia.

Besides, she'd been quite clear about her desire to return to her aunt's manor. Until their lunch with Sinclair, Hugh had not given much thought to the life Brianna must have led in Kincardineshire, of all the young men—besides Sinclair—who would have fallen in love with her. And he couldn't even begin to think about the followers she'd attracted during her London seasons, or the man she'd loved and lost.

It was the ultimate irony that Hugh was bothered by her pining for a man who had not fought for her. Hell, it did more than bother him. It infuriated him. First, because the idiot had caused her sorrow, and second, because Hugh hated knowing she'd loved someone else.

What a fool he was.

"Laird! Good day to ye," called Osgar Tullis, who was sweeping the cobblestone walk in front of his public house.

Hugh dismounted and tied his horse at the post. "Send someone for MacTavish, will you, Tullis?"

"Aye, Laird."

A very odd idea crossed Hugh's mind as he went into the tavern, and he found himself unable to ignore it, even when MacTavish arrived. Tullis joined them at the table, and Hugh checked to see if MacGowan had been seen in the vicinity since his disappearance. If the innkeeper in Stonehaven was correct and he was en route to Dundee with Roddington, their coach would have passed nearby. Might even have stopped to allow a passenger to leave.

MacTavish shook his head. "I heard naught of him."

"I saw no lights up in his cottage last night, Laird," said Tullis.

It would have been reassuring to have some guarantee that the blackguard had gone all the way to Dundee. Just because there had been no sign of life at his cottage did not mean the man wasn't lurking about somewhere.

"We'll need to suspend our shipments for a while," Hugh said. "Until after the inquiry, at least."

"Aye, Laird. 'Tis our habit every year to quit until the weather clears, anyway," said MacTavish. "Benoit willna come into these waters again until late January, or even February, depending."

"That's good. And even then we might want to delay the trade for a while longer."

"But the income . . ."

"I'll make up the difference for now," said Hugh. "And with the changes I'm considering, I believe there will soon be a more steady prosperity for all of Falkburn."

"What are ye thinkin', Laird?"

"A distillery."

Chapter 17

Wisdom is best taught by distress.
SCOTTISH PROVERB

His statement was met with silence.

"Where is the best whisky in the world made?" he asked.

"Scotland, of course. But we've never—"

"Which does not mean we cannot begin," Hugh said.

MacTavish leaned forward, his arms crossed on the table, while Tullis frowned prodigiously.

"We can do it legitimately. Pay the taxes."

"Pay the taxes!" Tullis exclaimed, though he kept his incredulous voice down to a hush. "Laird, ye must know it goes against m' Scottish blood to pay taxes to the English crown."

"I understand, Tullis," said Hugh. "But Kincaid's murder turned our trade into a much more dangerous business than it's ever been before. You must know that the crown will send someone to replace the surveyor, and we cannot hope the man will be as ineffective as Kincaid."

"Aye, that's true," said MacTavish.

"A new man might even report Armstrong for incompetence and see to it that he's replaced."

"And what about Pennycook?" asked MacTavish. "If MacGowan's been bribing him with our brandy for his daughter's favors . . ."

"Speakin' of it would land him in a world o' trouble," said Tullis.

"Yes, so I'm guessing he'll keep quiet. Even so, Kincaid's murder turned the magistrate's eye toward Glenloch, in spite of Pennycook's silence."

"Because of MacGowan," said Tullis. "He killed Kincaid."

Hugh shrugged. He felt sure Roddington was involved somehow, but the marquess wouldn't have been the one to smash Kincaid's forehead in. It was more his style to have pushed the man into the sea. "Aye," he said. "It seems likely.

A deep crease furrowed Tullis's brow, but MacTavish appeared to be more receptive to the idea of abandoning Falkburn's free trade.

"How would we do it?" he asked. "How would we start up a still . . . I mean, a legal distillery?"

"I haven't worked out any details yet," said Hugh with a distinct sensation of breaking with the past. A past that deserved to be broken. "But we've got a river full of good, rich water, and if every field is planted with barley this spring, we might be able to start when autumn comes."

"'Tis surely a . . . *different* solution," said MacTavish. "I canna say I ever looked forward to those late shipments down at the castle, when we could be caught at any time."

"Not that there was much chance of it wi' the lot who keep watch up in Stonehaven," said Tullis.

"Aye, but as Laird Glenloch said," MacTavish remarked, "tha's likely to change. And no' for the better, either."

As they talked, the idea of a legitimate distillery took on a more solid shape in Hugh's mind, as did his conviction that Glenloch's smuggling days were over. "I remember hearing of a new kind of still . . . I'll see what more I can learn about it." And about the distilling process in general. He would need to engage architects and engineers to build the distillery, and a manager to oversee the entire process.

Someone refilled Hugh's glass, and as he looked up into the smoky gray eyes of Tullis's comely barmaid, he realized she'd been hovering about their table, but he hadn't even noticed her presence.

Naught had changed about her. The lass's body was still as lush and inviting as ever. She smiled prettily at him, but her mouth did not create the same havoc in his brain that his wife's did, nor could her lusty eyes draw him into her arms the way Brianna's could do.

His throat tightened, and he suddenly felt as though he could not breathe. The prettiest lass in Falkburn had no sway over him. He felt no stirring. No desire.

He knew as well as Brianna that their marriage had been a mistake. He should release her from her vows. Surely the scandal of divorce would be minimal in

Scotland, freeing her to wed someone else . . . Someone like Lachann Sinclair.

Hugh's stomach burned at the thought of it.

"We can figure how much barley to plant," he heard MacTavish say, but Hugh was barely able to focus on the subject at hand.

But one thing he did realize. He had to be daft even to consider committing himself to a project that would require his frequent presence in Glenloch—only a short ride from Killiedown Manor.

Brianna placed the pendant on the mantelpiece. She did not know how she was going to bring it to Hugh's attention, only that she needed to do it. The ghost would not have shown it to her unless it was necessary.

Perhaps she would give it to him after she told him of her hope to remain with him at Glenloch, as his wife.

Her heart tripped in her chest at the thought of saying the words. She might very well have misread his signs of jealousy, and he was just as anxious to be rid of her as he'd been when they'd wed.

And yet she could not help but hope his attitude had changed, at least enough to give them a chance to forge a true marriage. She knew he must have gone out of his way to purchase the lovely shoes she now wore, and he had cared enough to arrange for a luxurious hot bath to be brought to the nursery for her that morn. They were small things, but signs of his true character, nonetheless. He was a kind and thoughtful man whose consideration went beyond the bedchamber, though Brianna had not mistaken the intensity of his lovemaking in the library, or when he'd reached for her during the night.

The force of his passions had created a torrent of confusing emotions in Bree, and she'd been too cowardly to face them. But now she risked unguarding her heart, slowly and carefully, unveiling her feelings in layers. *And in so doing, she knew that she loved him.*

Bree pressed one hand to her mouth and closed her eyes tightly against the flood of feelings that threatened to overwhelm her. 'Twas frightening, this emotion that had caused naught but pain for her in the past. She'd lost every connection she'd ever made, and been turned out of every house that had grudgingly taken her in. She'd hoped for a friend who would be true to her, and prayed that Bernard Malham would take her with or without her dowry, all without success.

It was only the isolation of Killiedown and her aunt's loyalty that had kept her heart safe.

And yet she was far beyond having a choice in the way she felt about Hugh. She wanted him, wanted to be his wife. She'd made a vow to take him with all his imperfections as well as his virtues. Bree understood now that she'd meant those words, though she had not been able to admit it, even to herself, on the day she'd spoken them.

With trepidation, she went up to the nursery and put on the gown she'd worn for their wedding, then pinned up her hair, using Amelia's combs. She told herself repeatedly that this was no mistake, that she felt more for Hugh Christie than she had any other man—even Bernard.

The servants left at dark, and Brianna waited patiently for Hugh to return and sup with her. But as it grew later and he did not appear, she lost all appetite for food. She started to feel unsure of her course, and had second thoughts about telling him how she felt. He had never contradicted her intention to return to Killiedown, and Brianna suspected he might very well be anxious for her to go.

She paced nervously in the library. The room that had felt so warm and inviting just the night before, so cozy and intimate, now felt cold and huge. And empty.

There was no good reason to remain there, dressed in her best gown and waiting anxiously, for it was clear that Hugh had found something far more engaging to do in Falkburn than to return home to her. She went up the steps, thinking she would return to the small nursery, but changed her mind when she reached the top of the stairs. She headed in the opposite direction, back to Amelia's bedchamber.

Brianna pulled her shawl tight around her shoulders and stepped inside the room as she considered the best way to approach her husband when he returned. Or whether to approach him at all. She felt a need to understand Hugh's first marriage a little better before speaking to him of their own.

But no answers came to her.

She turned her attention to the furnishings in the cold bedchamber. 'Twas likely Amelia had spent her nights there, rather than in her husband's bed. And if the miniature in her locket meant what Bree thought it did, then Amelia could not have been very welcoming when Hugh had come to her here.

Considering the possibility that Amelia might have hidden some correspondence that would shed light on her sorrow, Brianna went to the larger of the two wardrobes and slid her hands into the spaces between the folded clothes. Finding naught, she opened each of the drawers and searched inside, finding nothing but the usual stockings and smallclothes.

She closed the wardrobe and turned her back to it, leaning against it as she thought about Amelia's profound unhappiness. She'd been separated from someone she cared for, a situation that was far too close to that which Brianna would soon suffer, if she did not manage to convince Hugh that they ought to stay together. She did not want to think of the empty days— months—she would have to endure at Killiedown Manor without him.

Feeling as lost as she'd ever been, she let her gaze drift aimlessly, finally alighting on the dressing table. She frowned, noticing something lopsided about it. A drawer.

'Twas odd that she had not taken note of it before, but the table was carved very ornately, and the drawer seemed to be part of the façade, only it was slightly ajar now. She went to it and found an indentation, just below the top of the table. 'Twas in a concealed space where her fingers fit, just barely. She pulled it open and found naught but a few small sponges and a jar of water.

Brianna opened the jar and sniffed, drawing back at the acrid smell of vinegar. The discovery meant naught to her, and when she was startled by the sound of doors opening and closing downstairs, she left the room, anxious to see Hugh. To tell him how she felt, before she lost her courage.

She was just descending the stairs when he entered the hall, stopping abruptly when he saw her. They stood paralyzed in the moment, and then he turned his back to her and walked into the drawing room.

Brianna refused to acknowledge the snub, aware that their earlier parting had been uncomfortable. She followed him into the main room of the castle, watching as he poured himself a drink from a crystal decanter of brandy. He took one sip, then went to the portrait of Jasper Christie hanging beside the panel that led to the secret passageway. Hugh lifted it down, laying it flat on the floor.

To Brianna's amazement, he stood on one end of the heavy frame and pulled up the other side, breaking the frame in half. He carried the whole thing to the fireplace and tossed it in, causing the existing fire to flare when it caught.

"Hugh?" she asked.

"'Tis time for a few changes," he said.

"I see." She watched him do the same to a smaller picture, then take his brandy in hand and leave the drawing room, going into the study to repeat the exercise.

"What brought this on?" she asked, following him to the dining room, where he tore down the portrait that hung there.

"Naught but a desire to break with the past."

His words raised her sliver of hope to more of a shimmer. If he wanted to put the past behind him, then surely he was looking forward, toward a future together.

She opened her mouth to tell him of her wish to stay with him, but she'd anticipated a quieter, more romantic situation. Perhaps in his bedchamber as they undressed each other. Or when she straddled him, naked and needy. He would not deny her then.

But he was wholly occupied with destroying his father's likenesses. "There are probably more portraits, and even a few landscapes stored in your attics," she said. Perhaps they could go up and explore those rooms together in the soft, intimate lamplight.

"Those can all burn, too. These walls will remain empty until I can commission new paintings."

"New paintings?" Her heart sank, for it seemed to be a hint that he intended to leave for London soon. Where else would he go for artwork?

"Aye. I've decided to end the free trade at Glenloch and begin a new venture."

The discussion was not going at all as Brianna had planned, and her eyes filled with tears of frustration, not that he noticed. "What will you do?"

"Whisky."

"I don't understand. You just said you were going to end the smuggling."

"We're going to make it," he said, taking a drink of his brandy as he walked into the library. "We'll distill it ourselves. We'll call it Glenloch whisky and sell it all over Britain."

"Then you mean to . . . to stay?"

He did not look at her, but walked to the fireplace and set his drink on the mantel. In a very deliberate manner, he remained a few steps away from her, hardly looking at her as he spoke. "That won't be necessary. At least, not right away."

Brianna felt her small rays of hope slipping away. "So you're going to leave."

He started to say something, but his gaze caught on Amelia's locket, and he looked at it as though it were a venomous snake. "Where did this come from?"

"The ghost showed it to me."

He looked at her with exasperation. "You know full well there is no ghost. We've only encouraged the tales about it to keep the curious away from the brandy."

"You're wrong. The ghost is real, and it led me into Amelia's bedchamber. It showed me where the locket was hidden."

"Aye. This was hers," he said, his jaw clenching. "Where was it?"

"'Twas caught on a splinter on the side of her dressing table, next to the wall," she said, her heart tumbling to her toes at the distance he'd put between them. "Open it."

Gingerly, he picked it up, but his fingers were too big and he could not work the catch. Bree went to him and took it from his hand. As she worked the catch, she could not have been more aware of the way he avoided her touch, and she realized he'd come to some decision about them. Opposite to the one she'd reached.

Tamping down her anguish, she opened both parts of the locket, so that he could see the miniature, as well as the lock of hair.

He gazed at it for a long moment, then took it from her and closed his hand around it, snapping it shut.

" 'Tis Simon Parker. A gentleman from town."

He said naught after that, but his features darkened ominously, and Brianna knew that he was considering the ramifications of that portrait and the small lock of hair hidden behind it.

Hugh picked up his brandy and went to the staircase. *Simon Parker*, for God's sake!

He wondered what other treasures Amelia might have left for him to find—if he'd ever allowed himself to look.

The servants had cleared away all her belongings from his other houses, but his staff at Glenloch had been reluctant to spend any time in Amelia's bedchamber. As had he, but for an entirely different reason.

He entered her room, opening both wardrobes and pulling out every drawer. He dumped the contents on the bed and pawed through them, looking for other keepsakes, other clues of what had been in her mind.

He knew what a miniature in a locket and a lock of hair meant. She'd been in love with Parker, and he with her. But Hugh knew her father would never have allowed the match—just as Brianna's guardian had refused her first choice. An obscure baron was nearly as bad as a merchant's son.

Christ, he should have known there was more to Amelia's distance and despondency. She had loved another man. No matter how Hugh had tried to please her, his wife would never have been happy in their marriage.

He took a long pull of his brandy, then rubbed a hand over his face. Simon Parker would have made a perfectly fine husband, although he wouldn't have been accepted into the society Amelia's family valued so highly. Had she wed Parker, the daughter of an earl would have become a merchant's wife.

And spared him years of misery and blame. Of guilt.

Hugh sat down on the bed, his stomach clenching painfully. Their fathers had likely known of Amelia's preference for the other man when they'd arranged the match. Not that it would have mattered, for marriages among the titled elite were arranged every day by their parents with little regard to the parties' preferences. And Lord Benning would certainly have discounted any tendre his daughter might have had for the untitled Mr. Parker. It was astonishing that they'd ever had the opportunity to form a bond.

What a young fool Hugh had been. He'd felt attracted to Amelia on sight, for she had been beautiful and charming, and a little bit mysterious. Now he understood what had caused that aura of mystery about her. She'd been keeping a significant secret, and it had made her miserable.

"She was in love with him," said Brianna from the doorway. "That was why she—"

"I realize that."

"But you didn't know it at the time," she said. "You . . . You loved her, didn't you? And you thought you failed her."

Hugh stood abruptly. "You're damned right I did! What else should I have thought? That she was pining for another man—"

Bile rose in his throat and he pushed past her, walking away, fleeing down the stairs and through the scullery. He jammed his arms into the sleeves of his greatcoat and slammed out the door to head toward the stable.

He didn't want to think about Amelia or the grief she'd caused. He wanted to punch something.

There were taverns in Stonehaven, and likely any number of sailors or fishermen who would be happy to indulge in a boxing match that would leave both combatants bloody. And exhausted. It was exactly what he needed to burn out the frustration he felt. The pain.

It was well past dark, but the moonlight reflecting on the snow gave enough illumination for him to see his way. He entered the stable and lit a lamp, then saddled his horse, mounted, and started down the northern road. Passing out in some rundown tavern in Stonehaven was a far better option than having to face the truth in Brianna's eyes and in his own heart.

Brianna's tongue felt thick in her mouth. Naught had progressed as she'd expected. As she'd hoped.

She wrapped herself in the plaid blanket and curled up on her bed in dejection, holding the drawing of the sailing boat in her hand. Hugh had ridden away, and 'twas likely he would not wish to see her again. Not after the way she'd confronted him with his feelings toward Amelia.

As though *she* knew anything. 'Twas up to Hugh to come to his own conclusions, and not for her to tell him how it had been. How could she know what had occurred between them? She had not even been there. She didn't actually know Amelia's true feelings for Mr. Parker.

Why hadn't she kept the locket to herself? It could have dangled at the side of Amelia's dressing table for months, or even years. Or she could have disposed of it before Hugh ever had a chance to see it. Then Brianna might have had a chance to make their marriage a success. To show him that no matter what had happened between Hugh and his first wife, Brianna was the one who loved him now.

Her tears flowed freely. *This* was why she'd wanted to return to Killiedown Manor, where everything was clear, and she had no worries about losing what was important to her. Losing Hugh.

She pressed her face down on the bed, weeping with the knowledge that she would soon have exactly what she'd wanted from the moment she'd left Claire's gravesite a lifetime ago. And yet it had only been a matter of days. Little more than a week. Was it even possible to fall in love with someone in such a short time?

She feared the answer was yes, for she loved Hugh as he must have loved Amelia. Without reciprocation.

'Twas painfully ironic.

Deriding herself for the foolish revelation that had decided her fate, she wept until her eyes burned and her ribs ached. There was no point in trying to talk to him.

He was ending his smuggling business, and said he did not intend to remain at Glenloch. When morning came, she would leave Castle Glenloch early and alone, for she could not face a farewell that was sure to be painful. For her, at least.

Her decision made, Brianna fell into a deep but restless sleep.

The furious momentum that drove Hugh toward Stonehaven slowed only when he was more than halfway there, when the need to do some damage finally receded. He was not an aggressive sot like Jasper, who went looking for trouble whenever frustration or boredom took him over. Beating the stuffing out of some drunken sailor was not going to change anything.

His marriage to Amelia had been doomed to failure from the start. With her heart engaged elsewhere, she'd been uninterested in the warmth and affection Hugh had been so keen to give.

He might have been an inexperienced lover when he married her, but he hadn't been entirely incompetent. He'd known how to give and take pleasure, but Amelia's cold indifference had baffled him. There hadn't seemed to be anything he could do to alter her disinterest or her martyred response to his attentions.

God, what a naïve fool he'd been.

He halted in the middle of the road, swung his leg over his saddle, and slid off his horse. Walking to the edge of the road, he turned to look out at the sea crashing below him. The temperature had increased slightly and the clouds were thickening and obscuring the moon.

He could feel another storm coming, and he knew a few more inches of snow was going to delay his return to Glenloch.

Which was perfectly fine. He had no interest in facing Brianna and yet another failed marriage. She still spoke of returning to Killiedown, as though that would make everything all right, as though a retreat to her aunt's house would nullify all that they'd shared. That it would somehow cancel out their marriage.

Hugh let out a hard breath at the thought of going back to London while the Lachann Sinclairs of the district were free to pursue Brianna. There wasn't a man with eyes in his head and an appreciation of a naturally sensual woman who would be deterred by a bill of divorce. If it could even be granted.

He jabbed his fingers through his hair and started to pace. It would be up to him to put forth the petition for divorce, but what kind of man could do such a thing to Brianna? She was an innocent, caught up in a situation that was out of her control. All she'd wanted was to get back to Killiedown, a free and independent woman.

Bloody hell. *He didn't want her going up to Killiedown without him.*

And yet he had done naught to suggest he wanted to keep her with him. He'd gone along with her desire to go to Killiedown, and would already have taken her there if not for Kincaid's murder and the questions that had followed. He'd shouted angrily at her—at *Brianna*—when she'd shown him the evidence of Amelia's perfidy. At Brianna, the one who'd done naught to elicit his anger.

He put both his hands against the flank of his gelding

and hung his head between his arms as the leather folio he'd stashed in his wardrobe came to mind. The words written there were real, and they were final. Brianna had spoken her vows from the heart, without referring to any written document. She had promised to take him with his faults as well as his strengths.

But Hugh had been miserly with his own words. He'd merely promised to take her to wife, and said naught about his expectations in marriage.

Because he'd wanted no marriage. He could not face dealing with another wife who would feel cheated by the life he could give her. But Brianna was nothing like Amelia. She was the most audacious woman he'd ever met, full of spirit and life.

He should have said that he. . .

Christ, he should have said he cared for her. He loved her. He wanted her at his table every morn, sitting across from him at the chessboard, riding him on his sofa, moaning beneath him in his bed. He needed her, needed to convince her that they could make a very agreeable life together, even without children.

Bachelorhood was vastly overrated.

Brianna had been right about his feelings for Amelia. He'd cared for her, but his feelings had been met with disdain. Now he had some grasp of her cold response to him. 'Twas naught that he'd done or neglected to do. He'd had no ability to please her, for she'd loved another.

Such was not the situation with Brianna. Her past had been filled with scheming, untrustworthy "protectors" until her aunt had come along. Hugh sensed that Brianna was just as afraid to care, afraid to let herself love him. And that state of affairs had suited him up until now.

Everything was different now.

He needed to get back to Glenloch and repair the damage he'd done. He'd been such a fool he hadn't known enough to dispute her intention to leave him, or asked her to reconsider the life she wanted at Killiedown.

He had to make her see it as the mistake it was. Somehow, he was going to convince her to stay, going to convince her that he wanted her. That he loved her.

The snow started coming down hard, and Hugh noticed that he was covered with a thickening layer of icy crystals. He brushed them off and mounted his horse, then turned around to head south, toward Glenloch. The clouds had darkened the sky, so he proceeded carefully, averse to any misstep that might delay his arrival at home.

Sounds that were out of place woke Brianna.

She wasn't sure what she'd heard, but it did not sound like Hugh coming up the stairs. It was likely the ghost rattling some windows in the attic, trying to get her to go wandering through Amelia's bedchamber or some other closed-up room again.

It wasn't going to work this time. Brianna had seen more than she ever cared to see, intruding on a dead woman's privacy, causing more hurt and dismay than she ever intended.

Brianna could not tell how late it was, or how long Hugh had been gone. But the fire had burned quite low.

She got up from the bed, keeping the plaid blanket around her shoulders. Her throat felt sore, and her tears had dried on her face, so she rinsed her face and took a sip of water.

A strange creaking sound caught her attention. It wasn't the usual kind of crash or moan caused by the ghost, but a stealthier sound that raised goose bumps on Brianna's skin. Perhaps it was only a shifting of the foundation. Or a mouse scurrying across the corridor outside the nursery.

Hoping that she was wrong and it was Hugh returning home, Bree left the nursery and retraced her steps down the gallery, heading toward the north tower where his bedchamber was located, across from Amelia's.

Quietly, she turned the latch and opened his door, but the room was empty, the fireplace untouched in hours. Shivering with the cold, Bree drew the blanket tightly around her but recoiled at another sudden, wholly different sound. Of course, it was coming from Amelia's room.

Brianna stalked across the corridor to confront the ghost and tell it to stop bothering her, but when she pulled open the door, she saw naught. There was no shimmer of light, no hazy figure hovering over the dressing table or against the wall near the bed.

But the room had definitely changed.

Lifting the lamp before her, she rubbed her eyes, doubting what she was seeing. The wall had been pushed aside, and was standing ajar in exactly the same fashion as the secret wall in the drawing room. Glenloch's ghost had hovered near this same wall in Amelia's room every time it had led Brianna there, and had even disappeared through it.

Now Bree realized its significance.

She approached the wall-door and saw that it led to the landing and the stone staircase that stood behind the locked doors of the tower. "All right," she muttered as she stepped into the ancient tower, "where are you?"

Surely the ghost was nearby, if it had bothered to lure her to the site.

But Brianna had no intention of going any farther, if that was the phantom's intent. The tower—and obviously, the steps—was not sound. She started for the doors to see if they were unlocked again, but stopped in her tracks when she heard footsteps coming her way.

Chapter 18

Nae whip cuts sae sharp as the lash o' conscience.
SCOTTISH PROVERB

The voices belonged to two men, and neither of them sounded like Hugh. As they came closer, she could tell that it was Mr. MacGowan and the Marquess of Roddington. Bree slipped back into Amelia's bedchamber with the intention of fleeing the room altogether, but she could not resist listening to their hushed conversation as they climbed the old stone staircase, speaking in whispered tones.

"Ye've got yer money, Marquess. Now see tha' ye doona show yer face—"

"Me?" Roddington whispered harshly. "You are the dastardly one, MacGowan. First, poor Amelia. Now, Kincaid—"

"Ye were there wi' me every step o' the way, Roddy."

Shocked by their interchange, Brianna hurried toward the door, but not before they caught sight of the light from her lamp.

"Judas priest, MacGowan, you told me she'd be gone!"

MacGowan did not stop to answer him, but ran through the passage to reach her.

Brianna did not wait for him. She turned and ran, dropping the blanket as she fled. She barely got out through the door of the bedchamber when MacGowan grabbed the back of her gown and yanked her back.

She cried out in surprise, falling awkwardly against him as he dragged her into the room.

"What in hell are ye doin' here?"

"'Tis my home at the moment," she snapped, and tried to extricate herself from his grasp.

He muttered something ugly and shoved her toward Roddington, who had followed him through the passageway, letting the door shut behind him. The marquess caught her, laughing so incongruously that Brianna wondered if he was in full possession of his wits.

"I could never have imagined the irony, MacGowan. Could you?"

"Shut up, Yer Fancy Lordship," MacGowan responded venomously. "'Tis pure trouble we've got here."

"Release me!" Brianna demanded

"I don't see why we can't just have a bit of fun with her and then dispose of her the same way we—"

"Enough!" MacGowan bit out, and Brianna was shocked by the man's demeanor and speech toward the marquess, a peer with so much power and rank that he could bury MacGowan with but a word. She grasped that the two were functioning as equals here. "Ye and I will do wha' we mus' do. Wi'out a lot of bletherin'."

But Roddington continued to chuckle, and Brianna

took advantage of his inattention to break free of his grasp. She tried to run, shoving a delicate boudoir chair behind her to block them from following her, but MacGowan managed to get around it and grab her before she even reached the bedroom door.

"What do you want?" she demanded.

"'Tis no' a matter of wha' we want," said Mac-Gowan.

With an iron grip, he pulled both her hands to her back and ripped a golden bed tassel from its curtain. Wrapping the cord tightly around her wrists, he imprisoned her despite her struggles.

"Be still, damn ye!" He pushed her toward the passageway, and Brianna tried twisting and turning to get out of his grasp, then attempted to fall to the ground. But her antics only made him angry, and he cuffed the side of her head, making her ears ring. And still, he managed to keep her on her feet, moving forward.

"Where are you taking me?" Brianna cried. She feared that if they got her into the old tower, she was doomed.

"Ye'll see soon enough," MacGowan growled.

"We've more than enough time to enjoy her," Roddington said, his tone the bleat of a spoiled child. "We saw her husband heading for Stonehaven. Surely you don't believe he'll return tonight. And you know as well as I that the servants won't step foot in the place until the morn."

"Ye're a fool, Marquess. She goes now."

Roddington made a derisive sound of capitulation. "Which way? Up or down?"

"Down this time. He's already had one wife throw herself from the parapet."

"No!" Brianna screamed, redoubling her efforts against MacGowan. She lashed out and managed to kick Roddington viciously in the shin. It must have hurt him as much as it hurt her foot, for he yelped and slapped her.

"You bitch! I'll see that you pay for that!"

"No' now, Roddington! Close the door to the gallery, then come and snap open the tower door."

The marquess did as he was told, and MacGowan half dragged, half pushed Brianna into the passage, past a bulky leather satchel that lay the floor. Roddington bent to pick it up, but MacGowan stopped him.

"Leave it! Yer money'll be safe here until we're finished."

They'd left one lamp on the cold, stone floor, and Roddington carried it, lighting the way inadequately from behind.

The stone staircase was wickedly narrow, and curved its way down the walls of the tower. It was bitter cold inside, for the arrow loops she'd seen from the exterior were not covered, allowing the wintry air inside.

Brianna could barely see where she was going, and she feared that MacGowan was going to push her down the steps. Such a fall would likely break her neck, and she would end up lying at the bottom of the stairs, somewhere near the ancient, caved-in pantry. No one would ever know what had happened to her.

Hugh would likely believe she'd left him.

Tears streamed down her face as she walked as carefully as she could, keeping her body close to the wall, hoping there might be something she could do to save herself once they reached the bottom. If only she could get her hands free, she might be able to find a loose brick or an old wooden beam to use as a weapon.

She did not dare try to free her hands while she walked down the stairs. 'Twas important to pay close attention to each step, for her skirts might trip her at any time. She had to come up with some plan to thwart these villains when they reached the bottom, for neither Hugh nor anyone else would be coming to do it for her.

Hugh walked from the stable to the castle, and let himself in quietly through the scullery door. Closing it behind him, he made barely a sound as he went through the main floor to the staircase. He thought only of taking his wife in his arms and apologizing for being such a lackwit.

And then he would tell her he loved her and wanted her to stay with him. They might well visit Killiedown Manor, but her home was with him. Would always be with him, as his was with her.

He climbed the staircase and headed toward the nursery, where he was sure Brianna would have gone. She favored the snug little room, and he decided she should turn it into her own solar. She should feel free to make any changes she wanted at Glenloch and his other houses, for he intended to make her the true mistress of his estates.

Moving silently in case she was asleep, he lifted the

latch of the door and stepped inside the nursery. 'Twas empty, but it looked as though she'd been there. The fire had burned low, but the blankets on the bed were mussed, and there was a crumpled sheet of vellum on it. He picked it up and recognized the drawing he'd made long ago.

'Twas clear Brianna had held it as she slept, and Hugh felt she must have known he'd drawn it. It gave him hope that she was not indifferent to him, would not be indifferent to his proposal that she stay with him.

Leaving the nursery, he walked down to his own bedchamber, his hopes rising at the knowledge that there could be only one reason that she awaited him there. She wanted him. He would wake her and ask her to stay with him, then he would draw her into his arms and kiss away all her doubts.

He was an absolute skitterbrain for thinking marriage to Brianna would be anything but perfect. Brilliant and exhilarating. She was an exceptional woman who would not allow a lack of children to destroy—

Hugh stopped midway to his chamber at a sudden realization. Amelia's sorrow was due to her marriage to him instead of to Simon Parker. His understanding of Amelia's unhappiness was based on a false assumption. She hadn't cared about motherhood at all. Everything he'd believed about her was a mistake.

He continued to his room and opened the door quietly, but found it empty. And no fire had burned there recently.

A sudden thickness obstructed his throat as he perused the room. If Brianna was not there, and nowhere else in the castle...

Good Christ, could she have left him? Had his temper and his abandonment driven her away? 'Twas nothing less than he deserved.

The mare he'd bought in Stonehaven was still in the stable, so she hadn't gone on horseback. And he'd seen no tracks when he'd come in. Unless she'd gone before the snow had started again, she'd have left tracks.

In any event, she couldn't have gone far. Intending to go after her, he went out the door and came up short at the sight of a filmy light outside Amelia's bedchamber. It looked nothing like lamplight as it shimmered erratically, nor did it emanate from inside the room to shine under the door. Hugh frowned at the idea that he might actually be looking at the ghost Brianna had insisted she'd seen.

A cold sweat broke out on his forehead as the thing took on the shape of a woman and beckoned to him. *It could not be real*, not when tales of the Glenloch Ghost had merely been invented to keep curious customs agents and other intruders away from the castle.

Yet it was hovering in plain sight at Amelia's door until it had his full attention, then slipped through the wood and disappeared. Hugh shook his head to clear it and started back toward the staircase. There was no time to investigate the ghost now. He had to catch up with Brianna before she froze—

Unless the ghost knew where Brianna was. He could not believe he was actually entertaining the possibility that the Glenloch Ghost was real... But *something* had caused that light to appear, and it didn't seem to have been from any natural cause. It had actually taken the form of. . .

He muttered a low sound of self-derision and returned to Amelia's door. Hesitating for a moment, he braced himself and opened the door.

It was dark inside, and no fire burned in the fireplace.

And yet the hazy specter hovered there, as though trying to tell him something. Swallowing his trepidation, he approached the strange thing. Brianna said she'd never felt threatened by it, but it might have been trying to gain her trust. If the servants were right, and it was a fearful thing, it might have caused her some harm. And—beef-brain that he was—he'd left her in the castle, to face it alone!

Anguish flowed through him at the thought that the phantom might have lured her somewhere and caused her harm. "Where is she?" he demanded, as he nearly tripped over something on the floor. He bent down and discovered the plaid blanket he and Brianna had shared in the kelper's cottage. He picked it up and thrust it toward the ghostly apparition, and repeated his question.

Slowly, the ghostly form slipped through the wall beside the bed, and Hugh felt a moment of despair. He could not follow the damned thing, and he had the distinct feeling that it knew where to find Brianna. "You showed me the blanket," he said, his voice a quiet rasp of hopelessness. "Now show me where you've gone!"

He lit a lamp and looked around, but there was no

other clue. Only an open drawer with several small, absorbent sponges in it. Frowning, he lifted one of them, and then noticed the open jar of vinegar beside it.

A strange sound in the room caused him to set it aside. He followed the sound, and went toward the bed, where he'd last seen the ghost. The sound came again, almost like the flapping of a blanket in the wind.

And yet it had come from the other side of the wall.

He placed both hands against it and tried to understand what was happening. If the ghost was behind the wall, then it was hovering in the empty shell of the north tower, which had been securely locked after Amelia's death. So he could not imagine how Brianna could have gone inside. Besides, she would have no reason to go into those ruins.

He swore under his breath as the flapping sound returned, even more insistent this time, and he knew he would have to get inside the tower. There was probably a key to those doors somewhere, but 'twould be much faster just to break them down. He started to move, but caught sight of a piece of white fur.

'Twas exactly like the fur that had trimmed Brianna's wedding dress.

'Twas caught somehow, and when Hugh reached down to pick it up, he realized it was wedged *under* the wall. He suddenly knew that this had to be an arrangement like the secret door in the drawing room.

He ran his hands down the edges of the wall and finally found the latch, hidden just behind the head of Amelia's bed, and obscured by her bed curtains. He tripped the bolt and pushed the wall forward, then picked up his lamp and stepped into the locked portion of the tower, where the old stone staircase hugged the wall. All was quiet, and when he looked up, he saw the shadowy steps Amelia must have climbed as she prepared to jump.

The shimmering light of the ghost appeared on his right, distracting Hugh from his morbid thoughts. He realized it meant for him to follow it.

Complying with the phantom's wishes, he started down the treacherous stairs, but stopped when he came across a large leather pouch that was filled with coins and paper currency. He tossed it aside and went to the stairs, descending as quietly as possible. When he'd made it down a full flight, he heard voices. MacGowan's, if he was not mistaken.

And Brianna's!

He took a quick look to memorize the steps he needed to descend to reach her, then extinguished his lamp. Standing still in the darkness, he heard a crack, and then a whimper.

All thoughts of caution fled.

Chapter 19

Danger and delight grow on one stalk.
SCOTTISH PROVERB

"You'll never get away with this, MacGowan!" Brianna cried, tasting blood. "My husband will find you—"

"Can't you gag her, MacGowan?" asked Roddington, his voice maddeningly casual. *Bored.*

"No need. It'll all be over before long."

They'd come to a cellar at the bottom of the steps, and Brianna knew the caved-in pantry must be just above it. Or, no, 'twas beside it. MacGowan shoved her through the cavernous room, past all its rotting wooden arches until they reached a group of large barrels, stacked one on top of the other, against the far wall, and covered in dust and cobwebs. "Open that cask on the end, Roddy."

Roddington picked up an iron bar and pried open the top of one barrel that had nothing on top of it. MacGowan shoved Brianna toward it.

"No!" she cried, redoubling her struggle against the burly man who held her. If they forced her into that chest-high drum and sealed the lid, she would be doomed for certain.

MacGowan dragged her to it and tried to shove her into it. But there was something revolting inside, lying at the bottom in an acrid-smelling liquid. "Bend, damn ye!" MacGowan growled, trying to force Brianna over the edge and into the disgusting liquid. But she was not about to let it happen. She struggled mightily and screamed when he suddenly picked her up and tossed her over his shoulder.

Her hands were still bound, and her shoulders shrieked in pain as she tumbled down MacGowan's torso. She screamed as loud as she could as she lashed out with her feet, doing as much damage to the wicked man as possible.

"Shut yer trap!" he shouted, but he jumped back suddenly, and dropped Brianna to the cold floor. "Wha'?"

"Good God!" Roddington cried.

'Twas the ghost, her bright form nearly solid as she hovered over the barrel where they'd meant to stow Brianna.

Bree ignored the pains in her wrists and legs and pushed herself up to her knees, scooting away to wriggle out of the bindings at her wrists. She was never so happy to see Glenloch's specter as she was at that moment.

And then Hugh suddenly appeared at the mouth of the dark staircase. He took one look at her, then roared with fury and charged into MacGowan, knocking the man up against an arch that cracked and buckled when he hit it. Hugh took hold of MacGowan's coat and gave him a bone-crunching punch in the jaw, but MacGowan struck back, and they exchanged blows until their encounter turned into a full brawl.

In the thick of it, Hugh called out to her. "Brianna, are you all right?"

"Yes!" she cried, still struggling with the ropes on her wrists. She could hardly credit his arrival. It warmed her, and gave her hope, yet she was terrified for him. There were two of them—MacGowan and Roddington—and they meant to kill. "Hugh, watch out—"

MacGowan delivered a powerful blow that pitched Hugh violently into the same cracked beam. The ceiling and the rest of the beams creaked ominously, and dust and debris started falling from the ceiling. Another arch cracked.

"Hugh, we must get out of here! I think the ceiling is going to collapse!"

But MacGowan had the upper hand, grabbing fistfuls of Hugh's jacket to pull him up from the base of the arch. Brianna flinched when he drew his meaty fist back to deliver a disastrous blow, but Hugh blocked it with his arm and pummeled MacGowan's abdomen with both fists. Hugh gave no quarter, forcing MacGowan to back up, even as the man tried to defend himself.

Dust was raining down on them now, but the brawl continued, each man swiping at the other verbally as well as physically. They careened into the row of barrels, and two of the huge casks fell, crashing into pieces of rotting wood and copper as they rolled away, spilling their sour contents onto the stone floor.

"Is this where you hide your ill-gotten proceeds,

MacGowan?" Hugh demanded. "Down in this decrepit hole?"

"Ye should hae kept yerself in London, Laird," MacGowan rasped. "But doona fret, I'll see to it ye never return there."

"In your dreams, lad," Hugh said with a harsh laugh, and Brianna wished he would not be quite so cavalier. MacGowan's face had turned to a deep red and he was grunting with cruel intent. Brianna feared one of his vicious punches would eventually catch Hugh in the face, or knock him against one of the beams, perhaps a killing blow.

She wished her husband would finish the man, allowing them to flee the dangerous room, but MacGowan was Hugh's equal in stature, if not finesse. His blows made contact often enough that Brianna feared for the outcome of the struggle, and she knew she had to try and help him.

Roddington was slinking away toward the stairs. Hugh saw him, but he was fully engaged in the fight against MacGowan, and he knew it was a fight to the death. His former estate manager could not afford to let Hugh or Brianna escape.

They battled with fists and knees, grinding into one another as they fought, crashing into walls and joists as dirt fluttered down from the ceiling. He could hear the framework of the room splintering apart in his ears, and knew Brianna was right—the room was going to cave in, and he needed to get her away from there.

"Brianna! Go for the stairs! Get out of here!"

But Roddington was heading in that direction, and Hugh didn't want her anywhere near him. His heart jumped into his throat when he saw her free her hands and go after the rotten marquess, but his distraction cost him, and MacGowan got the upper hand. MacGowan delivered a cruel blow to the abdomen, but Hugh kept his head down and butted viciously into his adversary, knocking him to the floor.

Hugh started for Roddington, but MacGowan grabbed him by the ankle and pulled him down. Just then, Brianna picked up a metal bar from the ground near the barrels. Wielding it with both hands, she started for Roddington, but a huge beam crashed down from the center of the ceiling, with an attendant load of debris. She could not get past it to the marquess, but that was the only way out.

"Hugh!"

"I know! We've got to find a way—"

They needed an escape route, but the staircase was blocked.

"Come with me!" she shouted.

The floor above her groaned ominously, and a sudden mass of rubble fell directly in front of her, covering her with dust.

"Brianna! Move, love! Get—"

MacGowan suddenly shoved him away and made a wild dash for the steps, just as another huge piece of the ceiling crashed down, blocking the stairs entirely. Hugh regained his balance and went to Brianna then, grabbing the lamp and taking her hand to pull her toward the barrels. "Look! We can climb up and out this way!"

Hugh lifted her onto a closed barrel and pointed past her to a wide crevice that had opened between the top of the wall and the ceiling. "Climb up and slide through that space. Hurry, sweetheart!"

He climbed up behind her and when he looked back, he saw that the rest of the cellar was already falling in on itself. Below him was an open barrel, and he shuddered as he looked down and saw its gruesome contents.

The crashing sounds behind them propelled Brianna, and she managed to scramble quickly to the top of the next barrel. Once there, she wasted no time sliding through the opening, which placed her inside the precarious walls of the pantry. Hugh handed her the lamp, and she moved away from the opening to allow him enough room to get through. He managed to push his way out of the cellar just as he heard another loud crack. The entire room was collapsing.

"Come on, Brianna! We've got to get out of here!"

He scrambled to his feet and raised the lamp high so they could get their bearings, then grabbed her hand and made for one of the broken-down walls of the old pantry. With all possible speed, they slipped through a decrepit doorway and started running through the snow as far from the castle as they could go, before the entire tower cracked and split and crumbled to the ground below.

When he judged that they were far enough away from the disaster to escape injury, Hugh pulled Brianna into his arms. She clung to him, her face against his chest as she trembled violently. But she was right where he wanted her.

The sea crashed behind them, and snow fell all around, but Hugh did not need to look to know that the north tower of Castle Glenloch lay in a rubble of rock and dust before them.

"I feared I'd lost you," Hugh murmured against her head.

"No," she said, holding him tightly. "MacGowan meant to murder me, but you came for me," she added incredulously.

"I'm so sorry I wasn't here to protect you. I was wrong . . . about so many things."

She shook her head against his chest. "No. I had no right to interfere—"

"You had every right. You are my wife." He slid his hands up to her shoulders, then higher, cupping her face. "You are my love, Brianna."

She looked up at him, with doubt and disbelief in her beautiful eyes. "But I—"

He kissed her gently. "I love you, Brianna. Stay with me. Be my wife."

Her chin quivered, and he saw the glimmer of tears in her eyes. "I-I don't want to go back to Killiedown." She pressed her body against his in a tight hug, tucking her head beneath his chin. "I love you, Hugh. "

His heart seemed to swell in his chest. "God, Brianna, you have no idea how glad I am to hear you say it. You are all that I want. All that I need." He tipped up her face and kissed her again, then touched his forehead to hers. "I don't know what I would have done if I'd lost you."

She was still trembling, and he removed his coat and draped it over her shoulders. "I didn't think you would come."

"I was such an idiot . . ."

"And I was sure you would never find me."

"I wouldn't have found you, but for the ghost."

She drew back. "You saw it?"

" 'Twas the ghost that led me to you."

Brianna let out a quick breath of surprise. "She saved me from being drowned in that open barrel. She startled MacGowan and Roddington, and distracted them until you arrived."

"Brianna . . ." He had to tell her now, tell her what he'd seen in that cellar, and they would never have to speak of it again. "I know why she's been haunting Glenloch."

"You do?"

He nodded, still horrified by her close brush with death. She might have met the same fate as their glimmering ghost, and been doomed to roam Glenloch's halls and galleries forever. "There was a body—a skeleton, really—in the open cask."

"I saw something in the one they meant to drown me in." He felt her shudder. "Was that . . . Was it in there?"

"Yes. I saw it when I climbed up behind you," he said. "I think she must have been killed and her body hidden in that barrel of spirits."

"Oh dear heavens." Her trembling increased.

"Come on. You're freezing. We have to get you inside."

Hugh lifted the lamp, and they could see the disaster. The tower was completely gone. "I don't think MacGowan and Roddington could have survived that collapse."

Brianna took in a sharp breath.

"We'll have to excavate the site for their bodies," he said.

"How awful."

"'Tis no less than they deserved for what they planned for you."

"'Tis horrible, nonetheless. And the Glenloch Ghost . . . Might we recover her bones, too, and give her a decent burial?"

"Of course, love. Our ghost surely deserves to rest now."

Epilogue

A blithe heart makes a blooming look.
SCOTTISH PROVERB

St. George's Church, London. June 1830.

"I had a letter from Falkburn yesterday," Hugh said.

They'd left their carriage and were walking the last block to St. George's Church for Sunday services. 'Twas only an hour after they'd climbed from their soft, comfortable bed at Newbury House. The glow of their lovemaking still filled Brianna.

As did their child, who would make its appearance well before the year's end.

Hugh reached down and slid a wispy lock of her hair behind her ear, oblivious to the sidelong glances his intimate act garnered from the very proper matrons who passed them by. She supposed she should be relieved that he hadn't run his hand down the slight curve of her belly, as he was wont to do.

"Mmmm?" Brianna drew her hand more deeply into the crook of Hugh's arm and moved closer to him as they walked. Perhaps they should have stayed home in bed, for she craved his touch more than ever. "What did Mr. MacTavish have to say?"

"He asks whether we're ready to return to Glenloch. The new manor house is nearly finished."

Hugh had razed the entire castle soon after the bodies of Roddington and MacGowan had been recovered. The place had been fraught with unpleasant memories for Hugh, with its history of violence and the deceit he would no longer countenance. His father's whip, Amelia's locket, and the drawing of the sailing ship that reflected Hugh's futile pining for his lost friend had all been destroyed with the building.

Hugh had had to explain the significance of Amelia's sponges and the vinegar in her dressing table, and then they both knew the extent of her betrayal. Instead of giving Hugh her honesty, instead of living up to the responsibilities of her marriage, Amelia had become sullen and resentful, making both their lives as miserable as possible.

Even so, Brianna knew Hugh regretted that she'd somehow interfered in Roddington's dealings with MacGowan. The hints the two had given Brianna made it almost certain that they were responsible for Amelia's death, as well as Kincaid's. And the blackguards had nearly managed to cause Brianna's early demise. In spite of her narrow escape, she and Hugh were both glad to have discovered the body of the young woman in the cellar—the Glenloch Ghost—who had haunted the castle for centuries.

Hugh had seen to it that she received a Christian burial, in spite of the fact that her name was unknown. Everyone in Falkburn believed she must have been the daughter of an ancient laird who was said to have disappeared. In any case, it had not been too difficult to persuade the vicar to bury her in the village churchyard.

"Are you certain 'tis all right for you to be walking so far?" he asked her.

"This is not far at all," she said with a joyful laugh. The sun was shining, her heart was full, and she was walking beside the man she loved. "And since you do not want me to ride any more, I must find some way to exercise my legs. Tell me what Mr. MacTavish had to say about Glenloch."

"The barley is in and growing," he replied. "Our builder and the engineer are still up there, overseeing the construction of the new house and the distillery, and making sure all is being done according to the highest standards. We'll be ready to make whisky this autumn after the crop is in."

She smiled at his enthusiasm for the project. Visiting Glenloch was going to be an entirely different experience for Hugh now, with the castle gone, and the distillery standing in its place. The new house was being built much closer to Falkburn, to the village residents who would soon be earning their income from the new venture. Fortunately, they had the proceeds from Roddington's purse—money that had been swindled from them—to help carry them through until then.

"Do you regret tearing down the castle?"

"Not at all," he replied, his dark visage lighter than she'd ever seen it. "Naught has ever given me such satisfaction. 'Twas a horrid place, but for meeting you there."

"I will not disagree, husband."

"And I'm doubly glad that we're out of the free-trading business," he added. "No doubt Captain Benoit will have plenty of others to take our place, but there will be no more violence for the sake of Glenloch's brandy."

"I would like to meet Captain Benoit one day," Bree said. "I have a question I'd like to ask him."

Hugh looked at her curiously, but then smiled. "Whatever you wish, love."

They entered the church, and he steered her toward two seats that were as far as possible from where Lord Stamford and his family were already seated. Somehow, the Crandalls had lost favor with the more influential hostesses of the ton, and Brianna rarely saw them at any of the balls or soirees she and Hugh attended.

It did not bother her in the least.

She looked to the altar where she might have married Roddington had she not acted so impulsively that cold December night, and thanked God that she had been taken in by the Laird of Glenloch instead. Had they not been in church right then, Brianna would have kissed him, pouring into it all the passion and love she felt for him.

"I cannot imagine being happier, or loving anyone

more than I do you," she said, pulling him down slightly to whisper in his ear.

"Brianna . . ." He squeezed her hand and looked down at her, his eyes reflecting all the love and happiness they shared. Speaking so that only she could hear, he said, "You take my breath away. I would never have believed it a few months ago, but you have given me a life, and a future. I love you."